THE SHADOWMERE TRILOGY

Jaide Fox

Erotic Fantasy Romance

New Concepts   Georgia

The Shadowmere Trilogy is an original publication of NCP. This work has never before appeared in book form. This work is a novel. Any similarity to actual persons or events is purely coincidental.

New Concepts Publishing
5202 Humphreys Rd.
Lake Park, GA 31636

ISBN 1-58608-670-7
© copyright Jaide Fox
Cover art by Eliza Black, © copyright 2003

NCP books are available at special quantity discounts for bulk purchases for sales promotions, premiums, fund raising, or educational use. For details, write, email, or phone New Concepts Publishing, 5202Humphreys Rd., Lake Park, GA 31636, ncp@newconceptspublishing.com, Ph. 229-257-0367, Fax 229-219-1097.

First NCP Paperback Printing: 2004

Printed in the United States of America

Visit our webpage at:
www.newconceptspublishing.com

UNTAMED

CHAPTER ONE

"Lady Ashanti, we have captured a beastman. The curse that plagues you will soon be broken." Lord Conrad's voice echoed through the marble hall as he entered, the sound of his heavy booted stride preceding him.

Astonished, Ashanti dropped the heavy, leather bound *Grimoire* she'd been studying, her fingers gone weak at his announcement. It landed with a dull thud on the plush carpet covering the marble, forgotten.

A smile that chilled her blood slashed across his dark face.

Ashanti returned his smile hesitantly as she rose unsteadily from the scattered pile of pillows she'd been resting on. The light golden chains of her skirt jingled softly as she moved.

She had always hated the garments Lord Conrad insisted that she wear, which were more revealing than concealing. Under other circumstances, she might have found some appeal in the jewel colored, gossamer veils and intricately wrought, golden chains that made up her costumes, but she could scarcely stomach having Lord Conrad look at her at all. The lustful gleam that entered his eyes each time he looked upon her near nakedness made her feel far more than indecent. It made her feel befouled, and yet her mind was such a jumble from his pronouncement that she was only vaguely aware of the conflicting emotions that generally assailed her in Lord Conrad's presence.

An end to her torment!

Or would it be just the beginning? She knew he planned to claim her once the curse had been broken--if it was even possible.

"How can this be? The beastpeople are forbidden to enter this land, as we are theirs." An uneasiness assailed her at the implications and she frowned. What had he done?

Typically, the tinkling sounds of her chains drew Lord Conrad's attention. He ran his gaze over her body, his eyes a soulless black as lust filled him. Careful to conceal her revulsion, she endured his look, pushing it to the back of her mind as she generally did. "Please do not tell me you risked your men to enter Shadowmere."

Much as she despised him and her virtual imprisonment, she couldn't abide the thought of bloodshed and endangerment so needless. She wondered how many men he'd lost to his obsessions but knew it didn't bear thinking on.

Lord Conrad continued smiling as if she hadn't spoken, his black eyes glittering like a serpent's. She refrained from shivering, knowing it would not help her cause. He crossed the distance spanning them and clasped her in his arms, apparently completely oblivious to the fact that she went rigid, trying to hold herself aloof from his armor clad body. His musky scent filled her nostrils and she breathed through her mouth to avoid his familiar scent. His clammy hands smoothed over the bare skin of her waist, his clinging fingers bringing to mind leeches.

"Your concern touches me, beloved. Rest assured, we were careful and not detected. He shall not be missed. I suspect he was naught more than a rogue hunter, for the condition we found him in....He was easily taken." He chuckled, his cruelty seeping out like oil, tainting her with his foulness. She wanted desperately to be free of him, to go and bathe his stench and touch from her skin.

She'd learned in the time she had been with him, however, not to allow her revulsion to show, or to let it rule her life. She knew, despite his cruelty, or perhaps because of it, that the certainty that she found him vile would not persuade him to release her. More likely it would only inspire him to torment her more, and if she allowed these feelings to dominate her, she simply could not endure her captivity. She would go mad.

Moreover, she felt a strange compulsion fill her that forced everything else to the fringes of her mind, felt, but tamed by a need even greater than the desire to escape Lord Conrad's invasive touch.

She felt the need to see the creature that was to be sacrificed so that she might live.

She had never seen one of these creatures of legend, but it was far more than curiosity that sparked inside her and grew quickly to a desperate need to behold what few mortals had ever seen and lived to tell about.

Myth held that they were loathsome to look upon, that even when they assumed a human-like form, they appeared more monstrous than human, that only to look upon one was sometimes sufficient to drive one insane with pure terror. There were other tales, as well, that, with only a look, or touch, they could fell a powerful man....for what purpose could only be guessed, for in general they shifted and, in their beast form, slaughtered all within their path.

It was insane even to consider going near one of her own will, and yet she found that the need was near overwhelming. Perhaps because she hoped it would cleanse her of the guilt that was burgeoning inside her that it was to die only for the *possibility* that it might cure her?

Knowing it was useless to even try, yet unwilling to abandon the hope that he'd heed her, she dared to request something of him. Her voice muffled by his proximity, she said, "I would like to see him." Ashanti felt him stiffen, his arms like a rigid wooden cage, trapping her.

He pulled back and looked into her eyes, his expression a mixture of suspicion, reluctance and pleasure. "You are certain?"

The pleasure, she understood. He seemed to suffer from an overwhelming need to brag about every accomplishment and there was little doubt in her mind that he was eager to show her his prize.

His reluctance, she might have put down to concern for her safety, but she knew him far too well by now to allow that as a real possibility. More likely his reluctance stemmed from his suspicions, but she was at a loss to fathom how her motives could be suspect, or what he thought she might do.

Perhaps he suspected that the sight of the creature might deprive her of her wits and feared he would end up with a blubbering lunatic?

The thought almost brought a smile to her lips. She suppressed the urge even as she dismissed her anxieties about his suspicions. She didn't care what he thought, what he suspected, or how it might affect her in the future. She felt that, regardless of possible consequences, she *had* to see the creature.

"You will take his life. I wish to see the beast who sacrifices so much for me." It was rare that she made a request of him, and she hoped this time he would oblige her wishes.

He turned to go, and she felt defeated, but then he held his arm out to her. "Very well, but I warn you, 'tis not a fair sight."

* * * *

As they stepped into the dungeon and the heavy wooden door closed behind them, Ashanti noticed with some relief that a small circle of light surrounded them, provided by a solitary flickering torch. A guard sat in a rickety chair just inside the dungeon that occupied the nether regions of the castle. Stout and prone to drink, he stumbled awkwardly to his feet as they entered, bobbing his head more out of fear than respect. Lord Conrad fixed him with a long, cold stare but said nothing. Instead, after that one, hard stare, he seemed to dismiss the frightened man, turning instead to pick up a torch, which he held to the one on the wall until it, too, flickered to life.

Beyond, the dungeon seemed to stretch into an eternity of darkness. Ashanti shivered, but not from the cold and damp that permeated the air, crawling across her scantily clad form like the lifeless hands of a dead lover. The place reeked of sickness, torture and death. The darkness seemed almost a tangible thing.

Without a word, apparently oblivious to her distress, Lord Conrad strode down the narrow corridor leading to the cells. Closing her mind to the possibility of other occupants, Ashanti followed him, staying close only because the heavy blackness was even more repellent than Lord Conrad's proximity.

An odd sort of anticipation blossomed inside her as they traversed the narrow, twisted corridors that seemed to lead off in every direction with no apparent design. A part of her mind counted the paces and turns they took, an instinctual reaction rather than through conscious effort, as it flickered through her mind that it would be all too easy to become lost in this labyrinth of darkness.

She was more conscious of the tempo of her heart, which seemed to outstrip their pace. Fear? Unaccustomed activity?

She dismissed the last almost as soon as she thought it. Despite her affliction, she was not such a weakling as to become breathless and weak from so little exertion, so that her heart labored to support her.

The fear….She acknowledged she felt some, and had every right to it, all things considered, but she knew there could be no real threat or Lord Conrad would not have brought her…would not have come without men to protect them. He was not a coward, but neither was he a fool.

At any rate, it was more than just fear. It was anticipation, and it grew stronger as they progressed, more powerful, until she could not dismiss the fact that it was not altogether a product of her own mind. Some*thing* was reaching out to her, touching her in a way she had never been touched before.

She tried to dismiss those thoughts as purely fanciful imaginings, but, in her heart, she knew it was more than that. It was as if she was rushing to meet a long, lost lover.

That thought was so stunning that she stumbled and almost fell.

Lord Conrad stopped. Briefly, she thought it was because he'd heard her. Then she noticed he'd stopped before a cell and was staring fixedly at something within.

A rush of mixed emotions filled her. Almost reluctantly, she moved forward until she was standing beside him.

"Why is he naked?" Ashanti asked, her steel blue gaze drawn to the creature …the man… within like a magnet despite the dimness of the cell.

Lord Conrad blinked, as if awakening from a daze, but instead of answering, he turned and thrust the torch he held into a rusted iron brazier bolted to the wall outside the cell. The flames flickered, casting eerie shadows.

In the dappled light, she could see the trussed man who dwarfed even the large cell. His massive arms were stretched above his head and manacled with heavy chain to the damp stone. The muscles of his chest and shoulders strained in pain and the effort not to collapse, his legs spread and chained to the wall as well. Ashanti remained well away from him, the bars a barrier between them, but his size was still impressive even with the distance. He was tall--no--huge, towering above her height at least a foot, and she was as tall as any man. Ice blond hair, like pale gold, fell past an impossibly wide chest and clung to his narrow waist, baring and hiding tantalizing bits of tanned flesh. His sex was thankfully covered with a loincloth, but otherwise he was naked.

"This was how he was found. No doubt clothing restricts their capabilities. He's a monster, is he not?"

Knowing agreement with Lord Conrad was always an expected thing, Ashanti nodded slowly, absently, wonder widening her eyes as she looked over him again, letting the sight sink into her mind.

At the sound of Lord Conrad's voice, the man had looked up, his wild features hardening into a mask of hatred and rage. She felt Lord Conrad stiffen beside her. The prisoner's gaze then shifted to her, and she felt as if she'd been struck a blow to her solar plexus, the air knocked out of her lungs. She gasped, trying to retain her composure, but it was nearly impossible with him looking at her. Her heart quickened, the beating pulse pounding in her ears.

She shook her head, covering her eyes momentarily. Ashanti had never seen one of the creatures of legend. That he looked as human as she did startled her. She'd expected him to look like the beast she'd always been told they were…terrifying even to look upon.

But although his body was that of a human, his eyes betrayed the untamed animal hidden inside.

Ashanti looked away, her heart slowing as she did so, her breathing relaxing once more. Strangely, she felt as if he'd spoken to her with that one look, almost as though he begged her help, but he looked too proud a man to ever beg for anything.

"Damned animal. Do you see his defiance? I'll be glad to break the beast."

A well of sickness invaded her throat at Lord Conrad's comment. One of his many pleasures was tormenting animals…in fact any creature weaker than himself and although the beastman looked to be a capable warrior, he was chained and unable to defend himself should Lord Conrad yield to his propensity for torture.

Ashanti swallowed against a painfully dry throat to speak, eager to distract him, yet in too much turmoil to choose her words as carefully as she should have. "How can you be so certain that he is a beastman? He looks so ... so human."

"You've doubts? I admit he is not nearly so impressive as he is when in leopard form." He removed a key from his belt and opened the cell door, moving to a table with implements of torture laid across it in ascending order of size, shining metal flashing in the light. "I will allay your fears, beloved."

Inexplicably, the endearment sounded more foul in the strange man's presence, even more so when she realized her careless comments had precipitated just the situation she'd hoped to avoid. She felt a sick feeling in her stomach when she saw him pick up a cat 'o nine tails. He fingered the braids lovingly. Surely he didn't mean to use it? But she saw that he had every intention of torturing the man. Even as she cried out for him to hold, he whirled around and slashed the wicked barbs across the man's chest again and again.

Ashanti screamed, and he ceased his barrage, chest heaving, blood flecked across his face like a butcher's block. The braids dangled to the floor and she thought he'd strike again, but he returned the whip to the table. She darted a glance quickly to the man and covered her mouth to keep from cursing Conrad and inviting his wrath. Jagged splits of red cut across the man's tan flesh, blood flowing to the cold gray stone. The man jerked against his chains like he would tear Lord Conrad apart, silent, hating. His pain ripped Ashanti to the core. How could she have ever doubted Lord Conrad's intentions? The man had no conscience.

Bile rose in her throat, but she choked it back.

Suddenly, even as she watched in horror and pity, the man's bleeding slowed, then stopped completely. Her eyes widened in astonishment as the skin began knitting itself up, becoming whole once more, leaving naught more than angry welts.

It was true then. He was a shifter.

If the witch Lord Conrad had consulted could be believed, this man's blood would heal her curse. The time of the hunter's moon was fast approaching. If she was to live, he would have to be sacrificed. That was what she'd been told and what Lord Conrad held as truth. Nothing would stop him from getting what he wanted, and he'd lusted after her her entire life.

Apparently drained of energy by the effort to heal his newest wounds, the man's head slowly drooped, his chin resting against his chest, his defiant glare shielded as his eyes slowly closed. Ashanti thought he must have passed out. How could he have borne the pain so silently? She looked down, realizing that there was already dried blood on the floor. How many times had this happened?

And how had Lord Conrad captured the unattainable in the first place? They were more than human, faster, more savage, and could heal any blow save one made by silver. She knew if released, he would likely kill his tormentors, for that was the way of a caged animal. He was wild and deserved to be free, not taken against his will and sacrificed on the off chance that a girl's life could be saved.

No matter that she wanted to live, Ashanti knew suddenly that she could not allow the atrocity Lord Conrad proposed. She could not bear an innocent's man's death on her conscience. She'd had enough death in her life.

CHAPTER TWO

In the past, the fear of catching her affliction had saved Ashanti from Lord Conrad's intimate pursuits, but with the capture of the beastman, a change had come over him--one that made her shiver with foreboding.

She sat at his feet, wincing as he twisted a tendril of her dark hair around his fingers, her back rigidly straight, steadfastly ignoring his lascivious stroking behind her. Would that she were a warrior, he would cease his pawing of her when he drew back a nub.

The celebration had begun hours ago if the ache in her bones was any indication of the passage of time--the men eating and drinking with gluttonous abandon. It was unusual for Lord Conrad to be so forthcoming with his generosity, but circumstances had seemed to improve his mood.

She looked around the room at the fallen men, bested by drink. They wallowed on the floor, on the tables, heads resting on pillows of pies and meats, snores echoing through the great hall as untended fires burned low to ash. All was quiet save their labored breathing.

What before had seemed excess to her, now had become the miracle she had sought. Likely the whole castle lay in a stupor, complacency and ignorance breeding carelessness and stupidity. If she could only escape Lord Conrad's clutches....

With the thought, she noticed the incessant tugging on her head had ceased, and she couldn't recall when it had happened. Ashanti waited patiently, barely breathing until she felt assured her movement would not stir him. Slowly, when enough time had passed to give her confidence, she craned her head around to look behind her. Conrad slouched back with his legs splayed wide, his head lolling to one side, an empty tankard dangling from one hand on his lap even as his other held her hair in a lax grip.

He'd finally succumbed as the rest had. She breathed a sigh of relief and relaxed her unyielding position, wanting to groan as pain lanced up her spine and down her cramped legs.

Ashanti knew this was her one chance to help the beastman--she could not pass up such an opportunity. The danger Lord Conrad presented was culminating, and she dare not hesitate or they both would be crushed by his passions. That Lord Conrad would enact his obsessions with her, she was certain. He now had nothing to hold him back from destroying her. She would at least save one person, though the cost to herself would be great. Conrad would punish her severely ... and she had no healing abilities as the shifter did.

She would not think on that now--she couldn't or what little will she had left would flee her.

Ashanti shook herself, determined to put it out of her mind. She must tackle that problem when it arose, but for now, she would do what she had promised herself.

Certain that he would be incapacitated for the night, Ashanti pulled her hair gently free and stood stiffly, stifling her moan of pain as the blood rushed back into her legs. Taking a moment to recover, she stretched her legs as sensation awakened with painful clarity until she could move without groaning.

Bending over him, she worked at the keys tied to his belt, cringing as they tinkled softly, holding her breath against the stinging, foul scent of liquor rising off him. Finally, when she thought she could take no more before passing out on his lap, she freed the keys from his belt.

She straightened and looked down at him, watching the even movement of his chest as he continued sleeping undisturbed. Smiling at her success, she closed her fist around the keys and eased away from him. Wincing at every slight sound she made, she padded softly across the cavernous room, glancing nervously back at Lord Conrad with nearly every step she took. When no battle cry erupted from him, she relaxed and continued, avoiding the largest obstacles of drunken bodies as she eased away. Ashanti stepped over fallen men as she crept out of the hall, each time knowing that now she would be caught, but no man stirred, and she exited without incident, not daring to breathe thanks until she was free.

Near the door, she grabbed her cloak where it puddled on the floor and strode into the corridor, angrily recalling Conrad's gall as he pulled it off her shoulders and flung it away from her--he would not have her cover herself, no matter her own comfort.

Defiant, she donned the black velvet and moved through the dim corridors down to the dungeon, coming to the wooden barricade. Unlocking the door, she pushed it open, grunting with the effort and walking inside. It was then she remembered the guard--too late! Ashanti froze inside the frame, braced against the half closed door, heart hammering until she couldn't breathe, couldn't think. The alarm would awaken everyone--including Lord Conrad. He would tear the hide from her bones for her defiance. All her care was for naught.

The guard made no move to stop her, just continued sitting in his chair. Why was he not raising the alarm? Could it be he thought she was supposed to be down here?

He was a drunk but surely not such a fool. Of a sudden he snorted, mocking her, then his breath wheezed out his lungs.

Ashanti looked at him closely for the first time.

He was asleep!

Empty flasks littered the floor--wine flasks she discovered as she moved closer and the pungent odor greeted her. She could scarce believe her luck!

Still more than a little wary, Ashanti moved closer, gently waving her hand before his face. He continued to snore, blissfully unaware of her intrusion. Giving thanks to the gods for their help, she took a torch and headed down the corridor, using her memory to guide her down the labyrinthine passages. She shuddered in the slightly chill air that permeated the stone lair, grateful for the heavy velvet that protected her. She pitied the man who'd suffered in the cold so naked and helpless. She would remedy the situation soon, may the gods help her.

Ashanti paused as she reached the corridor leading to his lonely cell, wondering if she'd lost what little sanity she still possessed. If Lord Conrad even suspected she'd had a hand in releasing his prisoner.... But then spent blood pooled in her mind's eye, remembered and imagined tortures playing out in her mind, and she knew there was no choice. She *would* do this. She had to ... or she would never be able to live with herself.

Decision made, Ashanti moved quietly to the cell's entrance and peered through the thick iron bars at the bound man. The torch she held flickered, dancing as a secret breeze struck it, shadows engulfing the sparse golden light. Her heart ached at the sight of the defeated man. His head hung down, hair obscuring her vision of his haggard face. Had Lord Conrad continued torturing him? It was a possibility. The man appeared to be sleeping though, or perhaps he was unconscious…in which case, she had no idea what she would do with him.

It was all speculation, best banished by going to him. Unlocking the cell, Ashanti eased the heavy door open. Thankfully, the oiled hinges made no sound. She left it open as she stepped cautiously inside.

Fears assailed her now that the time had come, and she almost thought she couldn't do it. She wiped an errant lock of black hair out of her eyes, stalling as she tried to gain her courage. What would stop him from eating her alive once she released him?

Ashanti shivered at the prospect. She could only hope he was human enough to spare her in exchange for his freedom. But then, what did she truly have to lose? She was living on borrowed time, whether Lord Conrad discovered her treachery or not. Almost, she wished she'd studied the black arts, but her soul could not have withstood the jeopardy of eternal damnation ... or rather *more* jeopardy than she already faced.

She moved close enough his scent teased her, pleasantly musky and evocative as freedom despite his ill treatment. She was near enough to touch him and yet he remained still, his breathing so shallow she couldn't detect the rise and fall of his lungs. A different fear seized her in its terrible grip, making her stomach clench painfully. Was she yet again too late to save someone? She'd been unable to help her parents and now this chance for redemption was slipping through her fingers. Had Conrad killed him with his tortures? She had no way of knowing what had been done before, or since, his capture.

Tentatively, afraid of what she'd find, Ashanti reached up to lay her fingers against a pulse in his neck. It beat surprisingly strong and fast. She sighed in relief, then frowned.

A trick? Perhaps. Perhaps not.

His skin scorched her, the flesh eat up by unnatural heat and flushed splotchy red in places Ashanti noticed now. He was ill--likely dying. Studying him, she could see he hadn't healed completely. Something must have caused him more hurt than she realized, but she couldn't fathom what it could be since shifters had such miraculous healing abilities and strength. Had a hidden injury been the reason Lord Conrad had captured him so easily?

Unbidden, unwelcome, pity surged through her. Without conscious volition, she stroked his neck and head, feeling an instinctive need to comfort. He did not respond, assuring Ashanti that he was unconscious rather than merely sleeping or feigning sleep. Emboldened, as concerned with his lack of response as she was relieved, she trailed her fingers from his hair along his neck and shoulder ... still no response ... from him.

His skin was smooth, silky beneath the sensitive skin of her fingertips and palm, the muscles beneath that smooth sheath rock hard even in his state of unconsciousness. Her fingertips tingled with tiny shocks of energy that she found strangely unnerving and invigorating at the same time. The urge to comfort was usurped by another urge, one she neither completely understood, nor questioned.

A brazen urge to explore what had always been called a nightmare compelled her to bury her fingers in the pale blond, surprisingly soft hair that flowed from his scalp along his powerful neck and fell across his chest. She should have been repulsed to touch him so intimately, but it had the opposite effect, spurred her to touch him more. Tentatively at first, she glided her fingers down his hair sprinkled chest, wincing as she encountered the welts from his beating.

Anger surged through her. That bastard Conrad deserved retribution for his actions. Unfortunately she was not the one to deal out justice.

In that moment, it almost seemed as if she stepped outside herself.

The side she knew felt remorse that he'd been made to suffer in her name, compassion for his pain.

The side she barely recognized felt far more than anger--a rising heat, a consuming hunger--almost a sense of triumph that this powerful creature was helpless to her will. Brazenly, she leaned closer, bending her head so that she could run her lips along the angry welts, brush them with her cheek, lathe them with her tongue.

Heat curled between her thighs. She squeezed them tightly together and nearly gasped at the sharp stab of pleasure.

She was barely aware of the restless movements of her hands, stroking the hard ridge of muscles along his sides, down the rippling muscles of his abdomen, up along his sides again to the arms chained above his head. The muscles along his inner arms stood out in long, hard bands that she caressed. She touched the cold steel that bound his wrists, almost as if to reassure herself he was still within her power, then allowed her hands to drift downward again, fascinated by the contrast of cold metal and heated, silky skin, roughened by a sprinkling of hair. As her restless movements brought her hands once more to the hard chest beneath her cheek, she discovered a hard male nipple and paused to tease it with her fingers, then her tongue as her fingers sought new discoveries.

The rippling muscles along his lower chest and abdomen quivered slightly as her palms skated over them, but she barely registered it, caught up in her exploration and the heady sensations it evoked. When her questing hands at last encountered his loincloth, she hesitated. Dare she explore further?

She should not.

She did.

Almost timidly now, feeling her two selves converge as doubts surfaced, warring with forbidden desires, she skated her hand lightly along the band, oh so tempted to delve inside, but caution won out and she merely ran her palm over the supple cloth where she discovered to her surprise a very large, very hard ridge of flesh. Puzzled, a little confused, she cupped her hand around it, slipping it along the hard length.

More than a little dazed, it took several heartbeats for her heated brain to catch up to her mental processes. She looked down at her hand, cupping his sex through the thin cloth. Slowly, realization sank in and, still hopeful that she was wrong, she raised her head, lifted her gaze to his face.

He was looking right at her. And he bore not the look of a man at death's door.

Ashanti couldn't breathe for several moments, felt her jaw go slack with surprise. Complete awareness awakened very slowly ... the realization that her cheek still rested on his hard chest--that she still cupped the hard ridge of his sex in her hand....

She released him as if she'd just discovered a hot poker in her hand, leapt back, feeling the blood rush from her head and then back in a sickening wave that brought a wave of cold and blackness, then a flood of bright red heat.

What foulness had bespelled her, she wondered frantically. Shame filled her, that she'd taken advantage of an ill man, unconscious, barely clinging to life.

When had he awakened?

His slanted, tawny eyes, their pupils mere slivers, studied her with a mixture of bewilderment and ... and hunger. A shiver skated over her skin, leaving goose-bumps in its wake. She wanted to run from those alien eyes, to turn away, but mesmerized, she was held rooted to the spot, her legs refusing to obey thoughts of escape.

Without fathoming why, she *needed* to touch him again, like an unheard beckoning that had to be answered. Unconsciously, she stepped close and reached up to comb his hair from his face, her wrist brushing his lips accidentally.

She felt a jolt when his tongue snaked out and touched the fragile pulse that beat there, that tasted the salt of her skin. He watched her, watched her reaction to him and seemed pleased that a simple touch affected her thusly. But he couldn't know that she'd never been touched by anyone but Lord Conrad ... and that she hated him.

At his touch...her own reaction, Ashanti wavered, tempted to flee, compelled to stay. That other side of herself that she didn't know or understand seized control of her so that instead of yielding to her inner warnings and fleeing, she moved infinitesimally closer, curling her hand around the back of his neck, drawing him down as she raised up to meet him.

She closed her eyes as his lips touched hers and a fire burst inside her, searing heat scorching soft skin where she connected with him. Her knees weakened and she drew her other arm around him to support herself, not daring, nor willing, to pull away.

He kissed her ravenously as though starved, his mouth moving in hungry nibbles over her lips, debilitating what little strength she still possessed. She'd never imagined a kiss could be so powerful.

Something beat wildly in her ears and she realized it was her pulse, deafening with its quickening. She groaned against his mouth, molding herself to his hard planes, wanting to be closer still, unwilling to stop even to breathe.

The chains rattled as he strained to touch her, to be inside her. Sensing his need, she parted her lips and he thrust his rough tongue into her mouth, delving deep, and then drawing her into him. She gasped in the back of her throat, unable to believe the simple pleasure two mouths could conjure together, reveling in the wild taste of him, an untamed force that consumed her soul and gave it to him.

Vague and disjointed as the thought was, it connected with an earlier warning, that she had somehow been bespelled and fear knifed through her.

Ashanti broke away, stumbling back from him several paces, panting for breath as she stared at him in shocked dismay. A warmth suffused her limbs, weakened her. Her skin tingled all over. Her thoughts lay in the ruins of confusion, as if she'd drunk too much wine.

Touching a hand to prickling lips, she looked at him accusingly.

His fierce gaze swept her up and down, measuring, lingering on her intimate parts as if they caressed her. She regretted her wardrobe then, felt shame and guilt flood her as she saw herself through his eyes: the scarlet linen cut in a deep vee to her navel, slit up the sides and held in place by a gold cord wrapped around her to stabilize the flimsy fabric. By Lord Cornad's will she was clothed like a courtesan, not an untouched maiden…and yet, her actions had done nothing to lead anyone to believe her an innocent.

It angered her that she had left herself in no position to dispute the knowing look in his eyes.

He studied her a moment longer, until she thought she'd crack from the suspense. Gleaming eyes met hers once more, alien, angry. "Why did you come here? Were you curious about my people's legendary skills as lovers?" His voice rolled over her, as seductive as a purr.

She swallowed hard, passion leaving dust in the wake of mortification. "No, I did not." Speaking was an effort. Her lips felt swollen, heavy. She could still taste him on her tongue and wondered if he could her. She squared her shoulders, determined that he would not see her frailty.

"Your actions belie you." He looked pointedly down at himself, drawing her attention to the erection that steepled his loincloth. Warmth flooded her cheeks at her audacity. She turned her back to him, ashamed and not wanting him to see her embarrassment, all thought of defiance fleeing her. She was a woman full grown, not a child, and yet this man, this beast, brought out a side in her she'd never seen before.

"I came to free you, though I know not now if I should risk it ... What do your people call you?"

"I am know as Blasien, and it matters not to me, my lady, if you free me. I do not need your help."

She shuddered, thinking of what he would endure in her name. Lord Conrad would never let him live even had he not been a shifter. He'd dared to touch her when she'd invited him. She couldn't look on the doomed man. "You fool. You'll be killed if I don't. I want some assurance you'll not touch me if I release you."

Ashanti trembled, hating herself, feeling the heat of his golden eyes, though she couldn't bear to see him.

"I offer you no such promises. 'Twas because of you that I was taken."

A wave of shock and guilt went through her. She hadn't expected that he would know. No doubt Lord Conrad had bragged of it to him, she thought with a mixture of shame and anger. "I know," she whispered. She hid her face with her hands. Had she been in his position, she could well imagine her feelings would mirror his own. Revenge would be sweet in her heart.

"I do thank you, however, for allowing me to free myself, *my lady*."

His words chilled her, the hackles along the back of her neck raising in warning too late. She turned and saw him straining, the muscles of his arms and legs bunching with power. A shiver arced up her spine as the sounds of chains snapping reached unbelieving ears. Without hesitation, as metal links groaned and flew through the air, she whirled and ran, but a lightning fast hand grasped her cloak and pulled her back before she could escape.

Ashanti tried to scream but he knew what she would do before she did. He clasped a hand over the lower half of her face, blocking her cries for help, and shoved her against the wall, trapping her. A tremor ran through her at the contrast of warm skin to chill block. She struck him with her fists, flailing her arms to find purchase. Blasien released her mouth to pin her arms above her head, a massive hand encircling both her wrists.

His face hovered mere inches from hers. She sucked in a breath to scream. It died in her throat at the look in his eyes.

The dungeon was far below the castle--no one would hear her. It was down here for that very reason. There were no guards keeping watch over the empty dungeon, for Lord Conrad had dismissed all but the most necessary men.....and the guard at the main gate was dead drunk even if the thought of him challenging such a man as this were not laughable. No one would come. He could do with her what he would with none the wiser.

She wanted to believe he would not harm her, but his actions told her he would do something that could damage her mind and soul rather than physically wound.

And God knew, she wanted it.

He held her captive with his body, molding her breasts to his chest, his erection digging into her lower belly. The thin linen of her gown acted as little barrier to him. Her body was taut against the wall, and something coiled inside her, near bursting to be released.

He breathed heavily, as though strained by the activity, the wildness of his scent engulfing her senses. He leaned closer, speaking low. "The situation has been reversed. What shall you do now?"

CHAPTER THREE

Sensing her weakness like he'd read her mind, Blasien lowered himself until his groin matched hers, his hard length pressing through flimsy fabric at the juncture of her thighs. She remained still, gathering her strength for a fight.

Their roles had indeed been reversed, but she was of no mind to allow him to trespass as she had, to assume the role of conqueror.

He moved a leg between hers, easing them apart until he nestled against her cleft. She struggled then, an alien wetness soaking her with his intimate contact, panic suffusing her as she realized that she must fight her own responses to him to have any hope at all of fending him off.

He quelled her rebellion with a single thrust.

She stopped instantly, trembled, unable to believe his intent.

"You like it, don't you, Ashanti?" He sniffed her, his eyes growing dark and slumberous. "I can smell your desire."

"You have nothing I want," she gritted out, straining her arms, trying to free herself and avoid his touch.

"Ah, but I do."

As though incapable of stopping himself, he ground his erection against her moist cleft, pressing her flat against the wall. She had nowhere to go, could do nothing but take the force of his movement.

Ashanti bit her lip, nearly crying out at the unwilling pleasure he evoked. She shook her head. "No. Stop."

"I know you want this, sweeting. You cannot deny it." He moved again, grinding, the roughness of cloth stroking her as nothing had ever before.

Soft whimpers escaped her as he cupped her buttocks with his free hand and drew her closer, sliding roughly against her wetness through their clothing.

Ragged gasps tore from her throat, making her hate her shameful reactions, hate him for evoking them.

"You've awakened my beast, just as you wished. It can only be satiated now but by two things, blood or...." He looked at her pointedly.

Ashanti closed her eyes. She knew what the other was. She breathed deeply, tried to regain her composure. "I asked for no such thing. Release me."

He moved his mouth down her neck. How much more could she take before giving in completely?

"You did. When you touched me. When you kissed me." His voice was muffled, his breath hot, sending goose-bumps to race over her. "Your skin is like creamed chocolate." He nuzzled her neck, nibbling her ear. "And just as sweet to my tongue." He nipped it with his teeth, sucking the lobe into his mouth as he stroked it with his strangely coarse tongue.

"Oh ... please...." She was nearing the breaking point-- knew he sensed it too. With a strength of will that nearly killed her, she whispered, "I ... said ... stop."

Blasien halted his assault at the quiet strength of her words, leaning his forehead against her neck as though pained. With an effort, he released her from the cage of his body, though he kept her arms pinned.

"So be it. I shall stop for now. You could be the death of a man, Ashanti."

She could breathe again--could scarcely recall when she'd stopped. "How ... is it ... you know my ... name?"

Blasien eased back, distancing himself. "My hearing is far keener than any human's."

"Then ... you heard it spoken?"

"Aye."

"And you heard me come down here to release you?"

He grinned, predatory, making things jump inside her. "Aye."

"You bastard. You staged this. You could have left at any time, but you tricked me." Furious at his deception that had moved her to pity and near ruination, Ashanti tried to knee his groin, but he blocked her easily. He frowned at her, as though she should not offer repercussions to his deceit.

"No, I could not escape. If you hadn't come, I would have died down here." His face grew hard, his heavy brows drawn in an angry line.

Somehow, she believed him, believed that he would rather die than reveal this weakness to another being. She sensed that she bewildered him for some reason, but she was just as confused. "I don't understand."

"You possess a power I have never encountered in a mortal beyond my land. I was struck a debilitating blow in a battle before I was claimed prisoner. My body couldn't heal it completely without changing, and I was not allowed to shift. You have healed this wound inside with these." He bent and kissed her softly. "And with this," he said, cupping her sex briefly despite her shying away. His every touch flamed her and threatened to incinerate all thought of fleeing him.

"That is why you shall be coming with me to Shadowmere."

CHAPTER FOUR

"I'll go nowhere with you willingly."

At her fierce glare and frigid posture, Blasien sighed. "Then I regret that I must do this." Reaching his free hand around, he touched the side of her neck, willing the strength of his power into the simple touch.

Ashanti's scream cut off before it began as she slumped in his arms, unconscious.

Her head fell back, baring the sculpted lines of her long neck, her fair skin begging for the mark of his teeth. The inky black of her hair pooled around her shoulders, half braided, the other free to caress her breasts and hips.

His hands itched to touch the expanse of white flesh bared by her gown, the toned tautness of her stomach tempting him beyond reason.

He groaned, swallowing hard, controlling his beast and the lust it unleashed. In all his years, he'd never lost control, but this woman was different. He looked at the exotic slant of her eyes, remembered their cerulean blue, deep as the ocean of lost souls and just as much an enigma to him. She brought out something dangerous in him, and it took every ounce of strength to reign himself in. Had she but known her danger, she would have screamed and taken the hide off him with her teeth and nails--not that it would have done her any good. A single, unarmed human had no hope of stopping a shifter.

A female had less hope, for human females were nearly impossible for even the strongest of shifters to resist. But the females were as drawn to shifters as shifters were to them--a conundrum that had mystified the most learned in the land. This woman affected him as if he were a mere cub, and he had not known such effects in many years.

He'd nearly lost the battle once. He could not afford temptation so soon. Nor could he be allowed to mate with her, for he knew his carefully restrained beast would be unleashed should he lose to the insanity of bedding her. And humans could as easily be destroyed by a beast's passions as addicted.

It would be safer for them both if he left her.

He tried to release her, wanted to with a desperation unlike him, but his body refused to obey. It was something he was unable to accomplish, simple as it should have been to let go. He sighed.

It seemed he would, against his better judgment, be taking her to Shadowmere after all.

Lifting her easily, he positioned her over one shoulder to free an arm should he need to battle their way out.

Ignoring the intoxicating scent of her skin and the tempting roundness of her buttocks so near his mouth, he moved through the dungeon, his senses seeking the way.

He was silent as he crept through the dark, the torches having burned out with no one to tend them. He did not need the light to see, however, and moved as easily as if it had been day.

Blasien sniffed the air, following the sweet, fresh scent only one of his kind could detect….the fresh sweetness that meant freedom.

He came to an iron bound door at the end of a hallway, finding also the source of the stentorian snores that had helped to guide him. Having fallen from his chair, the single guard lay curled in a fetal position on the stone floor. Blasien studied him for several moments, but the man showed no indication that anything short of a horn blast could rouse him. With a mental shrug, Blasien dismissed him and grasped the door handle. The door groaned as he pushed it open to reveal a cavernous hall draped in darkness now that all the torches had burned out.

He did not need light, however, to see that men lay sprawled in drunken slumber throughout the huge chamber. Disgust and contempt mingled with triumph as Blasien surveyed the room. Lord Conrad was either overconfident, or a fool.

Dismissing the strange ways of men, Blasien moved through the room like a shadow, pushed open the heavy door at the entrance and stood for several heartbeats, surveying the outer keep. Nothing moved. Dimly, he detected faint sounds of movement here and there with his keen hearing, but those who stirred were too far to present a threat.

Blending in with the shadows, he worked his way through until he reached the outer wall. Only a imbecile would have so poorly protected a castle, more a manor than anything else. The lord's confidence in his safety was foolhardy, and it was only a matter of time before tragedy struck. It was good that he was taking Ashanti away, even if it meant she would be surrounded by enemies. He would be there to protect her.

The feeling itself should have unnerved him, but it did not. Inexplicably, it felt right, this need to protect. He had lived so long for only himself that something so alien was welcome.

Sprinting through the dark landscape, he ran faster than the human eye could detect even if they'd been watching, his body shifting as he ran to gain speed. Golden, black spotted fur covered his skin as he assumed his half-leopard form mid-run.

The border wasn't far from these lands. In the sky, the blood moon had set, but the silver still remained high. He should be able to reach Shadowmere before day, and by then they would not be found by her people. She should sleep through the night.

He only hoped they would both survive what awaited them once he reached home.

* * * *

Ashanti awoke to a sharp object stabbing her firmly in her right buttock. She groaned, wondering what had happened to her mound of pillows as she pulled the crippling rock out from under her before trying to sit up. She discovered she couldn't without a great deal more pain.

Subsiding, she lay on the ground, trying to remember when she'd been hit in the belly, for it felt horribly sore.

An eerie cry echoed through the air. Galvanized, Ashanti sat up, stifling her moan of pain, looking wildly around at the unknown landscape for the approaching danger, her heart thundering in her ears.

She spotted it as if the mere thought could conjure him up. Without being told, she knew she'd crossed the border. And only one person would bring her here--Blasien.

He trotted over a rise, sparse trees shading him from the blinding sun, a hunk of raw meat in his hands. Blond hair blew around his shoulders in a soft breeze, catching the light like gold. He'd be breathtaking if she wasn't so annoyed…and frightened.

And yet she realized almost the moment the thought occurred to her that her fear had been banished the moment she had spotted Blasien and an odd sort of peace had settled over her. Unwilling to examine that thought at the moment, she dismissed it as she watched Blasien's approach.

He stopped when he reached her and she craned her neck up, shielding her eyes from the sun. Small beads of water ran down his golden chest, gleaming like jewels in his hair as it clung to his face and arms. From no where the urge to catch those droplets of water on her tongue suffused her, flooding her with warmth. Resolutely, she ignored the unthinkable.

He had been hunting.

And she did not appreciate being scared just after she'd awakened. "Why were you howling?"

He ignored the grumpy tone of her voice as he answered proudly, "I've returned with meat. I've brought this for you, though we dare not light a fire. The smell of blood is enough of a draw in this land."

Ashanti's stomach heaved. She'd never had a big appetite, least of all first thing in the morning ... and *never* for raw meat. "Thank you, but no."

He frowned down at her from his towering advantage. "You'll grow weak if you do not eat."

She struggled to stand, ignoring his proffered hand. "I can safely lose a few pounds until I have *cooked* meat. That," she pointed at it in disgust, "could kill me." She'd fasted many times in the past with ease. The ability would a godsend now, she knew for certain.

"Many things could kill you. We all eat raw meat safely."

"Who is this *all*?"

"Shifters."

She was not convinced, and his weak argument did little to assuage her fears. He could heal *wounds* in a matter of *seconds*. She did not think diseased meat would affect him as it would her.

"Ashanti," he growled.

"Blasien," she growled back.

He threw his hands up, knowing defeat when he saw it.

She refrained from gloating and looked around at the deserted landscape. Save for the forest he'd ventured from, all she could see was dirt and rock. Despite the lack of appeal, however, she felt an inexplicable sense, almost of euphoria, settle over her. Again, she refused to explore it, yielding instead to curiosity. "Why have you brought me here? And why am I so sore?"

"Because I wished it. And I carried you here over my shoulder."

"Which explains much. You always get what you wish. I suppose next you shall want to share blood," she added dryly.

He frowned. "Blood sharing is sacred. To be done only between ... it is best you not know these secret ceremonies."

She almost laughed at his serious expression. She hadn't felt so free since she was a child and all at once she knew exactly whence the sense of euphoria had arisen. She was free of Lord Conrad, something she'd never expected or even dared to hope for. "I jest. Do not look so. Take me to water, now."

"Yes, mistress." He bowed, and she laughed, struck by his absurdity, though she wanted to strangle him. He had freed her from her prison, and for that she would always be thankful.

He led her to a small pool formed by a shallow creek collecting in a basin of rock. Strange tracks marred the dirt, and she shivered, imagining all sorts of horrors roaming freely here.

The unnatural, as they'd been called, all those of preternatural blood had been banished to this land, surrounded on three sides by an impassable mountain range. They were forbidden to leave, but a tentative truce prevented humans from entering, lest a new war should arise from their transgressions.

Her family had been lost in the last conflict a decade ago. A witch's curse had claimed their lives and her own soul.

Maybe the crone had felt guilt at the idea of killing a child, maybe not, but Ashanti had been allowed to live--at least for a time.

She had but about a week left to live. When the moons aligned in the hunter's eye, the evil eating her inside would lie dormant no longer and stake final claim to her life. Nothing could rid her of the malady. Lord Conrad had consulted a witch, who had convinced him that a shifter's blood would be her salvation, but Ashanti knew there was no hope.

And yet, strangely, she hadn't felt any of its exhausting symptoms the past few hours--not since last eve in fact. And she'd slept through the entire night--something she hadn't done in more years than she could remember.

Still, she had no hope. It was futile to allow herself to think that she did. The witch's curse would claim her in the end. It was best not to imagine any other conclusion but the one destined for her. She was thankful that Blasien had taken her from that place--to be allowed some measure of happiness in her final days.

Ashanti knelt and drank, then bathed her hands and face in the clear water, enjoying the feel of the cool rivulets that dampened her hair and skin. She looked up when movement caught the corner of her eye.

Blasien watched her. His eyes followed the trickles of water as they slid down her throat, past the valley of her breasts, pooling in her exposed navel.

She could almost feel him touching her, so intense was his gaze. Desire blossomed, the scent a drug that pulled him to her.

Impossibly fast, he moved to where she knelt, kneeling before her on his knees like a supplicant, though he was too proud to be dominated, commanding only submissive thoughts in her mind.

"I beg a drink of the lady." He did not await her leave, however. He leaned toward her even as he whispered the words huskily, flicking his tongue over her neck, catching the water in his mouth. Ashanti shivered with pleasure.

This was wrong. She shouldn't allow it. Couldn't--but he entranced her, holding her in thrall when she knew she should do anything but submit.

Gently, he lowered her to the ground. With his tongue, he traced a line of moisture between her breasts. She sucked in a sharp breath as his teeth grazed the supple skin and then moved on. He placed tormenting, nibbling bites down the concave of her stomach, his tongue teasing her navel, his lips breaking the dam she'd built inside herself.

Ashanti clutched his head in her hands, running her fingers through his silky hair, wanting more, wanting him to go lower, lower still. It was as though a rope connected him to her, coiling tighter with each touch.

A pulse throbbed in her sex, pounding, aching for him to touch here there--needing him as she needed air to breathe.

This was danger. It was death--his death, but she wouldn't let it go that far, she told herself. The witch's words intruded, pricked her fogged brain. *Let no man bed you, for he will suffer your fate. Your father's line dies with you.*

No, no! Her black hair tumbled around them both as she shook her head violently, willing the words away, wanting to enjoy her last days on earth, needing him in a way that she had never needed anything else in her life.

The god of innocents protect her, she couldn't stop. Her will had abandoned her.

Blasien stopped, drew away despite her efforts to hold him to her.

She nearly screamed in frustration.

Perhaps he sensed her internal struggle? Perhaps he fought his own. His body shuddered with the effort to pull away from her.

Shame at what she'd encouraged filled her. He had the will to stop when she did not. She would kill him if she gave herself to him. It was inevitable.

She looked away, unable to bear her image reflected in his cat eyes, unwilling to tell him death was so much a part of her. "Let me go back, please."

"No. I cannot leave you, and you would never make it back alone."

It did not matter over much. Hers was a finite time, come what may. "I do not belong here. Someone will kill me. I know the tortures humans can endure here." A chill crept into her soul as she found herself uttering the thoughts she'd refused to acknowledge when she realized she had crossed the border. There was death--and then there was death.

She had lived many years with the witch's curse, had feared it, and yet had grown accustomed to the hour and manner of her death. Blasien had freed her to face a far more terrible end should they be caught.

"I will not allow anyone to touch you. Even if it means ... I must ... kill you to protect you."

CHAPTER FIVE

"That is a comfort," Ashanti said dryly, sitting up and brushing the sand and leaves from her skin and clothing. "Send me back, I say."

"You little fool." He rose, pulling her to her feet. When she would have turned away, he made her face him, shook her as though he'd force some sense into her. "You have no comprehension of what could happen if we don't move forward. We must reach my castle before night falls. Did you not notice these tracks by the pool? They belong to the hunters. We risk attracting them if we do not make it in time. They only travel by night. Your ... scent will be irresistible to them and easily tracked."

Hunters. She'd been weaned on horrific tales of the hunters of Shadowmere. They were not merely shifters but something else. They had the cravings of both wolf and vampire. Once they were on your trail, you could only escape in daylight--the one time when they rested, and sometimes not even then if they were powerful enough.

They patrolled the borders, keeping the humans out ... and the Shadowmeres inside.

She was surprised they hadn't been caught already, as close as they were to their territory. Blasien would not be able to protect them from so deadly a threat. He was but one man--there was only so much one could do.

"Then why did you bring me?" Angrily, she pulled away from him.

"I had no choice."

There was something in the way he spoke that cooled the anger, that spoke of both confusion and yearning. Ashanti felt it as a painful clutching at her heart and knew a sense of defeat.

When her time was so short, was it really worth arguing? Particularly when she realized that she had found more pleasure in being with Blasien than she had known in many years.

But if she yielded to his demands, could she protect him from her curse? It seemed doubtful. Her resistance was tenuous at best. And yet, what point in debating the matter with herself? He would have his way. There was nothing she could do to stop him, nothing she could do to protect him, save hold her own desires in check.

"I will go with you ... for a time. Until I can return to my own kind."

"I would have it no other way." He nodded and looked almost relieved that she hadn't fought him more. "It is time we go."

They set off at once, but they hadn't gone more than a few paces before the ground began cutting Ashanti's bare feet. She said nothing, but Blasien had the uncanny ability of reading her thoughts, or perhaps he could *hear* them.

Without warning, he scooped her into his arms and began jogging over the rough terrain. She clung to his neck, thankful, amazed at his strength, for she was no delicate beauty. After a few moment's uneasiness, Ashanti nestled against him, breathing in the unmistakable scent of his skin--something wild and animal. Strangely, he made her feel safe. Even though he'd taken advantage of her position, she still felt comfort in his arms that mystified her. She only hoped nothing ill befell him, for he seemed far too pig-headed for his own good, as all men were.

No matter how hard she tried to dismiss it, though, it occurred to her that Blasien could not keep this pace all day. He would falter eventually, no matter that she didn't want to think about it, nor how capable he seemed.

She would only slow him down. And they would both pay the price.

* * * *

They were being hunted.

And it was her fault.

She'd begun feeling the cycle of the moon's alignment. Her body became weak. Despite her best efforts to disguise that fact, Blasien knew when it overcame her each time. He'd stopped repeatedly to allow her rest from the constant jarring of his stride. Foolish as it was, she'd been thankful. She prayed they weren't doomed now because of it. How much peril could her soul take before eternal damnation?

Night had crept up on them and pounced, and still they were leagues away from his castle. Leagues away from safety.

As she'd rested, she'd watched Blasien, pacing like a caged animal. He crouched low to the ground, moonlight glimmering on his skin like molten silver. He turned his head, listening, scenting the air for danger. He looked incredibly animal as he moved, muscles lithe, taut, hypnotizing.

Ashanti didn't know how long they'd been followed, or when Blasien had realized it, but his repeated actions were terrifying her. She expected any moment for something to leap out at them, and it set her nerves on edge. Being completely reliant on him for protection did not sit well with her, but the wound to her pride paled beside the certainty that if she had not been there, there would likely be no danger to either of them.

In her weakness, her selfishness, she had doomed them both to a horrible death.

Blasien approached and picked her up without a word-- began running once more.

"They're after us, aren't they? The hunters?" She looked up at him, studying his face at her leisure. She'd had much time to do so, and still the angular planes fascinated her. He looked grim now, his strong jaw clenched with tension. He must be exhausted but he hadn't faltered once.

Long moments passed as he continued in silence, and she despaired of him answering. Finally, he said, "Aye. I did not want to tell you."

"I'm not blind. You should have left me." Brave words easily spoken. She buried her face against his chest, enjoying his warmth, his smell, but as he jumped across a small creek and shook her she had to bite back a gasp of pain. He tightened his arms around her, sensing her discomfort.

"I could not have left you. You know this."

She was beginning to feel like she'd never want to leave him--a feeling that was frightening and, sadly, in vain. She felt an inexplicable connection to him that she'd never had with anyone else. Lord Conrad had been her sole company for most of her life, and his cruelty had not only repelled and horrified her, it had convinced her that she could expect nothing else in a male. Somehow, though, she instinctively knew that Blasien would never allow himself to be guided by cruelty, and she was both grateful and seduced by this strange mixture of warrior and tenderness.

Remembering she hadn't replied, she said softly, "I know. At the least you should not have allowed me so much rest. They'll kill us when they find me with you." Ashanti felt his muscles stiffen beneath her hands. He knew the truth of her words and did not deny them.

"What's done is done."

She was a weakling for allowing him to carry her so far, for not demanding that she walk on her own, but she could never have kept his pace and the end would have been the same regardless, perhaps worse. Had he found freedom only to face a worse death at inhuman hands?

Cries broke the stillness like ripples in water, high keening howls that closed in from all directions. They did not sound like any wolves she'd ever heard in her life. Ashanti felt her soul shrivel in fear.

The hunters had found them.

How many were there? The wails seemed to come from everywhere, drowned out all else but the pounding thump of her own heart.

Blasien increased his pace. Sweat formed on his creased brow as he strained to save them both. She wanted to pummel him with her fists and knock some sense into him, but the terror in the night froze her limbs and chilled her blood.

Struggling to breathe, to think, she said, "Put me down. NOW. You can go faster without me." She *was* a fool, just as he'd called her once before. They would *both* die now.

"No," he gritted out, breathing harshly. "I brought you here. They'll not take you without killing me first."

That was what she feared. He was too stubborn and determined to obey logic, but then, the animal world did not obey the rules that governed hers.

Blasien stopped suddenly, breathing loud in the silence overwhelming her own heaving breaths. She looked up from the safety of his chest, followed the line of his gaze.

The blood moon had risen and bathed the land in a crimson wash, sanguine light illuminating a horror she did not want to comprehend ... wanted to unsee and banish from her mind and memories.

Dozens of men, more wolf than human stood before them. In their dark visages, rows of teeth gleamed blood red with the moon. Their black fur absorbed the light like an eternal darkness.

"Don't look at their eyes, sweeting," Blasien murmured as he set her on her feet.

She nodded. The hunters had the power to enthrall anyone foolish enough to be captured with their gaze. Ashanti kept her balance on weak limbs as she stood, carefully avoiding the wolves' eyes that could capture as easily as any vampire. They had the powers of both shifter and vampire, and none of the weakness. They were the perfect border guards. The perfect killers.

Ashanti looked around, her heart sinking as she saw what they faced.

No hope ... no hope.

They were surrounded.

CHAPTER SIX

The wolf men parted and a man-beast strode forth from their midst to face Blasien. Ashanti felt almost like she was witnessing a stand off as he approached, for both men tensed with barely leashed savagery as if each knew he faced his equal and must find a weakness if he was to have a chance of victory.

As she watched his approach with deepening dread, Ashanti saw that the man-beast's body was adorned with what looked to be silver but couldn't possibly be. A ring of metal encircled his brow like a coronet and long cuffs of the same material encased his forearms. A wide silver colored belt shaped like two wolves fighting held a short leather kilt snugly to his narrow waist. Long midnight hair blew around him.

Ashanti was careful not to meet his eyes even as she looked upon his face. He did not bear any resemblance to the monsters around him. He appeared to be human, but no one could look on him and not see him for what he was--a monster.

"Blasien, he is one of them?" Ashanti whispered. "Does he wear ... is that ... ?"

"Silver? Yes, it is and he is one of them." The man approached them slowly, like a hunter stalking a doe. "It is a sign of strength and confidence. He does not need to shift to reign supreme over the hunters, and he can resist the pain silver causes us. He is their greatest warrior and the most feared hunter in the land."

"How do you--?"

Some emotion Ashanti couldn't decipher briefly crossed Blasien's hard features, but instead of answering her question, he said in a harsh whisper, "Silence, he nears."

The man stopped several feet from them. Blasien tensed, ready to spring, his hands clenched in tight fists. Never had she been so aware of their differences until now. This was his world. These were his people. He was savage, and she could never forget that.

"It has been long since I've seen you, Blasien. Long since you left Ravenel." The man's voice reminded her of a growl, a low rumble of sound ... as though unused for a long time.

"It has, Raphael."

Ashanti sensed an infinitesimal lessening in Blasien's guard. Clearly they knew each other. Did that mean there was some hope after all?

But she did not allow that to comfort her. They did not behave as enemies, but neither did they behave as friends, and, at any rate, the question seemed moot, for the horde that surrounded them did not seem as if they would stand down only because Raphael asked it of them, even if he was their leader.

"The law has not changed. You cannot bring humans here, no matter how... tempting." He paused to look Ashanti over and Blasien stepped in front of her, shielding her with his body. He looked almost amused by Blasien's possessiveness. "You know this."

Blasien's expression hardened. "I do."

"My men want her. They've followed her scent since you left the border. You know they cannot be prevented from taking her from you. She is unmarked."

Raphael sounded almost apologetic, but clearly he was issuing a cryptic message. Unfortunately, Ashanti wasn't certain of what he meant or what it might mean to her.

Regardless, she could not bear to remain silently by, awaiting her fate. Fear not withstanding, she moved from behind Blasien, pulled at his arm. He did not spare her a glance. "Blasien, of what does he speak?" They were speaking of her fate; she had a right to know what was going on. If she didn't, she would go mad with fear.

Some emotion she could not decipher passed briefly across Blasien's features before they hardened once more into a cold, dangerous mask. "I did not want to do this, Ashanti." Blasien pointedly did not look at her. His jaw hardened, teeth clenched.

Something in his manner frightened her far more than the known danger that surrounded them. She felt suddenly lightheaded as she recalled his vow to her, that he would kill her himself before he would allow them to have her.

"It is the only way," Raphael said, his voice solemn, almost resigned. The men behind him grumbled in a foreign tongue, but he quelled them into silence with a look.

Blasien turned to her and held up his hand. His fingernails elongated, curling like wicked barbs, the ivory claws stark in the dimness.

Ashanti's mouth dropped open as she watched the transformation, seamless as flowing water and just as fast. Too late, she took a step back in horror, stumbling in her haste to flee, but he grabbed her arm with his other hand, holding her prisoner. She struggled against him, her thoughts chaotic, but his strength was inhuman and she could not break his hold. She couldn't believe what was happening, what he was going to do. Not Blasien. She had trusted him with her life when she'd never trusted anyone before. Would he rip her throat out now?

He looked pained at her terror of him, regret darkening his eyes. "I am sorry for this," he said softly before lightly slashing his claws across her heart.

Ashanti screamed as the poison seeped into her and began pumping through her veins, small, hurt whimpers escaping her as a wall of blackness crashed in upon her.

Blasien caught her in his arms as she collapsed, feeling a welling of sickness. She looked like a broken doll, crushed by the heels of men. And she had been.

Four thin, crimson lines bloomed through the slices in her gown, marring her supple skin, and a regret he'd never known flooded through Blasien like bile.

Raphael came up behind him, touched his shoulder. "I'm sorry, my friend. It was the only way. You know what they would have done to her." There was only so much control a leader of the hunters could expect to retain. A human female was not something they could easily deny themselves.

Blasien nodded curtly, cradling her limp form close as a spasm wracked her body, but he was far more angry at himself than Raphael. He'd known when he took her that it might come to this.....or worse.

He wondered now just how selfless his motives had been. He'd feared Conrad would slay her when he learned of her treachery, but he did not know the man, could not be certain that she would've been in danger there. He *had* been certain she would be in danger if he brought her...and yet he'd yielded to his desire for her.

Or perhaps he'd yielded to his desires only because of her usefulness to him?

She had done what could not be done.....healed a mortal wound that he could not heal himself. With her, he stood a chance of regaining what was rightfully his...Ravenel. Without her, perhaps, perhaps not.

Disgust filled him...and fury ... at himself ... at the fates. He had wanted her as she was. He had not wanted it to come to this.

Raphael faced his men and announced Blasien's marking of the female, then turned back to him, ignoring the furiously muttered challenge several of his men barked at them. They were disappointed, but they would not challenge him outright, nor Blasien since the female was now clearly marked. It was the law of the land.

"We will give you escort. I do not need be told that something foul has befallen you of late."

Blasien hesitated, but clearly it was more than a mere offer of escort. Raphael would see to it that Blasien returned to his own territory. "My thanks."

Raphael nodded and prepared to leave.

Blasien smoothed the sweat soaked hair back from Ashanti's face, touching the delicate, petal soft skin, wishing things had played out differently.

Her face ... the pure horror in her eyes when he struck her ... never had he thought himself a monster before, but her damnation cut him to the core. He had done no more than many before him. It was a ritual that had been performed throughout the centuries, but the thought gave him no comfort.

She was going to kill him when she realized what he'd done. And that she could never leave Shadowmere again.

* * * *

Ashanti awoke in the middle of the night to the soft swaying of Blasien's arms and a fire in her left breast. The vestiges of sleep wore off instantly as she remembered what he'd done to her. A fury seared her mind of anything but escape and leaving him far, far behind.

As soon as the memory came to her, she fought him, bucking in his relaxed arms and kicking until he dropped her in surprise. She landed on her feet with a grace she'd never before known she possessed and took off running through the hunters in a crosswise direction.

None stopped her, though they ceased their progression. Dimly, she recognized Blasien's deep shout behind her, but she wasn't going to stop merely because he wished it. She was precious few seconds ahead of him, hopeless if she'd been thinking clearly. Her breast pulsed as he gained on her, and her newfound speed faltered.

Suddenly, he lunged forth and caught her, hurtling them both to the ground. He rolled quickly until she lay panting beneath him, alternately growling and bucking at his immovable weight. She cursed him for his advantage over her.

"Hold, she-cat." He pinned her flailing arms down and straddled her. "Why have you run from me? Stop fighting me!"

Ashanti glared at him, putting every ounce of animosity she could muster into her eyes. "You lost my cooperation when you struck me." She bit at him, but he remained out of her reach. Frustrated, she collapsed back, calmed for the moment, regaining her strength to fight again.

He regarded her warily, not trusting that she'd been so easily subdued. "I rescued you. Can you not understand that? There was no other way but to give you the mark of the beast. The hunters would have raped and slaughtered you, bathed in your blood."

She knew he had saved her, but she didn't want to hear it. For once she wanted her life to be her own. "How high handed of you! I can rescue myself." The fact that she sounded like a spoilt child did not escape her, but she ignored it.

He did not look convinced. Ashanti growled and attempted to free her arms, ignoring the way his total domination made her blood race and her insides quiver despite her simmering rage. The bastard did not deserve her desire, and she would be damned if she'd let him know she wanted him no matter what he'd done to her. She would be a fool to trust him with something that so lowered her defenses.

Blasien seemed to read her mind, knew the conflict warring inside her, mind and heart struggling with lust and desire. A change came over him, deepening his voice to a husky rumble that caused shivers to skate up her spine. "Much as I would love to give you what you want so badly, I am afraid I have not the time to properly devote myself to you."

Ashanti was shocked speechless, but only for a moment. "You bastard." She squirmed but her struggles only seemed to excite him. She went still as his hard erection spanned the short distance to her body and pressed into her stomach. Instantly, she felt her sex mirror his lust, warm liquid dampening her thighs. It was as though he could compel her to do whatever he wished and want everything he could give her.

"Stop that," she gritted out when he rubbed against her, leaning close enough she could feel his warm breath on her face, his hair teasing her sensitive skin.

"You've done this to me."

"No. No ... I ... did ... not." Her teeth were bared and gritted, and she didn't care how foolish he thought her, nor how wild she must look.

"Have you never seen the mating of two cats? The female always struggles before finally submitting to her mate."

She felt a strong desire to scratch the smirk of satisfaction off his face. "I am not a cat," she muttered through gritted teeth.

"But you will be."

CHAPTER SEVEN

"No. No, no," Ashanti said over and over, shaking her head, unwilling to believe. Claws ... Blood ... The marks on her chest that were already healing, though only hours old…. All were clues that had bitter truth in them.

"The change has already begun. You feel me as I feel you. The ordinary, dulled senses of a mortal will become hypersensitive as it progresses."

"I hate you. You've made me into a monster." She could never go back to her world, never find the freedom she longed to possess. It was amazing how devastating that thought was given that she had nothing to return to, nothing in her own world to cherish.

He looked saddened, almost guilty. She didn't believe his facade. It was part of men's nature to deceive.

Blasien sighed heavily. "I know, but it was the only way to save you. By the hunter's moon, the change will be complete."

Ashanti closed her eyes to the pain, almost relieved at his announcement. She wouldn't be a monster long. "I'll be dead by then."

"Why is that?" he asked sharply.

"I am dying. A witch's curse will claim my life on the night of the hunter's moon of my 20th year. It destroys my body even now."

"Can you feel it, truly?"

"Yes, I--" She was going to say of course she could, but the gnawing pain and weakness had left her. In its place she felt an unnatural heat mending, suffusing her with life and strength. Why had she not noticed? Had he somehow made her recognize the change? "What ... what has happened?"

"You are changing. No malady can harm you now. Your blood is not that of a mortal's any more. Will you continue to try to escape or can I release you?"

"I'll not fight you." She was far too stunned by what had happened to resist. Could it possibly be true? Would she be free of her curse? Had Blasien managed to save her when no one else could? Hope burgeoned in her chest despite a lifetime of cynicism and hard logic.

"How can I believe you? Trust you?"

Blasien rose and helped her stand. Already she was recovered from their encounter. Her legs were no longer cramping and weak, her breathing had returned to normal. She felt ... good, and it was a surprising change.

"When the eye of the hunter passes and nothing ill befalls you, you will believe. Now," he held his arm out to her, "let us see how fast you can run."

* * * *

The castle sat on a rise of land like a huddled, old man defending his property, a great wall surrounding it with protective ancient stone. The gates leading to the castle loomed to soaring heights above them, solid wood monstrosities large enough a dragon could pass through them without scraping his wings on either side.

Only Raphael remained with them now, having sent his men back to the others guarding the borders. She was glad they did not face this alone, for there hung an oppressive air around the thick castle walls. Deep foreboding lodged in her breast at what portents it told.

Pale amber light seeped into the gray sky as the sun rose above the horizon to banish the night and welcome the day. Raphael was not affected by the light as his men were, and so he would aid them if need be.

Blasien faced the center where the massive gates met in a solid, unscalable wall, staring unblinking at the obstacle, his body tense with concentration.

Raphael calmly watched him, waiting for something, though Ashanti did not know what it could be. The urge to scream at the both of them was strong.

"What is happening?" she asked, proud of her calmness, but she received only a mildly amused look from Raphael that made her want to slap him.

She realized then that she'd been able to meet his eyes for some time now and wondered if this was part of the new power overcoming her humanity. Unless he simply had no interest in mesmerizing her--which was a distinct possibility since he seemed to be friends with Blasien--her musings cut off as metal screeched, scraping and groaning with the movement of thousands of pounds.

The gate was opening! How and why were foremost in her mind, and then the fear that an army was about to greet them assailed her. She had no reason to think this other than Blasien's and Raphael's strange behavior, but danger was a palpable thing to her.

The iron braced timbers swung open with the ease and speed of a gate a quarter of their size, and she marveled at the ingenuity that allowed such a feat to even be possible.

The gates missed Blasien by inches as they opened, and Ashanti flinched when he did not. A man stood in the center of the entrance facing Blasien. Raphael straightened at once, but Blasien was unmoved.

The man strode forth, a smile on his face, his cerulean hair and gold skin contrasting sharply with the pristine white of his kilt. By his side, a wicked toothed blade hung, a jewel glowing with red fire in the pommel. She'd never seen such coloring on a man. His strange, exotic looks both intrigued and shocked her. Dimly she recalled tales from her childhood of an ancient race of beings, seers, but legend had it that the race had died out long ago. It could not be, of course, but the idea was intriguing nevertheless.

He clasped arms with Blasien as a friend would, and Ashanti released a breath she hadn't realized she held. The stranger could not be an enemy, and she was thankful. She couldn't recall a time when her nerves had been so strained.

"I heard your call, Lord Blasien. I could not believe it when I felt your mind touch mine. We'd been told you were dead."

Blasien nodded. "What news inside, Syrian?"

Syrian's smiling face grew grim. "Moran has taken the castle in your absence."

A cold fury settled over Blasien's features, echoing in Ashanti's soul like it was her own. "And the people?"

"They remain loyal to you, my lord. Moran took the castle by cowardice since he knew he could not best you in a fair fight, but he holds them captive with Mortalsblade. I could do nothing to break the blade's barrier that protects him."

"It was Mortalsblade which struck me."

"I wonder that you still live. How is that?"

"The woman, Ashanti, cured me." Blasien pulled her close and draped an arm around her waist.

Syrian's sapphire eyes widened in disbelief and astonishment. "She is mortal?"

"No longer."

Syrian glanced down at the four healing cuts showing through her torn gown. "I understand, though she will need to display them until it is complete."

Blasien nodded, stroking her back in soothing circles during their exchange until she felt she could purr. She was becoming less and less human and more in tune with the animal side of her nature. A need was building inside her blood, something she couldn't quite understand but frustrated her nonetheless.

She shook the cloud from her mind as Blasien caught her attention. "This is Syrian, sorcerer and advisor to me while he chooses to remain at Ravenel."

The sorcerer took her hand in his, pressing strangely soft, metallic lips to the back of her hand. "A pleasure to meet one of your rare gift, Lady Ashanti."

"You already know Lord Raphael, Syrian." The men exchanged nodded greetings.

"Take me to Moran. The gods will rejoice in the sacrifice I will give to them."

CHAPTER EIGHT

The sun beat down upon them, warming the air, feeling out of place with what was about to transpire. Night's cloak seemed better suited to bloodshed.

The challenge had been issued as they walked through an eerily silent courtyard to the main entrance of the castle. Moran had no choice but to answer it if he was to keep the seat of power over the pard. As they approached the main structure, the heavy doors seemed to open on their own accord, admitting them into the crowded great hall.

A sea of people, some half-cat, others wearing the guise of humans, parted for their true lord, their excitement at his return and the blood that would spill unmistakable to even her own dull senses. Blasien led with long, sure strides, Syrian and Raphael fanned out behind him. Ashanti trailed after them, feeling eyes watching her from both sides, though she kept her gaze ahead.

The hall looked like the dwelling of pagans. Great columns supported a domed ceiling that stretched far above them, the blinding sun shining through a skylight cut out of the stone and protected with a sheet of glass. Huge basins of flames lined the walkway, casting orange and gold light over the assemblage as it mingled with the sun's rays. She should have been over warm, but she was not. Despite her concern over what was to come, she noticed, and it made her wonder what sort of fire cast light, but little heat.

At the end of the hall a throne stood in the center, set atop a dais cut from ancient rock and carved with images of the leopard god, Durth, fighting his age-old enemy, Lorica, the lizzar temptress.

A man who could only be Moran sat upon the throne. He was huge, appearing taller than Blasien, who'd seemed a giant to her. His body was thickly over-muscled, bulging with hard tissue. On his dark head he wore a crown that resembled the face of a cat, two huge emeralds set in it like eyes. On his lap he held a double edged silver sword that glowed with an unholy green light--Mortalsblade.

Ashanti felt her heart skip a beat as she recognized it. The legendary weapon had been lost for decades, though eagerly sought by men hungry for power. How had he come by it when no other had? It was wholly unnatural for a beastman to claim the thing as his weapon--a bane to their very existence.

"I see you've returned from the dead, *Lord* Blasien," Moran said in a low, challenging growl. He stood, hefting the sword in his right hand as Blasien stopped at the stairs to the dais.

Blasien smiled coldly. "I've come to finish what you started. You issued the challenge. I will end this."

"So be it." Wasting no more words, no doubt hoping to catch Blasien off guard and deal out death swiftly, Moran charged Blasien, his sword slicing through the air with a whining whistle, green fire trailing in its wake.

Blasien leapt out of the way and the blade missed cleaving him in half by mere inches.

"Blasien!" Syrian called, throwing his own sword to the unarmed man.

Catching the toothed blade as it sailed through the air, Blasien brought it up just as Moran struck again. Green light blasted red fire as the magical blades clashed and sparked, the steel grinding together.

"You always were a coward, Moran," Blasien gritted out.

Moran feinted, landing a vicious blow to Blasien's ribs when he overextended. Bones cracked, deafening to Ashanti's ears and a wave of fear and nausea washed over her. The blow would have killed a mortal man, but Blasien faltered only momentarily, pushing the heavier man back where he stumbled over the steps. Moran had barely regained his balance when Blasien struck him. Moran screamed when the sharp teeth of the red glowing blade bit into his arm, ripping out a chunk of flesh so that blood spewed out in a shower of crimson.

Ashanti wanted to scream for them to stop, but she dared not break Blasien's concentration. Mortalsblade had nearly killed him before. If it had weakened him, he could spare none of his strength in this battle if he was to win. One scratch from Mortalsblade could kill him--the poison had already entered his blood once before. Moran knew this-- had to. No doubt that was why he had answered the challenge so easily. He knew he need only nick Blasien to reign victorious.

The blood gushing from Moran's wound covered the floor, forming a treacherously slick pool, making their footing hazardous. Her heart leapt to her throat with each encounter, threatening to choke her.

Ashanti couldn't stand to watch, but she couldn't look away. She crowded against Raphael, who sensed her horror and put his arm around her shoulder. "Why does Blasien not shift and end this?" she cried, looking away when both men nearly fell on one another's blades from the slick footing.

"The challenge was issued in this form. It must be fought as they are or the people will not follow."

Suddenly, Blasien slipped in the blood, his blade flying from his hand as he tried to catch himself and failed. He landed heavily on his back and half twisted as if to rise. Moran, grinning like a madman, closed in, raising his blade for the final, fatal strike.

Ashanti screamed and tried to run to him, to save him, but Raphael held her back. She fought against the bonds of his arms to no avail--could only watch in horror as Blasien's death played out before her eyes.

Enjoying his imminent victory and his enemy's helplessness, Moran paused, towering over him, gloating, taking his time in issuing Blasien's death blow. Blasien suddenly struck at him, crushing Moran's knee with a kick that crippled him. He screamed and fell to one knee, Mortalsblade hanging loose in lax hands debilitated with pain. Blasien moved in the blink of an eye to snatch the blade from his hands. The blade a whirling green, he spun and sent the metal slicing through the thick muscles of Moran's neck, cutting his head from his body.

Moran fell to the floor with a thud, blood pooling around his lifeless body. The head rolled across the floor, leaving a scarlet trail.

Blasien had won the battle.

Ashanti fainted in Raphael's arms.

CHAPTER NINE

Ashanti awoke on a satin covered bed large enough to sleep at least ten people. She had no idea how much time had passed, but felt instinctively that it had been no more than a matter of hours. Had she been drugged while she slept? Dimly, she seemed to recall wine being forced down her throat, could still taste its sweetness in her mouth.

Gathering her bearings, she eased into a sitting position, looking at the room beyond through black gossamer draped from the ceiling that surrounded the bed.

A fire crackled against one wall, housed in a huge stone fireplace, guarded by a limestone mantel supported by carvings of seated leopards. Before it stood a gold tub inlaid with black marble, curls of steam rising from its depths. Beside the bed, a table was set with roasted meat and cheese. Realizing she was famished, she slid to the edge and greedily partook of the fare. She couldn't remember the last time she'd eaten.

Satiated, Ashanti arose from the low-set bed, her hair loose and tousled around her shoulders. Black furs softened her approach to the tub, silkily rubbing against her bare soles. Heated, rose scented water beckoned her, and she stripped off her ruined scarlet gown, giving in to temptation that she could not have resisted had she wanted to.

She eased into the wide tub, dispelling the mist-like steam that hovered in the air. The hot water caressed her skin in soothing ripples, easing above her breasts, cleansing her body and mind of the ordeals she'd faced. It seemed many days had passed since she'd been able to rest her tired, aching body. It was difficult to believe so much had happened...that her life had been so completely altered in the short time since she had made the decision to free Blasien from Lord Conrad's dungeon.

She dipped her head back, soaking her hair in the fragrant water and watching it float around her. Black tendrils clung to her arms and breasts like vines. Ashanti closed her eyes, began to drift to sleep just as a voice brought her back to awareness.

"Have you found it to your liking, sweeting?"

Ashanti cracked her eyes open as Blasien walked noiselessly to where she bathed. He appeared unhurt by the battle, though he would have healed any wound he'd received by now. Dimly, she wondered how it came to be that he seemed immune to the poison of Mortalsblade ... but perhaps the legends were wrong...or perhaps, having been healed from it's bite before, he was now immune?

She dismissed the wayward thoughts, uncaring so long as he was unhurt.

He'd cleansed himself, dressed in a simple black leather kilt that fell mid-thigh and revealed his long, lean legs. His hair was clean also, brushed into a tawny mane and held back from his forehead by a circlet of gold that matched the bands encircling the bunched muscles of his biceps.

No man should ever look so desirable, so dangerous ... so forbidden.

He raked his cat eyed gaze over her, lust dilating his black pupils and darkening his eyes as he looked his fill of her naked body, clad only in her ebony tresses. She made no move to cover herself, compelled to remain still. Ashanti felt her blood begin to pulse with near pain between her legs. She'd begun to embrace her animal side.

He lifted his gaze to lock with hers, an unspoken urgency in their depths. "I've come to make certain you are well taken care of."

Her voice uncommonly husky, she said, "I ... am, my lord."

His mouth quirked as he crossed his arms. "Why the formality, sweeting?"

"For my own safety ... and yours."

"I see. Then I shall leave you."

Blasien turned to go but she grabbed his arm, half rising from the water and revealing herself. "Don't go."

"You don't know what it means if I stay."

He was wrong. She did. "Then stay for only a little."

It was all the invitation he needed. With a growl, he pulled her from the tub and crushed her naked, water slick body against his, arms wrapped tightly around her.

She moaned at the feel of his hard erection trapped against her belly. He kissed her then, taking advantage of her open mouth to plunge his tongue inside. Hunger drove her to kiss him back, their mouths devouring each other as he moved them to the bed.

He wouldn't leave her mouth long enough to find the opening and pushed through the curtains, trapping black gossamer behind her and ripping it as they descended roughly to the bed.

Her hair and body soaked the satin, chilling her even as he sparked a fire in her blood. He broke away from her mouth, leaving her gasping as he trailed his lips across her delicate jaw to her ear, taking the lobe between his teeth and tugging, moving his tongue over the whorls as he breathed hotly into the crevice, sending waves of delicious heat through her to gather at her weeping core.

Ashanti moaned, clutching his shoulders as he moved lower, down her collarbone to the valley of her breasts. She cried out when he seized a nipple gently between his teeth, and it excited him. He pushed a leg between hers as he engulfed her other breast in one hand and massaged it as he tugged and nibbled on the sensitive peak enclosed in his mouth.

She knew she shouldn't allow this, could not, but he knew right where to touch her to evoke the quickest responses from her. He moved his hand to remove his kilt, but she stopped him.

He met her eyes, his look smoldering, questioning.

"Not yet. You cannot bed me until I know you will be safe ... after the hunter's moon."

He sighed heavily, bracing himself above her on his arms. "That is tomorrow."

"Yes." She looked away, knowing it had been a mistake to do this--no matter how much they both wanted it. She just couldn't take the chance. If only she'd known that her desire hadn't diminished, even after everything that had happened. It seemed to have only increased.

"There are other ways besides coupling to find release. I would like to show you."

She looked quickly up at him, eyes wide. "But--"

"Hush." He stopped her speech with his fingers on her lips. She kissed the tips and he smiled lustily.

He dipped and moved his lips down the taut line of her belly, sucking the edges of her navel as he traveled lower. He moved off of her and Ashanti squirmed uncomfortably, wondering what he was about but trusting him as she never had anyone else. Cautiously, he circled her thighs with his hands and slowly parted her legs, revealing the deep red of her sex to him.

A hoarse groan escaped his throat as he looked at her then leaned down, and Ashanti was powerless to do anything but watch his golden head settle between her thighs. Hot breath moved over the sensitive, secretive skin, and then he touched his lips to her clit.

A jolt racked her body with the intimate contact. What ... what was he doing?

He stroked the nub once with his rough tongue and a rush of hot liquid saturated her sex. She gasped and clutched the satin in tight fists, eyes closed, head falling backward as her back arched off the bed.

He stroked her clit, nibbling ravenously, his own tongue combining with the moisture of her body, his hands massaging the insides of her thighs.

Each stroke teased her to the edge, made her blood pump and her breath come in pants. By the gods, what was he doing to her? She couldn't think, could only feel his mouth on her sex. He moved one hand to thrust a thick finger inside her and she cried, her body bucking as he stretched her again and again, the pleasure bordering on pain but receding each time.

She tossed her head, unable to take much more of this, unwilling to ask him to stop. He pushed his tongue into her cleft, lapping at her juices, pinching her clit between his fingers in smooth circles. All at once something burst inside her recesses, and she screamed, collapsing back and panting hard, debilitating waves radiating out, weakening her.

She was riding down the high when he moved up beside her, cuddled her close, nuzzling her neck. She smelled her sex on his hand as he smoothed her hair back, the musky scent intoxicating in the wake of what he'd done.

It took her a moment to find her voice. "That ... was ... amazing."

"I'm glad you enjoyed it." His voice was muffled against her neck. She shifted to her side and felt the hardness of his erection. Something told her that he hadn't achieved what she had just been given, and she felt guilty for being so selfish.

Ashanti sat up and pushed him back. He looked at her, puzzled. "You have given me much pleasure, warrior. A lady always returns the favor."

He grinned then and lay back, propping his hands behind his head.

She smiled at his complacency, wanting to shock him as much as he had her. Guessing that his own body felt pleasure much the same as hers, she touched him as he had done. She flicked her tongue across one small, flat nipple, gratified to hear his breathing quicken. She drew her nails over his chest, lightly scratching, and he moaned, causing her own body to tighten in response.

Ashanti moved lower, trailing her tongue and nails down his stomach as she reached his kilt. She freed it roughly from the belt, enjoying the way he grunted in response.

His erection jutted forth from a nest of golden hair, thick and long, as powerful as a spear. She had never seen a man's sex before and marveled at the shape of him. Looking upon him made her body clench with renewed desire, grow tight and achy once more. She wrapped a hand tentatively around its engorged base, the heat scorching her palm, and he moaned, spreading his legs wide for her as she eased closer.

A tiny drop of liquid beaded on the tip, and she touched her tongue experimentally to the helmeted tip, tasting. He groaned loudly in response, moving much as she had. He tasted a little salty and not unpleasant as she'd expected. Emboldened by his reaction, she wrapped her lips around him and felt him tense like a coiled spring. She sucked him as she would a confection, rubbing her tongue over the tiny hole and around the rim.

He bucked against her mouth, and a surge of power flowed through her like a heady wine. He was helpless against her in this position, relying solely on her mouth. She stroked his thick length, reveling in her newfound power, sucking him harder as she took him deeper into her mouth. When her teeth lightly grazed him, he moaned so loudly it startled her.

So he liked a little danger with his sex.

She did it again, gently, and he bucked once more, his manhood surging, pulsing.

"Take ... me ... out ... of your ... mouth," he ground out hoarsely and she complied, keeping her hands on him, kneading the hard flesh.

"Yes. Like that. Feels so good, sweeting." He groaned and shuddered in her hand, and then a creamy liquid burst forth from his manhood.

Startled, thinking she'd hurt him, she looked up quickly to his face, but his relaxed expression told her she'd done him no harm. Never had she thought a warrior could be so giving and undemanding. She wondered what other misconceptions Blasien would banish.

He grabbed her arms and pulled her atop him, cradling her close. "Thank you for that." He kissed her eyes shut and then gently brushed his lips over her mouth. She snuggled close, burying her face against him.

"If I am not to take you here and now, I must leave."

She sat up and looked at him. "But--"

"I must. You're enough to tempt the saints."

He was right. She'd told him she wanted to wait. Even though her fears had begun to ease about the curse, it was still safer not to tempt fate. She couldn't bear the thought of her taking him with her into oblivion. It was better this way.

Blasien left her after she'd fallen asleep in his arms, dreaming of new and unearthed pleasures.

CHAPTER TEN

Ashanti stretched languorously on the soft mattress, satiated as a milk fed cat from the night before. Then she remembered what day it was and her sense of peace and contentment disappeared in an instant. She searched her inner self, fearful of what she would find. She didn't feel weak or sick.

She felt *alive*.

Rising from the bed, she saw garments had been laid out on a short table for her to wear as well as wine and fruit to break fast. She walked nude to the table and picked up the garments. A bronze brassiere cut in whorl shaped designs and backed with leather went on first, covering her breasts in scant metal even as they pushed them forth and deepened her cleavage. A small triangle of tanned, bronze fur covered her sex, held in place with a thin gold chain that looped around her waist and connected between her legs.

Normally she would have scoffed at wearing such an outfit, but she knew the sparse garments would please Blasien, just as they pleased other men....as such things had pleased Lord Conrad.

She shook off that thought, unwilling to allow that hated memory to tarnish the thrill she felt at awakening that heated look in Blasien's eyes.

As she looked in the gilt framed mirror that stretched as tall as a man, she felt like a pagan nymph and very unlike herself. Her skin seemed to glow a light bronze, no longer the pale white of her imprisonment. Health seemed to suffuse her, and she prayed the new changes overcoming her would prevail.

Nibbling on the sweet citrus of a *kwamquille*, she leisurely untangled her hair with the golden comb that had been left for her, brushing until the black locks fell around her shoulders like midnight silk, the ends dangling to her hips and teasing her bare buttocks.

Finished with her preparations, she went to seek out Blasien, eager to see his reaction.

* * * *

Blasien sat upon his throne, Syrian updating him on all that had passed in his absence, when Ashanti entered, however, it drove all thought of business from his mind.

Slowly, almost shyly, she approached the dais, hips swaying, her body lithe and nearly bare. His mouth went dry looking upon her, and his manhood swelled instantly.

Syrian had ceased talking, observing that his lordship no longer listened to him. With a faintly amused smile, he bowed and left, aware that Blasien's absent dismissal was as much as he could expect at the moment.

His cats rubbed against his legs, sensing his pleasure, purring as he rubbed them absentmindedly. Ashanti stopped on the wide stone steps, a seductive smile on her face.

"Does it please you, my lord?"

Blasien nodded, unable to speak. She would be the death of him. He didn't know how much longer he could hold out without burying himself deep inside her. Her body begged for him to touch her, and his beast nearly burst out with the desire.

She stroked one of his leopards as it abandoned him and wandered over to her, curling around her, then she sat on the dais steps, tormenting him, making him jealous of the attention she lavished on the cats.

Abruptly, he stood, ignoring her smile as he left the hall. His mind had gone to chaotic mush. His beast threatened to escape his careful control. If he didn't get away from her, he'd take her right there in front of everyone, whether she wished it or no.

* * * *

Ashanti watched him leave, desire and honor warring inside him. She smiled to herself, scratching behind the ears of the cats, enjoying their purrs of contentment. Her power over him astounded her…pleased her no end. She'd never realized the hold a woman could have over a man, and the sudden insight was intoxicating, tempting beyond reason. Had she known it sooner in her life, things would have been different.

A man approached her where she lounged on the dais with the cats draped around her. She had never seen him before, and the bold way he looked her over grated on her nerves despite the fact that what she wore was meant to invite such looks. She restrained the strong urge to cover herself and regarded him coldly.

"Good day, my lady."

"Good day," she said, her voice chill, arching her brow when he sat beside her without invitation. One of the cats growled in warning but eased down when she touched it soothingly.

He smiled, revealing rows of sharp teeth. Ashanti blanched inside, feeling her bravado vanish as it occurred to her that her protector had vanished and she was alone in a world completely alien to her. She knew nothing of this people, save that they were savage as any animal, ungoverned by the dictates of mortal man.

"I am called Bram." He ran a finger slowly up her thigh and she knocked his hand away, sitting up straight, edging away from him. "You're nervous. You don't have to be."

"Don't touch me. Lord Blasien will see you."

"No, he won't. We all saw that he left you, and none see any reason why he would unless you are free for the taking."

Ashanti felt her mouth grow dry with pure terror. "You're mistaken. I am no one's for the taking," she said sharply, hoping to infuse a conviction she did not feel into her tone.

"Our law does not say so. You are an unmated woman in a pard dominated by males. Lord Blasien has not laid his claim. He did not spend the previous night with you. You are unbreached--any man may take you by law."

Because she had sent him away ... and he had been too honorable to ignore her wishes. Or, perhaps, he had not cared enough to protect her as his own?

She would not allow herself to think that. In any case, she had more immediate concerns. "And I suppose you are that man?"

"If you so desire it ... or if I should."

Had Blasien known what the males of his clan would do to her? He'd left and she had no idea where to find him. Bram crowded close, sniffing her, his eyes gone animal.

She backed up and stood, putting the now sleeping leopards between them. He continued his advance. Ashanti looked around for help, saw that only a few men were in the hall and they watched with excitement.

"I will scream if you touch me."

He stood, crouching low as if to pounce. "Please do. It makes it so much more exciting."

"Bram! You touch her and you will have to deal with me." Raphael's voice echoed through the hall. Ashanti nearly cried in relief as she saw him coming toward her.

Bram turned to face Raphael, his fingers sprouting claws. "You have no power here, Lord Raphael."

Raphael sent him a black, malevolent glare, full of the power the leader of the hunters possessed. "Do you challenge me?"

For a breath of time, her fate seemed to hang in the balance as Bram hesitated. Without a word, however, he skulked away into the shadows with the other beastmen.

Ashanti ran to Raphael and clung to his chest, shivers racking her body. Raphael closed his arms around her reluctantly. "Oh Raphael. I didn't know what to do. I thought he was ... that he would...."

He smoothed her hair down her back. "Hush. The danger is over for now." "But Blasien...he left me."

"Yes. He did not know that Bram was a follower of Moran. Syrian has just now told me."

"Where is he? He needs to do something about Bram before he causes more trouble."

"He will. Syrian is apprising him of Bram's situation even now."

Ashanti nodded against his chest, finding comfort in his words and soothing actions. She knew she was implicitly safe with Raphael. There was an honor about him that prevented him from breaking her trust. "Raphael, Bram said I was unclaimed. That ... that any of them could take me. Is this true? What am I to do?"

Raphael stiffened at her words then continued stroking her. "Lord Blasien will take care of everything. I give you my word."

CHAPTER ELEVEN

Blasien attacked Raphael when he returned to the great hall after he'd escorted Ashanti to her room.

"I'll kill you, you bastard," he growled, lunging for Raphael with razor sharp claws bared. Raphael sidestepped him, holding his hands up to fend Blasien off.

"Hold, you great fool. I kept her from Bram."

Raphael's words struck him like a blow, and Blasien's fury immediately dissipated. His shoulders slumped visibly. "I am sorry. Forgive me for my folly."

When he'd seen Raphael embrace Ashanti, the world had gone red. He couldn't bear the thought that she would give herself to another. He wanted her to be his, forever. That another man protected her when he should have been there cut his heart to the quick. He had failed her, when he had said he never would.

Raphael clasped his shoulder, squeezing it reassuringly. "All is forgiven. I know the way of men's hearts."

What a fool he was, that he could ever doubt Raphael's honor, Blasien thought. He'd not been acting himself for some time now, and he wondered what could have effected such a change. Whatever it was, it had a firm hold of him. He thought perhaps burying himself inside the woman would assuage his hunger for her. Then his life would return to normal.

Raphael watched him, knowing his thoughts.

"Yet it has never affected you nor your judgment, friend," Blasien said, smiling solemnly at him, leaning heavily against the wall.

"No, it is one snare I will never fall in to."

"Much luck to you." Blasien grimaced, remembering a similar vow he'd made himself, once long ago, before a human temptress walked into his life.

Raphael frowned, puzzled. In truth, he couldn't altogether fathom Blasien's behavior. Since he had known him, Blasien seemed to have more of a tendency to be cool and level headed. Granted lust could cloud a man's mind, and his judgment, but...mentally, he shrugged. It was pointless speculation. The fact was that Blasien was obviously not thinking clearly or he would have known what must be done without prompting on his part. "Your actions leave her vulnerable. You will have a time of it if she remains unclaimed."

"Who would challenge me?"

Raphael gave him an unfathomable look. "Perhaps I would."

"Raphael," he growled.

A predatory smile passed over his face but was quickly gone. "You know what is to be done. She is a changeling, not a beast as we are. Her human half is still a powerful draw, but the beast will come tonight. You must show the pard she is yours."

Blasien closed his eyes, cursing the old law and what must be done. She would never forgive him. "Yes, I know." He did not wish to go forth this way, no matter how much he might crave it. Ashanti made him want to change his ways--the old ways. Ancient customs could not be overcome in mere days, however. There was no choice. Whatever the cost to himself, he *must* conform to the old ways in order to insure Ashanti's protection.

"They must all see it. It is not the way of their kind--the females crave gentle wooing, but the pard sees that only as weakness."

Blasien nodded, grim. Raphael spoke the truth, his advice logical and measured as ever. Ashanti would always be plagued by his males as long as she was unattached. She must go through the blood ceremony tonight. He could not afford to be swayed by her argument as he had before.

He only hoped when it was finished, that she would not hate him.

* * * *

Ashanti spent the remainder of the day in her room, alternately crying and despising her weakness. Blasien did not come for her, and when she finally received his summons, she had worked herself up into a holy terror.

Her body was undergoing strange changes that frightened her, and she could have used his guidance, his reassurance that all was well, and yet he remained away.

She dried her tears and washed her face, the red surrounding her eyes vanishing before her skin was completely dry. Healing from the change? Perhaps. She wouldn't know and damned sure wouldn't admit to Blasien that she'd been crying for him all day.

Straightening her spine, she left the room, walking down torch lit corridors to the great hall. Dusk had fallen, but the moons had not yet arisen. The blood and silver moons would align in the hunter's eye tonight, so called because it resembled an eye with a blood colored iris. She would either die this night or complete her transformation into a monster. She shivered despite the warmth of the hall but vowed she would show no more weakness to Blasien or his people. If she was to live among them, they must respect her.

Yielding to an urge to torment Blasien for his neglect, Ashanti exaggerated the sway of her hips as she walked down the long path to the dais where Blasien awaited her, his cats lounging on either side of him. His clan was assembled inside, but Raphael and Syrian were absent from Blasien's side. She did not wonder on it long as the crowd parted at her approach. Their murmuring buzzed in her ears but she ignored it, looking straight ahead.

Blasien watched her, seemingly mesmerized by her gait and the rise and fall of her breasts with each step she took.

In spite of her anger, she felt her heart pound looking upon him. He *had* saved her from Lord Conrad and the hunters, carried her across leagues of barren, rock strewn land, given her pleasure and listened to her requests when she'd asked them--all this from a warrior leader of a barbarous clan of savage beasts. Gentleness was as alien to them as shifting was to her. How much more could she expect from him?

Was she living in a dream to expect love in a world that destroyed innocence? Would lust be the only emotion he could ever give her?

And he was handsome tonight, more so than she'd ever seen him before. Something had altered in him, made his eyes gleam with a new, different hunger than she'd experienced. His golden hair shimmered in the flame's light behind him, his face hard lines and angles, his eyes so intense they made her breath catch.

He stood when she reached the first wide step leading to the dais, held his hand out to her. "Come to me, Ashanti." His face was solemn as she ascended and accepted his hand.

"Tonight we will perform the blood ceremony." His voice carried through the hall, and the crowd fell silent.

Ashanti watched Blasien warily, wondering what this new turn was and wishing she'd been told about it beforehand. But he hadn't seen her since the morning-- there had been no interaction between them since. He had said before it was a sacred ceremony. She only hoped it did not portend ill for her.

"Are there any here who wish to challenge me for the woman?"

Ashanti glanced at the assemblage. Their faces were immobile, but she sensed a suspenseful edge in the air. When no one spoke, he said, "And so it is." They faced each other, their profiles to the people.

"Do you wish my claim upon you to go forth, Ashanti? I give you this one chance to leave now," he said softly, for her ears alone.

She felt a thrill course over her at the thought of him claiming her, of being his woman. She knew no other man would protect her as he did, knew that she could never deny what she felt for him. Desire from him would have to suffice--she would never demand more when he could not give it.

Ashanti nodded, unable to speak the words, and he accepted her assent.

Moving slowly, Blasien took a small silver dagger from its jeweled scabbard on his belt and sliced the sharp blade diagonally across his left breast. A thin line of blood oozed from the narrow cut. Touching his fingers to the wound,

Blasien wet them with blood and wiped them across her forehead in two lines. Her forehead felt seared by his touch, and she resisted the impulse to rub her tingling skin.

"Blood of my heart," he said and paused, wiping a vertical line across her lips, "I give to you."

His part performed, he handed her the blade, and she repeated the ritual on him and returned the dagger. Their wounds had already begun healing, and she marveled at the change as the blood ceased its flow and skin closed, smooth and unmarred.

"My body, I give to you." His intense, amber gaze bore into her and she shuddered with pleasure. He was hers now, as she was his.

Knowing this was the final act, she repeated, "My body, I give to you."

Blasien closed his eyes and nodded slowly before opening them again. "Now you must mate with me." Blasien watched her steadily.

Ashanti was confused. Surely he didn't want them to leave now, with all his people waiting on him? She had imagined there would be some sort of celebration after the ritual. What could he be thinking? "Blasien, I told you--"

"Here. Now." His voice was calm, though his eyes seemed to burn a hole through her.

Ashanti blanched, her heart in her throat. She swallowed painfully. He couldn't be serious. They were ... they were surrounded. "No."

"You must."

He grabbed at her arms, but she evaded him, running to the throne to keep it between them. She quickly scanned the crowd, seeking help but saw none forthcoming. Alien eyes watched her, eager, excited. This was for their benefit then. A wave of nausea washed over her. How could she ever have believed that she could live among them?

"No!" she screamed as he came for her again.

He stopped, his face hard. "The ritual must be completed. If you go to someone, *anyone* else now, you will be theirs, damn it! Would you have *Bram* for your mate? *Raphael*?" Blasien demanded in a harsh whisper.

"Why?" she cried, even as he lunged around the side and caught her arm. She twisted and fell over the throne, the thick stone arm pushing into her stomach.

He leaned over, trapping her firmly, and she felt his erection as it pushed aside the thin golden chain between the cleft of her buttocks and pressed against the sensitive opening. Hard, heated flesh scalded her. He was going to do this, take her in front of them all. It didn't matter if it was a necessity or not, she would kill him for this humiliation.

Ashanti struggled, kicked back with her legs until he held them trapped against the throne with his own. She clawed backward, trying to tear him apart, but he manacled her wrists in one hand.

He held her still a moment, his body shaking as hers trembled. "Forgive me." His voice cracked with emotion as he pushed inside her with a single thrust, tearing through her maidenhead.

She screamed like her soul had been ripped from her body, her voice filling the hall. He shuddered against her, his chest heaving.

"Out!" he commanded, and the hall cleared immediately.

"I ... hate ... you." Hated tears fell from her eyes and onto their locked hands. She wanted to murder him for what he'd done. She blinked her eyes and forced the tears away.

"I know," he whispered, his voice full of regret that she didn't believe. He held his body tense, his arms shaking with the strain of controlling himself.

Inside, she could feel her body repairing itself, soothing the hurt until the pain subsided. She felt her insides stretched to the limit with the breadth of his erection. She squirmed, seeking freedom now that the final act had been completed. He grunted low to her ear, a growl, and pushed deeper inside despite his efforts to control himself. Little quivers started in her sex, and she hated him even more as her body began its betrayal against her mind.

"Release me," she gritted out, struggling anew, increasing the friction between their bodies.

"Hold still!" His arms shook more. He breathed raggedly above her, his hot breath scorching the back of her neck with each pant. "I ... can't," he gritted out between clenched teeth.

Grunting with the effort, he painstakingly pulled himself out, inch by inch. Jolts shocked her core at his bumpy, hesitant withdrawal. Before he removed himself entirely, he growled in rage at his weakness and plunged deep inside her again, her own damnable wetness easing his way.

She cursed him. Cursed herself for responding.

"I ... cannot ... stop ... myself," he growled low to her ear, nipping the hollow as he moved slowly out and back in, taking many seconds to repeat the movement.

Warmth spread through her limbs even as the moons shown above the skylight, beginning their alignment.

Ashanti realized she wanted this, even after his humiliation. A part of her recognized its need--the animal side. She struggled against it even as she enjoyed it and craved more. The beast was waking--her beast. She could feel it uncurl inside and spread its limbs through hers, increasing the tempo of her heart, the warmth of her body, the acuteness of her senses.

"More," she said in a voice she didn't recognize, more a husky growl than speech.

Incredibly, he'd been holding back, and he filled her more fully than ever with his thick erection. She bit her lip at the near pain of it stretching her, the wild, raw pleasure that filled her. Her body felt engorged with feeling, achingly sensitive, the slightest whisper of breath a heady caress.

He released her hands and she propped up on her straightened arms. From behind, he slipped his hands underneath the fur trimmed leather covering her dark curls and cupped her sex, his fingers finding her clit and moving in firm circles.

She moaned, pushing back against him, shaking her head, wanting more. He bit the back of her neck, moving his rough tongue over the tender skin as he sucked and marked her.

It wasn't enough. She wanted--needed--more. "Harder," she said huskily.

When he continued as he had, she said, "*Harder!*" She pushed back, grinding her cleft against him, enjoying the rough feel of his hair on the sensitive skin.

She felt him tense, sensed his struggle. Though it was foreign for her to feel this way, she didn't want his newfound conscience--she wanted *this*.

"If I go any harder, I could hurt you."

"*Now*. I shall take it."

He took her at her word, moving into her with force and speed, pounding his hips against her buttocks, his fingers pinching and teasing her clit, slipping in her juices. Her thighs slapped against the throne with every thrust.

She was building to something. Something more than an orgasm, and she could feel it in him too.

Her body shuddered uncontrollably as the moons aligned. Was she now dying and taking him with her? Her skin rippled before her eyes as the hunter's moon emerged. She was changing--the beast had come.

The climax took her suddenly and powerfully as Blasien rammed into her a final, soul shaking time, claiming them both in its wake, ripping through her even as she shifted into her secret half.

Claws sprang from her hands as she changed. Ashanti screamed as the pleasure wreaked havoc on her senses, scorching the humanity that clung by a thread to her soul.

They both collapsed, spent, bodies shaking as the climax faded away. Seconds later, her furiously pumping heart eased into its normal rhythm and her body melded slowly back to normal. She wasn't horrified as she'd supposed she would be. She'd been given her life in return for living as a beast that had been humanity's enemy. Death was no choice at all.

Blasien stood and took her with him, cradling her back against him. Ashanti looked at herself, her smooth, hairless skin. Confusion gripped her. Why had she changed back so suddenly?

"It is always brief the first time, sweeting. As a changeling and not a pure blood, shifting will never be complete for you for years to come," Blasien murmured against her ear as if he'd read her thoughts.

She nodded and pushed away, faced him. "Did you find much pleasure, my lord?"

His look was smoldering. "Yes, I did."

"Good, for you will never have me again after this night," she said coldly.

Something flickered across his features, emotions she could not decipher. His brows drew down as he frowned at her, but in a moment he seemed to dismiss both her comments and his doubts. He pulled her to him and kissed her gently. "Then I must use my time wisely."

CHAPTER TWELVE

Ashanti said nothing as Blasien scooped her into his arms, turned and strode in the direction of her own apartments. She was simply too angry to care what he had in mind. As they neared her door, however, she began to struggle to free herself.

Blasien's arms tightened around her.

"Loose me, you bastard!"

The look he gave her was one of mild surprise, but he did not release her until they had entered her chamber, where he set her gently to her feet before closing the door firmly behind him.

Ashanti straightened. "Leave me," she said imperiously.

Blasien grinned. "You have promised me the night," he reminded her.

Ashanti was speechless for several moments. "I did no such thing!" she finally managed to splutter.

His expression was all innocence. "Those were your very words."

Ashanti ground her teeth. "I said, you will never have me again after this night!"

"Precisely. It is still night."

Ashanti's eyes narrowed into near slits. "You know very well what I meant."

His look of stunned amazement was feigned, she was certain. It took an effort to curb the desire to knock his head clean off his shoulders, but she managed it, reminding herself that she was human, not savage beast.

"I'd forgotten."

Ashanti looked at him suspiciously. "What?"

"Humans have no honor."

Outraged, Ashanti could only splutter, could find no words to counter such an unjust comment. She decided she would not deign to respond. Turning, she left him by the door and moved across the chamber.

Food, she saw, had been laid out for her on the same table used earlier. The very sight of it nauseated her, but after a moment she picked up a piece of fruit and a small knife, sat on the edge of the bed and began paring it.

If he was not a complete idiot, he would take it as the warning it was, for she had every intention of castrating him if he took one step in her direction.

"It's a rather dull blade for that job, wouldn't you say?"

She almost nicked her finger. Had she said it aloud? She frowned. She didn't think so, but perhaps he was more clever than she'd thought. In any case, she had no intention of allowing him to draw her into further conversation.

After a moment, he released a sigh, apparently of resignation, and moved toward the fire place. Ashanti continued pretending to ignore him, though she was well aware of his every movement.

The tub, she saw, was once more in place. She wished she'd noticed it earlier, for the steam wafting from the hot water seemed incredibly inviting after the humiliation she'd endured at that beast's hands. She felt a strong desire to scrub her skin till she bled. Perhaps then she could cleanse her mind of the images tormenting her; visions of her bare bottom turned over the stone throne, of Blasien pumping into her.

It took her several moments to realize that the heat washing over her was not the heat of embarrassment.

At the sound of splashing water, she jumped, nicking her finger, her head coming up with a jerk. Blasien, she saw, had dropped his loincloth and stepped into the tub.

His back was to her. Without conscious volition, her gaze traveled over that broad expanse of bare, well muscled back to his narrow waist and his firmly rounded buttocks, her heart beating out a drum roll, hot moisture weeping into her sex.

She promptly returned her attention to the fruit in her hands as he turned to seat himself, his proud erection burning into her mind's eye despite the fact that she'd caught no more than a glimpse.

"Rutting beast," she muttered under her breath, feeling dismay seep into her as she saw that she'd nicked her finger and bloodied the fruit. Before her eyes the blood ceased to flow, the tiny wound closing, but the fruit looked far less appetizing now than it had to start with…which was to say it took an effort to curb her nausea.

She would have simply tossed it away except that she needed something to hold her attention and keep her from staring at the naked man in her bath not two yards from where she sat.

Resentment swelled in her breast. The bath had been intended for her! She had a good mind to march over there....

She broke off that thought. She wasn't going near him unless it was with a length of kindling to beat him into an unrecognizable blob of quivering, bloodied flesh.

She mulled over it for a time, relishing the look of stunned surprise on his face just before she clobbered him with the stick of wood, taking his head off at the neck and sending it flying into the fireplace beyond the tub. His face would still be wearing that expression of stupefaction when his head came to rest on the burning fagots in the fireplace.

A faint smile curled her lips at the image. She realized after a moment that she was no longer looking down at her hands. She was looking directly at Blasien.

Blasien was looking directly back at her, a tentative smile curling his lips.

Stupid man! How could he think for an instant that she would forgive him so easily. A blush, part embarrassment, part irritation flooded her cheeks as she quickly looked away.

It occurred to her then that what she really, really wanted was retribution. She wanted to make him very, very sorry for what he'd done to her.

Realistically, she had no hope of overpowering him to teach him a lesson. There was no doubt in her mind that that would give her the most satisfaction, to exorcise her demons by physically abusing him until he was nigh dead from blood loss.

She had only a woman's recourse, however.

She could poison him and watch him die a slow death...which wasn't realistic either, considering his powers of healing himself.

Or she could torture him as only a woman could.

Resolutely, she placed the ruined fruit, and the paring knife, on the table and rose slowly from the bed.

* * * *

Blasien eyed her warily as she stopped beside the tub.

As well he might. It took a supreme effort on Ashanti's part to maintain the faint, seductive smile she'd pasted on her lips, to refrain from grinning at his uneasiness…or grasping a handful of hair and shoving him under the water and holding him until the bubbles stopped.

He lifted a brow, questioning.

She lifted a brow, questioning.

"If you're of a mind to try to drown me, I feel I must warn you that I have no intention of cooperating."

Given her thoughts of only a moment ago, Ashanti chuckled. She couldn't help it. "If you were any sort of gentleman, you would," she said, only half teasing.

His expression became almost a sulk and Ashanti felt a new surge of amusement. He turned away. "I'm no gentleman. One must be human. Have you forgotten? I am a beast man."

"Hardly," Ashanti said dryly, her amusement vanishing.

He glanced up at her sharply.

She smiled her best seductive smile. "Shall I wash your back?"

He was instantly suspicious, but after a long moment, he offered her the sponge he'd been half-heartedly slopping water over himself with.

Instead of taking it, Ashanti began removing her garments.

Both his brows rose.

Ashanti lifted both her brows, as well, pretending nonchalance, though she could not prevent a faint blush of color from rising to her cheeks. "I shouldn't want to ruin this. I mean to keep it…always to remind me."

Blasien looked uncomfortable, though his eyes had begun to gleam with hunger as he watched her disrobe. "I would think you'd prefer to burn them."

Ashanti turned away, folding the garments carefully and placing them a short distance from the tub. "Oh no," she said through gritted teeth. Knowing he could not see her expression when her back was to him, she saw no reason to maintain the facade that was starting to make her teeth and facial muscles ache with effort. "I shall cherish them always as a reminder."

She saw when she turned, her smile firmly in place once more, that Blasien was flushed. With lust or discomfort, she wasn't certain, but she finally decided that it was a combination of the two. Good!

"Ashanti, I would give all that I am to undo…that I had not had to.…"

"Shhh!" Ashanti knelt beside the tub, placed a finger to his lips briefly, then took the sponge and lathered it. Taking his shoulders in her hands, she turned him away from her and began scrubbing his back. "I understand that it was custom in this savage, uncivilized land. You are their leader. They look to you to uphold the traditions they value. You are but one man. You could scarcely change the laws!"

"You don't understand…."

"I have said that I do." It took an effort of will to keep from snapping the remark at him, but she controlled herself.

"It was the only way to protect you from the likes of Bram…."

"Yes, and I want you to know I have no desire to be bruti…ravished by anyone but you." Try as she might, she could not keep the sarcasm from her voice. Instead, she distracted him by dropping the sponge.

She was busily searching for it in the murky water when he turned to her.

"Ashanti?"

"Ah!" Ashanti responded, lifting the sponge triumphantly, pretending distraction. "Yes, heart of my heart?" she said at last, smiling at him lovingly.

"You will never forgive me, will you?"

Deception, even for a good cause, did not come easily to Ashanti. What she wanted, in that instant, was to scream NO! at the top of her lungs and claw the flesh from his bones.

But she wanted revenge.

She had only one way to take it.

She did not trust herself to speak. Instead, she leaned forward until her face hovered only inches from his, closed her eyes and nudged his nose with the tip of her own, then placed a light kiss on his lips, his cheek, and finally touched the tip of her tongue to his ear lobe. Sucking the lobe into her mouth, she bit down on it gently.

She meant to.

She really did.

She was almost as surprised as he was when she drew blood.

He yelped.

She raked her nails, gently this time, down his chest, across his belly and finally wrapped her hand around his erection, all the while soothing his injury with gentle kisses. "You are mine…I am yours," she whispered into his ear.

He pulled her into the tub, in an instant positioning her beneath him, his erection probing that part of her that wept for his possession.

She hadn't expected it. It had been no part of her plan to come into such intimate contact with him…ever….

She stiffened as he lowered his head, taking her breast into his mouth, teasing her erect nipple with his tongue. The rough lathe of his tongue sent a sluice of wetness through her inner recesses, engorging and sensitizing her sex.

She drew in a deep breath, commanded her body to remain aloof.

The plan, she reminded herself, was to torture him, not sate him.

It was no use. No matter how she tried to prod her mind and body, they answered his call as if they belonged to him, not her.

She bit down on his shoulder as he forced his erection inside her, but she could not even convince herself that it was retribution, not lust.

Her body was on fire…for him.

It was many hours later, when he had satisfied her over and over again, brought her to screaming, clawing climax, as she lay exhausted and both sated and discontented, that she realized that she had failed. She would always fail.

CHAPTER THIRTEEN

Ashanti stood before Raphael's chambers, her fleeting bravery nearly deserting her as she thought of what could happen should she be caught here.

Screwing up her courage, she rapped quickly, softly, on his door before she could change her mind. Her ears discerned the slightest movement inside. She held her breath, awaiting his reply.

"Enter, Lady Ashanti."

How did he know ... ? Mayhap he could see through walls. He was a hunter after all. Releasing her pent-up breath, she eased the heavy door open and entered, closing it behind her before daring to look at Raphael.

Looking utterly decadent, he lounged back on the bed, laying atop vivid red satin, pillows piled up behind and beside him. He had removed his binding silver adornments in readiness for bed and lay watching her with glittering eyes.

Ashanti felt immediately uncomfortable and wondered what madness had possessed her to form such a plan. Raphael, for all that he was dangerous, had never seemed so to her until now.

"Why have you come here? If I were pard, I could be killed by having you alone in my presence."

Ashanti blanched and backed toward the door. "I apologize. I did not know...."

He held up a hand, beckoning her forth. "Stay. Pard law does not concern me. What does is why you have risked Lord Blasien's wrath by leaving his bed this morning."

"I need your help."

"I expected as much." He leaned back into the pillows, looking amused.

Ashanti frowned. "You are the only ... man here who could help me escape."

"Escape?" He laughed, a cold, mirthless bark of sound that would have chilled a lesser man, but Ashanti was no man ... and she was desperate. Ashanti stood her ground, body rigid.

"What has brought about this change of heart in you, my lady?"

"The ... the blood ceremony." Her eyes stung, but she had vowed she would not cry, not for herself and never for *him*.

"That is what I suspected."

His casual attitude infuriated her. "You have no idea. You weren't there." Her voice cracked, but she continued,

"Because of what he did, I can *never* face anyone here ever again."

Raphael was on his feet in an instant before her. He grasped her shoulders and made her face him. "It is because of his actions that you *can* face the pard. If he had not made you submit and mated with you, nothing would have stopped them from taking you as they would. He cannot beat them all for daring to touch you. Now no one can and live."

"I don't care if it *was* the only way. I hate this place. I must return to my own people." She had thought desire could be enough to hold her here, but it would *never* be enough. She would be living a lie if she chose to believe otherwise.

"Shadowmere is your land now, Ashanti. You have crossed over. Ours is a savage land. The people do not understand gentleness. They only know war and fear ... humiliation. They respect power alone."

"You talk as though you regret how things have come to pass. You seem to mourn for something, something lost...."

"No. I was never an innocent like you were. I was born to this. It is all I know."

"Then spare me, help me. I must leave." Ashanti blinked back the tears that threatened, put her hands on his where they rested on her shoulders. "What would it take to convince you to help me, Raphael?"

He gave her a long, measuring look, down her body and back up to her face. "Are you offering yourself to me in exchange for your freedom?"

Ashanti's stomach fluttered nervously. Could she sacrifice her body to save her soul? Had she misjudged Raphael as she had Blasien? Taking a deep, fortifying breath, she said, "If that is what it will take."

He leaned close, sniffed her skin, his intense eyes never leaving hers. She wanted to back away but his grip wouldn't allow it.

"I am but a man, Ashanti. Do not tempt me so." He pulled away and turned his back to her, hands clenched into tight fists.

"Please, you need only take me to the border." He didn't answer. "If you will not help me, I will go alone, though I do not know the way."

He turned, studied her for a long moment. "Very well."

She could not believe he'd agreed so easily. A thrill raced through her, but it was not altogether joy. It occurred to her to wonder if he meant to take her offer, or if he had merely yielded to her desperation for aid. Somehow she could not bring herself to ask, however, and decided she would face that possibility only when she must. "Truly?"

Raphael nodded, faced her once more. "We must go now, before dawn's light. I will make sure we are not missed."

"I'll collect my things." Ashanti turned to leave, but he stopped her.

"No. I am all you will need from now on."

* * * *

They left in the gray twilight before dawn. Ashanti wore a black cloak that covered her fully from detection, though none took note of their departure. Any pard they encountered fell into a stupor when Raphael bent their mind.

Essentially, his powers made them invisible because he could command it. She had never witnessed anything more terrifying in all her life and hoped such dark talent would never be directed at her.

Once they reached the outlying grounds, Raphael ripped off his kilt and handed it to her. She stuffed it into a satchel with his silver. Kneeling on the ground, he fell to his hands, fisting them in the dirt as he shifted into his beast form. His skin rippled like wind blowing through water, black fur sprouting in its wake. In seconds, a solid black wolf the size of a small pony stood before her, shaking its body like a wet animal, though he was dry.

Fascinated by the speed and ease of his change and new form, she longed to question him, but he could not speak now. He bade her ride his back by lowering himself to the ground. Not feeling her usual reluctance, Ashanti climbed on and clung to his long, soft fur, clamping her legs tight around his middle as he took off running into the dusk at a dizzying speed.

Unable to stand the blur of the countryside in her peripheral vision, Ashanti closed her eyes and lay against him, his heightened warmth soaking into her limbs. Wrapping her arms around his neck, she fell into an enchanted sleep as they escaped.

She only hoped Blasien would not be too angry when he discovered them gone.

* * * *

"I'll kill them both." The hall shook with the fury of his voice. Blasien pulverized the carved stone goblet he held in his fist and shook the dust and rock from his palm. Wise pard members avoided the hall, and it stood empty save Blasien and Syrian.

Syrian watched Blasien warily. He was not pard and unable to attend their most sacred rituals, but he knew what had happened during the blood ceremony. He could not blame the girl for running from their savagery. She was more human than anything else, despite being a changeling.

The sound of a whip cracking and a man's hoarse groan carried from the courtyard where Bram was being punished for his transgressions. He would be healed and then expelled from the pard. Syrian thought only that it was a pity it had not been done sooner. It was not his place to interfere when he hadn't been asked, but he did not need the *sight* to know that evil had been set in motion that would not be easily remedied, and Bram was at the heart of it.

"I want you to find her for me, Syrian. I thought Raphael only jested about claiming her, but I have been taken for a fool by my old friend."

Syrian sighed. In all his years of companionship with Blasien, he had never seen the man so angry before nor so ... he searched his mind for the appropriate emotion and finally settled on *anguished*. Blasien was *anguished* at their supposed betrayal, but they both knew Raphael. Raphael was amongst the most honorable men in Shadowmere.

Syrian knew Blasien did not *truly* believe his own words, but he was lashing out in any direction to spare blame from himself.

"I will Time-See, but only to gainsay this notion that Raphael and Ashanti have betrayed you."

Blasien growled, his eyes gone leopard, wild. "If not that, what then?"

"I believe you frightened her in the blood ceremony," Syrian said cautiously.

Blasien froze and his face crumpled in a mask of misery. He covered his eyes with a hand, guilt shaking him. "She told me I would never touch her again. I ... did not believe her when she said it."

Syrian regarded him thoughtfully. He'd never seen Blasien so affected by a woman, so regretful of his own actions. Perhaps the proud man had at last found humility in the arms of his chosen. "You thought your desire would be enough to keep her by your side."

Blasien nodded, his eyes still shielded. "Yes. Only you, Syrian, see so much. And only you and ... Raphael would dare speak so to me."

Syrian placed a warm hand on his friend's shoulder, squeezing reassuringly. "I warned that she would not take well to public subjugation. Human women must be gently wooed. They do not understand the wild."

"She understands it better than I do her," Blasien muttered, feeling his anger surge anew at his own helplessness. He had had no choice. He should have realized even before he brought her that he would be forced to perform the blood ceremony and that she would not forgive him. But then, in his arrogance it hadn't occurred to him that he would not be able to overcome her revulsion…..or that it would tear his heart from his chest that he could not have her forgiveness.

The poison of Mortalsblade was as nothing compared to the torture he now endured.

Syrian remained silent a moment. "Have you revealed-- told her of your feelings?"

Blasien growled and shook him off. "I am not a man of sweet words. She knows my feelings when I touch her."

"But was it enough?" Syrian said softly.

Blasien did not answer, but, despite his anger he began to see hope. Perhaps all was not lost? Perhaps if he told her….

Disgusted with the weakness inherent in his thoughts, Blasien felt his anger flare anew, felt his resolve harden. He would have her, will she, nil she. She was his! She had given herself to him. He had claimed her. Half mortal or not, she *must* accept him now!

Syrian sighed heavily. No man was more stubborn than when confronted by his own shortcomings. Even he, with all his powers, could not force Blasien to face himself. "I will Time-See and try to discover what has happened. If I find anything, I will alert you at once. We will find out the truth if it is not too late."

CHAPTER FOURTEEN

"What have you found, Syrian?" Blasien asked as he entered the sorcerer's dark chambers.

Syrian was kneeling upon the stone floor. In his hands he held the only source of light in the sparse room: a thick glass orb that contained a small blue fire--the Eternal Flame.

This was only the second time Blasien had seen it, and still the magic fascinated and amazed him. The flames, which matched Syrian's cerulean locks, hypnotized any who looked on them overlong, but Syrian was not affected as others were. The flame was a part of him, a piece of his soul. He was among the last of a race with the power to control the magic and see into the past and possibilities of the future. It was a power that had caused nearly their entire race to be hunted into extinction, and in fact, Syrian was the only one of his kind Blasien had ever encountered.

To use his gift for Blasien was a demonstration of how loyal his friend was to him.

Syrian did not speak immediately, his eyes were glazed as the magic coursed through his blood. His golden fingertips glowed blue where they touched the orb. "They have joined other hunters on the way to the border."

Blasien moved fully into the darkness, facing Syrian. "Why did he take her?" His gut clenched in anticipation of the answer.

Syrian stared into the flames, his gold skin blue hued in the light. "Raphael was moved to pity for the lady."

"A rare emotion for him," Blasien said slowly, thoughtfully. Ashanti had affected them all to some degree or another--even moved Raphael, a man normally under supreme control. She had a way of crawling under one's skin. He didn't know if it was her soulful blue eyes or the way she fought so hard for her freedom that made him want to protect her, but he knew her reaction to him from their first meeting made him want to cherish her forever ... That and the fact that she'd saved his life when she had no reason to spare him. She was the only one who could have. He was not sure he could go on with his life as it had been. A piece of him was missing, and he wanted it back. *She* would give it to him.

That she cared so little for him was enough to rip his insides to shreds and leave him to bleed a slow death. He was such a fool.

"She is in danger. Raphael does not go with her across the border."

Syrian's words snapped Blasien to immediate attention. He clenched his jaw against the pain the thought of losing her caused him. Voice hoarse, he said, "From whom?"

"I do not know this person. There is a shadow blocking him from my sight--magic."

A possible sorcerer? In human lands? Humans relied on magical objects, not trusting those who could wield magic, and sorcerers were rare even in Shadowmere. An uncommon anxiety gripped him, but, furious at the weakness, he ignored it. "Where do I find her?"

"Near her homeland. If you do not go now, she will die."

* * * *

"This is the border, Ashanti. Are you certain you wish this? You know you can stay with me." Raphael's voice was soft as he spoke to her. He'd regained his human form and clothed himself to spare her embarrassment, though she suspected he could walk about nude with ease.

A pack of wolves and wolf men surrounded them, but she felt an ease amongst the brethren that she never would have sensed before when she was still human. Now, half beast, she took comfort in their presence when in the past she would have shrunk away in terror.

An inexplicable sadness had come and took hold of her heart, an unwelcome reminder of crumbled dreams ... for what had been and what could never be. "My thanks, Raphael. You know I can never repay you for your kindness, and yet still you offer more."

"Anything to help a lady in need," he said, his face solemn.

For all his uncommon, kind words, she knew he felt little emotion for the fairer sex. The hunters lived a hard, dangerous life, one that suited the warrior better than playing hero to a damsel in distress.

She smiled sadly, looking beyond to the land she would soon cross to find a new home for herself. "I am not Lupa. It would never work if I stayed." Raphael was an honorable man. He deserved to find a life mate that would match him in every way, one who could break through his careful control and bring him happiness ... of which she knew he had seen little and perhaps none. Ashanti would only bring them misery. It seemed sorrow was her destiny.

"Yes, I know." He followed the line of her sight. "We cannot cross the borderline with you. The law prevents it, and I would not risk my men."

"I'm not afraid. You've taught me more about my powers. I'm stronger now. I can defend myself if need be." Ashanti hugged him and he stiffened as if he wasn't sure what to do, then relaxed in her embrace. "Good-bye, Raphael. If Blasien should come tell him ... tell him I will always remember him."

Deeply saddened, Ashanti walked slowly away, crossing the border even as the sun rose above the horizon and streaked the sky in crimson and gold. She turned to look back one last time, her hand raised in farewell, but no one remained. Ashanti shivered and pulled her hood over her head against the light of day.

She was now alone.

CHAPTER FIFTEEN

Ashanti trudged all day through the foreign land. Though she'd been born here, she'd not been allowed to roam free, and she remembered nothing from Blasien's flight to his own homeland. At nightfall she reached a small creek that cut a swath through the brush. The water was shielded by dense growth, and trees of a forest grew thickly near the life giving liquid. Exhausted from her travels and unsure what else she could do, she collapsed in a bed of ferns, huddled in her dark cloak against night's chill.

She slept soundly until she heard a sudden crashing through the brush. Instantly, Ashanti froze, wide awake. Opening her eyes cautiously, she peered through the tangle of fronds to the source of the sound.

A man was moving through the hip high weeds, intermittently slapping at insects and cursing. No doubt fresh water had driven him to face the wild.

Moving slowly, protected from sight by the thickness of growth, she drew up into a seated position, watching as other men rode up to quench their thirst.

Soldiers! She wondered how they came to be here and why on such a night.

Ashanti's pulse raced as they surrounded the area and more men kept coming as though piling into a battleground….or perhaps from one. She couldn't seem to find enough air to breathe. What was she going to do? Panic threatened to overcome her senses, but she strove to remain level headed. If she lay still, surely she could avoid their detection and escape when they left. It was as good a plan as any, and in any case she dared not move. The men were too thick to avoid notice of any movement, no matter how slight. Only the blackness of her cloak and the weeds could help her now.

Flattening herself to the ground, she curled as small as she could and lay with her eyes wide, listening intently. Snapping branches cracked with deafening noise as more men moved toward the water. Ashanti's heart stopped when she realized one man was closing in on her hiding place.

Silence and the darkness was her only hope, but she did not think she could've screamed if her life had depended upon her doing so. Her throat closed with terror, even as her mind remained strangely calm, racing with possibilities. For several painful heartbeats, the man towered above her and she nearly sobbed in relief when he didn't see her, his eyes only on the creek ahead. But as he stepped high to clear the scrub, his toe caught her leg and he went careening down into the brush.

Loud guffaws carried in the air as the other men laughed at him. He cursed and struggled to right himself ... and then he saw her. His eyes widened in shock.

Without thinking, she kicked him with all her might in the face, jumped to her feet, and took off through the tangles, flying over the impediments and running for the thick woods as hard as her legs could carry her. Heart pounding wildly, Ashanti raced for her life, knowing the ways of men and their love for blood sport should they catch her.

The men fell into stunned silence as she revealed herself, seconds ticking by as no one reacted, and then they roared battle cries when they realized prey had just been unveiled for their hunting pleasure.

They gave chase as she darted between their outstretched arms.

Ashanti could outrun common men now ... but she could not outrun the man on horseback that she heard pounding up behind her.

Apparently momentarily stunned as the other men had been, he nevertheless recovered himself far too quickly and charged after her, crashing through the water right behind her, the horse easily leaping over obstacles before it that barred her own progress. The horse landed with a thunderclap on the ground directly behind her, but she didn't look, could only keep staring ahead, her goal within sight. If she could reach the trees she could lose them.

A mighty arm swooped down from above and captured her in a forceful grip. Pulling her high into the air, the rider dropped her onto his lap as if she weighed naught more than a child. Ashanti flailed her limbs even as she landed hard on the pommel of the saddle, the man's force and her own impetus driving the air from her lungs as the pommel drove into her stomach. She gasped for breath as the horse halted as though commanded.

Lungs filling with air, she screamed in rage and fought against the man that held her, kicking and biting, digging her hands into his leather armored thighs. She wished more than ever that she had the ability to change at will. If she had, he would have been dead before he knew what struck him.

Unbelievably, the man easily trapped her arms in one hand and flipped her around, bending her backward over his lap, keeping her off balance.

The heat of Ashanti's fury froze like the blood in her veins. She felt her jaw drop and her eyes widen in terror as the enormity of her situation caught up with her brain.

She was looking into the face that had haunted her every waking moment for ten years.

"My little kitten has come back to me. We've been looking for you, Lady Ashanti," Lord Conrad said in a voice like rock crumbling down a mountainside. A cruel smile twisted his lips even as he descended for a kiss.

*   *   *   *

Ashanti bit his lips when he touched their slimy surface to hers. Blood gushed into her mouth and she spat it out, feeling it ooze down her chin from her supine position. It took an act of will not to gag at the foul taste, but she refused to give him satisfaction or show weakness.

Surprised at the attack, Lord Conrad jerked away from her, but the surprise lasted only momentarily. Ashanti more than half expected fury, possibly retaliation. Instead, she saw his black eyes glitter in the moonlight with an emotion she found far more unsettling. Her violence had excited him. She should not have been surprised. The household had been terrified of him. She had known he had a cruel streak. She simply hadn't realized that he found sexual stimulation in pain. "I see you've acquired some spirit, kitten. Or should I call you she-cat. That is what you are now, are you not?"

She lay still, despite the excruciating pain she felt at the hard pommel digging into her back. To allow him to see her pain would give him far too much satisfaction. "How did you find me?"

"I was informed of your ... untimely departure from Lord Blasien's castle."

"That's not possible. I don't believe you."

"How can you think anything else?" He bent and slid his tongue up her neck, leaving a trail of saliva that made her skin crawl and made her itch to be free of his nauseous touch. "Did you see the crown Moran wore? The cat with emerald eyes? They were seeing stones. I could see everything that happened and communicate with him as if he were standing right before me. How do you think I captured Blasien so easily? *I* gave Moran the Mortalsblade."

Stunned, Ashanti could only stare at him speechlessly for several moments. "No. No, you speak lies." The horror of his words rang as truth in her head, however. He'd captured Blasien far too easily for treachery not to have been at the root of it. He'd known everything about Blasien and Moran's battle, had tried to have Blasien killed. Why? The answer came to her suddenly--he'd needed a shifter to heal her curse. There had been no other way to achieve his ends.

What else could he have done with such power? And he'd known she left. She had not stupidly, or by chance, stumbled into the midst of Lord Conrad's army. He had been waiting for her, expecting her. That meant there was still a spy in Blasien's midst. It meant that Blasien, too, was in danger, for she did not for a moment believe that Lord Conrad would be willing to allow bygones to be bygones now that he had her back. He would be seeking a way to punish Blasien for escaping.....for taking her.....for claiming her when he had waited so long to claim her for himself! Who could it be? She would never be able to warn him in time to save him.

At her silence, Lord Conrad said, "I speak truth. Did you think I would give you up so easily? No one can help you now."

Anger blazed inside her. She was sick of betrayal, sick of cruelty and fear. Only one man had lifted her from evil's clutches, and she'd abandoned him because she'd been afraid of the savagery of their law. She realized now that no one else would protect her as Blasien would--he'd bound them together for life even though he did not realize it. "Blasien will come for me. There is a connection between us you can never sever." Lord Conrad laughed cruelly. "Blasien is dead."

Ashanti blanched. If he had stabbed her, she could have felt no more pain in her heart at his words. For several moments, she could not catch her breath, could not think beyond the pain. He could not be dead! She could not live without him. She had no wish to live without him.

It dawned upon her suddenly how utterly childish and stupid she had been to run away. She had been mortified, certain she could not face the others after what they'd witnessed, but it had meant nothing more to them but that she was taken and they dare no longer even entertain thoughts of touching her. There would have been no sly smirks, no tittering comments to follow her about the halls. It had been *expected*. It was their way.

But she had felt she *had* to punish Blasien in the only way open to her.

And now he was lost to her forever. She could not give him her forgiveness for doing what he had to to protect her, nor ask for his for doing her utmost to hurt him.

"No. I don't believe you," Ashanti managed to say. She felt unbidden tears bleed into her eyes even as she tried to deny his claims.

Was this truth or could it possibly be a new form of trickery designed to torture her? Had the spy killed Blasien? Could he possibly be dead and she unaware that the world had gone cold? For a moment, hope flickered inside her at that thought. Surely she would have felt it if he had died. Surely she would have known.

But hope withered and died inside her at the look in Lord Conrad's eyes. He fully believed what he said.

Ashanti turned away from him, feeling a single tear creep down her cheek.

"Gear up," he called out to his men and they mounted their own horses to leave. Lord Conrad smoothed a gloved hand down her neck and chest, cupping her breasts. A rough groan escaped him. She did not resist his touch. The will to fight had abandoned her.

"I have many delights to show you now that I am free to touch you. You would not believe the beauty a simple knife can create on a body such as yours."

CHAPTER SIXTEEN

"I've wanted you since I first saw you as a girl, lost in the ruins of your father's house." Lord Conrad leaned against the sole piece of furniture in the cell, a table with silver tools laid across its surface.

Ashanti stood with her back pressed against cold, rough stone, chained to the wall with silver manacles that burned her wrists. It was ironic that she was being held in the same place Blasien had been. Only she had not the strength to break her bindings, and there was no one coming to release her.

She had yet to think of a plan of escape, but she was determined not to give up.

Once the shock of Conrad's claim had worn off, she had realized that it was a lie…whether he realized it for what it was or not. Conrad could not know, or understand, the connection between her and Blasien.

He was alive.

She would have known it in the depths of her soul if ill had befallen him.

She would escape. She would return to Shadowmere where she now knew she belonged…to Blasien.

She knew Conrad's weakness was violence and sex. She would have to turn it to her advantage somehow.

"If you have waited so long, why have you kept me here the past few days waiting for your tender touch? I grow tired of your games."

Lord Conrad grinned blackly. "Easy, kitten. A secret admirer comes. An audience makes the pleasure so much ... sharper. Wouldn't you agree?"

His reference to the blood ceremony brought flaming heat to her skin, boiled her blood. "You bastard." He knew everything that had happened, how could she forget that? He would use all her weakness and experiences against her--as he had always done and would continue doing unless she freed herself.

And she had fallen into his hands yet again by allowing him to see that he'd enraged her.

Lord Conrad sauntered close, his boots echoing hollowly through the empty chamber. In his hands he held a long bladed dagger. He fingered the edge almost lovingly, looking down her naked body in a long, measuring look that clouded his eyes with lust.

Ashanti struggled against her bonds, her hands clenching with the anticipatory need to rip the hide from his bones and erase the smirk from his face. Metal clanked against stone as she strove to reach him but couldn't. She collapsed back against the wall, breathing hard, teeth bared to bite should he come too close.

Lord Conrad chuckled at her futile struggles, twisting the dagger so it caught the light and gleamed gold, reflecting onto her face.

"I could do so much to you, kitten." He shuddered with pleasure, fondling the blade and cupping his groin. Ashanti nearly gagged with revulsion.

"Cut me, if you are so eager," Ashanti growled, her eyes blazing blue hatred.

"I am glad you've regained your spirit. A lifeless wench holds no appeal for me."

Violence ... forcing her to submit to his will--these were the things he craved above all else. "I am so glad I please you, my lord. But why do you wait to share your prize?"

"'Tis the price I pay for your lover's death."

Ashanti felt a stabbing pain at the reminder. She'd tried to deny his words in the days since her capture, to forget he'd ever uttered such hated words to her ears. She thought she had convinced herself that it couldn't possibly be true, but she doubted, and that was enough to bring pain such as she'd never known, a different fear than she'd ever known. Even the shadow of a doubt was enough to weaken her, to throw her into utter despair. She hung her head, unwilling to allow him to see on her face how much she hurt.

A subtle, familiar scent teased her nostrils, coming from beyond the edge of light cast by the lonely torch, past the open cell door. Ashanti lifted her head, scenting the air.

Lord Conrad straightened, smiling as he sensed the foreign presence even as she did. "I'm glad you could join us."

* * * *

A tawny, black spotted beast roamed the darkened passages, sleek fur and silence allowing it to blend into the dark despite it's immense size--twice that of a natural leopard.

He had traveled many days, hunting, following the woman's scent to this fortress, followed it down deep into the underground.

A single lighted cell stood at the end of the long hall, a woman's anguished voice carrying above a man's. The cat felt excitement at the hunt and the faint smell of fear and sweat, the sound of blood flowing in human veins.

Blood that would soon be spilled.

He padded silently to the light's edge, crouching low to the ground, legs tensing for action. The man standing so casual and without fear, turned his head slightly and spoke the language of humans.

The cat sprang from the darkness with a roar, his ivory claws bared.

* * * *

Ashanti screamed as the huge leopard leapt into the cell. This was the spy. Her life was over. She closed her eyes to the anticipated blow, but the creature's claws never struck.

A man screamed and something wet and warm splashed across her bare skin. Ashanti opened her eyes and saw blood streaming over her breasts and abdomen, looked up with startled eyes just in time to see the great cat meld into the form of a man.

Long blond hair hung down to the man's waist, clung to his sweat dampened skin.

Ashanti felt her heart stop as the man stood and faced her briefly before turning to his foe.

Blasien.

Blasien had come for her.

Lord Conrad looked as shocked as she felt. Blood coursed from long gaping wounds in his shoulder and arms. The metallic scent of blood tinged with fear permeated the chamber.

Recovering quickly from his stupor, Conrad darted forward and sliced a wide swath across Blasien's abdomen, jumping back as Blasien twisted to avoid the blow. Blasien growled at the minor pain and struck again, his speed far superior to Lord Conrad's. From his hands sprouted wicked, curved claws stained crimson in the light.

Conrad grabbed the torch with his wounded arm, keeping the knife in his good hand. He swung the torch at Blasien to keep him at a distance. It scorched Blasien's hair as it swept above his crouched form. Blasien sprang and knocked the flaming torch from Conrad's weakened hand. It fell to the ground, casting distorted shadows across the two men.

In a move faster than her eyes could completely follow, Blasien darted past Conrad's outstretched arm, ignoring the long blade the man stabbed into his exposed ribs and slashed his claws across Conrad's bared neck. Lord Conrad backed away, clasping his fingers to the wound, red soaking his fingers as his life's blood flowed from his veins down his chest, dripping onto the floor and sputtering as it dripped onto the torch's dying fire. His eyes widened as he dropped to the floor, looking up at death's dealer.

He tried to speak but his wounds prevented speech. With a final, malevolent look, he collapsed to the floor, his life extinguished as darkness flooded the room.

Ashanti was blinded without the light, and she could barely hear Blasien moving about the room. Suddenly, he grabbed her shackles and she nearly cried in relief.

"Blasien, oh, how can this be?" She trembled as he unlocked her manacles and she fell into his arms. He hugged her to him, and she felt like her body could melt into his as his unnatural heat warmed the ice in her soul.

"Hush, sweeting. Nothing will ever happen to you again, I swear it." He stroked his hands through her hair and over her back, easing her tension and fear.

"You ... he said you were dead." She looked up at his face in the dark. He gathered her up into his arms, carrying her from the place of death and torture.

"I know."

A voice spoke in the darkness, "Bram nearly killed him when he reached the border, my lady."

Bram! Bram was the traitor. She should have realized it sooner.

Ashanti looked up from the protection of Blasien's chest. A light moved down the passage, carried aloft by Raphael.

"Raphael!"

He bowed. "My lady."

Blasien clutched her closer, nuzzling her hair. "We have Raphael to thank for our departure. And now the debt he owes me is paid."

"What debt?"

"I saved his life once. He does not bear my speaking on it well, and so I will say no more."

"Come, let us go," Raphael said curtly as he led the way out.

"How is this possible?" Ashanti asked, shivering in the night air. The castle was deserted. No one came to stop them.

"I've taken care of his soldiers. He had so few and most ran when I challenged them," Raphael said.

Raphael's powers always amazed her, and she'd never imagined the extent Blasien would go to to protect her. He'd risked everything in coming here--his lands, his life.

Raphael continued walking, but Blasien stopped, sensing the change in her mood.

"I have traveled long and hard for you, Ashanti."

"I know, Blasien. Why?" Ashanti looked up into his eyes, cradling one side of his face with a palm. She felt her breath catch in her throat at the look she beheld, something more than lust, deeper than desire--concern and ... dare she think beyond?

"When you left, you ... took a piece of me with you. I couldn't forgive myself for what I'd done and knew I'd driven you away."

"I forgive you," she said softly, holding his gaze. "Think on it no more."

He closed his eyes as though something broke inside. When he opened them again, she knew all his wounds had healed ... the grief and guilt had gone. "I don't want--no--I *can't* live without you in my life, Ashanti," he said huskily, his voice cracking.

Ashanti felt her heart swell, and she pressed her lips to his, kissing him, putting every ounce of feeling she had into the kiss before withdrawing to look at him once more.

"I love you, Blasien. May we never be parted again."

SEDUCED BY DARKNESS

CHAPTER ONE

Shadowmere, Northern Borderlands

Swan of Avonleigh had no knowledge of where she was and no memory of how she had gotten here. There could be only one explanation--dark magic.

She nursed little doubt that the source of the dark magic, the instrument of her torture by terror now, was the same-- Morvere, the sorcerer who had cursed her to live by day as a swan, only resuming her human form at night, the sorcerer who had had clipped her wing so that she could not even fly away to protect herself when the spell overtook her and changed her into a swan.

Not content with the misery he had already inflicted upon her, he had dropped her into this nightmare world, prey to the baying pack that now pursued her, where a horrible fate awaited her the moment she faltered.

Terror surged through Swan's veins, near deafening her to the sounds of the pack that surrounded her, almost seeming to toy with her as they herded her onward, closing in now and then to drive her in a new direction. Pushed almost beyond endurance, her muscles screamed in agony, but the threat of being eaten left no room for anything but the instinct to survive, to continue placing one foot in front of the other.

Keening howls tore through the night, wolfen, yet strange. They surrounded her from every direction, closing in now for the kill. Ignoring the sharp nettles of underbrush slashing her arms and legs as she forced her way through them, tearing her naked flesh, Swan forged onward in desperation. Blood shivered in thin rivulets down her skin, scenting the air and driving the howls wilder, louder ... the chase faster.

They were toying with her, she knew with certainty now, yet she could not give up hope that she would elude them.

Something crashed through the brush a short distance behind her but she dared not look--could only forge ahead and pray she could evade the monsters in pursuit.

Her heart choking her with its thunderous beating, the air burning her ragged lungs, she darted around a tree, ducking under its slapping branches as she passed. The hair rose on the back of her neck as she sensed something close, something bearing down on her. She whirled around, looking frantically for an avenue of escape, but everything was black in the night shaded forest. Movement caught the corner of her eye--death close at hand. She twisted away from it in vain hope, the scream she'd held back for so long tearing from her throat as a dark shape lunged for her. Jerking away from its grasp, she lost her footing.

Leaves and dirt churned as she crashed to the ground. She screamed again as hands grasped her arms and a heavy body rolled with her until she lay beneath it, her arms trapped behind her back against the cool earth. Bracing her feet against the ground, Swan heaved upward, desperate to escape the ravaging blows she expected momentarily. A leaden weight settled over her, tight against her thighs. Hands pinned her shoulders to the ground. She was trapped. Thoroughly bested, unable to move the slightest inch, exhaustion forced her to collapse and cease her struggles. Breathing harshly in the overwhelming silence, Swan braced herself mentally, expecting to feel curved talons rake into her flesh, slicing down into her heart.

No attack came, no bestial growl broke the stillness. Quiet had descended around her. The howls had receded into nothingness, and the forest was still save for her own pounding heart and ragged breath. When no death strike fell, her sanity returned, and she realized a man lay atop her instead of a beast as she'd feared. The touch of him scorched her own feverish skin, the sheen of perspiration doing little to cool her unnatural heat.

Blinded by the darkness, she could see nothing of him, his shadow eclipsing what meager light made its way beneath the thick foliage of the forest. Hard muscles clamped tight against her hips, their grip strong and unforgiving, but still human. He seemed as human as she, someone she could face and hope to win against ... if she could just gather her strength. A deadly calm settled over her.

"Why come you to these lands?" a deep voice rumbled above her.

Startled, Swan looked up at him, too surprised to do anything but blurt out the truth. "I know not where I am, nor how I came to be here."

He was quiet a long minute, weighing her words. "I think you do not speak the truth, but I will humor you for the moment. You lie in a forest of Shadowmere, on the Northern Borderlands. You have ventured far from your home, little bird. Now--who opened your cage?"

Gooseflesh rose on her skin, chilling her despite the hint of amusement she detected in his tone. Morvere had more power than she'd ever dreamed. If such was truth--and she held onto little doubt that it was not--then she could not hope to defeat the sorcerer on her own. It would take someone of equal power, someone versed in magic ... someone from Shadowmere.

An insane possibility, spurred by the sheer hopelessness of her situation, occurred to her. She ignored his question, voicing one of her own. "Are you going to kill me?"

"It is not often we attract spies of your ... ilk. I would not have you die so soon." He leaned toward her and sniffed her throat as if he would taste her. Swan held perfectly still, unwilling to give him cause to attack. The plan she'd only begun to formulate fled. No man behaved this way, this animalistic. She'd jumped to the wrong conclusion--a mistake that could easily make her life forfeit. He was not her kind. It had been foolish to think so--to believe for a moment that she had been rescued.

Inches away from her ear, his breath hot and invasive, he whispered, "My question remains unanswered. I may be tempted to ... eat you, little bird ... if you do not satisfy me."

Swan swallowed hard, ignoring the unfamiliar trembling that flickered through her. "I don't understand it. What spy of any worth would get caught?"

"One who had allowed it. Do you aim to disarm us with your charms?"

It was an intriguing question, provoking a spark of renewed hope. He would not have mentioned it, surely, if the possibility had not existed. "I'm no spy. You are mistaken."

"Rarely." He seemed to study her. "We have ways of making men talk. I can think of much more pleasurable methods to ply on a woman."

She would die before she allowed an unnatural to touch her, let alone use torture to gain information from her, even if she'd had information to withhold from him, which she most certainly did not. With an effort, she hardened her will. "You can not information I do not have, nor wield any force that could pry it from me if what you suppose were true. You don't frighten me," she said with a bravado born of rulership.

"You should be." He chuckled darkly, pushing himself up so that he no longer lay fully against her, though he still held her pinned to the cold ground. His knowing laugh crept over her with the intimacy of a caress. She couldn't escape the feeling that he could see every inch of her body, despite the darkness, that he invaded even her thoughts and knew her as no one ever had.

A callused thumb brushed the edges of her collarbone. Her skin tingled with heightened awareness, near burning at the points of contact. She shivered. Never before had she considered her nudity a danger. In her world, no man would dare touch her. And though the dark shielded her, here ... there could be no guarantees of safety in old illusions. Swan jerked away from his invasive touch. His gall was unbelievable.

"I did not give you permission to touch me."

Despite her command, despite her certain knowledge that in her own world he would not have dared so much, would have instantly begged pardon for a presumption that could easily have been a death warrant, she knew very well that she was powerless in his world.

He was an unnatural, of that she was certain, yet what powers did he possess? She could not know, nor even their extent, but even if he did not possess night vision, he would certainly have felt her nakedness, pressed against her as he was. Would he dare to press his advantage, to take what had not been offered?

Meager as the tattered robe had been that had covered her nakedness, even that had been lost in her mad dash for freedom ... snatched away by a tree's groping fingers. Nothing protected her now but her own tangled locks and the dusting of dirt clinging to her skin.

She should have felt frightened, or revolted. Instead, her sudden awareness of him as a far different sort of predator, sent a strange sort of expectancy humming through her blood.

"I did not ask it." He'd noticed her reaction, his senses uncanny. "Most women would welcome finding themselves in your position."

"And what is that, as a meal?"

He laughed. At another time, Swan might have thought the sound pleasant. Now, it only made her more uneasy. "There is more than one way to eat a woman. I would gladly demonstrate."

Strangely, although she had no very clear idea of what he referred to, her heart quickened, heat gathering in her loins. It disturbed her that he could command a reaction from her body with no more than his words. Irritation surfaced. "I never knew beasts were so obliging. I thought your kind only raped and destroyed."

His hands tightened on her shoulders. "It is humans who cannot be trusted. You break the pact coming here. Death has been dealt for less," he said, his voice deadly soft.

"I face it gladly," she said slowly. Her jaw clenched with the effort to remain calm, but her heart drummed in her throat with the new threat.

The man was silent a long moment, studying her, building the tension strumming through her aching muscles. At last the vice of his hands relaxed. "You lie, little bird. Your fear is as potent as a perfume. You would do well to remember where you are. I tire of these games. Why have you come here?" he demanded again, quietly. "The scent of prey is sweet ... and you have ventured where you don't belong. I will have my answer."

"I have told you what you asked. You don't want the truth. I have no one to turn to, nowhere else to go."

Morvere had sent her here, of that she had no doubt, though she could see no advantage to telling him of a man he would not know for his treachery. She could see no way to make him believe her tale, and it was possible that mentioning the sorcerer might only convince him that she and Morvere had formed some plot together, to use sorcery to get her beyond the border for some dark purpose.

In her homeland, it was well known humans were killed in Shadowmere on sight. Those few that survived its horrors turned mad. Morvere had sent her because he wanted her death and torture. He knew the unnaturals horrified her. To be made one and thrust into their midst to die was a vicious revenge for denying him.

He could not even be brought to pity and end her life quickly. How long had he conspired to claim her and her lands? She'd trusted him with her life, with the lives of her people, and he'd betrayed them all.

That reflection did much to steel her purpose. She would survive, if only to see him fall.

"Shadowmere is not a haven for your kind."

Despite his assurances to the contrary, it occurred to her that it could be, if she could convince him. Dare she pin her hopes on the people of Shadowmere? They had fought for so long, it was unlikely she would gain anything but a swift death. Still, she had nothing more to lose and everything to gain by asking. "I require your assistance."

The demand caught him by surprise. "You do not know me, and I feel I must point out that you're in no position to make any sort of demands. I fear I must refuse."

In some long buried sense, she felt he reserved a softness toward women--many men did. He had rescued her, after all. Of course, he might only have saved her for some darker purpose, but instinct told her she was right. "You have not heard me needs and I am not accustomed to being refused."

His eyes narrowed. "Arrogant. And naive. Obeying a woman's demands is beyond my experience."

"You cannot possibly refuse me help," she said, astounded, her voice tinged with doubt. What would she do? She could not go forward unassisted, and most certainly not back to Avonleigh. Morvere would likely do something worse, perhaps kill her on the spot for not having the grace to die the first time.

He shook his head, intrigued despite what he'd said to the contrary, to find his beautiful captive making demands upon her captor. But was it strength, or nothing more than a lack of understanding of the dire situation she found herself in? "I could, far more easily than you seem to think. I am bound by nothing from your world, not the position you held in your own world, certainly not your notions of chivalry. It's obvious you have no clear notion of your peril. Did not the pack fill you with terror at their call? The hunters answer but to one master ... and worse terrors roam these lands."

If had he meant to frighten her, it had worked. The blood froze in her veins as his words sank in. Why had she not realized what it was that pursed her the moment she learned where she was?

The hunters. Borderguards of Shadowmere. The pack was the essence of nightmares. They'd chased her, endlessly it seemed, but she had thought them beasts of the natural world, drawn by the scent of blood, not... the hunters.

Still, she lived. If what he said was true, why was she not dead?

It occurred to her then that there could be only one answer. "Who are you?" she whispered fearfully.

"I am Raphael, Lord of the Hunters." His hands shifted to grip her upper arms as he dragged her to her feet with ease. "And you are my prisoner."

They were surrounded in the next instant, wolfen men melding from the trees as though summoned with a thought. Some growled in the language of wolf. Others spoke in muffled tones, guttural, their menace palpable.

Knowing instinctively that to stare at them was to provoke them, Swan kept her gaze trained on the man who held her, Raphael, though she felt more than saw him. She'd baited one of the most powerful men of Shadowmere, but she couldn't dwell on that. Her initial fear faded, replaced with a sense of purpose.

She lived because he willed it. Whatever his purpose might be, she saw at once that he was a potential ally capable of defeating Morvere. And while she would never have considered allying herself with such as he under ordinary circumstances, desperation made strange bedfellows. She was not so haughty that she couldn't recognize this "man's" worth. She had only to convince him to help her.

A feat quiet possibly easier said than done, but she could

not allow doubts to sway her from her purpose. Her people needed her.

She sensed a presence near her from behind, warned by the crackle of dead leaves beneath softly padding feet. The movement halted a short distance behind her.

A voice rumbled from the dark, gravely and coarse as though unused, "My lord, we are sworn to uphold the pact...."

Raphael's hands tensed on her arm. "You need not remind me of my duty, Arion."

"That was not my intention, my lord--"

"Good. She is mine. Until it is decided what to do with her." He prodded her forward.

Swan was near blind, helpless to find her own way--and it rankled, as did his possessiveness. "I belong to no one, man or beast. Release me."

He ignored her demand. Swan attempted to jerk her arm from his grasp, to no avail. Her strength was no match for his. She stumbled with the effort, but he righted her before she could fall.

His grip tightened as he guided her through the forest, as though to dissuade her from further escape attempts. The precaution was unnecessary. It was less than futile to run again--not while under heavy guard, as she knew she must be.

In any case, where would she run to if she succeeded in escaping? Into the loving arms of the man who'd placed the curse upon her to begin with?

Raphael, Lord of the Hunters, might offer little hope, his possessiveness, his arrogance might rankle, but he represented the only hope she had at this point.

As she struggled blindly to keep up, the wound on her hand, the magically clipped finger, began to throb anew, forcing itself to the forefront of her mind. The pain from the myriad of cuts, scratches, bruises and aching muscles of her flight receded into the nothingness of minor twinges as raw agony from the injury pounded through her with every step she took. Had it only been a day since her life had been shattered irrevocably? The terror, the rushing adrenaline of her flight had vanished, leaving her weak, susceptible once more to the pain she had not felt in her shock. She began to realize she had nothing to sustain her, that she not could remain on her feet much longer. Unused to vulnerability, to being one of those needy females now made her despise herself. A simple wound should not affect her thus, she chided herself. The blood of kings ran through her veins. She shamed her ancestors with her weakness.

No thought could bolster her flagging endurance, however.

Each second weighed like a minute, each minute an eternity. The world slowed around her, sounds distorted like screams under water. Her legs, leaden from running, weighted her down. It was becoming increasingly difficult to move one foot in front of the other. Raphael's pace allowed her no reprieve.

"Let me go," she demanded again, a wave of dizziness washing over her in a nauseating wave.

"You should never run from the pack. It increases their appetite. How can I trust you would not do so again?"

The absurdity of her outrunning the hunters nearly made her laugh, especially considering her current condition. She would not be such a fool as to try again with their hunger unappeased, but it seemed unlikely he would believe her assurances. She was loath to reveal her weakness, but much longer and she would be unable to hide it from him. "I can only assure you that I will not," she said finally.

He seemed to consider her a long moment, then said, "Share with me but your name, and you may walk freely. Unless you enjoy my touch...."

That he would concede some ground was all the incentive she needed. "Swan of Avonleigh," she said. He released her, to her immense relief. Swan cradled her left arm, terrified to feel the heat of infection suffusing her hand. It was as she'd feared. Her steps slowed as she probed the wound, hoping she was mistaken. A sharp stab lanced up her arm with the light touch, and she groaned without thinking.

He stopped her with a hand on her shoulder. "What is wrong?"

"Nothing."

He cursed in a strange language. "Do you make a habit of lying?" He touched her hand, and she gasped and stumbled against him. Tears sprang to her eyes.

"Who has dared harm you?" he demanded angrily,

gripping her shoulders.

"Morvere...." she whispered, clenching her eyes tightly shut. She was fading away. Faster and faster. Was day approaching? Was she changing yet again? It was her last thought as warm arms closed tenderly around her.

* * * *

"What ails her?" Arion asked, kneeling beside the fallen woman. Her ragged garment had been retrieved and draped around her shivering form.

Raphael looked down at her, his anger building. "Other than an abundance of pride? She is injured. Someone has broken the heart line ... taken her finger." He despised the harming of women. The pack members who had disobeyed his word were being punished even now. That he knew not who maimed her, and therefore could not exact vengeance, infuriated him beyond measure.

Arion spared him a look before turning back to examine her. "Sounds like foul magic to me."

"Yes," Raphael said. It was undeniable that she was under an enchantment. Magic clung to her skin like an invisible film. He would have sensed it even if he had not seen her change into the swan near the border firsthand. He had ordered his men to keep watch. He had not expected they would give chase. She'd nearly paid for that misjudgment with her life.

"It smells unnatural, tainted by some magic. Illness has set into the wound. She is likely to die if it worsens." Arion looked up at him, his face grave. "We've not the skill to care for humans, let alone one bewitched."

Beastmen had no need of healers, for they had the ability to regenerate and heal their own wounds. "I know of another possibility. But it cannot be done here."

"If it works, you must teach me the skill that can break a spell," Arion said.

"If it does, all beasts should learn."

He could spare her the indignity of more exposure, but there was no guaranteeing what he planned would even work. The kharez was a phenomenon so rare, he'd only heard of it happening once in the entirety of his life. His friend, Blasien, had been healed by just such and still knew not the nature of the kharez.

A melding of essence and sexuality--the basis of creation-

-the powerful healing could only be used between normals and beasts for reasons unknown. And humans never mixed with their kind unless to kill them. Certainly never sexually.

Still, it was the one chance the woman, Swan, had. If it worked, she would likely kill him when she recovered, but he thought it a small price to pay for life.

Bending, he gathered her effortlessly into his arms. She trembled but remained unconscious. He nodded at Arion as he stood. "Let us make haste. We must reach Barakus before the silver moon sets."

CHAPTER TWO

Touching an unconscious woman held no appeal for Raphael. But the actions of a few rogue hunters forced him to make amends.

The woman had been bathed, and her wounds cleansed and tended to the best of their ability. It had done little to ease the fever racking her body. Doubtless her flight through the woods had only worsened her injury.

She'd been placed on his bed, soft furs draped around her body. In the room, lit dimly by basins of flame and the watery light of the red moon, she appeared unnaturally pale. Her skin was dry when it should not have been-- should have been soaked through with perspiration at her heat. He wondered that the wound affected her so harshly, but suspected dark magic had more to do with her illness than any natural cause.

Raphael climbed into the bed and knelt beside her. He smoothed a gold threaded lock of hair from her face. Her eyes moved rapidly beneath her lids, her body twitching slightly, her mouth parted on a sigh. She was dreaming, likely of the chase or some other horror he could only imagine.

Anger seeped into him. He clenched his hands into fists, then realized what he was doing. Deliberately, he drew and released a slow breath, forcing himself to remain calm. Reckless anger would do neither of them good.

From Blasien, he knew the kharez was inherently sexual.

Blasien's woman had healed him with her body and unintentionally formed a connection between them. Sensual touch sparked the reaction. And it was time to begin, before she worsened ... or roused enough to refuse him.

Raphael traced a finger lightly over her parted lips and down her right arm. Her skin was soft as down, smooth and perfect. Taking her hand in a gentle grip, he lifted it to his face and pressed his lips to her fingertips, feeling the rapid pulsebeat of her heart. He moved over each slowly, lingering, sucking each small pad into his mouth to rake lightly with his teeth and soothe with his tongue.

She moaned softly and shifted, drawing closer. The furs slipped down at her movement, revealing the soft globes of her breasts, golden tipped in the light.

His hands itched to curve around them, test their weighted softness in his palms. Heated blood rushed to his groin, his length swelling, hardening beneath his short kurt. Long had he been without a woman to touch ... to taste ... to bury his hard shaft deep inside. This woman--the human--tempted him.

Smoothing his palms over her alluringly defined collarbone, he moved lower, watching her face for reaction as he skimmed her breasts with the softest touch. Her lips parted on a breathy sigh as her nipples pebbled, begging, needing more.

He swallowed hard, his mouth suddenly dry. He pinched the tight buds, rolling each between his thumb and forefinger until she moaned and arched her back, thrusting her breasts closer to him.

Unable to hold his baser side, Raphael growled low in his throat and descended, brushing his lips down the column of her neck. He lathed her flesh, dipped his tongue into the hollow of her throat, felt the fragility of her life beating against his tongue.

His teeth elongated with the bloodlust surging through him, the pulse beating at the base of her throat tempting him to taste her life's essence. He'd not felt such longing in many years--had banished that side of himself.

He wrenched away from that temptation, breathing ragged and harsh, but she caught him, held his arms tight. Looking at her face, he saw that she watched him. Her eyes were slumberous, dark and glazed with lust and fever. She licked her lower lip, drawing his gaze, maddening him beyond reason.

Descending on her with a ferocity borne of long denial, he crushed his mouth to hers. Sucking her lips, he nicked her with his sharp teeth. Traces blood mingled with the sweetness of her mouth, fueling the lust consuming his senses, threatening to push him over the edge of control.

Swan made small throat noises, whimpers of pleasure as he thrust the furs aside and settled his body against her naked flesh. He groaned into her mouth as she rubbed her tight body against him. She closed her arms around him, digging her nails into his back, clutching tight as he ravished her mouth. Sliding his tongue inside, he probed her dark crevices, curling his tongue around hers as she sucked him deeper.

Her heat enveloped him, searing sanity, banishing reason. His hands moved with a mind of their own, down her taut stomach, past the thatch of hair hiding her sex. His fingers teased her slit, moist with her desire. The evidence of her arousal was near his undoing. Raphael dragged his mouth away, along her jaw to her ear. Tracing the shell with liquid heat, he plunged his tongue inside as his fingers sought and found her clit.

She moaned loudly, gasping as though she could not get enough breath. She spread her legs wide, tilting her hips to him. Fingers rapid, he worked the nub in tight circles until she lay panting beneath him. He broke his hand away from her lushness to rip his kurt away, until nothing barred him from taking her.

His cockhead nudged her opening, wet with her juices. She was smaller than he'd reckoned, tighter. Bliss beckoned his possession.

"Yes. Please," she begged, her voice husky as she wrapped her legs around him.

He stilled, poised above her, tense. He'd lost his damned mind. Strained, his arms shook with the effort to control himself. A cold sweat broke out on his body. It would take little movement to sink into her depths. She was slick and needy for him.

Swan arched beneath him, and his cockhead teased her entrance, jerking with need. He groaned, slipped infinestimally inside. His arms shook more violently as restraint slowly crumbled. Her wet heat enticed, threatening to snap the remainder of his control.

"Don't stop. I beg you," she cried, tossing her head back and forth on the silken furs, her eyes squeezed shut.

"You know not what you ask," he said through gritted teeth, pained with resistance.

"I do," she whispered and went still of a sudden, collapsing back.

Raphael drew up as though the tension between them had shattered, surprised as her arms and legs fell away. Moisture beaded on her body, sliding down her curves. Her skin pinkened, suffused with life, healthy and perfect. The fever had broken.

He moved from between her legs, beside her prone body. Kneeling over her, he touched her face. She slept. Her skin was cooling. No longer did the scent of illness cling to her.

Had the kharez worked?

He could not know, but it was likely so. And dawn was fast approaching. If his suspicions were correct, she would be changing soon.

Raphael stood and covered her once more. His body thrummed with need, unsated. He touched his hard length and groaned at the pleasurable pain. He would have this human when next he saw her, until the unbidden lust she aroused as woman and prey was cleansed from his body.

* * * *

An alien hardness nudged the opening of her sex, probing, painful. She arched her back, welcoming the intrusion with all her being....

Swan awoke with a start, gasping with remembered sensation, a cold sweat broken across her brow. Shivering, she wiped the moisture away, realized she was trapped in place. An unfamiliar heat lay at her back, cradling her length. She shifted, but a heavy weight held her in place, draped across her hip.

Looking around from her vantage point, she saw she lay in a strange bed, covered with dark furs. Beside the bed sat a squat table with the remnants of her robes. Bed posts rose from the corners, carved in the likeness of rampant wolves. In their teeth, dark gauze stretched between them--a net that could be dropped to protect from annoying insects, she presumed. Large stone blocks made up the walls of the room. An arched window was cut into the side wall she could see. Further down she could see a basin of flame that gave off flickering light and warmth.

Her attention returned to the bed, the other occupant, and the hand draped possessively around her. She had no memory of coming here. And she was as naked as the day she was born. Swan wondered frantically if she'd been sodomized, but a mental body check confirmed there was no tenderness, no aching, torn flesh. Her sexual muscles were relaxed and whole as the rest of her body.

The weakness she'd last recalled was gone, as was her nagging injury. Swan flexed her left hand in wonder, the consistent pain had vanished though the shock of the missing digit still greeted her. What magic did these beastmen possess?

From her position, she looked out of the window that faced her, though she could see sky and nothing else. Twilight reigned, that hazy darkness that warned of approaching dawn ... or coming night. She could not remember changing, but then, she usually did not, no more than the barest sense of it. Could an entire day have passed without her knowledge?

And if she had changed back and been healed, who then lay at her back? Logic dictated it would be her captor, Raphael. He would naturally be the most powerful hunter if he ruled them. Spoils always went to the victor. Seized by curiosity, Swan turned into his embrace for a glimpse at the man who would call her prisoner.

His hand slid down her hip at her movement, dangerously close to her femininity. She stilled, held her breath as she awaited some sign he'd awakened. The deep rhythm of his breathing greeted her. He'd not been disturbed.

Laying at an angle now, all she could see from the corner of her eye was a shock of black hair. Her hip began cramping from the twisted position. She couldn't hold it for long. She wondered just how deeply he slept. With the time, she must've changed a short while ago, so he could not have slept near her long. Certainly he'd not fallen into a deep sleep so quickly. The sky steadily darkened to pitch as she waited. The moons slowly began their ascent.

As she lay studying him, an outrageous plan began to take

form in her mind. She dismissed it at first, daunted by the enormity of it, unnerved that it had even occurred to her, feeling her pulse quicken with an odd mixture of excitement and alarm. Still, it nagged at her, refusing to be quelled until she examined the idea for flaws.

There were, she concluded, a wealth of them. On the other hand, she was in no position to dismiss a plot she perceived as holding tremendous potential for gaining what she needed. With an effort, she forced her doubts to the back of her mind, forced herself to calm reflection. The plot would only work if he was sound asleep as she suspected. It was wicked, not at all the thing for a lady to do, but it was her one chance to convince the beastman she was serious. If he wouldn't willingly help her--she'd force his hand.

Swan listened once more to confirm her safety. Satisfied, she began inching away from him. Sweat dotted her skin as she concentrated on small movements, moving with excruciating slowness. Finally, she managed to dangle one leg over the side of the bed. She was near spread eagle from the position, and his hand slipped steadily down, until it rested between her thighs. She gritted her teeth at the contact, flushing. Her body felt like a flower thirsting for water, thirsting for the heat and feel of him. Long had she been without a man's touch, not since she'd lost the seal of her body so many years ago in one careless act of defiance. An inch more and he could delve into her womanhood--

She closed her eyes, willed the blossoming desire down. He knew not what he did. It was abhorrent the thoughts flooding her mind. He didn't knowingly touch her--she could be any woman for all he was aware. It was insane to react to the touch of a beast, a stranger.

Slowly, she regained her purpose and used the strength of her leg to slide out from under him. She freed herself enough to rise from the bed. Almost at once, he sighed and turned, lying flat on his back with his arms upraised.

Swan stopped breathing as she awaited discovery. Watching him suspiciously, she got her first look at the man who had captured her. When he didn't stir immediately, when it was certain he slept on, she took her leisure in examining this manbeast. He was different than she'd thought, not at all the monster she had visualized.

Long, black hair shrouded his face, streaming over the

sharp line of his jaw. A single strand caught in the part of his full lips. She itched to remove it, part the flow of hair to see him fully, but she didn't dare. Almost, she wished he would open his eyes, just so she could see the color, but that time would come soon enough.

The rising moon increased at the window and sculpted the hard lines of his chest in the silver light. It slipped along his tapering waist and the flat hardness of his stomach, drawing her eyes down. He was completely naked, but she couldn't quite bring herself to look at his sex. Not the smallest measure of fat existed on his body. He was all muscle and rampantly male, more so than any other she'd ever known--and far more dangerous.

She wondered what he looked like awake. Would his muscles play fluidly with restrained power? Would his smile be as feral as she imagined? Swan shook herself from the arresting vision of him in repose. Now was not the time to dawdle. She had no notion the ways of servants in this castle, but she couldn't chance discovery before she'd had the chance to put her plot into action.

She quickly searched the room for some implement to bind him. There were no tools or ropes that she could see, no drapery but the fragile gauze that even she could rip through with ease.

The furs would be of no use either. They were too tough and thick to bend as needed. She looked back at the squat table. All she had were the sad remains of her robes. Sighing, she picked the robe up and walked softly around to the opposite side of the bed where he lay.

With quick efficiency, she twisted the length of fabric into a thick cord and looped the ends into knots that she could slip over his wrists and tighten from the top once in place. She knew she would have to move quickly, before he could rouse. Thankfully, he'd angled enough in his sleep that she saw she could bind him to one bedpost.

She wrapped the length around the post and took a deep breath, willing her nerve not to waver. It was now or never. Her heart drummed in her throat, choking off her breath. Steeling herself for action, she gently slipped the loops around his upraised wrists. The moment she had the loops around his wrists, she snatched the knot at the crux of the post, tightening the binding.

He awakened at once with a startling growl. Swan leapt atop the bed and straddled him, holding him down with her body while she clamped her hands over his mouth. He went still immediately when he saw her, though his arms tensed with leashed power.

Alert, he was more frightening than she'd imagined he could possibly be when she'd thought about tying him up. Slanted brows drew down in anger. Fierce black eyes, flecked with gold, stared at her above the level of her hands. Swan watched him warily, swallowing hard past the lump in her throat. She'd caught a wolf, and now didn't know what to do with him.

"Are you going to call for help if I take my hands away?" she asked. "Blink once for no, twice for yes."

He blinked once.

Swan regarded him suspiciously for several moments before she slowly withdrew her hands.

"Why have you bound my arms?" he said, his voice tight, his gaze watchful.

Swan felt a surge of victory as she realized he was well and truly caught. She'd done it. He was at her mercy. She needed only the strength of will to enact her plan. "Now you are my prisoner," she said triumphantly.

CHAPTER THREE

"What do you plan to do with me?" he asked, his voice carefully neutral.

"Quiet! I'm in control now. You will answer my questions or I shall be the one dining on wolf."

"Yes, my lady," he said, condescension evident in his tone. His mouth quirked in a half smile that was as inherently sensual as it was annoying. His lack of an appropriate response spoke volumes--he didn't believe the seriousness of his situation.

He leisurely raked his gaze down her body, lingering for long moments on the tips of her breasts, peeping through the curtain of her hair.

Swan flushed at his encompassing look, wishing she'd

thought to consider covering her nakedness before proceeding, but there was no time for regret. In any case, she had known she must act fast. There'd been no time to look for something to cover herself if she'd thought to consider it.

She was in control--she had to remember that fact. Until he satisfied her--she blushed at the turn of her thought, wondering when she'd turned into such a carnal creature. Was it an effect of the spell? She firmly pushed the wicked thoughts from her mind.

Shadowmere was a barbarian land. She had to make an impact on him, no matter how distasteful it was to her sensibilities.

She corrected herself--until he appeased her by agreeing to help, she would use her wiles to whittle down his resistance. After all, he'd promised to practice much the same torment on her. Fair was fair.

"I want you to agree to help me, Lord Raphael."

"I've answered you once before. Nothing has changed."

"I think you'll agree much has." She indicated the cloth binding his wrists to the bed, limiting his movement.

"What have you planned? I warn you, pain is of no consequence to a beastman."

"There are other methods much more pleasant, as you so graciously pointed out, that can be just as effective."

He laughed and slanted her an appreciative look. "Do your worst, my lady. My answer will remain the same."

His stubborn unwillingness to listen infuriated her. Though he was beast, she could not believe he was not the same as any other man she'd ever encountered, who fell to their knees and begged when presented the opportunity to bed a woman, promised anything for the chance of it. "That is not satisfactory."

His mouth quirked, revealing a dimple on one side. "What would it take to ... satisfy you?"

The heat of a blush crept up her neck. Her eyes narrowed. "Don't speak to me that way again or I shall gag you."

He chuckled knowingly. It infuriated her, but she couldn't stomach violence--there could be no other choice but the one she'd set out on.

Leaning forward, she drew her tongue up his neck in one long, slow stroke. Instantly, he went quiet, tense. She raised up, met the heat in his eyes and felt an answering fire spark in her depths despite her reservation. Power strummed her veins with potency.

Swan's lips curled into a slow smile. She'd gotten his attention. Bending once again, she nipped one earlobe, secretly thrilled to hear a soft gasp as she sucked it into her mouth. He turned his head to allow her easier access. It was only a matter of time until he was hers.

Releasing his ear lobe, she licked a trail down his chest, and rounded one small nipple. She circled it, staying just beyond reach. Flicking a nail against the opposite nipple, she raked her teeth over the tiny bud. He groaned, his skin jumped in response, heating with each grating pass of her teeth.

"Do you like that?" she asked. "I can give you more, if you'll only agree."

"No," he said through gritted teeth.

"It will only worsen."

Something glittered in his eyes. His jaw hardened, teeth clenched.

"So be it." It was altogether different being in control. She'd been freed by circumstance, allowed to do as she willed with no repercussions. The shock of power was heady, addictive if sampled overlong.

Swan straightened above him, smoothed her palms over his chest, reveling in the feel of his taut muscles, teasing his nipples with every pass. A trickle of moisture leaked from her sex down her thighs, until she could slip easily against his hard stomach. She rubbed experimentally against him, the ridges of muscle abrading her clit. Swan bit her lip at the sensation, at the goosebumps that rode across her flesh as she rocked against him. He groaned as she rubbed her slit back and forth along his lower belly, her folds held open by the spread of her legs. His erection dug into the cleft of her buttocks, insistent, demanding.

She reached behind, grasped it firmly, massaging it's engorged length. He sucked a breath in sharply, jerked against his bonds.

"Take me inside you, Swan," he said, his voice hoarse.

Swan opened her eyes, met his dark, heavy lidded look. His eyes glittered as the black depths were swallowed by golden flecks. She hesitated at the leashed wildness in his eyes. "Do you agree to help me?"

"Yes."

She stared at him a moment, uncertain she could accept such an easy capitulation. Finally, however, she decided she could take him at his word. He'd given it. He surely would not go back on it. "Good. I-I will release you to tend to your own ... needs."

He shook violently, his look thunderous. She gripped him with her thighs to stay upright until he stilled. "To tease a man is foolhardy. To tease a wolf is perilous."

Swan shivered. She'd not intended to provoke him so far. Her control had lapsed. "They say all is fair in war." She shifted to get off him, not so sure now that she wanted to untie his hands.

With a deep growl, he snapped the bonds like paper. In the blink of an eye, he grabbed her and rolled until she lay beneath him, trapped by the cage of his body. The color of his eyes bled to purest amber, near glowing with ferocity. Wolf's eyes.

He captured her hands before she could flay him, drew them up over her head until he'd manacled her wrists in one hand. Swan opened her mouth, and he covered her lips with his own, muffled her scream. She bit his lip as he sawed his mouth across hers. He bled but a little before the wound closed.

Her legs splayed wide round his hips, she could do nothing as the enormous head of his erection parted her folds and prodded her opening. He growled once more, forced her jaw open with a hand. Closing over her, he sucked her tongue into his mouth as he thrust his full length deep inside her.

Swan screamed into his mouth at the blissful friction. It was too much--she'd split in half. He ground his pubic bone against her clit as he buried himself in her tight passage, sparking a reaction in her core. He stilled a moment, leaving no doubt he possessed her body in totality, that she was his to do with as he willed. He allowed her to adjust to the immense girth of his erection. Pleasure and pain mingled as one.

With agonizing slowness, he pulled his hardness out until the head teased her opening, then drove inside once more, gaining momentum with each stroke until he pounded against her.

Swan arched her back, her blood racing, her clit throbbing with each grinding movement. He continued sucking her tongue, sliding his own against hers, cupping one breast with his freehand. He pinched her nipple hard, broke from her mouth to bite her ear. She gasped as the tremors increased. She locked her legs around his hips, her mind shutting down to pure animal lust, until there was only the tempo of his cock ramming into her passage.

The orgasm blinded her with its sudden intensity, slamming through her body until she panted for air. She trembled, her inner muscles tightening and jumping against his erection as he continued pumping to his own release. He groaned, collapsed against her as the hot wash of his seed emptied into her womb.

Breathing heavily, he lay atop her, nuzzling her neck until he released her hands. Swan pushed his shoulders, bucking against him to be free.

"Get off me," she gritted out.

He raised up, held her gaze steadily. He slid a finger along her jaw and she snapped at it with her teeth. Grinning ferally, he rolled off her and stood, stretching. Swan grabbed a fur and covered herself with it, flashing him a look that should have killed him on the spot.

"That is what happens when you tempt the beast, my lady."

"I hope you enjoyed yourself," she said, oozing sarcasm.

"I did."

"You bastard."

"You should never start something you don't intend to finish." He gave her a heated look that left her skin feeling singed, as if the fur was no barrier to his vision. Swan glared at him. "I will send someone with garments. We leave within the hour."

She started to say she wanted none of his charity, but his second statement stopped her cold. Surprised, she blurted out, "You'll still help me?"

"I always intended to."

Rage surged through her as his words sank in. How dare he! He had played her like a complete fool, enticed her to behave so outrageously! Swan fumed inside, unable to believe her lot in life. She'd gone through all that trouble for nothing, nothing but humiliation. Her pride was stung. "You could have gotten loose at any time, couldn't you?" she demanded furiously.

He smiled at her and strode from the room.

She wished she'd had something to throw.

* * * *

Raphael summoned Arion with the Flow. A current of thought known to beastmen, the Flow was necessary to them for communicating when they shifted, for they could not talk while they were in animal form. Though it did not work over great distances, it was invaluable to their way of life. Raphael used it now rather than wasting precious time locating his second in command.

He was in the great hall when Arion found him. Seated on the mantiam throne, he was staring pensively into the darkness, troubled by his reaction to the human woman. Never had he been so tempted to break old laws. And yet, he was disturbed to find the urge within himself to do so, particularly since he was no youngster, but a man full grown and aware of the consequences of doing so. His friend, Blasien had done so--he'd nearly lost his woman because of it.

Arion bowed deeply with respect and straightened. "I felt your call, my lord. What is it you wish of me?"

Raphael stood and descended the wide steps to stand beside Arion. They were of an equal height and look, much as all the hunters were ... dark haired and animalistic, wild as the humans would say. Arion, unlike the elders now gone, had supported his rise as leader of the hunters. He trusted Arion as he would a brother. "The pack is restless. The scent of new prey drives them mad with the blood lust." Their disquiet rippled through his mind. Violence and passion were easily read, and the growing danger disturbed him.

Now that he'd had the woman, he could easily understand their provocation. Her scent clung to his skin, fueling his own lust. Already he hardened, thinking of driving into her again. He'd taken her once, and still his appetite was unsated. If anything, burying himself in her body only seemed to have magnified his desire tenfold. Angrily, he pushed the madness back, tempered it with resolve. Even to consider touching her again was beyond foolhardy. It was dangerous to both of them.

Arion nodded. "Yes. They can not help but be so driven." He paused, looked his lord and master over as if weighing the wisdom of saying more. Finally, he said, "She cannot stay, else she will be devoured alive. Their restraint is not as it should be. I fear much blood will be spilled along our borders if e'er any cross."

Arion saw the root of any problem, much as he, himself. Raphael clasped Arion's shoulder. It was more affection than hunters usually showed one another, but he and Arion had shared much in the past. And he was leaving a heavy burden for Arion to bear alone. Unfortunately, there was no alternative to the decision he had made. "I know. I leave the pack to you until my return. I trust you, Arion. Not merely as my second, but as a friend and brother."

Arion nodded once more, clasped Raphael's arm in return. "It means much to me, old friend. I'll not fail you. I will await your return."

Raphael dropped his arm and walked down the centerway, Arion at his side. Avonleigh lay just beyond the Northern border of Shadowmere. Although many leagues distant, it was still a land easily reached without overwhelming hardship. The night was young. However, they needed to begin their journey to Avonleigh soon if they expected to cross any measurable distance in the darkness that remained. He did not relish the trek or breaking the pact, but he'd made her a promise. He would see her home. "I expect to return before the waning of the red moon."

"That does not give you much time."

"No. And the vampires have awakened." He'd sensed their presence before. It explained the unexpected bloodlust he had experienced during the kharez, and the sudden unruliness of the hunters. Once the vampires had sought to rule their creation, the hunters, but they had been gone many decades and the hunters had adapted to freedom. Still, their ties to their creators were strong and difficult to resist. He wondered how long it would take for the vampires to find them. They had never recognized any law but their own--for that they would be eradicated eventually.

Arion tensed beside him, surprised at the news. "Ill portent. Will you not take guard?"

Taking his men into human lands would only provoke a war. It was the last thing they needed now. He liked not the thought of traveling Shadowmere with a woman so tempting to predators, but he had little choice. He could not fight their own great numbers and still protect her from outside forces. The woman had nearly been killed by trusting his hunters before when he should not have. "No. If fate chooses our deaths, so be it. But I will not knowingly bring trouble. The bloodlust has risen with the rise of the vampires. I dare not trust our own with her."

CHAPTER FOUR

After he'd called the hunters and announced that Arion would oversee the pack while he was away, Raphael returned to Swan. Silently, he set the tray of food he bore on a table just inside the door, watching her.

She sat looking out the window, the glow of the moon limning her form. She'd not noticed his return, and he stopped in the shadow of the doorway to study her. Dressed in the loose flowing gown he'd appropriated, she appeared far more lush and at the same time more innocent than he remembered. The deep red heightened the pale translucence of her skin, highlighting the fragile blue tracery of veins in her breasts that caught his gaze even at the distance. Leisurely, he traced her profile with his gaze, settling on her full lips--a tight mouth he ached to feel wrapped around his engorged member. His groin tightened painfully at the thought, and he angrily tempered the burgeoning lust.

Now was not the time.

He crossed the threshold, stepping from the cloaking shadows and catching her notice. She gasped in surprise at his entrance, a hand flying to her chest. Holding her green gaze with his own, he moved forward and helped her rise from the low seat. She flushed under his scrutiny but grudgingly accepted his help. Once on her feet, however, she snatched her hand from his grasp as though bitten.

She looked him over, frowning. "You removed much of

your silver. Why?"

He'd kept only the arm braces and the circlet of his rank. "I won't need them for the journey." They could only be a hindrance.

"My own garment is hardly suitable for everyday wear, let alone travel. Have you nothing more I might wear that would be less...." She hesitated, pulling the edges of the neckline closer, nudging the deep armholes wide and exposing the sides of her breasts to his view. "Revealing?"

"I'm afraid not. Many here do not wear garments at all. Those of us that do must be able to strip it loose quickly for shifting. You are fortunate I was able to procure you a gown at all." It was only a slight fabrication, he mused. The women always enjoyed adorning their bodies with fabric, jewels, and metals--none went completely nude as the men wished.

"I thank you, then, my lord." Nervous, she smoothed her gown. The motion drew his gaze. He followed her hands as they molded the fabric of the gown against her ample curves.

She was strangely subdued, but the quick flash of her eyes as he met her gaze once more told him that it was a mere facade. A tempest brewed under that calm surface--one that would likely kill him if he turned his back.

"Though I much prefer the ... alternative, you are most welcome," he said silkily. Doubtless she knew not how inviting her subtle actions, how it increased the blood flooding his groin ... else she would cease her movements and hold still. If anything, clothed as she was, her charms were only enhanced. He had yet to feast his eyes fully on her nakedness--not to the degree he would have liked.

At the look in his eyes, Swan felt her body heat with remembrance, at her own boldness and attempts at seduction. She tried to quell both the memories and her reaction to them, and to him, and yet she couldn't help staring at him, allowing her gaze to roam down his chiseled form to the bulge cloaked by his kurt. He had been inside her, when she'd allowed no man to touch her in many years.

But then, she reminded herself, she'd not allowed Raphael. He'd taken, without permission.

Realizing she was staring at his manhood, Swan glanced

quickly at his face--wondering if he'd been aware of her assessing gaze. The perfection of his form made it difficult to conceive that he was in truth, a beast, and yet the look in his eyes could leave no doubt an animal lurked inside. Nor could his actions of before. Only a manbeast would dare to force her without the slightest guilt over his actions. If she were in her own world, she'd have punished him, but here, she tread on dangerous ground.

Privately, she could excuse him--she knew very well that she'd pushed too far to withdraw. She could excuse herself and say she had not meant to, that she'd been caught up in her own game, but that did not change the fact that she had provoked what had happened between them.

Regardless of her own culpability, she was appalled at her continued response to him after what had passed between them, disturbed that his nearness alone could provoke a heated response from her.

The crooked smile on his full lips answered the question that he'd noticed her perusal, but it vanished as he followed suit, examining her with equal interest. As his dark gaze moved over her lingeringly, she had the conviction that he'd missed no detail of her appearance; from her tousled hair curling over her nude shoulders and near bared breasts, down to the length of her legs exposed by the deep slits up the side of the gown. Swan flushed under that deliberate, sweeping stare, reminded of what he'd done to her and the desire that left her sex moist with want.

"Do you like what you see?" Swan asked belligerently, determined to quash any burgeoning feelings she might have.

"Is that an invitation?" Raphael smiled and moved closer.

Swan took a step back before she realized it. "No, it is not. You've had as much of me as I am willing to give." More than I was willing, she thought. She clutched the edges of her neckline together and held one hand up as warning to come no closer. He stopped, his chest inches from her fingertips, near enough she could feel the heat from his body.

His eyes narrowed. "Do not make idle promises you cannot keep, my lady. Think you I failed to notice your response to my touch? You may lie with your lips, but your body betrays you." He indicated her death grip on her clothing. "Think you I will rip your gown away?"

Swan straightened but did not relax her hold. "I would not be surprised if you did. You've already demonstrated a certain lack of control."

His brows drew down in his anger. "I don't make a habit of ravishing women."

"You've done so. Twice. Today and the night before."

He chuckled and rubbed a thumb along his jaw. "So you remember that time as well?" His voice dropped by a finite degree. "Do you remember ... everything? How you begged for more?"

Swan blushed. "You're lying." The dream she'd awakened to, urging him on, had she really done that? The fever had been brought on by magic, there was no telling what she could have done.

"I would not lie of such a thing, not a woman's sweet entreaty for pleasure."

The suggestiveness of his voice caused heat to flare along her nerves. Swan swallowed, her throat gone dry. His words evoked an erotic image in her mind, of lips and teeth, sucking, nipping, driving her to the edge. In all truth, she could not remember all he had done, nor how much she had encouraged him. Had she truly begged for his caress?

He'd held back before. She was certain of that. Some shred of honor had restrained him. It was not until she'd tempted him that he'd broken control. She would never allow that to happen again--tempting the beast, he'd called it.

"Would you like me to refresh your memory?" He moved forward until her palm was pressed flat against the hard plane of his chest. "I healed you with the touch of my hand." Slowly, holding her gaze with his own, he stroked a finger up her arm.

Swan shook her head vigorously. "Never touch me that way again. I would rather die."

"Are you so certain?" He continued his slow, lingering stroke. "I think your will wavers...."

"Please do not begin this," she whispered.

Something in her eyes halted Raphael's advance as her words could not. "You are afraid." Frowning, he withdrew his hand from her arm. She thought he would say something more, but after studying her for several long moments, he turned away. "Very well. We have too little time, in any case, to properly pursue the matter. For the moment, it would behoove you to explain the circumstances surrounding your arrival in Shadowmere. Come, I have gathered food for you. Explain to me as you eat." He gestured toward a low standing table near the room's entrance that she had not noticed before.

Swan regarded him warily, not certain she trusted the reprieve. Had he hated bedding a human as much as she did a beastman? Their species were too different to coexist. It was inevitable that they would hate one another. The thought sickened her, inexplicably.

Disturbed by the direction of her thoughts and her reaction to it, she changed the subject abruptly, forcing a light tone to her voice. "Surely such a task as this is too menial for the lord of the hunters?"

He was silent a long moment. "It is best for now if I see to your needs. Now, before I take you to your homeland--"

Swan gaped at him, so stunned by what he had planned that it took her several moments to react. "No! I cannot go back there, not as I am, not with him there! He would kill me on sight were I to return."

Raphael bade her sit on the bed's edge. Standing with legs braced apart, he crossed his arms over his chest. "You'd best explain."

He'd promised to help her. As uncomfortable as it made her to tell the whole, sordid tale, and the blind naiveté that had led her to such a pass, she couldn't expect him to walk blindly into danger.

She thought it over for several moments, but decided she must begin at the beginning of her troubles. "I came to rule Avonleigh at a young age. I would by far have preferred the lives of my parents to the power that was my birthright and my responsibility, however. Other than my younger sister, I had no one, certainly no one to guide me. Morvere, my father's sorcerer, seemed... an ally, a man I could trust to advise me. He was always there for me over the years. I knew not that he craved our lands ... and me in his bed." She shivered in revulsion, toying with the cheese she'd taken from her plate before continuing. "Finally, he revealed his lusts to me. When I refused his advances, he cast a changeling spell upon me, taking my finger as his prize."

Uncomfortable with the admission, she found herself unable to meet Raphael's gaze. "Morvere has a malicious humor. By day, I am cursed to be a swan, as my namesake. By night I return to my human form."

Strangely, she found when she had finished that it was a relief to have someone to talk to, to finally have the sordid mess out in the open. For some reason, she did not feel so hopeless now, having told him.

"I sense you've not told me everything," Raphael said quietly.

"No, I have not. I told the truth before, in the woods. I knew not how I came to be here. Morvere is powerful, more so than I ever imagined. Some spell transported me here ... to die...."

Raphael studied her for a long moment, as if searching for the truth in her eyes. Finally, he turned away, pacing the room, deeply in thought. Swan watched him, hopeful, unnerved also that a solution had not immediately presented itself to him.

"If what you say is true," he said at last, "I must consider another possibility, rather than taking you directly to Avonleigh."

Swan nodded, feeling relief seep through her. "What is that?"

"Magic can only be fought by magic. I know of a mage who may have answers for you. Have you finished?"

She looked down at her nearly full plate in some surprise. "I've lost my appetite."

"You could lose more than that before we are done. Come, follow me." He strode toward the door, but her voice stopped him.

"Can I trust you?"

"Can you afford not to?"

* * * *

They packed light, for travel was harsh if overburdened, and her change with the day almost certainly slow their progress. He had planned for that, however. One basket held their provisions and space enough for their garments, the other was empty. Raphael did not inform Swan that it would be for her when she shifted. Likely it would disturb her, but even dumb animals recognized predators when near, and he could take no chance she would harm herself while she was trapped in the form of a bird.

It seemed no one took note of their departure from Barakus. From what Swan could see, the castle, built into the ground and foothills, was empty. True, she had only been there a short time, but she had seen no one else, not even so much as a servant, nor heard anything but the haunting call of wolves in the distance.

Regardless, she had the eerie sense of hungry eyes following her every move as they set out, watchful but unseen.

She was glad to be going from this place and wondered how he could stand it. But then, the beastmen were his own kind. She could never adjust to such a place, could not imagine ever wanting to. It was alien, brutal. Her place was with her people, her sister, who even now was in grave danger.

She was more than a little dismayed to discover that the common mode of travel, when magic was not used, and what was expected of her now, was running. This might well be easy enough for those accustomed, but she was unused to the constant physical exertion she'd been subjected to since arriving. Riding horseback kept her muscles lithe, but she was a ruler, not an athlete.

Unfortunately, due to the nature of predators, there were no common beasts of burden willing to carry beastmen and, that being the case, none were available for her use.

They set out at a steady paced jog under the rising moons, guided by plentiful light, the landscape washed with watered red that revealed as much as it hid.

Watching the silver and blood light mingle and play on the muscles of his naked back, Swan was struck by the raw power he exuded with each movement, with each breath that he took. It was difficult to reconcile him as one of the monsters. Wild yes, but monster? She was no longer as certain as she had once been that he deserved such a judgment.

Strength was ingrained in the people of Shadowmere. Until ill had befallen her, she'd never before realized just how vulnerable she was as a human, helpless even to cast magic. The best defense she'd had was training with a blade, as all women must learn, but she'd seen no weaponry with which to arm herself since her arrival in Shadowmere.

It rankled being dependent on another for everything, including protection, particularly when she trusted nothing about the man save the fact that his nature alone precluded trust.

She had only these thoughts to keep her company, for Raphael said little and responded less. The darkened landscape afforded no distraction, lying indistinct beyond the circle of her vision, without even the shelter of trees to break the monotony. Gradually, the loam, softened and pungent with fallen, decaying leaves, gave way to hard, barren ground. Thousands of rocks littered their path, as though mammoth stone had once been moved across the earth and rubbed to pieces.

Swan was grateful for the sturdy boots she'd been given, but still the stones made their mark felt on her soles, made walking difficult and hazardous.

Raphael pushed her to the boundaries of her endurance and beyond. Each league felt like a hundred, and she soon realized that no matter how much it galled her that she could not hide her weakness, she simply could not hold out. No training could match that of a shifter. Her stamina had collapsed, and he had not even broken a sweat.

Finally, when she could run no more, she dropped to the ground. She gasped, clutching a stitch in her side, her lungs heaving as she struggled for breath, her heart pounding as if it would explode in her chest.

He stopped and stood over her while she gathered herself. She wanted to strangle him, even if he was doing this for her. At that moment, she felt like she could gladly curl up and die, if only for the rest.

Without a word, he bent and swept her into his arms. She yelped, shocked, and threw her arms around his neck for support. He stooped and grabbed the fallen baskets before taking off once more at a full run.

She was no petite bit of fluff, no lightweight, and yet he carried her effortlessly, as though she were no more than a part of himself. Weary beyond belief, she settled her face against his neck. Within moments, her nostrils filled with him. His subtle pheromones sent her blood to roaring. The burning need began to surface like a live thing, insidious, creeping through her being and devouring logic and control. Desire this potent was not, could not be, natural. Swan jerked away, and his arms tightened around her, holding her tightly.

"Put me down," she said, thinking only that she must put distance between them before she shamed herself.

As he had from the time they had left, he ignored her.

The fact that he did not even dignify her request with a response only fueled her fear and anger. "Now, beast!" she commanded, her tone harsh, her voice shrill with consternation. The moment the words left her mouth, she realized what she'd said was unforgivable, but it was too late to snatch the words back, and her control was too tenuous for her to care greatly. She could not desire him. It would have been impossible were he any stranger, but this was far worse even than that. He was not of her own kind. He was a beastman.

His jaw clenched, the muscles working. "Your prejudice is ugly. It taints your beauty," he said, biting each word off.

Swan glared at him, thankful for the dowsing anger that curbed her unwelcome appetite. "There has been little enough proof that beastmen deserve my regard."

He tensed as if she'd slapped him. "And yet you expect the help of a beastman?"

"I do not need a lecture on the virtues of Shadowmere. Let me down and I will seek my own way," she snapped unwilling to yield even knowing she had spoken in a way she should not have.

He'd shamed her. She had acted abominably, throwing his charity in his face. Never would she have done so to another. Diplomacy had always been one of her strongest assets, but with Raphael, she lost all sense of reason. She should apologize, she knew, but it had been so long since she had, she found she could not force herself to speak the words. Her throat closed up, her pride refusing to budge.

He'd done nothing but pick her up when she'd fallen, help her when she required it. Still, the words would not come.

His arms tightened around her, and he continued his pace.

"I warned you not to touch me," she said, voice soft with reproach.

"I think perhaps you require a lesson in manners and

humility."

Alarmed, she tensed. "How dare you threaten me! How dare you suggest that you have any right to teach me anything!"

He glanced at her, but said nothing.

Swan swallowed with some difficulty. "What do you mean to do?"

Raphael would not answer her, and despite attempt after attempt, she could not lure him into speaking any more. She could blame no one but herself, ungrateful wretch that she was. He was silent well into the night, though his anger was palpable with every mile they crossed.

Eventually, the tension and worries overcame her, and she slept, guilt plaguing her dreams.

CHAPTER FIVE

With the morning, she changed into a swan. One moment, he was cradling her in his arms, the next, a mist gathered and when it cleared, he held the graceful bird.

If he had still harbored any doubts that she was under an enchantment, it had been dispelled. A true swan maiden would shift much the same as he did when he shifted into his beast form, with bones melding, their outer skin shivering as fur or down cloaked them.

To change instantly was unnatural.

Rising, he placed the squawking bird in the empty basket he'd brought to carry her and latched the lid. Although he studied her for some time, he saw no sign of the intelligent, vibrant woman she was as a human. Did the spell consume her entirely each day?

He thought o the Flow, the mind force, and an idea occurred to him....

* * * *

She was sleeping in down, surrounded by comforting warmth and softness. Something pricked her consciousness, quiet, insistent. Swan snuggled deeper into the darkness, wanting nothing but blissful rest. She was so tired. Her bones ached from the run, from fighting to stay alive and continue going. Here all was peace, no troubles plagued her. Only sleep.

A low growl of sound nagged her, buzzing in her mind like a fly. She waved it away, felt it tickle her lips, then her nose, and finally settle on her lobe.

"Swan," a voice whispered in her ear. She made no move to acknowledge the husky voice, instead struggling to burrow deeper into the comfort of nothingness.

"Swan." The voice was louder this time, substantial, obviously not the stuff of dreams. Something shook her shoulders. Still, she resisted. It was the none too gentle swat on her buttocks, followed by a soothing caress that finally drove the vestiges of sleep from her mind. Swan roused, groggy, struggling to turn and sit up.

A hand pushed her down, on her back. "Keep your eyes closed, little bird. Lay still."

Raphael! She obeyed him, because she could do nothing else. Her eyes were sealed shut, heavy, as if made of lead rather than thin flesh. Instead of alarm though, she felt only a drunken restlessness.

What was he doing here? Where was she, for that matter? This was not her bed, and neither was it the mass of furs she'd awakened on before. It felt nothing like either of those, and yet of both, a blending of memories that eluded her.

Still, she could not open her eyes. Blinded, she had no defense, could not run or save herself. Her senses seemed unfocused, confused. If she didn't know better, she'd almost suspect she'd lost herself entirely, existed as nothing but a thought in the darkness. Despite this handicap, she felt no fear, only a heightened awareness. "Where are we?" she asked softly, anxious to distract him from whatever his intent, listening for the sound of his movement but hearing nothing.

"You changed, Swan."

She startled. He was above her now, but she hadn't heard him move. "That's ridiculous. I'm here."

He chuckled darkly, by her ear once more. No heated breath stroked her skin with his nearness. Swan shivered despite herself. His body settled over hers, trapping her between his hard thighs. His sex weighed heavily against her belly as he leaned over her.

"I'm reminded of a promise I made."

She was not so sleep drugged that she missed the slight menace of those words. It did not bode well for her. Swan struggled to sit up but he pinned her arms above her head, until she lay helpless beneath him.

"What do you mean by this?"

"You'll know, soon enough. First, an experiment."

If anything, she liked that suggestion less. Under his domination, he could do anything to her. Swan shivered as something akin to fear and desire thrilled her blood. "What have you done to me?"

"I haven't done anything ... yet."

A palm skated down her upraised arm, along the sensitive underside. Her breasts were drawn taut at the angle, easily plucked from his position. She was naked and wondered when she'd lost her gown, and how he had removed it without her knowledge. He could do anything he wanted apparently, with her none the wiser. The beastmen were renowned for their skills in the bedroom, legendary. The thought had always appalled her, but now she could not help the curiosity that filled her every fiber.

Swan shook her head, shoving the persistent, erotic thoughts aside. "You're lying, else this is a dream. You are here, but not." She had to be dreaming. Never would she allow a beast to touch her this way, to dominate her so completely with no fight.

"Would you like me to prove how very real I am?" he whispered against her ear, cupping one breast in a firm grip.

Swan gasped at his familiarity, at the near painful puckering of her nipple in his hand. He squeezed, kneading her firmly. She could almost picture him smile at her unbridled response.

"I warned you not to touch me. I want nothing from you ... ever again."

He chuckled, knowing her words as lies. "No lasting harm will come to you."

"You are wrong. You cannot know everything." She bit her lip as he pinched her nipple, tweaking it harder. An ache spread from the peak of her breast and lower, crept down to that place between her thighs.

"I know your desire, Swan. You cannot deny your

craving to know a beast's every touch," he murmured huskily against her neck, his lips pulling at the tender flesh. Placing a hand on her neglected breast, he repeated his taunting actions, massaging until the globe lay swollen and heavy beneath his hand.

He stilled, pulled away from her neck. "This bud is shy. What will it take to awaken it, I wonder?"

A soft roll, as of lips moving over the small bud followed his words, and then his teeth raked across her, dragging a groan from her throat as the nipple hardened beneath his touch.

"Don't do this." She whimpered as he latched on to the peak, pulled hard with his mouth. A pulse started in her sex, quickening with each hard drag, each sharp tease. She arched her neck, bending her head back, moaning as he moved down her stomach.

Heat flared at his path. Her blood rushed in her veins, pooling in her sex, a pulse beating in her hidden nub. She shouldn't want this. It should stop, but her mouth couldn't form the words. She was as mute to say nay as she was blind.

Raphael released her hands and moved, freeing her legs of their cage. He cupped her breasts as he drew lower, then released them, nuzzled the apex of her thighs with his nose. His lips teased the top of one limb, nipping the sensitive flesh as he spread her legs with callused palms.

He rubbed his face against her inner thigh, faint stubble roughening her skin. She shivered at the contrast of silken lips and harsh stubble.

Swan's breath hitched at the first probe of his finger in her folds. He traced up and down her slit, parting her like a blossom, edging nearer and nearer the opening of her womanhood.

"Say but my name, Swan. Tell me you want me. Say you want a beast to pleasure you as no man ever will."

"No, I don't," she said shakily.

He slid up, circled her clit with his finger, driving her mad with his teasing nearness.

"I can end it, Swan. You have only to admit your desire."

She shook her head, ignoring that unbearable touch. She realized then her wrists were free. The bonds gone. He'd released her when he let go of her hands.

Hesitant, with growing strength, she opened her eyes. The pleasure disappeared in that instant. He was gone.

* * * *

As night fell, Swan changed into human form once more. Shivering, she slowly opened her eyes to dusk and the cool air of coming night. She stared at the dying rays of the setting sun, feeling an overwhelming sadness. She had always taken daylight for granted, never known how much the sun could be missed, but she was a creature of the darkness now, doomed never to see the sun again with the eyes of a human, unless the spell could be broken.

Her thoughts turned to another creature of the dark, to Raphael.

More specifically, her thoughts returned to the strange dream she'd experienced earlier. Had it truly been nothing more than a dream? Had guilt provoked the fantasy of admitting desire for a man not her kind? She was loath to say anything. If it had been a dream, she would be mortified to reveal the extent of her fascination with him. Lust could form no lasting connection--and she didn't desire to be chained to any man.

A fire flared to life, and she sat up, startled at the sudden flash.

Raphael knelt across the way, watching her over the small, orange flame, his dark look blistering.

Cloaked with trailing hair, she nevertheless felt completely exposed by his intense scrutiny. Swan covered her breasts with her arms, breaking eye contact.

"Your gown is in that basket. You need to eat and warm yourself quickly. We dare not keep the fire long."

Swan complied, waiting until he turned his back to rise and dress herself. The muscles in his back were tense as he crouched, watching the growing darkness.

She ate dried meat and cheese, studying him. Sipping sparingly on the water bladder, she finally could contain her silence no more. "Is there something I should know? You are acting most strange."

Standing, he faced her and pointed to the East. "Ravenel is but a league distant."

He must have carried her straight on through the day to cover so much ground. Had he not rested at all? "That is not what I asked."

He smiled briefly. "Your persistence is admirable."

"That is a pleasant way of saying that I am bull headed."

Raphael kicked dirt over the fire and packed their few supplies. "We are being followed."

There was no need to ask if she should be alarmed--she was already. "Are we in danger?"

He didn't look up from his task. "There is always danger in Shadowmere."

"How do you know we are being followed? Have you seen them? Who follows us and why?"

"It is vampire, but their mind is shielded. I believe they will not act until they know our purpose, and by then, we will be under Ravenel's protection. Getting out again is another matter entirely." He stared off into the distance, back the way they had come. "I may return to Barakus to find it under their sway."

Swan was appalled. "You risk your rule for me? Why?"

"I made a promise. I am a man of my word."

His words brought her no comfort. When she said nothing, in fact, stood rooted to the spot, he said, "We'll need to travel faster. I must shift. I warn you now, you'll likely be frightened."

She watched as he set the baskets down and unbuckled his kurt, averting her eyes at the last minute to avoid searing her mind with the image of his nakedness. He packed the black garment in a basket and crouched on the ground.

"Will it hurt?" she asked, backing up a step as she watched him, unblinking.

"There is some discomfort if you are a changeling or it is your first time, but I was born this way. I have shifted for decades."

"Decades? How old are you?"

Raphael looked at her once, his eyes glowing with amber light, though he didn't answer. He hung his head, allowing his long hair to shield his face from her view. His muscles tensed, jumping as though a surge of power coursed through his body. A wave of black fur flowed over his flesh like a rising tide, enveloping his bronze skin and leaving none of the man behind. His curled fists formed into great paws with black claws that scoured the hard earth. Ivory teeth flashed from the long muzzle as his hair shortened and turned to fur, revealing familiar amber eyes. In but a moment's time, the man before her had shifted into a wolf the size of a pony, as seamlessly as water flowing.

She was held by those golden orbs, mesmerized as he padded close and dropped to allow her to ride him. Swan hesitantly gathered the baskets and climbed atop him. His fur was incredibly soft and long enough she could gather a hand hold. When she was settled, he rose and took off at a full run.

His speed raised chill bumps on her skin, cool air whipped her hair in a frenzy at their passing. The land rushed by in dizzying starkness. Swan bent and cradled her face against his warm neck, burrowing into the fur.

There was no doubt in her mind they would soon arrive at Ravenel. She only prayed they would not be stopped.

CHAPTER SIX

The fortress loomed above, crouched on a rise like a great cat ready to pounce. The gates of Ravenel cracked open as Raphael bounded up the final stretch of land toward them. She didn't wonder how those inside knew them as friend-- could only be thankful there would be no wait for entrance. Swan clung to the baskets and Raphael's neck, pervaded by a sense of fear and desperation that had grown with every mile they crossed. She glanced over her shoulder at the dark, could see nothing, but knew the vampire was closing fast now that their destination was known.

A howl erupted from the sky behind them, like the earth gasping for breath as a cyclone of wind gathered. Raphael's hackles rose at the sound, her own responding as her blood froze. A black shape swept past her peripheral, swooping down from the air. They passed inside, inches before it touched them. The massive gates slammed shut just as they cleared. The creature dared not come inside.

Swan breathed a shaky sigh of relief and dismounted. She stood with Raphael at her back as he changed into human form and dressed. The gatemasters nodded their welcome but, strangely, no one approached. The courtyard teemed with people, curious to see their arrival but hanging back.

"Why do they not give greeting," she whispered to Raphael as he came beside her.

"There is no need. I come here often and am considered friend. Come, we shall pay visit to the lord of Ravenel."

He led her toward the main entrance, the two great doors opening at their approach. The crowd parted for their passage, some bowing respectfully. As Swan walked past, they sniffed the air behind her, as though a succulent piece of meat had just been dangled before them. Her heart jumped in her throat at the gleaming looks. She tore her gaze away, keeping them straight on Raphael's back as she kept close to him, not wondering a minute at her trust in him to protect her.

Would she always be considered food in this land? There was no greater reminder that she could not stay--ever.

The doors shut behind them at their passing, cutting off the greedy, hungry stares. The great hall stretched wide and cavernous, their footsteps echoing before them. The ceiling expanded above into utter dark, supported by immense columns, its blackness relieved only by a skylight cut into the rock above, raining faint moonlight on them. Basins of flame flickered golden near walls carved and painted with legends of old, of battles between the lizzars and the leopards.

"Raphael!" a deep voice bellowed across the hall. Swan peered over Raphael's shoulder to see a blond giant of a man striding toward them. In the next moment, he was before them, clapping Raphael on the shoulder jovially.

"Welcome, my friend. Long has it been since you've visited us. I wonder that you'd not forgotten the way."

"I am glad to be back," Raphael said, returning the friendly greeting.

The blond man glanced away from Raphael, noticing her for the first time. He looked her over from head to foot. "Who is this lovely creature? I've never known you to travel with a companion."

Raphael stepped aside and presented her. "This is Lady Swan of Avonleigh. She is under my protection. My lady, our host is Lord Blasien of Ravenel."

Swan curtsied to Lord Blasien's bow. "Thank you for your hospitality, my lord."

"She is tired, and I wish to speak with you alone."

Raphael missed the glare she directed at his back, but Lord Blasien saw, and his eyes alighted. He chuckled and summoned a servant. "I will have her taken to your room. My ladywife will see to her."

* * * *

Blasien waited until Swan was escorted out by an elder retainer before clapping Raphael on the back. Grinning broadly, he said, "You told me once it would never happen, my friend. Love turns us all into liars. Who is she, truly?"

They moved up the dais and sat on the ancient carved rock, neglecting the throne for ease and affability of nearness. "She is but a thorn in my side, Blasien. I do this only to be rid of her."

"Strong words that have not the ring of truth. I see it in your face, you desire this woman."

Desire? If this insatiable need to claim and possess her was desire, then yes, he felt such feelings, but fire eventually burned itself out, leaving only ash behind. He could not give over to insanity. It would spell her demise, and likely his own. "You know no human could rule beside me over the hunters. They are too savage. She would be torn apart. Your own people lick their chops when she passes by."

"You needs must mark her, until her scent is your own. Their control is hard pressed. Times are lean. The land has been hunted until kill is scarce. Each day we go deeper into the wilds."

"It is the rise of the vampires. They leech the land until it is nigh barren."

Blasien rubbed his chin thoughtfully. "They will sate themselves and soon go underground, as they have in the past."

Raphael shook his head, slowly crossed his arms over his chest. "I fear it is different this time. Something calls, yet I do not know what. I feel war is brewing, distant but palpable. That this woman is here only proves the humans have lost their respect for our borders and fear of retaliation."

"They think us a dumping ground then?"

"For undesirables. They have no respect for the land, devour its resources with their greed. Shadowmere is tempting with its unspoiled riches. Your own capture proves they grow bolder. The rise of the vampires will only worsen the situation. The pact may soon be null."

Blasien tensed in surprise at his words. "Ill news you bring from the border."

"It is suspicion only at this time."

"I've learned to trust your instincts with my life, Raphael. Your senses are the most canny of any I've known."

"I thank you. There are times I feel my age in the weariness of my soul."

Blasien smiled faintly. "I know a cure for your ills, but you do not listen."

Raphael waved the matter away. He knew all longed for him to settle with a woman and produce an heir worthy of carrying on after he was gone, but now was not the time to consider such things. "That is not my concern this day. I came here seeking Syrian."

"He is seeking within the flame. Mayhap he felt this call, as you put it. He is acting most strange."

"I wish to be alerted the moment he returns from the portal."

"Even this night?"

"Even so. The woman is human but not. She lives under an enchantment that sees her change with the sun's rise. She must speak to Syrian when I do, and yet I feel we cannot wait for tomorrow night. The morning will be too late."

Blasien clasped his shoulder in sympathy, and they both rose from the stone step. "I will send for you when he comes from the seer's flame. For now, you must follow my advice and mark the woman as your own." At Raphael's scowl, he added, "You need not bond with her, as well you know. Under this enchantment, the old laws are hazy."

Raphael nodded. He knew well ancient law. Had she not been part changeling, he would never have taken her so deeply into Shadowmere. He was a keeper of the law, bound by it as all inhabitants were bound.

There were but two ways to be marked, one was permanent, the other was sexual claiming. Marking Swan would be distasteful--not because he didn't desire to bury himself inside her, but because she forbade him to touch her--a request he would honor were circumstances different. Danger was afoot, however, even here in this protected alcove. The vampires' presence was proof enough of that, even had he been blind to the gathering of leopards to the scent of prey. He liked not the thought of forcing her to his will, but if she did not give in, worse would befall her ... and that was a possibility he would not allow happen.

* * * *

The elder bowed deeply at the door to her room before leaving her. Swan opened the door and allowed it to swing open slowly, half expecting to be jumped where she stood. No attack came, and she chuckled at her overactive imagination before entering.

Swan took one step into the room and stopped dead in her tracks. A bed swallowed the space, obscenely huge and dripping blood red satin, from its coverings to the canopy draped in flowing crimson. Never had she seen a room so blatantly designed for pleasure. Anyone else entering would leap to the same conclusion.

Hesitant, she walked fully inside, close enough to touch the decadent satin. She took a corner in her hand, smoothing her fingers over the shining material, reveling in the silken feel, so rich and rare in quality and color. The deep red came from a fragile flower, that was notoriously difficult to find and harvest. Even in her own realm such luxury could only be afforded by the most wealthy among them. That this house expended so much on a guest was a mark of extreme generosity and riches.

Thinking on it recalled painful memories. She missed her home--and her sister. Swan wondered how Nila was adjusting to rule, and how she faired with Morvere at her side. He would not harm her--she was too valuable as heir apparent--but Swan prayed Nila would not be bound to him in marriage before she could return. Marriage was his best chance for gaining rulership. If Nila didn't give in willingly, Swan had no doubt Morvere would ensorcel her will. Her disappearance would buy Nila some time, but not much.

"You must be Lady Swan," a soft feminine voice spoke behind her.

Swan guiltily dropped her handhold and turned to see a woman standing in the door bearing a tray of meat, cheese, and fruit. Her raven hair hung well past her hips, longer than Swan's own waist-length locks. It was tamed with braids that swept back from her temples. Her skin was the color of creamed chocolate, pale and rich looking, as exotic as the slant of her eyes. The woman moved into the room and set the tray down on a squat table beside the bed, then turned back to her.

Her gown, flowing loose around her legs, emphasized her breasts and couldn't quite conceal the swell of her belly. She was most definitely with child.

"I am," Swan said, nodding.

The woman smiled, friendly and graceful. Swan felt immediately at ease. "I am Lady Ashanti, Blasien's wife."

"I thank you for your hospitality, my lady. Please, call me Swan."

"And you must call me Ashanti." She gestured toward a pair of chairs sitting before the fire that Swan had scarce noticed.

Ashanti sat with little grace, her heavy belly making her awkward. Swan followed suit.

"I came to offer you some company. Shadowmere can be a brutal land."

"Yes, it can."

"It has been too long since I've seen a woman of my kind. You are an outworlder, are you not?"

Swan looked at her, surprised at her canniness. "Yes, how did you know?" It was to be expected she would be regarded as an outsider--she was, but Lady Ashanti had seemed ... well, like a normal to her. Not one to pick up on the subtleties of human or not. But then, she'd never ventured from Avonleigh before, customs were likely different in other parts.

"I was human once. Those alike can recognize one another. Though, I'd never thought Raphael to break old law and bring another into Shadowmere."

"You were human? And now you bear a beas--forgive me. My mouth runs away with me." Swan blushed at her rude remark.

Ashanti chuckled. "I was much the same as you, in the beginning. I find no offense in the term beastman, or beastwoman. That is what they are, what I am."

How she could be both was beyond Swan's reckoning. It

seemed an improbability, yet she couldn't deny that the woman lived here among the beastmen when humans did not. There had to be some truth to it. And if so, she would bear her husband's child--a halfling? The rules she'd thought herself just beginning to understand were dashed away. "How can you be human, but not?"

"Circumstance brought us together. I was cursed, much the same as you. Blasien saved me, as I did him," Ashanti said, elaborating on the matter no further.

Ashanti's eyes shone with love, happiness. Such depth of feeling warmed Swan's soul. That such could be found between two races astounded her, for it did not seem possible for her. Here, Swan was only food.

"I warn you, though, if Raphael seeks the blood bond ceremony, you must wrestle a promise from him for it to be completed in private." She laughed softly, a far away look in her eyes. Ashanti continued, "They can know your mind once a connection is formed. It is why they are such renowned lovers. Ah, you do not know this?"

That couldn't possibly be true. It was too ... too unbelievable. They were not mages, to delve into the minds of others. Even Morvere had not the power to read her mind. She dismissed it as fable propagated by old wives. "There is nothing between us."

Ashanti slanted her a shrewd look that spoke volumes. "Nothing but reluctance, I gather?"

Swan colored at her knowing look, feeling as though her transgressions were scrawled across her face. Could everyone read her so easily? It was no wonder she'd landed herself in such a predicament. Raphael had not helped matters at all either. She'd become so distracted from her purpose by him it was disgraceful. No responsible ruler would put anything before her people, and she must remember to do the same. Any less would be a betrayal of trust and duty.

"Raphael is a hunter. They are different than other beastmen. Vampiric powers flow through their veins, allowing them the ability to touch without being near. Or so I've been told."

"Why do you tell me these things?"

"Just as warning. I had no foreknowledge myself. I would not have my brethren helpless to defend herself. Besides, I enjoy the thought of Raphael having to work hard for a lady's favor." She laughed softly, cradling her belly. "The men here are used to getting their way in every thing. A challenge is hard to find."

"Thank you, but I have no need to protect myself from Raphael. He helps me of his own free will." And there was no challenge as far as she was concerned. No one would possess her let alone control her mind. To believe talk of mind magic would drive her mad. It couldn't possibly be true, but she realized she would have to question him to make certain. Then again, what man had ever told her the truth?

"I think he may have more on his hands than he is aware."

Ashanti struggled to sit forward, and Swan rose and helped her to her feet. "My thanks, Swan. I will be glad to hold this babe in my arms rather than my belly. Come, eat. Raphael joins you soon. You should be ready for his arrival."

Surprised, Swan stopped mid-motion, unable to resist looking at the bed. There would be no avoiding it once he was in the room. Nobility fled in a rush of unbidden heat. "He can't possibly sleep here. It isn't proper."

"But it is. Human rules do not apply here, dear Swan." She gave her a pitying look. "As women, we adapt. I suggest you not leave this room. You'll find in Shadowmere, as a human, having a man's protection is vital to your survival."

CHAPTER SEVEN

Swan heard soft footsteps stop before her door and knew immediately who stood there. Determined not to be caught without defense, she hurried from her position near the fire, around the largest obstacle in the room--the bed.

The door opened and Raphael stepped inside, closing it behind him with a finality that tightened her nerves. He leaned back against the wood paneling, crossing his arms over his chest, looking pleased. A slow smile curled his lips as he caught sight of her across the wide space and dragged his gaze down her body.

She'd bathed the dirt of travel off and changed into a gown Ashanti lent her. If anything, the loose robes that covered her with no peep of skin showing save her head, hands and feet only seemed to incite him further. Swan's skin tingled beneath the garment with as if caressed by his leisurely appraisal. She gritted her teeth to control her response, incensed.

"What makes you smile so?" Swan asked tightly.

Again that slow, lazy smile that set her nerves on edge. "Mayhap your continued demureness, hiding behind that bed as if it would protect your purity. I rather thought to find you lying in it, awaiting my pleasure."

He baited her, of that, she was certain. To what purpose, she didn't know. Her eyes narrowed. She'd been in a foul mood ever since she discovered she was to share his room ... and his bed. If she hadn't known better, she would have surmised the lord and lady of the house deliberately set out to provoke a relationship between them rather than for the protection she'd been told she needed. "Your assumption is wrong. Lady Ashanti and I talked."

He arched one black brow. "Oh?"

"I know what you expect. What other reason could there be in placing me in your room when there are doubtless many others to be had?"

"Perhaps you were put here for your protection?"

"Ha!" She laughed derisively, dismayed to hear him echo her thoughts. "And what of this ... this bed...." She could hardly look at it without blushing, without imagining being tangled in its covers, covered by a hard male body, Raph--

He continued grinning, wolfish as his look encompassed the decadent barrier between them. "I assure you, there is nothing quite like the feel of such finery beneath you when making love."

She glared at him. "That will never happen."

A long moment passed between them. He stepped from the door, gestured with a sweeping wave of his arm for her leave. "Go then, if my company is so undesirable. Choose another, but be warned, you may not enjoy the welcome you receive."

Swan made no move to withdraw, could only watch him

warily. She couldn't help but feel she was over-reacting, yet she'd been cornered into a fight of which she had no understanding.

His black eyes glittered dangerously as she remained still, watchful. With his hair loose around his shoulders, he looked very much the savage of old lore. "Better the beast you know, my lady?"

Yes, but she had tempted that beast before ... with results that melted her core and turned her knees to water. She couldn't fathom why his presence disturbed her so much, why being near him made her heart stop and yet beat faster. She liked not the dizzying rush he aroused, the loss of control he invoked.

Swan swallowed, moistened her suddenly parched lips with her tongue. His gaze seized on her mouth. Her heart skipped a beat, then pumped furiously to recover. She stilled, her voice strangely hoarse. "I'll not give you what you want."

Raphael advanced, consuming the safety of her circle with his aura, blocking all avenue of escape. "Of what do you speak? Afraid to voice such forbidden desires?" he asked, his voice a deep rumble that raised the fine hairs on her skin.

Swan held her ground, straightened her shoulders, strengthened her resolve to remain calm. "No."

He halted, the wide bed offering little restraint. She'd fooled herself to think it would keep him from her. He was a beastman--there could be no escape. Her muscles tensed with his proximity.

"Then what?" he asked silkily.

"My talk spurs you toward greater gall. If I had more sense, I would keep my mouth closed."

Raphael's voice dropped. "I could think of ways to keep it occupied. You'd have no time for talking...."

Shivers skated over her flesh, trailing chill bumps in their wake. "You think only of one thing."

He moved around the bed. Swan took a step back. "I'm inclined to agree with you." Raphael sighed heavily at her wary look, leaned against the carved bedpost. "Swan, delightful as this game is, I needs must forego such play for more important matters."

"What do you mean?" she asked, slanting him a

suspicious look.

"I must mark you with my scent. It is not enough to touch you." He watched as she edged further away. "My hand is forced."

It was unthinkable that he sought to assuage himself by denying guilt. "As mine is? I did not ask to come to this place."

"But you wanted my help, and I intend to give it. Now I offer protection."

Swan laughed mirthlessly, a stranger to herself, thoughts of honor and nobility fleeing before her anger. "You wish only to satisfy your lusts." Oddly, the thought of being nothing more than a tool for his desire hurt. It should not be so important to her. Women more often than not were subjugated to worse--she was no different here.

"I offer a mark that leaves no permanence. If you wish to survive, it will be done."

Swan shuddered with the mental imagery, remembrance sharply defined as she recalled the ravenous looks she'd received since coming. She realized in that moment he was right, but just because he was did not mean she enjoyed that fact. Her experiences since Morvere attacked balled into a mass of flaming anger. Some demon stoked the fury in her soul, urging her to folly.

Defiant and seething, Swan placed her palms on the bed, bent over it like a supplicant. Her hair parted around her shoulders, pooling on the satin. Refusing to meet his eyes, she said, "Do it and be done."

"You sorely test me, Swan." Raphael bit off each word, his voice deadly soft.

Menace resonated from him. She'd gone too far, but there was no stopping now. He'd seen to it that she would go through with her actions. She was not one to back down in cowardice and didn't believe, despite his veiled threat, that he would harm her, else she would never have dared such boldness.

She didn't know what drove her to push him, to test his limits. But Shadowmere's very deviance, its savage people and customs grated. She'd be damned if she would relent without a fight. An insane urge struck her, caused her to blurt out in taunting fashion, "Is this not the way of animals?"

He roared, a sound of such agony and rage it rent her soul. She jerked her head up, felt her body freeze. Anger burned in his eyes, in the heavy slant of his brows. He shuddered, overcome, muscles jumping with tension as his eyes bled from cold black to fiery gold in an instant.

"If this is how you wish it, so be it," he gritted out, voice pained.

Raphael ripped his kurt away, throwing it to the floor. His erection jutted forth from the thatch of dark hair at its base, swollen with anger and lust. His shaft's length and breadth were enormous, a weapon should he so choose. It was small wonder her sex had ached from his rough possession. She shrank inside as she watched him round the bed and move toward her, knowing full well she could not go through with this now, not after meeting the haunted look in his eyes. Her childish, goading bravado vanished.

Swan lunged across the bed, desperate for escape, knees and hands sliding in her frenzy. He caught her in the middle, grabbed her ankles and pulled her back to the edge until she knelt on the floor with her chest pressed flat on the bed. With her hair in her eyes, she clutched at the satin, her hands slipping in the silken finery, unable to pull herself to freedom.

Rending cloth greeted her ears, followed by the soft caress of air on her naked flesh. He'd bared her completely with so little effort, it was frightening.

Swan struggled as he bent, his skin scorching as he cradled his form against her, muscles molding to her back, his hips hard against her tender buttocks. He pinned her flailing arms to the silken bed, manacling them in one hand as his shaft nestled in the cleft of her buttocks. The lips of her sex moistened with his nearness, spurring her ferocity.

Swan growled, but could do nothing but shout obscenities. He'd secured her beneath him, so that she could not move unless he willed it.

Raphael lay still a moment, letting her feel the weight of his domination.

He buried his face in her hair, breathing deeply, expelling it in a hot rush against her neck that made her blood beat faster. With one hand, he pushed the mass aside, nuzzled her neck, shuddering against her as he drew a heavy breath. "I want to give you pleasure, Swan, gentleness," he murmured near her ear. "Why will you not allow it?" He dragged his hot mouth down her neck, nipped her shoulder when she did not answer.

Swan trembled, desire warring with reluctance. He sucked the curve of her neck, rubbing his tongue against her, weakening her resistance.

Gentleness and sweet words tendered the heart. She'd been deceived by sweetness before, had been ripped asunder by the betrayal that followed her submission. To allow a man to touch her heart was unthinkable. To allow a beastman was death. There could never be anything but the fire of need between them--she could allow nothing else. Anything else would destroy the last shreds of her soul.

To continue resistance could be just as detrimental. There was but one choice she could make. "I'll not fight you, on one condition," she said, muffled by the bed.

He ceased his perusal of her neck. "Yes?"

"Do not ... kiss me." A kiss was too intimate, too impossible to ignore. Some said souls crossed and mated when mouths joined as one. True or not, it weakened her resolve to remain aloof. It was a risk she could not endure again--not from him.

A long minute dragged by until he sighed heavily. "Agreed." He released her wrists and stroked his palms down her arms, down further, teasing the sides of her breasts exposed by the torn edges of her gown. She shivered as he moved lower, along the dipping curve of her waist, his mouth raining kisses down the length of her spine.

Smoothing her hips, he backed away from her, teeth skating the top of one cheek as his fingers traced the bottom crease of her buttocks.

She felt him smile against her. "You have a delightful dimple ... here." He pointed the spot out with his tongue, lathing the smooth flesh.

Swan jerked at that wet heat, cooling rapidly as he moved lower. He dug his hands between her thighs, his thumbs rubbing her nether lips. She shivered at the unfamiliar sensation.

"Part your legs for me, Swan."

"Why?" she asked, her breath stolen.

"I want to taste all of you," he near growled.

A hot flood saturated her cleft, her sex spasming at the rush. She leaned forward, resting on her stomach as he spread her legs and stroked a finger up her wet slit. Swan grabbed fistfuls of satin, bit the fleshy part of her hand as he nuzzled her nether lips, breathing hot against that forbidden, secret place.

It was too much. She'd die from anticipation.

"I've not nearly begun," he murmured, muffled by her depths. The wet probe of his tongue slid into her swollen folds, teasing the entrance to her womanhood. He wrapped his arms around her thighs, massaging the tender inner muscles from the front as he drew a heated line down to her needful, throbbing clit.

She widened the part of her thighs around his legs as he knelt between them, tilting her buttocks high to allow his access. He grunted, delved deeper. The first stroke against her swollen nub made her gasp for air. He flicked his tongue at a rapid tempo, slipping easily in her juices. A shock wave radiated from her core--she jerked against it, grinding back into his face, unable to control her response.

He broke away, replaced his tongue with his fingers, cradling her clit between the stroking digits. Nipping the crease of one buttock, he moved over the roundness until he cradled his hips against her once more, his fingers still working her in steady strokes.

"Do you want me inside you?" he asked, hoarse with desire. The head of his shaft teased her nether lips insistently.

She nodded, unable to give voice to her wants, knowing only that he was bringing her to that brink once more, and she ached to fall over the edge.

He stroked his satiny length up and down her slit, his cockhead slickened with her own wetness, maddening her with thorough agony.

"Say the words, Swan. You want this." He edged her sensitive opening, drawing his fingers from her clit to grasp her hips.

"I want this," she gritted out, pained with need. She wanted it more than anything at that moment.

He shuddered at her admission, tensed as he plunged his hard shaft deep inside with one stroke. She cried out as he filled her completely, his own loud groan mingling with her voice. The angle was odd, pleasing her in a way never felt before. She bit her lip as he pulled slowly out, a withdrawal that jerked her with sensation.

A madness overtook him, and he withdrew, only to sink inside again, faster, faster, until his hips slapped against her buttocks. He pulled her hips back to meet each thrust, guiding her movement. She bent her head down, slamming back against him, reveling in the ragged sound of his breath as pumped into her slick passage.

Her heart drummed in her ears, nerves alighting with fire, burning with need. Her arms tensed to support her upper body, arching her back as he bent close, his fingers sinking back to her soaked clit, moving in a maddening circle. Swan gasped as the climax thundered over her with a suddenness that stole her breath, her muscles quivering.

His erection jerked at the spasm of her sex, and still he plundered, sinking further each time, until he nudged her womb. He drove into her again and again, urging the waves of orgasm to build to greater heights and crash over her. She moaned, bliss and pain melding until she could stand no more. She dug her fists into the bed, the orgasm consuming every fiber of her being.

He cried out hoarsely as his shaft pulsed one final, soul rending time, jerking as his seed spewed his release.

Collapsing against her, he breathed raggedly against her neck, pressing soft kisses along the curve. He pulled his shaft out with a heavy sigh, leaving her feeling strangely bereft.

"You feel so good," he murmured against her ear, kissing the tender hollow. "No other could replace you."

Swan shook, utterly exhausted, wondering over his admission.

A knock at the door saved her from responding in kind. Raphael rose, taking with him the heat that warmed her. Swan sat up on her knees and clutched the pieces of the gown to her chest, watching as he crossed the room, heating once more at the sight of his muscular back and tight buttocks.

Raphael cracked the door and spoke in hushed tones before closing it and turning back to her. "We have been summoned."

* * * *

With her gown torn beyond repair, Swan was forced to go to Ashanti's chamber and beg another. She couldn't go about the castle indecent. A large tear ripped from the neck to the base of her spine, leaving her back exposed as she awaited entrance. Raphael watched her, smiling at her nervousness as he leaned against the stone wall. He claimed he guarded her modesty--not that she believed him. She would have to be blind to miss his appraising looks.

After her brief knock, Ashanti called softly and Swan opened the door, surprised to see Lord Blasien on his knees, his ear pressed against his wife's belly.

Ashanti chuckled at her startled look. "He imagines the babe talks to him."

Blasien looked up at his wife, grinning broadly. "My son knows his father."

"Daughter," she corrected.

"Son," he argued, smiling. He stood, rubbing her belly one last time. "I will leave you both alone. I expect you in my bed, wife, before my head hits the pillow."

Ashanti swatted playfully at his backside as he left and returned her attention to Swan.

"I've had an ... accident, Ashanti. I apologize for disturbing you."

"It's not a bother. He would sit all night with his ear pressed to my belly if not for these little interruptions." She moved to a chest and took out another gown. "Be sure Raphael is more careful with this one."

Swan blushed to her hairline and dressed with Ashanti's assistance. Once she left Ashanti's chamber, Raphael took her arm and silently guided her through the darkened passages back to the great hall.

She couldn't help but wonder why they would be summoned so late--the witching hour if the sky could be trusted--but she appreciated being included in any discussions that concerned her. It was great evidence they began to respect her.

Raphael led Swan up the center walkway, guided only by the watered light of the moons shining through the skylight. He took her past the dais, to a chamber cloaked by an indistinct tapestry. Drawing the fabric aside, he pushed the oaken door open, releasing a flood of amber light into the darkness.

Inside, a fire warmed the close room, flaming braziers lined the walls, and padded chairs hugged the space nearest the blaze. A man sat in one of the leopardesque chairs. He stood at their entrance, facing them.

Crossing the threshold, they stepped into the room. Half blinded by the brilliance so sharp against the darkness, Swan's eyes widened as her vision adjusted to the light, halting before the man. Raphael and he each exchanged greetings and still she looked on, amazed. What she thought to be only a trick of the light was not--his skin was the color of gold, his hair a cerulean wave around his shoulders.

"I'm am called Syrian, Lady Swan," the strange man introduced himself, his sapphire eyes flashing as he took her lax hand and pressed soft metallic lips to its back.

"I'm pleased to make your acquaintance. But ... how do you know me?" she asked, withdrawing her hand and glancing at Raphael. She hadn't thought he'd been away from her long enough to speak to more than the lord of Ravenel.

"Lord Blasien spoke of your predicament. I am sorcerer and adviser to him while I choose to stay."

Of course he'd done so. It made sense that her presence be made known. Her thinking was clouded from her encounter with Raphael. Syrian beckoned they sit, and Swan smiled and complied, Raphael sitting in a leisurely manner beside her.

"Pray tell, why have you asked to see me this night, Raphael? Looking to the flame is wearying."

"My apologies, Syrian, but I did not think the matter could wait. Swan, tell him how you came to be here."

At her hesitation, Raphael took her hand and cradled it in his callused palms, offering silent support. Her fingers tingled from the contact. Swan took a deep breath, and slowly related Morvere's betrayal, his spell, her suspicions of continued machinations.

Syrian's eyes darkened as she finished. He rubbed his jaw line in contemplation. "Such a spell is easily laid, for even the amateur mage can curse when weaned from their master. When your finger is returned, the spell will be broken. His death will most likely break the enchantment.

What disturbs me is this spell that transported you to Shadowmere. Such as that requires a great swell of power ... a sign the humans are advancing in their abilities, though it is not easily recovered. It takes time to heal from a spell of this magnitude. If he aims to take Avonleigh, he must replenish it soon."

"I'd not known sorcerers had need of recovery," Swan said.

"Humans have not the ability to regenerate as we do. Expelling energy is much the same as receiving a mortal blow, though more akin to a strike on the spirit."

It made sense. Power did not come without great cost.

"It is risky striking in Avonleigh. His forces would cut us down, not to mention an attack would signal the beginning of war." Raphael leaned forward, releasing her hand. "What think you, Syrian? I sense your thoughts echo mine."

Syrian smiled grimly, steepled his forefingers beneath his chin. "In the Skarlothian mountain range, there lies a secret, hidden from mortals save but a precious few. It is a pool of water unlike any known, liquid like molten silver."

"One of the seven pools of Lysia," Raphael murmured.

"One of two now, unless there are others across the Rycarthian straights. The rest were destroyed. The only other Lysian pool is in Shadowmere. It takes a coven to destroy one, my skill is not enough, but if the Skarlothian pool is disabled--"

"He will be forced to come to Shadowmere." Raphael smiled darkly. "How soon can you be ready to make the journey, Syrian?"

"Balian's call drained me. I will likely sleep through the day."

Raphael nodded, thoughtful. "I had not considered the disturbance in the land was his doing."

"The ocean of lost souls churns as never before."

"It explains much. I fear our journey to human lands will only worsen the situation. It is good the Skarlothian pool cannot be destroyed. I'd not give the humans more reason to invade."

They may as well have been speaking Lizzarian for all that she understood their doom and gloom predictions. What irked more was the distinct feeling that Raphael planned to go to the pool with Syrian--alone. "Where do I fit in with your plans?" she asked, crossing her arms over her chest.

Raphael slid her a glance. Syrian fell silent--wise man that he was. "You will stay here, under Ravenel's protection."

Swan had been patient during their exchange, but the thought of being abandoned was too much. "This is my fight. I go too, where ever you may roam."

He gave her a long, measuring look. "You would only hinder us." He appeared to regret his words, yet she was not fooled by his facade.

She seethed inside, unable to believe he'd uttered such nonsense. She was a ruler as much as he, a person of responsibility. Never had she been accused of hindrance to another. "You have no knowledge of my skills. On human soil, I can hold my own. Give me a blade and I will prove my worth."

"I respect your courage, Swan, but it is misplaced. I'll not have your life placed in Morvere's path again."

"And your life is less valuable than mine own? My sister is in danger. I cannot sit idly by. I will go mad with worry." His jaw remained stubbornly set, his will as hard as stone. "I can't stay here! Th-they want to eat me!"

Raphael gave her a pitying look. "You'll find that everywhere in Shadowmere. It is the spell you are under--they smell prey beneath the surface. Until it is removed, you'll not be safe. Blasien controls Ravenel. No harm will come to you here."

"If that is so, then why the marking?"

His jaw twitched. She'd discovered a flaw in his thinking.

"No. My word is final," he said tightly.

Pig-headed, stubborn, mule of a man! It mattered not that he wished to protect her. She was not some jewel to be hidden away, nor was she his to control. She'd sought help, not a master. We shall see whose word is final, she fumed mentally.

CHAPTER EIGHT

The distance between them was immeasurable. As long as she was human and he beast, it would always stand as a barrier. He couldn't see her as anything but helpless, vulnerable to attack. She'd had no chance to prove otherwise.

Swan listened to the soft click as Raphael closed the bed chamber's door. "Dawn approaches. You've but a few hours to rest as you are now."

She hadn't realized so much time had passed. "How can you know?"

"Those with the bond of vampires, their blood and lusts, know the rise and fall of the sun without looking. Few hunters venture into the daylight." He moved behind her, too near for comfort. Placing his hands on her bare shoulders, he nuzzled her hair, breathing deeply of her scent.

Swan resisted the temptation to pull away, still angered over his refusal to listen to reason. He stood there, just holding her until her agitation dissipated. Slowly, she realized such hostility was futile. It would not help her achieve her goals.

"You walk about in the sun," she finally said. Or else, she assumed he did. Daylight was beyond her ken as long as she remained under the enchantment.

He chuckled against her hair, smoothing his hands up and down her arms as if he couldn't touch her enough. "I am not as most hunters. I rule my appetites. They do not rule me."

But it was not true. She'd seen his loss of control. If she could affect him that way, surely she could entice him enough to take her with him when he left? Honey lured when vinegar would not.

He pulled away and walked to the bed, removing his kurt with a jerk of his hand, dropping the heavy black material to the floor with a soft thud. Swan averted her eyes from his nakedness, not wishing to encourage him to carnal pursuits with her interest.

He smiled as her skin pinked with embarrassment. "You have seen me before, Swan. Why blush now?"

"I do not believe I will ever adjust to it."

"Nor do I wish it. I enjoy your reaction to my body." He chuckled, climbing into bed, leaving the covers folded back. Patting the mattress, he said, "Come to me, Swan. I would hold you in my arms while you sleep."

Swan took a deep breath, firing her courage. Slowly, holding his gaze, she pushed the neck of her gown off her shoulders and let it drop to the floor, shielded only by the thick length of her golden shot tresses. His eyes flashed with heat, raked down her body in a heady caress. "You are lovely, Swan, full deserving the elegance of your namesake. Would that I had time to devote myself to worshipping you this night."

He held his hand out to her and she accepted. The bed dipped slightly beneath her weight, and he pulled her, smoothly rolling until she lay beneath him. He twined a lock of her hair around two fingers, looking deep in her eyes, his black gaze unfathomable.

His gaze lowered to the peaks of her breasts. "At times, I cannot help even myself," he murmured huskily, drawing a lazy palm around the soft curve of one breast.

Her nipples pebbled. A sharp stab of pleasure spiked from the hardened buds as he grazed a thumb across one tip. Torturous heat flooded her womb. She stopped breathing a moment, waiting in suspense of his next action.

He cupped her breast fully, leaning nearer. His exotic scent teased her, searing her senses, intoxicating. "Your heart beats wild for me, Swan."

She swallowed, managed to find her voice. "From fear."

"From desire."

With but one simple caress, he distracted her from her purpose, stirred desire best abandoned. His power over her was frightening. Struggling to regain control, she took a deep breath, willing her heart to calm its crashing tattoo.

"There are other ways to garner my grace, my lord," she whispered, recovered enough for coherent thought.

He removed his hand, used the backs of his fingers to push the frame of her hair from her face. Stroking a lone finger down her cheek, along her jaw, he said, "I know what you wish. Much as I desire to fulfill your wants, I dare not risk it. With the vampires roaming the night, if I were killed, you'd be helpless."

Her blood chilled with his words, heat lost in the tide of fear. They wanted him. He'd hinted of the bond between hunter and vampire before. Leaving with no guard but

Syrian at his back was suicide.

"I would have a kiss ere I die."

"Do not jest of such things."

"I implore in all seriousness," he murmured, his voice husky, his eyes heavy lidded. He descended for a kiss. She turned her head at the last moment, felt the soft graze of his lips on her cheek, hating the sudden tension of his arms.

He said nothing as she turned from the enclosure of his embrace onto her side, facing away. He pulled her tightly against him, smoothing her hair from her shoulder and neck. Cradling her, his arm draped around her waist, he seemed at ease, but she couldn't ignore his subtle reaction to her rejection. Had she, a mortal woman, hurt the mighty lord of the hunters?

* * * *

Swan awoke to the scent of freshly cooked bread and fowl wafting in a delightful haze round her nose. She slowly opened her eyes to see a steaming plate of food sitting on the table near the bed, and Ashanti preparing to leave.

"Wait. Ashanti, please, stay with me. I miss the company of women."

Ashanti turned from the door and smiled. "As you wish. I admit I feel the loneliness at times." She sat heavily in a chair, propping her hands on either side of her swollen belly.

Swan returned her smile and sat up in bed, silken covers tucked around her chest, her hair a mass of tangles.

Ashanti talked of her child and Blasien's excitement over the babe, his plans for expanding his holdings. She couldn't help noticing Ashanti was younger than she, and soon to be a mother. Like as not, Swan would have no such similar fate. The thought should not disturb her as it did, but she couldn't help being reminded of Raphael's seed washing her womb. But then, shifters could not mate with humans-- everyone knew that.

Swan turned her mind from the disturbing thoughts, concentrating on eating. She nibbled at the food on her plate, grateful for Ashanti's consideration in bringing food to her. She couldn't quite remember the last time she'd eaten. Knowing it was the next night, however, she wondered if her plans had gone awry before they even had a chance to be implemented. If Raphael was gone....

"Has Lord Raphael left?" she asked, casually taking a sip of wine.

"Syrian has not yet arisen. I know they plan to leave you." Her fine, arched brows drew down in displeasure.

"I see you feel much the same as I." Swan hesitated a moment, wondering the wisdom of pursuing her plans. She felt instinctively that Ashanti could be trusted. Finally, believing it could do no more harm, she said, "I know it is forward of me, but can I ask a favor of you?"

"An inkling germinates." She grinned. "Ask."

Swan set the plate aside, tucked a wayward strand of hair behind her ear. "Could you help me outside ... to leave I mean? I do not intend to be abandoned."

"Shhh." Ashanti held a finger to her lips. "Do not think loudly."

Swan affected a blank stare, wondering if Ashanti had gone suddenly daft. How could she think loudly?

"I warned you before they could know your mind. With distance, it lessens, but we can take no chances he will hear your thoughts."

Again with old fables, but Ashanti had reacted so strangely she couldn't help but wonder if it held some merit. "How can I tell if he ... well...."

"Reads your thoughts? If you concentrate, you feel a tickle, a buzzing, like an insect. Long was my time here before I realized Blasien had this gift. All beastmen can, though some are stronger than others. It is how they communicate when they shift." She hesitated. "I should not say this, for I don't want to frighten you, but Raphael's powers are ... different ... vampiric. He can control the weak willed with his mind. I know not the extent of his gift."

Suspicion dawned at Ashanti's description. That nagging sensation when she'd slept.... Swan frowned. The fantasy she'd had before, of Raphael coaxing her desire in what seemed an eternity ago. Had he, in fact, invaded her dreams? Ashanti's serious expression lent credibility to her charge. Raphael had pressed advantage while she'd changed, with no reason but to see if she would relent. How dare he!

If she'd had any doubt of proceeding, it disappeared with

that revelation.

"I think we will be safe if we hurry. It is past time these men learn a lesson in respect."

Swan agreed whole-heartedly. Ashanti struggled to her feet, going to the door. "I will be back in a moment."

Swan hurriedly finished her meal, and afterwards, brushed the tangles from her hair as she awaited Ashanti's return. Knowing the long tresses would hinder, she braided her hair in a coronet about the crown of her head.

As she finished, Ashanti returned, grinning wickedly, her arms loaded. "Get dressed. It's designed for travel and protection. Blasien had it made for me. You and I are of a size, or would be were I not with child. They should fit."

Swan picked at the mass of metal warily, unsure. She'd never worn armor of any description before. What she had seen was very complex, near impossible to put on by oneself.

"I'm not certain I can handle this alone."

Ashanti waved her concern away. "It slips on. There are no buckles save at the neckline to worry over."

She looked up from the pile, seized by a thought. "Can you get me a blade?" Raphael would soon know her skill.

"I believe I can find one. It's rare to use blades in Shadowmere, but there were some from the war stored in an old weapons room. I'll not return until I've found something."

After Ashanti had gone once more, Swan stood and examined the pile she'd been given. She'd likely not be able to move once dressed. Trust a man to give a woman such unwieldy garments.

She picked up a mail skirt, lined with heavy flesh colored fabric, and slipped it over her head. The skirt dropped down to rest on her hips. It was lighter than she'd first supposed, easy to move in with the short length that barely covered her thighs. Next, she tied a wide scarf around her breasts, similar in color to the skirt's lining, and pulled the chain top on, buckling the neck piece in the back. She was taller than Ashanti, and the mail left a thin band of her waist exposed, but otherwise, the mail fit as though made for her. She had some doubt, given its light weight, that it would protect her from a heavy blow, but it allowed some protection regardless.

Looking down at herself, she couldn't help but notice it looked as though she wore nothing beneath the mail but her own skin. The chinks were wide enough to show glimpses of flesh and lining. She wondered if perhaps the outfit were more for titillation than protection, but shrugged it off.

As Swan finished slipping her boots on, Ashanti returned and presented her a sword. She took it, examining its workmanship in the light. It was short and light for easy carry. Running a thumb down the silvered edges, she also discovered the curved blade was sharp enough to slice through silk ... or flesh with equal ease.

Ashanti helped her buckled it around her waist. She was as ready as she would ever be. She only hoped when Raphael discovered she was following, he wouldn't offer unpleasant repercussions.

Ashanti held a finger to her lips for silence, then bade her follow. After a quick glance down the hall, assuring no one was there, they left, each taking a torch for light. The night was young, but it would be dark as pitch outside until the moons rose.

Moving with quiet stealth, they crossed intersections of large corridors until a downward channel emerged from the labyrinthine passages. The faint jingle of her mail made her grit her teeth with fear of discovery, but Ashanti led her down a seldom used corridor where none dwelt. Dust stirred at their passing, a testament to its lack of usage.

Swan realized as they continued that Ashanti was leading her to the belly of the castle. The air grew steadily cooler at their descent until she was certain they walked below the earth. The torches illuminated but a small circle, and she was dependent entirely on Ashanti's guidance.

A grate came into view as the passage narrowed to a dead end. Cut into the wall, she could see nothing past the metal slats but wet darkness beyond.

"This is as far as I dare take you," Ashanti said, whispering as though someone would overhear them. Taking a key from her pocket, she unlocked the heavy bolt and pulled it open with Swan's help. "The path is straight and true. Follow and it shall lead you up past Ravenel, a league's distance."

"What is this place?"

"It is one of many escape routes from Ravenel. This one

takes you in the direction Raphael and Syrian will travel. You can gain advantage on them if you hurry."

Overcome at her kindness, Swan hugged Ashanti. "I thank you, Ashanti. You have my undying gratitude."

Ashanti nodded as Swan released her. "I know how it is to feel helpless, trapped. Go now. Remember to guard your thoughts. I wish you luck. Do not give Raphael an easy time of it." She grinned broadly as she closed the gate behind Swan.

"I assure you, I will not."

Ashanti left her then, her torch fading away until Swan was swallowed by darkness, her own meager light weak in the cavernous blackness. Swallowing an unreasonable fear, she began walking, occupying her mind as she traveled with plans on what she would do once she was returned to normal.

She'd been too trusting, that was certain. Never again would she allow danger to come so close to her sister and Avonleigh. Her parents had toiled too long to allow its destruction.

She wondered at Raphael's involvement. He seemed determined to help her, even against her will. With Barakus endangered by the vampires' return, she couldn't help being curious on his elusive reasoning. She finally decided that the attack upon her on the borderlands had doubtless raised his protectiveness, for despite her annoyance, she knew he was a man of deep honor.

Turning the matter over and over again in her head, she barely registered the climb in temperature, the increase of fresh air. A breeze struck her skin, fingered through her hair, and she realized she neared the opening Ashanti had described. Eager to leave the close confines, Swan quickened her pace, running the remaining distance.

She stopped at a chain of steps leading up. Glancing skyward, she saw that stars winked in the blackness above. Swan breathed a sigh of relief--she'd made it. Climbing the steps, she reached the top, stooping beneath a stone grate. Swan threw down her torch and pushed the heavy covering aside until she could squeeze through the opening. It took some effort to finally heave over and pull her body out.

She pushed the grate back in place and collapsed on the ground, looking up at the sky as she rested. Raphael would be so surprised to find she had defied him. Delighted most nearly described her mood, delight to prove she had her own brand of resourcefulness--that she could take care of herself when necessary.

She chuckled, imagining the look on his face, how much it would rankle. He wouldn't be able to take her back, not without losing valuable time. All in all, she was satisfied with her decision not to allow herself to be trampled on. Now she need only watch for them, and she could follow at a safe distance.

It was as she struggled to gain her feet that a black shape blotted the stars from the sky. She froze instantly, unable to tear her eyes away.

A scream bubbled from her throat as the wind gathered in a deafening gasp.

CHAPTER NINE

Syrian met Raphael in the courtyard. Cloaked in black robes slit up the sides for easy movement, he wore the shrouding robes to hide his golden skin, the hood drawn close to shield his unusual hair. Should they encounter mortals, he would not be readily identified as an inhabitant of Shadowmere. Syrian's people had been hunted to near extinction. He was one of the last of a dying race. He risked much traveling with Raphael.

Round his waist, his sword belt buckled, the toothed blade wicked in the light as the red jewel glowed softly in the pommel. Beyond a few pouches hanging from his belt, he bore nothing else.

Raphael carried but one sack of supplies himself and held no blade. He'd been born a weapon. He needed nothing else.

Blasien came out to the courtyard as they prepared to leave, no other there to witness their departure. The feline people had retreated to the great hall for their nightly meal when dusk settled and would not leave for some time yet.

Blasien looked to the gates as he reached them, the gatemasters preparing its opening. "What do you plan to do about the vampire?"

Raphael finished knotting the sack to his belt before regarding Blasien. "If he remains, I will kill him should he hinder us, but I suspect he has gone."

"My men found nothing, but vampires seldom leave evidence of their presence." Blasien clapped them both on the shoulder. "Let it not be so long until next you visit."

Raphael nodded, watching the great doors that marked the entrance of the castle. "I will return to see the woman home."

Syrian and Blasien followed the line of his gaze and exchanged a look.

"She does not come to see you go. Will you not say farewell to the woman?" Blasien asked, stroking his chin thoughtfully.

Swan's nature was turbulent. He could stoke the flame of desire within her, but her mind remained cold to him, beyond his reach. His fists clenched, arms bunching with tension. His every fiber burned with the need to go inside, break the door down and kiss her until she was mindless to anything but him and the feel of his tongue claiming her mouth. That he was so repugnant she would not allow his kiss seared the shreds of his sanity.

Almost he considered going to her, allowing her her head, yet it would change little and only reveal his weakness to her. It was a weakness he could not afford. The impotent were killed in Shadowmere. "She cares nothing for me. I will always be but a beast in her eyes. Her place is with her people. I cannot deny that."

"We beastmen are drawn to strong, proud women. They do not bow easily."

"I wish to hear none of it, Blasien." The gates opened. It was time. Raphael turned to go, but Blasien caught his arm, glancing at Syrian a brief moment before returning his gaze to Raphael.

"A friend cautioned me once on my pride. Sometimes it is necessary to go to a woman and lay bare your soul to capture her heart."

His jaw tightened with the effort to control himself. Raphael turned fierce eyes on his friend. "And what of the woman who has none?"

Blasien made no answer, released his arm.

He and Syrian left through the slight opening of the gates, silence thick with his tension. Setting the pace, Raphael followed Syrian, no thought but the torture of his own guilt.

The moons had yet to arise, but they needed no help, knowing their footing. Each had traveled the land a hundred times, and would so a hundred more. The run ate the miles in minutes. He felt the increasing distance from her pull like a rope threatening to snap.

A northerly wind suddenly shifted the still air. They stopped, recognizing the threat instantly, hackles raised. Raphael peered ahead, his senses stretching.

A woman's scream ripped through the night--cut off abruptly.

"The Lady Swan," Syrian whispered, cursing.

Raphael took off, recognizing the voice immediately.

He would kill who'd harmed her.

Nothing more than blurs of motion, they ran, instinct guiding them to her. A sudden fog gathered, viscous, white mist clouding their way. Raphael tore through it and the thick undergrowth, heedless of slashing thorns and broken rock. A clearing opened before them without warning. Raphael halted abruptly at the edges, unable to believe the sight that greeted him. Their breath was harsh in the ensuing silence.

"Raphael!" Swan shouted, restrained from going to him. She stood in the center, a man cloaked in darkness holding her arm.

Raphael's eyes narrowed. "What are you doing here? If you have harmed her, I swear you'll not live to regret it."

The man smiled, sharp, ivory teeth flashing. "I've found something you did not know you lost, brother...."

* * * *

The man looked down at her, stroked the underside of her arm once before releasing her. Swan pulled away to the fog's edge. Her hand going to her sword, she glared at him and resisted the urge to scratch her arm where he'd touched her.

His crimson eyes glittered with amusement. "Something so precious should be guarded."

"Her defiant nature makes such a task impossible, Vachel. How did you find her?" He gave Swan a hard look that would have killed a lesser woman. She wasn't altogether certain she wanted his rescue, if he thought he could punish her--and likely would try.

"Do you believe me such a novice? I caught your mark on her, Raphael ... else I would have taken her for myself. Long has it been since I found a woman so tempting."

"You keep your hands off her." Raphael's feral smile promised pain.

"Of course." Vachel returned his grim look with one of mirth.

Raphael nodded, satisfied. "Come to me Swan, he offers no harm."

"Are you so certain?" she asked, giving the stranger a wary glance. Vachel set her nerves on edge. She didn't want to turn her back on him, let alone release her weapon. Beneath the amused air lurked danger.

"Swan," he growled, capturing her attention.

She watched Raphael in her peripheral, not quite believing the man so harmless, sidling away. She told herself if he had intended harm, she would be dead by now. She could feel it with such potent certainty the knowledge chilled her marrow. She reached Raphael's side and stepped behind him, her flank protected by Syrian's comforting presence. Swan clutched his hard biceps, leaning close as she continued watching the man, Vachel.

"Is he truly your brother?" she whispered, drawing Vachel's eyes. His coloring was naturally pale from living in the dark, but his hair was the same shade of midnight as Raphael's, highlights almost blue from the striking moon. His frame was leaner than Raphael, but that appearance could be attributed to his greater height. The structure of his face was harder, more angular and sharp, but the eyes-- in the eyes she could see their similarity.

Raphael's eyes narrowed. "He is. Vampiric blood flows in our veins, and when a hunter female is taken by one, her children are born more vampire than wolf. Vampiric women cannot bear children. Their men steal ours to propagate their lines."

Vachel chuckled darkly. "My blood shames you, does it not, brother?"

Swan couldn't answer for Raphael, but she did not like the thought that he shared blood with this man. Vampires were monsters. But then, she'd been told hunters were monsters, also, all her life, as were all the people of Shadowmere. It was with a sense of surprise that she realized old prejudice had been slowly stripped away.

"I find I do not think of you at all, Vachel. Why have you followed me?"

"I was curious to see why the rabid watchdog of the borders allowed a human inside."

"I would have told had you asked."

"Now Raphael, what is the fun in that?"

"Your sick humor will spell your end one day."

Vachel nodded his dark head, his hair caught in the current air around him. "Of that, I have no doubt. One cannot live by blood alone."

Syrian interrupted, breaking the tension. "Time passes we can ill afford, Raphael."

"Yes, enough of this talk. Swan, you will come with us, if only so that I can watch you."

"I join you as well, brother."

Raphael glared at him. "You know not where we go."

"It matters not. I have need of amusement. But if you go to Barakus, I carry warning."

"And that is ... ?"

"Barakus is besieged. The elders resent your denial of women and blood. They feel it is their due."

"You do not, of course ... ," he said, his jaw tight.

"I have never been one to bow to another."

"This changes everything, Raphael," Syrian said, coming up beside them. "We cannot risk a delay at the borders. The Lysian pool is strongest when the silver moon shines alone. We have until the red moon wanes. Already it fades. If he comes, it will be then."

"You journey to human lands? Because of a woman?" Vachel laughed at Raphael's fierce glare.

He thought the matter over a long moment. "If we cannot go around, we will go under. Vachel knows the way."

Vachel crossed his arms over his chest, his black cape cracking like a whip in the wind. "I could be persuaded ... for a price." He advanced across the circle, appearing to glide, watching Swan alone. "Let me ... taste the woman."

Swan gasped in outrage, fingered her sword, but Raphael held her back from slicing him in two.

"Touch her and die."

Looking smug, he chuckled as though Raphael had reacted exactly as he intended. "It is as I suspected. You are besotted. We run a fool's errand."

"No one asked you to come," he growled.

"I'd not miss this for a seat on the council. I will show you the way."

"Fine. You hinder us, I may forget you are my brother. You," he pointed at Swan, "I will deal with later."

The hard look in his eyes promised it would be unpleasant, but Swan was too shaken to disagree. She didn't trust Vachel, even if he was Raphael's brother. No man that looked so ... hungry could be trusted near a woman. That he was now a traveling companion as well as their guide did not bode well for them.

* * * *

Vachel made no further contact with her. If anything, he ignored her completely, his brother's threat enough to warn him away. She was thankful. Raphael alone was enough to make the strongest woman faint. His brother's nearness only compounded her problems.

The fog Vachel shrouded them with disappeared at his command, and he leapt into the air, hovering at a height just above their heads, his cape fluttering in the wind like wings. They would follow him, not out of want, but for lack of an alternative choice.

She only prayed Barakus would not fall before Raphael could return. A pain stabbed her heart at how much he risked.

She glanced briefly at Syrian as he murmured soft words and a red glow surrounded his body a short moment. He'd cast a spell that increased his stamina for the journey.

Raphael caught her attention with his movement, stripping nude to shift. She blushed as she always did seeing him naked, the lean muscles of his body powerful and silvered in the light, his manhood rampant at her regard.

She touched his shoulder hesitantly, halted his movement, averting her eyes from his groin with an effort. Now was no time to allow longing to get in the way. She had to at least try to beg him from this course. "You should go to your people. They need you. Syrian can help me face Morvere."

His eyes were shielded, amber flecks swallowing the black irises as the change began. "No. I made a promise. I will keep it. Arion will hold the fortress until I return." He exuded confidence like no other, his belief firm when her own wavered. She sighed, glad he'd not been swayed, but saddened too.

Swan watched, breathless, as he shifted before he'd even dropped to the ground, fur rippling over his body like wind. A wolf stood before her, rubbed against her legs in assurance. She climbed atop him, the sack he'd carried slung over her shoulder.

There would be no changing his mind, she knew that now. He was as stubborn as she, perhaps more. Her gut clenched with nervous worry; worry over Morvere, for Raphael's people. She dared not look for meaning behind his words and determination. To hope for something more would be the final crack in her facade.

They traveled well into the night. Unhindered by human weakness, each used their own gift to enhance their speed.

Swan squeezed her eyes shut, terrified at the blur of the land whirling past. Fear and need hastened them, fear that they would be too late. If Morvere reached the pool before them, there would be no chance to defeat him. This was her only hope to return to the life she'd known. To stay a swan maiden would eventually strangle her will--it was no way to live, trapped by the night. Yet Vachel did, and many of the hunters. A newfound pity for them stole into her mind. They were not so unlike.

Hours dragged by as they ran. Her hands cramped from clutching Raphael's fur, and her legs and hips ached with the effort to stay upright. Raphael slowed, and she opened her eyes. When the Northern mountains loomed into view, Swan breathed a sigh of relief. They reached the base of the range as the moons set.

The harrowing trip seemed to last an eternity. Swan had never been more grateful in her life than she was when they reached the Northern pass. She thought coming here would take them directly into the vampire's midst, but no one else was concerned of the danger.

Suspecting they knew more of their land than she did, she trusted them.

Rock skidded and bounced down the foothills, the footing

dangerous for the unwary.

Old warnings told that the mountains were impassable to foes, cupping Shadowmere like a hand shielding a flame. Only the vampires knew the passages, having long lived underground in hibernation.

Vachel guided them to a sheer face, seemingly unscalable. The black rock stretched above, dark clouds gathered around its peaks.

Raphael shifted form, touching the stone as he looked up at Vachel. Nodding, Vachel grasped Syrian under the arms and soared high above their heads, disappearing over a lip. He returned moments later, landing lightly on the ground.

"It is your turn, my lady," Vachel spoke softly, walking near.

Swan pulled back, looking at Raphael for reassurance. "Is there no other way?" Heights had never before terrified her, but the thought of leaving the ground in the arms of a questionable man would make even the most stalwart quail with fear. Flying was unnatural. She did not even do so as a bird.

"There is not. Does my touch repel you?" He grinned as if pleased.

"Enough taunting her, Vachel," Raphael growled warningly.

Vachel shrugged. "I only wish to see if she deserves you."

"I've no need of a mother hen."

He laughed and scooped her into his arms before she could protest, rising into the air. "I will go slowly with you, fair Swan."

She refused to look at the ground, could only watch his face. He smiled at her, the derisiveness gone from his eyes. "Only the most extraordinary woman could capture Raphael. Never has a mate claimed his heart."

And with that nugget piquing her curiosity, he set her down and went below for Raphael.

Vachel returned a few minutes later, landing on the stone lip with ease. Raphael stood distant from her once above, giving her a long, measuring look. He walked past her into the yawning maw of the cavern behind Vachel without uttering a word to her. Swan followed, if only in want of anything else to do. With only a little over an hour before dawn and her changing, her nerves were wound tight.

Vachel went deep into the cavern, away from possible sunlight to rest, while Syrian remained outside to keep watch, preferring the fresh air to the staleness of the mountain. She suspected they had only departed to allow Raphael an opportunity to vent his spleen.

She was alone with Raphael, for the first time in hours, and she suddenly dreaded it, remembering his warning earlier. A depression in the rock held remains of an old fire, enough wood Raphael easily lit a blaze for her comfort. The weak flames flickered with the air sucked through the space. Shadows danced on the wall and Raphael's back, his tension illuminated.

A storm brewed. His silence and that long look should have warned her his foul mood had returned. She expected any minute to be struck dead by a thunderbolt. Waiting, her patience ran thin when his silence continued. She couldn't take it anymore, the thick unease and discomfort. It would be best to air his feelings than go on this way. "Are you going to pout all night?"

He didn't turn around, a sign that he was very, very upset with her. Her hope that he'd forgotten his promise dashed away--if she'd learned nothing else, she knew Raphael always kept his word.

"Why did you disobey me, Swan? I had my reasons for telling you to stay."

Why had she? Her excuses seemed shallow now, foolish. Her damnable pride had always gotten her into trouble--that and the urge to show him he couldn't control her. But deep inside, she knew such reasons were only smoke covering the truth. She'd been terrified she might never see him again--furious that he would dare risk his life. She could not tell him, however. He wouldn't understand, and it infuriated her to have such weakness, to need another person as she needed him. She turned anger with herself on to him. "You don't own me. You can't tell me what to do."

"I thought I had made myself clear."

He'd made it perfectly obvious she was more trouble than she was worth. And now his holdings were being attacked. He would blame her. He was like every other man, attacking when they thought they'd been wronged. It mattered not that she'd told him to go back. "You did, with perfect clarity," she said tightly.

"I told you to stay for your protection."

"You are not my father," she said, biting each word off as if pained.

His hands clenched into fists, relaxed, and clenched again. "No, I am not."

"I-I don't need your protection. I don't need you." She repeated the words mentally, a mantra to keep her whole, uninjured.

Raphael turned then, his eyes blazing, his muscles bunched with power. He was on her in an instant, his arms wrapped tightly as he crushed her fully against his body. Her curves molded to his hard planes, the chain mail heating from contact, searing her senses as though nothing stood between their melding as one but skin.

She tilted her head up in her fury, foolishly, unable to believe his intent. His mouth descended, his lips crushed against her own, his arousal digging hard against her belly. She gasped in shock, energy coursing through her body like a lightning strike. He took advantage of her weakness, thrust his tongue into her mouth, possessive, sweeping aside her protests. He utterly dominated, his kiss ravenous and consuming as he tasted her dark crevices and the sweetness of her tongue.

He broke away from her as abruptly as he'd started. Swan shook with desire and anger, her chest heaving for air. She slapped him before she realized what she was doing. The crack of her hand on his flesh echoed loud in the enclosed space. He'd ruined her, ruined her last chance to pull away without tearing her soul in two. "I warned you not to kiss me."

His eyes flashed gold, near glowing with animal lust. He advanced on her, moving forward with each step she took back, until bare stone trapped her.

"Can you deny your need? Do you dare deny it?" he demanded, his voice hoarse with want.

"Nothing has changed."

He snatched her wrists before she could strike him again, pinned them to the smooth stone above her head. "Deny this," he growled before he kissed her once more.

Swan tensed, expecting harsh punishment, but his lips were soft. He coaxed her response, nibbling, tugging at her bottom lip with his teeth. She'd not anticipated gentleness, knew that his tender urging would be her undoing.

Desire unfurled in her belly, liquid heat trickling in her sex. He trailed kisses along her jaw, up to her ear, nipping the sensitive lobe.

"Stop this," she whispered, begging.

"You don't want this to stop." He shifted, pressing his groin against her, the sensation muffled by the mail skirt.

Tracing the shell of her ear, he thrust his tongue inside, and she moaned, unable to deny him any longer.

Raphael slowly released her wrists, smoothing his hands down her arms. He kissed her again, sliding his tongue easily inside, his palm cupped behind her neck allowing no escape.

She sucked him greedily, didn't resist as he unbuckled her top, protested only when he broke away long enough to pull it and the skirt over her head. He untied the scarf binding her chest, and when his palms cupped her aching breasts, she forgot why she'd fought him. At the pace they'd set, this would likely be their last time together, making each heady caress bittersweet with regret.

He pinched her nipples, rolling the buds between his fingers until they hardened unbearably. Sucking her neck hard, he grazed her with his teeth, releasing her breasts to rip his kurt away before sliding his hands down to her buttocks. He grabbed each cheek with a palm, lifted her.

Her legs spread at the movement, opening for his hips, laying her wide and vulnerable for the taking. She wanted him to claim her, wanted nothing more than the feel of his shaft deep inside her. He teased her cleft with his nearness, so hot and hard. Swan ran her hands up his arms, touching every part she could reach, urgent and greedy for all of him. He groaned against the corner of her jaw, his tongue lathing the line as he pressed the length of his shaft against her slickened cleft.

Swan gasped, arching her neck, clutching his shoulders as he burned a trail down the column of her throat. He rotated his hips, sliding the heat of his erection along her slit in long torturous strokes. His cockhead nudged her swollen clit, breaking a moan from her.

"Please, Raphael. Dawn...."

He broke away from her throat, meeting her eyes with a heady look as he pressed her to the cavern wall and plunged his engorged length deep inside her. Swan bit her lip to keep from crying out as he sank fully, his hips grinding against her clit.

"Don't hold back from me, Swan," he murmured, burying his face against her neck as he pulled out and plunged deeply once more.

He moved faster and faster, each rippled vein spurning quivers to run through her body. Swan hooked her heels under his buttocks, tilting against him, rocking as he thrust again and again. She dug her nails into his back, the tremors climbing with each pounding second.

He bit her neck, piercing the skin, and ecstasy rolled over her in a heart stopping wave. Swan cried out at the sudden bliss. He pushed into her harder as his own release neared, her orgasm building upon itself, liquefying muscle and bone to only heat and need. He groaned as he climaxed, breathing raggedly against her neck as the warm seed spewed into her belly.

Tears streaked her face. She hadn't realized that she was crying. He lifted his head, meeting her gaze with an unfathomable expression on his face.

He lifted her away from the wall then, remaining inside her as he settled them near the fire. Rolling to his back, he held her cradled atop him. He smoothed his hands down her back, through the hair that had fallen from her braid.

Swan reveled in the feel of his heart racing against her cheek, the gentle comfort of his arms. It couldn't last. Swan lifted up, regarding him with the sorrow she felt in her spirit. "It is the last time. You feel it as I do."

"Yes," he whispered, cupping a hand behind her head as he brought her down to meet his kiss. Emotion hovered under the surface, elusive to ken.

Swan pulled away, moved from atop him. She draped a leg over his, cuddled against his chest. She feared the change as never before, knowing when next she awoke, their fates would be decided.

CHAPTER TEN

Raphael lay with Swan until she fell into a deep sleep as she always did before the change. At the sound of her even breathing, he slipped from under the drape of her arms and legs. He tied his kurt around his hips, standing over her, caressing her sleeping form with his gaze, drawn to her soft curves and the cloud of her hair spread beneath her. Looking on her, he could forget their differences, what had drawn them together, yet pushed them apart. He hated Morvere for what he'd done, but had he not, Raphael would never have known her. A fierce ache blossomed with the knowledge, undeniable.

He knelt and touched her cheek, brushing a strand of hair from her lips. They parted on a sigh, drawing him unerringly forward to taste her again. He leaned to kiss her once more. Their breath mingled as one. He pulled away, pained, and left her, unable to be near when she shifted.

He walked quietly through the cavern to the outside, leaned against the lip's edge as he watched fingers of dawn creep across the darkened sky. He rubbed his eyes, lack of sleep and their insane pace wearying him. An hour of rest would set him to rights, for then he could heal torn muscle.

"She changes?" Syrian asked, drawing his attention. He was crouched on a crop of rock, looking out toward Shadowmere as the light slowly pulled back the blanket of dark.

"Yes," he said, his voice soft. Raphael stepped from the edge, moved until bare rock stood at his back.

Syrian stretched and faced him. He'd been silent most of the journey, withdrawing into his mind to prepare facing Morvere and disabling the Lysian pool. "She accepted punishment?"

Raphael laughed, a harsh bark of sound. There'd been no punishment except his own. Touching her was pure torture ... when he knew he could never be with her. He leaned against the sheer rock, gratified to feel its rough hardness dig into his back. Pain kept him alert, alive. He'd do well to remember that fact.

"She needs you, Raphael. You more than anyone know the ways of women."

Truth, he couldn't deny. But Swan blinded him. He couldn't think straight when she was near, and her persistent denial infuriated him like nothing else. "I take her to Avonleigh when this is through. A wolf cannot love a swan."

"She will not always be so."

"She will always be human. Her heart is against the beast. No mark can change her will--and I cannot force her to see what she will not."

Syrian looked thoughtful a moment. "Love coaxes. Force can only destroy."

Raphael grunted. "You do not know Swan. I can see with my own eyes."

"You are as blinded by pride as she is." Syrian rose, stretching muscles tired from holding his position so long. "I'll see to Swan. The bird likes not the scent of predator."

He nodded, watched Syrian go inside. That was wholly the problem--he was a threat to Swan, a threat to her way of life. He turned back to the sky, disturbed to have his faults laid out before him, faults that couldn't be changed.

They rested briefly before pushing onward. Raphael could take no chance with Swan's life. Vachel led them through labyrinthine paths, moving steadily down, darkness swallowing their descent. Needing no torches to see, they passed through the range quickly, moving with a speed borne of urgency.

Hours passed and still they ran. The climate changed in the tunnel, growing warmer as they approached the outside. Vachel hung back as they neared the entrance, waiting in the dark. Raphael and Syrian continued on until they reached an edge much the same as that where they had entered. Outside, the sun dwindled in the sky. In the valley spread a small village, near enough to be a danger should they be seen. Beyond its borders lay the Skarlothian mountains, black and shining like glass.

One single, hidden path led to the Lysian pool. Only a mage could reveal it, and while the sun shone, they could not chance discovery by the villagers. They rested while the sun dipped, waiting for cover of darkness before proceeding.

* * * *

Swan awoke to Syrian's golden face, his sapphire eyes full of concern. "You were asleep longer than expected. I believe he nears. You've only just now changed and the sun set an hour past."

She sat up, stiff, her left hand tingling. She flexed her hand, looking around. "Where is Raphael?"

"He awaits you outside. We must hurry if we are to succeed."

She dressed quickly and joined them outside. They watched the sky as gray clouds uncovered the lonely silver moon. "The red has gone," she whispered. "Have we come too late?"

Syrian looked at her. Raphael remained silent. "We've no choice but to try."

Vachel carried them down the mountain, one by one. Distant fires lit the town. Raphael took no chance on being spotted as a beastman, and so remained in human form just as Vachel ran alongside them instead of taking to the air. By the time they reached the steep hills leading to the range, Swan was winded. A cramp stabbed her left side with each step. She said nothing, just gritted her teeth against the pain and continued on.

Syrian stopped suddenly and pushed back his hood. They'd reached the path, though she could see nothing. He turned his face skyward, his eyes closed and palms clasped open against his chest. The wind stirred as he murmured strange words that tickled the mind, gaining strength as he pushed his hands forward. His hair flew around him with the force, his robes whipping in the wind, cracking like sails.

A golden glow spread down his arms, energy traveling toward his fingers, curling through the air.

The hairs rose on the back of her neck as she watched him, and she stood under Raphael's arm, seeking shelter.

Syrian stopped as abruptly as he began, opened his eyes and pointed toward the mountain. A small path she hadn't seen twisted up the mountain, disappearing beyond a crevice, invisible to the naked eye.

"So lies the path," he said, moving forward.

They walked up the steep incline, the stone smooth and unlittered with even the smallest pebble, the slightest crack. A crevice broke the mountain, dark and tight. They continued climbing until they reached a wide platform. From there they walked into the jagged rip that split the mountain. Light flared at their approach.

Swan jerked back, shielded her eyes until her vision

adjusted. Slowly she withdrew her hands, blinking. Her mouth gaped as she beheld the sight before them. Above the silver moon hung in the center of a huge opening, shining down on a pool of glittering water, illuminating the cavernous room. The water rippled at their approach, sensing the presence of magic. It moved toward Syrian as he walked around, silver ripples undulating like reaching fingers.

"It's beautiful," she whispered, walking nearer.

Raphael stopped her, held her arm. "And deadly to all but those with the gift."

"Indeed," Syrian said. "I sense no disturbance, but he cannot be far. I must work quickly if we are to leave before he comes. Stand away from the entrance."

"What is he going to do?" She'd never once thought to question how they would disable the pool. She had foolishly thought perhaps they could break it apart, but remembered it was protected with powerful magic.

"Drain it. I can create but a small opening in the pool's base, but it requires much of my power. The runes protecting it meld cracks in the rock. I can hold it open for a time, but do no lasting damage. To destroy it would take a coven with a century's experience."

They moved aside as he instructed, standing flat against the wall. To touch the liquid was poison without the knowledge to channel its energy. Even beastmen were susceptible.

Syrian stood before the opening, his legs braced. He pushed his sleeves up and focused on the base of the pool. Sweat beaded his brow as his skin began to glow. The light slithered up and down his arms, coating his skin, climbing beyond the cloth, covering every inch of skin.

The air rippled with energy, heating the atmosphere, scorching their lungs. The stone walls sweat with the heat, gasped as a crack formed in the pool's base. Silver water burst through the opening, rushing along the floor the way they'd come.

Swan watched, mesmerized, unable to tear her gaze away from the silver stream. It moved like a live thing, a serpent slithering along the ground, suddenly freed. Syrian breathed harshly, his arms shaking from holding the crack wide as though his fingers pried the rock apart. His skin shown brilliantly as the Lysian water drained away, down the mountainside. White streaks formed in his hair, and still he continued chanting, drawing out the last drop.

He dropped to his knees as the flow stopped, breathing raggedly. Swan and Raphael rushed to his side, helped him to his feet.

"It ... took more than ... I thought it would," he said heavily, a wry grin on his face.

Swan touched his snowy hair, overcome. She hugged him tightly, and he patted her back soothingly. Pulling back, she held his hand to her heart. "Thank you, Syrian. Had I but known, I never would have allowed you to take such a risk."

"You are most welcome, my lady." He nodded at Raphael, who gripped his biceps in a gesture of thanks. "Now if I may say so, we must hasten our return to Shadowmere. Morvere will go there now that the pool is empty."

"I agree. Vachel, come. We go," Raphael said.

They needed no prodding to leave the haunted cavern. The presence of ancient magic had disturbed them all. As they moved through the crevice, the stone shifted, groaning. Swan glanced over her shoulder to see the opening close, melding together as though never cracked asunder.

She shivered and hurried behind Raphael, Vachel close behind her.

As Syrian stepped outside, on the cavern's ledge, a bolt of light shot from the sky and struck him full in the chest. Smoke billowed as he fell to the ground.

Swan gasped, too shocked to scream. Raphael ran, reached the edge first, his eyes straying right, away from Syrian. Vachel rushed past her, brushing her aside as he joined his brother. Desperate to reach them, she followed quickly, not knowing what had happened.

A roaring growl ripped from Raphael's throat just as she crossed the darkened threshold into the light. She knelt beside Syrian, checking his pulse, turning only after she made sure he still lived to see what had captured Raphael and Vachel's attention.

A black fog spread up the mountain path, slithering up the sides like snakes, tendrils groping for their feet. It emanated cold like the grave, chilling the marrow, drawing the heat from their bodies.

Vachel leapt from the ground, summoning the wind to clear the black obscurity. It parted before them, revealing a man shrouded in robes of blackest velvet, steel gray hair streaming from his head, the ends crackling with chained energy.

"Morvere," Swan hissed, then fell to her knees as a force wrenched her insides. She gasped in pain, clutching her stomach, unable to tear her gaze from the horror playing out before her.

"You are supposed to be weakened," Raphael gritted out. They'd all thought so. It had been their only chance for success.

"I have enough strength to kill you all," he snarled.

"You cannot kill me with such foulness," Vachel growled, diving for him. Raphael moved in, racing toward Morvere as Vachel caught the sorcerer's attention.

Morvere raised his hand and another bolt lit up the sky, flying toward Vachel. He dodged it--too late. The bolt ripped through his side, smashing into the mountain. Rock shattered, raining down on them like broken glass, littering the ledge with deadly slick debris. Vachel yelled in agony, diving still for Morvere, his hands curled like talons. The smell of scorched flesh filled the air with nauseating thickness.

Morvere waved him away with a glancing blow of power, and Vachel whirled in a somersault. He fell behind the sorcerer, plowed into the stone path and went still.

It was enough distraction. Swan struggled to her feet just as Raphael struck Morvere in the chest, his fingers grown into black claws. Blood, black in the darkness sprayed from a slash in Morvere's throat. Morvere laid hands on Raphael's biceps, smoke rising as he scorched Raphael's flesh.

Swan ran toward them as they locked in a deadly embrace, pushing back past safety toward the edge of the mountain as each man grappled for domination. Raphael stumbled on the rock littering the ground, his greater weight pulling them both toward the edge.

Swan screamed as they went over, her cries mingling with Morvere's own.

CHAPTER ELEVEN

Swan ran to the edge, but could see nothing with the distance. He couldn't be dead. She scarcely noticed her missing finger had returned, could think of nothing but Raphael.

A hand grasped her shoulder. She startled, half expecting Morvere, and cried when she saw Syrian standing beside her.

"We must go to him," he gritted out, clutching his chest. He coughed, bending nearly double.

She turned to rush down the mountain.

Vachel was gone, she'd not seen him recover, so couldn't know what had happened to him. Had he been dragged over the side as well? Swan raced down the mountain, Syrian trailing behind, moving as quickly as he could, each minute agony. Tears streamed down her face. She wiped them away, only to be blinded by more.

An eternity passed until they reached the bottom. Syrian limped behind her, too injured to keep up as she scrambled over the steep hill, her fingertips bloodying as she struggled not to fall, to reach him as quickly as she could.

She cried in relief when she found him, crumpled on his side, Vachel beside him. Morvere lay a short distance away, broken over a crop of rock, his head lolling at an obscene angle. She turned away from him, unable to bear the sight.

Vachel looked up at her as she dropped beside Raphael. "He's broken inside," he whispered.

"Don't say that!" she screamed, kneeling beside him, touching his skin. He was cold, chill as the grave. Her heart ceased beating as she stared down at his still form.

Syrian came up behind her, quiet.

She turned to him, clutching the hem of his robe. "You have to do something, Syrian. He'll die if you don't."

Syrian gave her a pitying look, his eyes saddened. "There is nothing I can do for him. My power is drained."

"No!"

"I can't wake him. There is nothing we can do," Vachel said softly, rising.

"Leave me be," she cried, gathering him in her arms. They left her quietly, moving away for her privacy.

Swan rocked him, her tears gliding down her chin, falling on his face. "Raphael, open your eyes, please. Please! You have to wake up." She shook his shoulders. His head fell back limply. "Raphael! You need to change. Do it for me, Raphael."

He lay limp, his skin growing steadily cooler. Swan collapsed against his chest, crying brokenly against him. "Don't leave me, my love. I'm healed," she whispered, kissing his cheeks. "Morvere is dead. You kept your promise," she said, throat closing on her words.

She curled beside him, draping her arms and legs around his still form, watching his face for some sign of life. She couldn't warm him. He was so cold. She smoothed his hair back from his face, barely breathing, her heart breaking.

"You said once, you would have a kiss ... ere you ... die." More tears flooded her eyes as she leaned close and pressed her lips to his mouth, willing what spirit or force gave her life to go into him. She cupped his jaw, rubbing her thumb softly against his cheek, heating his body with her own.

She pressed her palm against his heart, sawing her mouth across his lips, suffusing him with warmth. His lips twitched and she pulled back, startled, watching him, seeing no movement. She descended again, nibbling his lips, hoping against hope her sanity had not broken.

A faint beat thumped against her hand. She stroked the hard plane of his chest, grazing his nipple, feeling for the beat. It grew strong, heat spreading out from her palm.

His lips moved again, responding to her. She stroked her tongue against them, soothing the parched surface. He groaned softly, his lips parting. She pulled back and his eyelids fluttered open.

A buzz tickled her ears and then his voice filled her head. *Don't stop. The kharez....*

His eyes closed and he went still once more. Swan frantically touched his face, kissed him again, pushed her tongue into his mouth--anything that would provoke a response. She stroked her palms over his chest, and each time he grew warmer, the heat spreading. It dawned upon her suddenly. Her touch was healing him.

She moved further, touching the ripples of his stomach, lower, feeling his skin coming to life at her as she caressed him. She pushed past his kurt, touched his hips, the soft thatch of hair at the base of his sex, further, to that central part of him.

Her fingers tingled with energy as she gently laid them against his manhood. He hardened instantly, and she looked up at his face, saw that he watched her, his eyes lucid.

Slowly, he lifted an arm, cupping a hand behind her neck to bring her down for his kiss. He plunged his tongue into her mouth, growing steadily stronger with each liquid glide.

Swan cried again, gripping his shaft, feeling life pulse through him. He groaned into her mouth, his fingers tangling through her hair as she continued to caress him.

Breaking away, he kissed her cheeks, moved brokenly along her jaw. He pulled back, held her gaze steadily. "You've healed me, Swan. There is no need to go on. You can release me."

She did so, reluctant to break contact. She drew her arm up to hug him tightly, gratified to feel the strong beat of his heart pounding against her cheek. "I thought we'd lost you."

"You brought me back from the brink."

"And you saved me, Raphael." His chest was wet from her tears, she laughed softly, embarrassed at her emotions, wiping them away as she sat up.

Swan could hardly believe he lived. She couldn't touch him enough, couldn't bear to leave his embrace.

Reluctantly, they both stood, holding each other for support. Vachel and Syrian walked up.

Shock etched across Vachel's face. "She has powers I've never before seen. I am glad to have you back, brother." He leaned in to embrace him.

"Let there be no bad blood between us ever more," Raphael said, returning his brother's embrace.

Syrian clasped his shoulder. "The kharez is powerful indeed." He looked past him to Morvere's broken body. "What will we do with him?"

Raphael glared at the body. "Leave it, as warning for others."

Syrian nodded. "You go to Avonleigh now?"

"Yes," Raphael said, his jaw clenched.

"I will return to Ravenel. Vachel, will you give your aid?"

"I will. And I may seek nourishment from these strange lands." He looked into the distance, clutching his side.

"You'll be killed if they discover your origins," Raphael warned.

"Only if I'm caught. And I do not plan to be so obvious. Farewell, brother, until next we meet."

He and Syrian limped away, back down the steep foothill. Swan watched them until they disappeared in the darkness.

It suddenly occurred to her that they had succeeded. She stretched her hand, amazed to see it whole once more. The spell had lifted with Morvere's death. She was free! Her blood soared at the knowledge.

Swan hugged Raphael again. "Your promise is kept, Raphael," she said, her voice muffled against his chest.

He was silent a long moment. "It is not yet complete. I said I would return you home, and I will. Your sister and your people need you."

Her chin wobbled, but she fought the urge the cry again. "Yes, they do." He'd not heard her words when she thought him dead. It was best for them both that she not repeat them. A human could not live in his world. She could never forget that.

* * * *

They traveled until they passed the village--the danger in exposure for Raphael too great if they stayed near. Beastmen were killed for trespass, and she couldn't bear to take the risk only for the comfort of an inn.

Her body weary beyond belief, they stopped to make camp at the border of a shallow forest. Soft, thick moss coated the ground near a small, gurgling mountain stream. They drank their fill and collapsed into the moss bed, falling asleep in each other's arms.

The night passed in haunting dreams.

Swan awoke to the glare of light beating upon her eyelids. She cracked them open, not quite believing she lay with the sun kissing her skin.

The horror was truly over, and with it came the end of her existence with Raphael. She couldn't dwell on that sadness. She craned her head to look at him, a thrill running through her body to wake with his arms wrapped around her.

He grinned at her, lazily moving a hand up her waist to the underside of her breast. She pushed it down, coy, batting her lashes.

He growled playfully and rolled on top of her, kissing her with a thoroughness that curled her toes.

There was no need for words. Each knew these moments alone were precious. Desire unfurled as he turned serious, stripping away the barrier of their garments until they lay in the moss with nothing between them.

Raphael wedged a knee between her legs, parting her thighs. He rubbed the hard, thick muscle against her, increasing the moisture soaking her cleft.

Swan moaned as he pinched her nipples, massaging her breasts. They moved rapidly after that, hands groping, need furious. He moved between her thighs and thrust into her barely slick channel, the friction causing her to gasp.

He moved in and out, kissing her deeply, his hands braced on either side of her head. He broke away from her mouth, dropping his face to her neck as he gained tempo. Swan curled her legs around his hips, raising up with every thrust, her hands roaming over his back, reveling in the play of muscle with each potent stroke.

The climax took her quickly, suddenly. She cried out at its intensity, bit his shoulder, her nails digging into his back. His own release followed soon after and he collapsed, rolling onto his side and holding her close. He crushed her to him, laying still until the furious beat of their blood returned to normal.

He pulled away from her, kissing her closed lids tenderly, then her mouth. "We dare not linger, Swan."

She nodded and rose to bathe in the water, reluctant to wash his wild scent from her skin but needing its coolness to steady her calm.

Once dressed, they left.

He kept their pace consistent, stopping only to hunt and break at night. In the dark, they came together again and again, until they fell into exhausted sleep, knowing these passing nights need last a lifetime. She couldn't speak of parting, couldn't think about it, and so said nothing.

It wasn't until a fortnight had passed that the roads became familiar, and the fear she'd held at bay for so long returned full force. They had reached the border of her lands.

* * * *

Day drew to a close when they reached the first village, the sun dwindling in the sky, a deep burnt orange that turned to clouds to flame.

Children ran through the streets, laughing, kicking dirt at one another as they raced home to their mother's call. An old man shook the trash from his pipe on the ground, standing near a squat stone hut, giving them a suspicious look as they walked up the wide dirt road bisecting the center of the village.

He paused, studying them, and slowly his face crumpled into a wrinkled smile. He cried out and ran to them, dropping to the ground before her. "My lady!" He kissed the hem of her mail skirt. "My lady, you've returned. They spread the word you had been taken from us."

Swan looked down at him, flushing as more men and women came to their doors to see the commotion. As they saw her, they rushed into the street, crying and laughing. Nila must have been searching for her, she realized. Dimly, she heard the clop of horse's hooves racing away from the village, but she was too overwhelmed by the people to think anything of it.

Raphael watched Swan, saying nothing as the families slowly thinned out and went back to their homes so she could leave. They walked on, leaving the town as the sun settled.

He couldn't take her to Barakus--there was too much danger, too much risk she'd be killed.

He'd come to Avonleigh to see if there could be another choice. If there was some chance.... The lands prospered under her rule, if the health of her citizens could be evidence. They needed and loved her, recognized her face. If he'd had doubts of her place before, he held them no longer.

"Why do you not ask to stay with the townspeople?" he asked, watching her reaction.

They'd stopped past the outskirts, far enough away the lights from the town were dim. "I couldn't chance they would know you, Raphael."

"You should stay. In the morning they can take you to

Avonleigh."

"No, I--" She stopped, listening as did he. "Horses," she breathed, looking into the distance. The rider she'd heard leave, he must have gone for help or to give notice.

He tensed, ears perked. "Armor shod. A patrol."

"Nila. She must be looking for me." Her heart thrilled at the prospect. She would soon see her sister.

After but a few minutes, horses crested the horizon, thundering down the wide dirt road. Swan awaited, fearless, recognizing her guard immediately. They pulled to a halt, a circle around them. Seeing Raphael, they drew their swords.

"Wait!" she yelled, pushing in front of him. Raphael glared at the horsemen, his hands clenched into fists. "He is no threat. Lay down your arms."

They slid their swords back in their sheaths, still giving Raphael a wary eye.

A man dropped to the ground, their leader. He removed his helm and bowed before her. "My lady, we'd near given up hope of finding you," Captain Sade said. "Blessed are we. The gods have returned you home."

"How fairs my sister?" she asked, worry etched across her face.

"Well. She would hear nothing but news of our progress."

"I wish to see her at once. We can wait no longer."

Captain Sade nodded. "We'll take no rest until you are safely ensconced."

The men broke the circle, preparing to leave. He pulled Swan up onto his own horse. "The men will double up for you and your compan--Oskar, where is Lady Swan's companion?"

"He was here but a moment ago, Sir! I swear I only just took mine eyes off him."

Swan glanced behind her, felt her blood freeze. Raphael was gone. She'd heard no sound of his leaving. "Raphael?" She walked back down the road, looking for sign of his passing and saw none. "Raphael!" He couldn't have left her. He'd promised to take her home. "Search the woods, now, Captain Sade."

"Yes, my lady."

They beat the edges of the woods, but could make no headway in the brush, weighted in their armor. She continued calling for him until she was hoarse. The men came back to her, subdued with failure.

"My lady, we can find no trace," Captain Sade whispered, touching her arm when she would not move from the road.

"He can't have gone," she said, tears falling as she collapsed onto her knees. She pushed Sade away, concentrating on calling him with her mind, reaching out to him. There was no response. She had not the power of mindspeak--he couldn't hear her.

The words she'd held back from uttering burned her throat, tears blinding her. "Raphael," she whispered brokenly into the dark, "I ... love you...."

She received no answer, and in her imagination, she thought distantly, a wolf cried.

CHAPTER TWELVE

Swan said nothing as Captain Sade helped her onto the horse. She remained silent until Avonleigh castle came into view. Word had been sent ahead that she'd been found.

Bonfires lit the streets with the brilliance of daylight. The heavy gates were thrown open, allowing them inside.

People cheered the triumphant return of the patrol guard. A groomsman helped her down, and an excited roar went up from the crowd. They parted suddenly, and Nila ran through their midst, grabbing Swan in a fierce hug.

"I thought I'd lost you forever, sister," she cried on Swan's shoulder, burying her face in her hair.

"And I you," she breathed, smoothing her sister's dark hair back. This was where she belonged. Raphael had been nothing but a dream--she must remember that.

Her throat ached with unshed tears. She still couldn't quite grasp that he was gone, never to return.

Nila released her and they walked through the courtyard inside, Swan waving to the crowd as she passed.

"Prepare a bath in Lady Swan's room. And a plate," Nila said to a servant, guiding Swan with an arm to her solar.

Nila couldn't stop touching her, held her hand as they climbed the long stairs and finally settled inside the comfortable room. They sat on cushioned chairs, pulled close to the fire. "You must tell me what happened, Swan. I don't think I can bear the suspense much longer."

Swan nodded, looking into the flames. She slowly told of Morvere's betrayal, of Raphael's rescue, of their hard journey to the Lysian pool and the sorcerer's death.

"By the gods!" Nila exclaimed, clutching her sister's hand to her chest. "I had no idea. Were it not for your intervention...." She shuddered. "He collapsed after you disappeared, said you'd been abducted from us. He told me we must join to face the threat on Avonleigh. I could think of nothing but searching for you. The guards have patrolled the borders, searching for any sign, any ransom. But a sennight past, Morvere grew well enough to leave his room, and I haven't seen him since. I wish I could spit upon his grave for the heartache he's caused."

They hugged again. Nila could always be counted upon for her passions. She should never have doubted her safety. She'd proven herself capable of handling anything, and keeping the people going.

A servant came in announcing her bath was ready, and she left. After she was bathed and fed, she went to bed, clutching her pillow like Raphael lay beside her, wishing for the comfort of his embrace. She fell into a fitful sleep, her dreams filled with Raphael's brooding face and glowing eyes.

* * * *

Swan's heart wasn't in overseeing the lands, and so Nila continued ruling. She was proud of her sister's accomplishments, proud of her commitment to their health and prosperity.

Still, nothing could pull her from the dark mood that consumed her every waking hour.

A week passed, and she recovered. She worried about Raphael going back to Barakus, wondered how he faired against his enemies. Thought of his failure and death never crossed her mind. Were she to dwell on such things, she'd go mad.

At night, she examined her belly, hoping a babe had been planted. And as the weeks passed and her monthly flow came, she cried again for chances lost. Eventually, the well of sorrow dried, and she could cry no more.

That was when the dreams began.

Subtle, at first she could remember nothing but the barest details, but each night her imagination grew. He came to her, tangled in her arms in legs, taking her again and again.

A month passed, agonizingly. Desire grew with each erotic dream, until her every muscle ached for release only he could give. She tried touching herself, her fingers stroking her swollen, saturated lips, her clit begging for the callused fingers of her lover. She imagined his hands and lips upon her skin, pinching her nipples, smoothing her belly and thighs, but it was no use.

* * * *

"Swan, I worry over you. Has the spell some lasting harm we do not know of?" Nila asked. They ate together each night in Swan's solar, since Swan had no desire for the excited chatter of the masses.

"I'm saddened for friends lost." She couldn't tell her sister the reason behind her morose mood. She knew it was past time she got on with her life and stopped feeling sorry for herself. He wasn't coming back. He'd made his promise and kept it. "You are right. I have been selfish. I promise things will be better from now on."

Nila smiled and they chatted about the harvest and her many suitors. She was a prime age for marrying and should choose a husband soon. Swan made no response to Nila's claim she, herself, deserved to marry.

Swan climbed into bed that night, determined to put Raphael completely from her mind. It was time to heal. She didn't know it would only intensify her dreams....

* * * *

A hand stroked her hair, pushed the mass away from her face. Swan turned into it, sighing, drowsy.

The bed dipped as a heavy weight settled into it. Swan rolled toward it, encountered hard, hot flesh. She snuggled close, breathing deeply of his scent.

A hand flattened on her belly, smoothed up her ribcage, a finger light under one breast.

Swan arched, sighing, not daring to open her eyes and dispel the dream. Feathery light, the palm circled her breast, drawing closer and closer to her nipple. The sensitive tip puckered in anticipation, begging his attention.

Wet heat latched onto her nipple, sucking hard. Swan gasped, pleasure arcing through her body, settling between her legs. Her eyes flew open. She looked down to see a dark head at her breast.

He massaged her other breast, teasing her nipple as his teeth grazed her distended flesh, breaking a moan from her throat. She ran her fingers through his hair, not daring to close her eyes for fear he'd disappear again. He looked up at the contact, his eyes flashing with gold.

"Are you real?" she asked, breathless as he covered her with his body, eased between her parted thighs. His hard shaft lay heavy on her hip. He braced his arms on either side of her head.

"I never should have left," he said, voice gravely with disuse. He descended for a kiss, crushing his lips to hers.

Swan clung to him, kissed him back, their tongues dueling, fueling desire.

He moved a hand between her legs, past the thatch of hair covering her sex, to that nub that needed his touch so badly. He probed her and she moaned into his mouth, sucking his tongue, silently begging for more.

He hooked a hand under one knee, rocked his hips against her, letting her feel his hard length. His cockhead slipped along her folds, teasing her clit, the opening of her womanhood. She broke away from his mouth, whimpering at his torment, digging her heel into his buttocks.

"Please," she begged, arching, unable to hold still.

He lifted her other leg, tilting her hips up as he plunged deep inside her, his shaft stretching her to the limits. Swan cried out as he nudged the blissful spot inside her, her heart hammering against her chest.

His arms tensed with the effort to control himself, to plunder her slowly, thoroughly.

"Don't hold back from me," she whispered, meeting his gaze.

He held her gaze as he thrust inside, harder, his control slipping. His eyes glowed amber as she tightened around him, dug her nails into his back. She gasped for more, until each deep thrust lifted her hips, faster, harder, his pubic bone grinding her clit.

She shook her head, her eyes squeezed tightly,

determined to ride with him until the end. Energy coursed through her veins, speeding, drawing her nerves tighter and tighter.

She opened her mouth to scream as the climax claimed her, but Raphael smothered her cries with his mouth, his body jerking with the force of his own release. He kissed her all over her face, brushed her tears away.

His heart thundered against her breast. She gloried in the feel of him, alive, holding her.

As their blood calmed, he rolled off her, cradling her in his arms. She craned her head up, watching him in the dark. She feared to break the spell, feared not asking him the question that seared her mind. But she had no choice, if she was to remain sane. Her heart could take no more. "Have you come only to leave me again?"

He was silent a long moment, stroking her hair. He breathed a deep sigh, shuddering. "I've come to take you with me."

She stiffened, unable to believe his words. "Truly?"

"I need you, Swan. More than water or air, I need your heart, for I lost mine to you long ago." His voice broke. "I love you."

"Raphael, Raphael, my love." She hugged him tightly, kissing his chest, his face. "I died the day you left."

"Forgive me." He shuddered again, crushed her to him. "I thought I did what was best. I found I could not live without you. I died that day, as well."

She laid a finger against his lips. "Shh. There is nothing to forgive. You resurrected my heart with your kiss. I love you, Raphael, with every beat of my heart, with every breath I take."

THE END

THE DRAGON KING

Prologue

Before the birth of Shadowmere, at the dawn of time, when men and beast were one, a single, aged race ruled the land ... the dragons.

Magic flowed through their veins, their scarcity of numbers strengthened by their power, and the fear they invoked.

The race of man was not content with their lot. They craved the immortality of the beasts and dragons, and above that, their power. In great numbers, they swarmed their brethren born of magic, sweeping across the land as locusts, killing all who stood in the way of gaining that which they most coveted. Elusive was the beast's secret, however, forever remaining out of man's ken.

One by one the great dragon kings fell to the horde, betrayed by those they'd taught the essence of quickening to--their magic used against them.

Their kind overcome, the beasts fell back, until the edges of a dark land lay at their back, shielded by heavy mountain and desolate plains.

To survive, the ragged remains of these strange peoples banded together, led in force by a dragon king of immense power. There could be no other choice for freedom, for they would not be slaves.

In a final battle, the gods wept as their children lay dying, the sheer gray landscape awash with blood.

A tremulous peace was struck amid the deafening cries of the dying, and the beasts of magic retreated to a land they called their own.

And the last dragon withdrew to the raging sea of lost souls, alone, his brethren lost for all time.

Chapter One

Time had never been his enemy, until now.

Sleet pelted Balian of Memnon, driving against his hide at the altitude he flew, slashing against the thick, protective lids covering his eyes. He raised his shoulders, closing his wings slightly to duck beneath the cloud cover. There, above the pitch black landscape, he hovered. His wings lazily stirred the air, crystals of ice tinkling as they broke from his scales with each beat of his wings.

He blinked his lids back as he looked down on the castle. The sheer rock of the valley protected its flanks. Its spires seemed to grow from the very ground itself. From the land, the fortress below him was impregnable--immune to any force that dared to assault it. Many had tried ... and failed.

His keen eyes picked up the glow of fires, the faint, frosted breath of horses in the courtyard, traced the movement of guards watching the lay of the land. He could hear the boasting laughter of one guardsman to another, the quickened steps of a servant rushing down cobbled hallways. Unaware that their oldest enemy hovered above them, life carried on there as it always had.

None expected attack from above, nor had they reason to. They could not reach such heights themselves, their own abilities having deserted them in a long ago age, leaving them barely capable of flight at all, and his race had died long ago--though the loss felt as fresh now as if it had only been yesterday.

His lips pulled back in a semblance of a smile over jagged teeth the length and thickness of a man's leg--razor sharp, designed for one thing alone ... rending a foe to pieces.

They had everything to fear ... they just didn't know it.

Inside those stone depths, his bride awaited--in the tallest tower, in the land of Wyverns, at the stronghold of their domain ... so he'd been told. Here was a woman worthy of his claim, with a strength to match his own ... a mate for the last of the dragon kings.

He'd best not keep her waiting, he thought with a combination of amusement and anticipation.

Heaving a breath of thin air, he tilted and flattened his wings to his body, diving, his quarry in sight. He cloaked himself in darkness as he approached the tower, shifting into human form as he neared, landing with light feet upon the dark and lonely balcony. Fine glass doors opened with a soft push, and he was soon inside the black chamber.

The bed dominated the room, and his eyes were drawn instantly to its occupant.

With silent footfalls, he approached the bed, easing back the sheer drapery to better view her. She lay with an arm flung carelessly above her head, her fingers tangled in nut brown hair shot with streaks of gold. Silken sheets rode high upon her chest, obscuring the bounty of her figure but not wholly hiding her beauty.

His gut clenched with sudden, fierce desire, awakening the beast betwixt his legs with painful intensity. How long had it been since he'd lain with a woman, supped on the honey between her thighs, felt the heat of her body wrapped around him? Ages of abstinence had honed his need until it felt like the thrust of a blade in his belly with each beat of his heart.

He groaned under his breath, gritting his teeth against the pain, against the savage desire to take her and ravish her where she lay. He welcomed the agony as an old friend, knew its nature and how to control it. He slid his fingers through the ends of her hair, and up, across supple, pouting lips that begged a taste. How easy it would be to steal such treasures, but conquering her mind and body until she succumbed willingly? 'Twas a test he was willing to engage.

She sighed and stirred in her bed, the sheets slipping down her body, constricting his strength of will. One taste would suffice, would tame the wild beast.

But no, it wouldn't be enough. He closed his hands into fists and thrust away from her, moving across the room before he could make a mistake. His chest heaved, his nostrils flared as he breathed the cool air flowing through the window. Blood rushed to his clenched fingers, pulsing like heartbeats, prickling with awareness. The memory of silken skin against his fingers seduced, warred with his mind.

He couldn't leave without a sample of her delights.

* * * *

A cold sigh of air caressed Kisah's skin, nipping her with cool teeth. The breathy coolness moved through the room, fluttering the netting about her bed until it crawled across her skin in slinky movements. Fingers seemed to glide through her hair, making her scalp prickle, drawing her up from the depths of sleep.

Kisah awoke with a start, gasping, certain she'd been touched, certain she'd heard something move about in her room.

Darkness blinded her. The room was black as pitch without any relief. Not even her window revealed a speck of light. She knew the moons must have set hours ago for it to be so dark inside.

As if to give the lie to the reassurance that leapt so readily to her mind, light winked palely as something moved in front of the window, revealing the source of the darkness.

Kisah startled, nearly jumping out of her skin, sure her eyes were playing tricks on her. Perhaps she still slept....

"You're awake," a man spoke, the timbre of his voice deep and tinged with an accent from an unfamiliar land.

Kisah sucked in a breath to scream, but his next words choked the air from her lungs.

"No one can hear you. I have laid a muting spell on the room."

That explained the tingling feeling when she awoke, the feel of lightning dancing across her skin, raising the hairs on her arms and legs. "What do you want of me?" she asked, feeling beneath her pillow for the sheathed dagger she always kept there. Her fingers found nothing.

"I've taken care of your blade as well, princess." His tone was almost apologetic.

More startling than the knowledge that he'd done away with her blade was the fact that he could apparently see her in the dark as well as if it had been light. She wondered briefly what else he'd done while she slept.

Kisah stayed her hand, searching her mind for any other weapons she had nearby. She could think of none save throwing huge pieces of furniture, and that was not feasible.

"You didn't answer my question," she gritted out in helpless frustration, clutching her blankets in a tight-fisted grip. "What do you want?"

"You," he said, amusement tingeing his voice.

Kisah stiffened, glaring into the shadows. "I am not for the taking."

"If I choose it, I could take you now," he said, so quietly she barely heard the whisper of sound.

Nevertheless, the threat in his statement set her nerves on edge. "You will draw back but a nub if you come near." She gathered herself on her knees, preparing to make a run for the door.

He seemed to sense her intent, though her movements were subtle, for he moved deeper into the room. His footsteps were soft as he progressed. She lost track of him, couldn't place where he'd moved. Her hackles jumped with warning, her skin interpreting every breath of wind as his touch.

"I think Syrian to be right," he said, suddenly, his voice a few feet to her right--and blocking escape through the door. "You are worthy of me."

His audacity stunned her to silence for several moments. "I'm gratified to know that," she said tartly. "It changes nothing. Touch me and you will regret it."

He laughed, so deep and husky, it touched something inside her, warming her, as the affectionate laughter of a dear friend. What strangeness this was? She wondered, for it was not a laugh of cruelty, but true amusement. Never had she heard a more pleasant sound. That in itself stoked the warning fire inside her, warned her that more magic surrounded her than merely a muting spell. Kisah shook the strange kindling off, curling her hands into talons.

"Easy, princess. I came only to look upon my future bride, to see for myself if you are the one."

Knowledge dawned with that bold statement. He had to be one of the contenders for her hand, come to participate in the games that would decide her fate. Boastful bastard. She could not fathom how he'd managed to reach her room, but she would discover it on the morrow if she survived tonight. By his words, he intended to collect the bounty of her dowry, which meant he would not harm her-- not yet.

The thought gave her little comfort.

"Until next time," he whispered.

The bed dipped abruptly. Kisah shrieked and scrambled

away. He was faster. He caught her legs just as she freed herself from her heavy covers and dragged her to him, underneath him. Suddenly she was trapped beneath a wall of hard male flesh.

Kisah slapped at him, squirming, kicking her legs. He pinned her with his body, locked her hips down as he straddled her. Two massive hands closed around her arms and brought them above her head, pinning her wrists to the bed.

Kisah growled in fury, biting at him. She tasted hair. It tangled all around her, choked her. She blew it out of her mouth just as he bent his head close.

His lips touched hers, and a wave of enraged heat enveloped her. The kiss was brief, more a flutter of air than a merging of souls. He pulled back before she could bite him.

He paused above her, silent as she fought the anger threatening to overwhelm her thoughts. He transferred her wrists to one huge hand and trailed his free one down her face, cupping her jaw, skillfully avoiding her teeth.

Kisah stilled, waiting to see what he would do, if he would finish what he had started. The men of this land were violent, not above rape. She would endure it if she had to, and when he was done, she would try her utmost to kill him.

He progressed no further than the column of her throat, explored the fine tendons, up and down, the curve of her jaw. She didn't understand what he was doing, why he didn't press his advantage, for she was powerless to stop him.

Her stomach fluttered as his thumb brushed against her bottom lip. She sucked in a sharp breath, ignoring the sudden, tingling throb of her lips. She wanted to bite him, but she couldn't. He threatened no violence now, only explored with feathery strokes.

She wondered for one insane moment what it would be like to allow him to steal a kiss....

"Another time," he said, as if in answer to her thoughts.

Kisah stiffened at the promise.

He stood abruptly, releasing her. Before she could sit up, he ran toward the open window. Kisah caught a glimpse of silvery limned, muscular shoulders and long dark hair, and then he leapt out the window and off the balcony.

She gasped, hopped out of bed and ran through the portal, peering down over the balcony, expecting to see a broken body on the parapets. There was nothing but the patrol guard manning the walls, the fires of torches. She continued looking down in stunned amazement. It was as if he'd never existed, and yet her heart still pounded in her chest, her lips still tingled.

He was a sorcerer of some type, of that she was certain. Magic sparked in the air, tasting like flame on her tongue.

Kisah stepped back and closed the window, shivering from the cold.

Tomorrow, she would have the window bricked up, or new locks placed on the latches. She crawled back in bed, but she knew sleep would not come, not this night.

The games would begin with sunrise. She would find this man in the contests, and she would have him put to death for daring to touch her.

Chapter Two

By her father's decree, the best warriors in the land had gathered to compete for her hand in marriage. They cared naught that they gained a king's daughter as their bride, only for the chance at the riches of her dowry.

Women were of no value to them beyond the wealth they brought their husband and the ease they took of their bodies. These warriors felt no tenderness for their mates. They cared only for wars, for letting blood. At times, Kisah cursed her bloody, violent heritage. She had no desire to be any man's possession, and yet, by these contests alone, her father guaranteed that only the strongest and fiercest would win--the warrior who most personified that which she detested about her race. She would have no chance against a man such as that. She could not blame her father for his thinking--he wanted a strong man as her husband, one able to protect her as a royal deserved.

As a man, however, he was prone to overkill in every task he undertook, and finding her a husband was no different.

Her protestations fell on deaf ears, and she was inclined to believe much of these games were for his benefit alone ... or rather, his entertainment alone.

She could not allow hopelessness to creep in. She needed her wits about her to formulate a plan to retain her independence ... or at least guarantee marriage to a man easily manipulated and controlled.

As if fate chose that moment to taunt her hopes, she spied ahead of her one of the contestants waiting to waylay her. A faint smile curled his lips, his gaze raking her as if he had stripped her naked in the hall. She gave him a withering glare, and then promptly ignored him to allow him to know that he was beneath her notice.

He stepped away from the column where he had been lounging as she came abreast of him. "A token, my lady?"

Kisah would have brushed past him, but there was something about his voice that seemed unnervingly familiar. She turned a suspicious gaze upon him, measuring his height and breadth. Like most of the other warriors who had descended to claim the bounty of her father's kingdom, this one was tall, broad shouldered, muscular of build. Unlike his counterparts, he wore no armor. Beyond the loincloth that drew her eye, he was dressed only in boots and bracers. His long, inky locks of hair were not even restrained.

His build was suggestive of her night prowler, but she saw nothing of the swaggart in his expression. Nothing that suggested he had intimate knowledge of her. His features were pleasantly angular, well-defined, and would have come together to produce an attractive visage even if not for his eyes. His eyes were exotic, mesmerizing, with long, black lashes and deeply arched eyebrows. He should have looked feminine with those eyes, ridiculous--anything but devastatingly fascinating. Her belly fluttered with unaccustomed nervousness, and she laid a hand upon her breast to calm the sudden speed of her heart.

His lips curled at the thoroughness of her examination, her apparent absorption in his features. Irritation surfaced along with the determination to wipe that smirk off his face. She smiled at him coolly. "I've already promised my token to another."

To her surprise and annoyance, the faint smile widened

into a grin, his eyes gleaming appreciatively. "This one who milady favors, by what name is he known?"

Kisah gaped at him blankly. She had lied and had not thought to cover her lie. "Why?" she asked, sparring for wind.

"So that I may kill him first."

Kisah felt her heart skip several beats. "You are so certain of your prowess, sir?"

He allowed his gaze to travel lingeringly down her body. A flush of heat followed in his wake and flickered in dark, secret places. "You will have to be the judge of that, my lady," he said with husky, sensual promise.

She glared at him, angry at herself for reacting to but a simple gaze, but more irritated that he had cleverly maneuvered her into a corner. The remark was *plainly* sexual, but she could hardly acknowledge that. And yet, if she pretended that his innuendo had escaped her, she would appear short on wit. She could not, in fact, think of any clever retort. A thought occurred to her suddenly, however, and she smiled sweetly at him. "Alas, but it is my father who is judging the contestants. After all, it is his...." she paused significantly, " ... bounty that has enticed the treasure seekers."

Something flickered in his eyes. Empathy? Understanding? It disturbed her far more than his brazenly suggestive comments.

"There is only one treasure I seek," he murmured.

She studied him a long moment, but once again, he had rendered her speechless--something she was not accustomed to. "I am expected to take my place beside my father," she said abruptly. "If you will forgive me...." Without waiting for a response, she turned away.

"Most anything, my lady," he said quietly.

It took an effort to resist the urge to glance back at him.

* * * *

Kisah was still more than a little unsettled when she reached the boxseat that had been set up for the royals and their guests.

Her father glanced at her in irritation. "You are late, daughter. We could hardly begin the games without you."

Curtseying deeply in respect, she smiled at her father as she stood upright once more. "Pray, forgive me, father. I was detained by a minor annoyance."

Her father looked her over suspiciously as she took her seat at his side. He didn't question her further, however. "Will you choose a champion? It might make things more interesting."

Kisah smiled in genuine pleasure this time, that her father's thoughts fell in so well with her needs. "Anything to please you, father."

Rubbing his hands together in anticipation, he stood up, holding his hands out. At once, the crowds gathered in the stands began to fall silent. "Princess Kisah has expressed an interest in choosing her champion for the day. Let the contestants come forward."

Kisah was not particularly interested, but still she found herself looking around for the encroaching oaf who had delayed her arrival, bringing her father's wrath down upon her head. She saw him at the very edge of the lists, mounting his horse as the others rode forward. A mixture of irritation and contempt went through her as she saw that the fool still had not donned his armor. Could any male be more cocky? Or more foolish? One thing was for certain, this contestant would not be one that she would need to concern herself with for long. Nevertheless, she waited until all of the men had lined up before the royal box.

Rising slowly, she moved to the front, examining each man carefully ... except the half-naked oaf in the loincloth. They were all the same to her, but she saw that Nkunda, a warrior known far and wide, both for his ferocity in battle, and the battle lust that rendered him brainless, was mounted on a horse near the center.

Untying one of her scarves, she leaned on the low wall, smiling at Nkunda as she waved the scarf at him, trying hard not to glance at the swaggering braggart at his side. Nkunda, grinning like the jackass he truly was, spurred his horse forward, skidding to a halt just below her.

Leaning forward until she was certain he had a clear view of her cleavage, she dropped the cloth. A glazed look had come into his eyes as she leaned over the wall until her breasts were on the verge of leaping from her bodice.

If not for the fact that the crowd roared with approval, the numskull would have simply sat there drooling on himself and missed her token entirely. Belatedly, he surged forward, catching it in his hand and then spinning his horse, holding it out like a trophy for all to see before he tied it around his upper arm. Smiling at her, he gave her a nod, turned his horse, and rejoined the group.

Her father stood up. "Let the contest begin!"

Almost immediately after her father's announcement, there was a commotion on the field. Her father irritably summoned one of the guardsmen from the field. "What goes on here?" he asked with a scowl that quaked most who saw it.

The guard's eyes widened, and his throat bobbed as he swallowed. "There is a contestant who asks to be first combatant against Nkunda."

"He's a fool then. He would do better to wait until the others wear Nkunda down. Who is this man?"

"It is the barbarian who wears no armor, your highness. He goes only by the name Balian."

Her interest perked with the guard's words. Kisah interrupted them. "Well, if he insists...." She deliberately allowed her words to trail off.

Her father stroked his chin, considering the matter. He waved his hand in annoyance. "Bah. So be it. Let Nkunda kill the simpleton."

To her surprise, Kisah felt a stab of alarm at her father's words. It was nothing to her, one way or the other, she assured herself, who won the match, or who was killed in the rush. The truth was, her own battle began only when this one ended. Still, as the men took their places for the first contest, she couldn't restrain a flicker of disappointment. The barbarian, Balian, had seemed genuinely interested in her, not just her dowry. He, alone, had seemed different--clever as well as strong and capable as a warrior.

It was a shame she would see no more of him after today.

The first competition was the joust. This would eliminate the pure amateurs from the serious contests, which would become progressively more difficult and require more strength, stamina and skill as time wore on. In the center of the field, a half wall had been moved into place. The wall, breast high to the horses, would prevent the contestants from crossing into their competitor's path. Along the length, hazards had been placed to simulate field battle conditions which would have natural obstacles that the warrior and his mount would have to overcome.

Her champion was given the position nearest the royal box. She watched as the barbarian took up his position on the opposite end, accepting the lance and shield that were handed to him and moving them into position. Nkunda, she saw, when she finally glanced his way, had already received his lance and shield and had twisted on his saddle to give her a salute. Knowing it was expected of her, she pasted an insincere smile on her lips.

The master of the tournament gave the signal. Abruptly, Nkunda dug his spurs into his mount's sides and his horse lurched forward. Balian could have taken advantage of Nkunda's inattentiveness and gained ground and speed. Instead, to everyone's surprise, he waited until Nkunda had launched his attack before he spurred his own horse forward.

Down the length of the field they raced toward one another, gaining speed despite the obstacles the horses were forced to avoid, each man striving to reach a point of advantage--a straight away--at the crucial moment of impact. Despite Nkunda's delayed reaction to the signal to start, he reached the point of advantage first.

Chapter Three

Kisah found that she was gripping the arms of her chair tightly, holding her breath as she waited for the sound of clashing lances. She gasped as the blunted tip of Nkunda's caught the upper edge of Balian's shield. It slipped upward with the force of Balian's own impetus. A sigh of relief escaped her as the tip of Nkunda's lance slipped free, passing over Balian's shoulder. Both men rocked backward in their saddles as the lances caught them, Balian's shattering on impact.

After a moment, they recovered their balance, brought their horses around and returned to the starting position. Fresh lances were brought out and, again, the men were given the signal to attack. Kisah slid forward in her seat, watching as the two horses thundered down the field in a second pass. This time, Balian had the advantage. Nkunda's lance failed to find a mark. Balian caught him fully in the center of his shield, pitching him backwards from his horse.

The crowd roared their approval as Balian brought his horse to a rearing stop. They fell silent in surprise when he leapt from his horse and strode purposefully toward Nkunda, who was still lying stunned on the field. Placing one booted foot in the center of the fallen man's chest, Balian snatched Kisah's favor from the man's arm, and held it up triumphantly. For several moments, everyone merely gaped at him in disbelief, for the lady had bestowed her favor. Never had a warrior had the audacity to conqueror it. After a moment a roar of laughter and approval erupted from the crowd.

Kisah blushed with a mixture of annoyance and embarrassment when he threw her a roguish grin and climbed onto his horse once more, trotting the horse around the perimeter of the field. She was still gaping at him when he passed beneath the royal box.

He winked at her.

Kisah could not believe his audacity, could not even think of how she should react to such a thing. Chuckling, he turned his horse and waited while Nkunda was helped from the field and a new contestant rode out to meet him.

The day passed in much the same manner, though Balian did not give up his position as her champion. Occasionally, a man would manage to remain seated through two passes, but none made it through the third and final pass and there were far more who were unseated in the first pass.

The crowd was mad for him. Each time the signal was given to begin a new match, they would stamp their feet, clap their hands and begin chanting his name. Each time he won a match and rode the perimeter of the field they would leap to their feet, screaming wildly, the ladies tossing their own tokens at him.

Kisah was torn between rising alarm, annoyance, admiration and a strange, suffocating weakness that overcame her each time he passed beneath her box and threw her a smiling glance. When, at last, the day's events were declared at an end, she sprang to her feet, desperate to remove herself from the watchful eye of the public. She was the princess, however, and, ever aware of her position, she knew she could not simply dash from the box and rush to her room to hide. Pomp and ceremony were expected of the royals. To disappoint the crowd was unthinkable.

Stiffly, she moved to the front of the box, pasted a smile on her lips and, for the benefit of the crowd, blew her champion a kiss.

He stunned her once more. Leaping from his horse, he sprang over the low wall, landing beside her. She was still gaping at him in stunned surprise when he seized her shoulders, almost jerking her from her feet as he pulled her against his hard chest, bent his head and covered her mouth and kissed her thoroughly before she could even recover sufficiently from her shock to protest. The crowd went mad, but Kisah was barely aware of the screaming mob. She was too caught up in the feel of the rock solid body pressed so tightly against her, and the heat of his mouth as he explored her own with a thoroughness no one else had ever dared.

He smelled of battle and horseflesh, but the intoxicating taste of his tongue overrode all else, suffocating her senses until she aware only of the roughened slide moving in and out of her mouth. Prickles of heat burst along her nerves, surging through her veins with the potency of heavy wine. His touch felt like a summer storm, thrilling as lightning, frightening as thunder.

When he released her at last, her knees were so weak she swayed. The crowd roared their approval at Balian's prowess as both lover and warrior, and Kisah felt a rush of heat to her cheeks. It took an effort to smile for the benefit of the crowd.

She glanced at her father a little helplessly and saw that he was looking Balian over speculatively. He rose from his seat, held his arms up for silence. Slowly, the crowd complied.

"Well done, Balian of....?"

Balian merely bowed without volunteering his origins.

The king's eyes narrowed, but after a moment he went on, glancing around at the crowd. "We will all wait anxiously to see how well Princess Kisah's champion performs on the morrow. In the meanwhile," he returned his attention to Balian, "I hope you will do us the honor of joining us at table tonight for the feasting."

Smiling his acceptance, Balian bowed again.

Kisah excused herself, summoned her ladies and departed. She found by the time she reached her apartments, that she had a headache. Her ladies chattered excitedly and unceasingly about the barbarian, Balian, all the way there, giggling while they exchanged ribald comments about the length of his loin cloth and their curiosity as to what he might be wearing beneath it. One swore it was nothing at all, that she'd gotten a peek at the serpent that dwelt there.

Kisah gave her a look and the girl retreated into silence. When they reached her apartments, she dismissed them, saying she would rest for a while before she needed their help in preparing for the feast.

The maids exchanged uneasy glances, for they knew very well that the princess was expected to make an appearance in the great hall in short order, but they didn't dare argue. Instead, they closed the doors to her bed chamber and left her in peace, tiptoeing around the day room while they prepared for her bath and laid out a selection of clothing for her to choose from.

Kisah rose from the bed the moment they had gone and began pacing, her nerves taut, her thoughts chaotic, her emotions vying with one another for dominance. She was furious at the man's outrageous behavior. She could still taste the wildness of him on her tongue, still feel the hard press of his muscles against her chest. Her knees went weak just thinking of how thoroughly he'd kissed her, how much he'd embarrassed her before the crowd.

How dare he manhandle *her*, Princess Kisah, like a common woman before their subjects? His boldness knew no bounds. Granted, she could not help but admire the way he had handled himself in the tournament. She had dismissed him as a country bumpkin, easily routed after their brief encounter on the way to the games. He had surprised her with his skill, his speed, his strength. Almost as surprising, he had come through the entire trial without so much as a scratch or even a bruise.

Despite her reservations over the entire tournament, and the objective of it, she had found herself enjoying watching him as he vanquished foe after foe, eliminating almost half the contenders on the first day of the tournament.

That had become a sticking point, however, as it dawned upon her that he was systematically eliminating the competition, that her choices were narrowing far more quickly than she had anticipated, when she had not even had the chance to observe the men vying for her hand or to decide which man among them would be the least threat to her freedom.

Plainly, Balian was determined that he would win her. Just as clearly, she saw now that his chances of doing so were far greater than she had anticipated.

She couldn't decide how she felt about that. On the surface, he seemed to have a surprisingly sweet nature for a warrior, and infinite patience. He was not, unfortunately, stupid, though his easygoing nature might lead others to that mistaken conclusion.

He would not be easy to manipulate, she realized. He might, willingly, concede to her wishes, but she doubted very much that she would be able to trick him into doing anything that he was unwilling to do.

He was not, she was certain, a man whom she could rule. That made him dangerous, and undesirable, to her way of thinking, as a husband.

The word 'undesirable' had no sooner popped into her mind, however, before she remembered his kiss yet again and a raw flush of heat suffused her. He was certainly not unappealing in a physical sense. It would be no great sacrifice to perform her duties as his wife, but there, too, she found a flaw. She did not at all care for the way her body had responded so readily, and excessively, to his touch. It boded ill for her should she find herself in the position of having to try to exert control over him by way of sexual favors. She could not be certain that she would not be as much a slave to desire for him as he was to her.

Unbidden, the thought leapt into her mind to wonder if it would even be possible for her to enslave him with the pleasures of the flesh without finding herself in the same position.

Chapter Four

The feasting and festivities were well underway by the time Kisah arrived in the hall. Her father favored her with a disapproving glare as she took her seat.

"You are late, daughter. Is this the impression you wish to give our subjects? That you are too spoiled and lazy to consider anyone but yourself?"

Kisah flushed. "I beg pardon, father. I had a throbbing in my head that would give me no peace and had lain down in the hope that it would pass. I must have been weary, for I fell asleep."

Her father looked her up and down frowningly. "You are a woman. Allowances can be made for a certain amount of weakness, but I would not like for our people to begin to think that you were not robust, for then doubts might arise as to whether or not you were capable of producing a strong son and heir."

Resentment swelled in Kisah's breast, but she bowed her head respectfully. "I am certain I will not fail the people in my duty, father."

Despite her discomfort, or perhaps because of it, she could not help but glance at Balian in the hope that he had not heard her father's comments. As her champion, and the winner of the day, he had been seated to her father's left, one seat down from her own.

To her surprise and dismay, he met her gaze. His expression was carefully guarded, but there was that in his gaze that gave her to know that he had heard all. It was not condemnation, or sympathy ... but understanding, desire, and strangely, sadness.

The sadness surprised her, but, thinking back, she realized that each time she had looked deeply into his eyes she had seen it, lurking always in the background, even when he smiled.

She looked away, troubled by the observation, wondering if she had imagined it, wondering what terrible thing must lie in his past that he would carry such deep sadness with him like a well worn cloak, a thing so familiar that he was scarcely even aware of it any longer.

More troubling was the realization that it touched

something inside of her that she could not discard or ignore.

"You have traveled far to take part in the tournament?" she asked politely.

He shrugged. "Nay. Not far."

Kisah frowned. She had only intended to make polite conversation. It seemed odd that someone who appeared so open should be so evasive in answering such a simple question. She lifted her brows questioningly, but he merely smiled and returned his attention to his food.

"It is fair, the land you hail from?" she prodded.

He frowned, slid a glance sideways at her and finally a faint smile dawned. "You must tell me when you see it."

Kisah felt her jaw sag. Irritation surfaced. "You are so certain that I will?" she asked primly.

His smile widened into a grin. "Yes," he said, and returned his attention to his food.

Kisah glared at his profile for several moments. "Confidence is a trait to be admired, but cockiness so often spells disaster."

He chuckled.

The man had a hide like ten year old tanned leather.

"What have I done, I wonder, to earn the sharp edge of your tongue?"

Kisah glared at him. Before she could speak, however, her father spoke. "She has the tongue of an asp. Take care, barbarian, she can wither your manhood with it, or shred your hide to ribbons."

Kisah blushed. He'd spoken in a chastising manner as he so often did, but there was a note of pride in his voice, as well. Moreover, Kisah prided herself both on her intellect and her ability to smite with her words those she could not physically overcome. Still, for some unfathomable reason, she didn't particularly care to be cast in the mold of a shrew. "I am not so ill tempered as to use it against the unworthy," she responded a little stiffly.

"Then I take it as a compliment that you consider me a worthy adversary," Balian said with amusement, and then lower, for her ears alone. "I confess, I am anxious to discover what other uses you might have for your clever tongue."

Kisah's jaw dropped as she gasped in outrage.

"There is a problem?"

Kisah whirled to look at her father when he spoke, his words soft with threat. "Uh ... it was only that I suddenly recalled something I had forgotten--nothing of any importance." She slid a narrow eyed glare at Balian, fuming inwardly. She knew very well that he had not misunderstood her comment, knew she'd meant 'undeserving' not 'capable' when she'd said unworthy, but he had twisted her words, again, to wring a compliment for himself from it. The blatant sexual innuendo of his other remark was even more infuriating. She could not address it at all without making it clear she knew what he was suggesting.

It made it worse that she was not offended--as she should have been--so much as stunned that he would risk making such a remark to her when he sat no more than a few feet from her father, who could have him executed on a whim. Was he foolhardy? Or just that fearless?

She glanced at him assessingly. "In kindness, I feel I should warn you that it is not at all wise to provoke my father," she said quietly. "You are a stranger here or you would know that."

He glanced from her to her father, but he seemed more pleased than alarmed. "Strong, beautiful, clever and kind-- you are indeed a rare jewel."

Kisah blushed fiercely, torn between annoyance, amusement and pleasure. "I am a princess. If I were a drooling idiot with a squint and hunch back, I would still be considered a rare jewel of great beauty," she responded tartly. "Somehow, I had expected more sincerity from you. You do not strike me as a court fop."

He looked troubled. "I swear upon the graves of all I held dear that I am absolutely sincere."

"Then you are either blind, deaf and amazingly dull or laboring under the impression that I am. I am clever enough not to be taken for a fool, but I am not beautiful by anyone's standards and I have never been accused of being kind."

"It is often said that love can produce that effect upon one, but, perhaps, it is not so much that I am, blind, deaf and dull as it is that I see you and not the position you occupy?"

Kisah frowned. "This is most unkind of you," she responded with a touch of humor. "To profess love on so short an acquaintance makes it impossible for me to enjoy your compliments as an honest observation."

"You do not believe in love at first sight?"

Kisah threw him a laughing glance. "I insulted you and your were instantly smitten?"

He chuckled, but sobered almost at once. "The moment I saw you."

The words sent a shiver of warmth and pleasure through her, but touched off a shock wave of warning, as well. Somehow, the way he said it brought to mind her night visitor. He was certainly bold enough to have done such a thing, but her night visitor had seemed far more dangerous- -let alone, and despite the skill he had displayed on the field today, she could not think a man of his size would have been able to scale the wall and enter her room so swiftly and quietly. Then, too, her night visitor had spoken of magic--wielded it--and this man did not strike her as possessing the abilities of a wizard.

She shook the suspicion off, dismissing her pleasure as well. Even if she were inclined to favor him above the others--and she wasn't certain that she was--only his skill as a warrior would determine who won her 'heart' and hand.

"Unfortunately, you waste your time in wooing me," she said coolly. "The contests will determine who wins my hand in marriage."

He shrugged. "Why would I deprive myself of the pleasure of wooing you when the outcome is as certain as the fact that the sun will rise on the morrow?"

She didn't know whether to laugh or be outraged at his remark. "It is certain you do not suffer from self doubt."

"No."

Her eyes narrowed as her suspicions rose once more. "Skill, not magic, will determine the outcome."

"You doubt my skill?"

That was not the response she had been angling for, but she wasn't really surprised. She hadn't truly believed he possessed magic, or that he would admit it if he did, but it had seemed worth a try to see if she could prod him into admitting, or disclaiming, sorcery. "It matters not, what I think. That is the point."

"It matters to me."

"Unlike you, I can not presume to judge on so short an acquaintance." She was relieved when their conversation was interrupted by the servants clearing away the remains of the feast. At her father's signal, the entertainment began and she did her best to focus on the succession of dancers, tumblers and singers, biding her time until she could retire, for she found she had developed the head ache she had claimed earlier. As much as she enjoyed the banter between Balian and herself--and she was surprised to discover that she had--it only brought home more forcefully the unpalatable situation her father had put her in.

Looking about the room at the revelers, she studied the men who had come to vie for her hand, wondering which of those present would claim her. Not one among them, save, perhaps, Balian, looked the noble warrior this night. Most were more than half drunk before they had even finished feasting. Many were already slumbering with their heads on the tables before them, or stumbling about the room groping any maid who happened to pass within reach.

Revulsion filled her as she imagined their callused hands pawing at her, their soured breath in her face. She had never regretted that she had been born a woman, instead of the son her father desired and needed, quite as much before as she did now.

When the hall at last reached a crescendo of drunken revelry, she excused herself and rose, making her way from the room. She had reached the winding stairs and just released a sigh of relief when she was seized roughly from behind and slammed against the stone wall hard enough that she bit her tongue. The taste of blood filled her mouth, but the pain in her head far surpassed that discomfort. Dazed, she was only half aware of the rough hand that found its way up her skirt.

As abruptly as she had been seized, she was released.

Turning, she watched in stunned surprise as Balian slammed Nkunda against the wall hard enough that it shook loose mortar from the crevices where the stones were joined. With one hand around Nkunda's throat, Balian shoved him against the wall until he had lifted the man clear of the floor.

Chapter Five

"Did he hurt you?"

It was several moments before Kisah realized that Balian had turned to look at her, that he'd spoken to her. Gone was the smiling, amazingly even-tempered courtier. In his place was a cold stranger who seemed unnervingly dangerous. She looked from Balian to Nkunda, whose face was the color of ripe cherries, his eyeballs bulging. "No," she finally managed to say, still too stunned by the swiftness of Balian's attack to come to grips with what had happened.

Balian's eyes narrowed as he returned his attention to Nkunda. "You are fortunate, dog. Tonight I will allow you to live."

Kisah glanced from one man to the other, feeling alarm slowly seeping into her. "He won't if you do not loosen your grip upon his throat."

Balian turned to look at her for a long moment and finally allowed the man to slide down the wall until his feet were touching the floor. With an effort, it seemed, he loosened his grip on Nkunda's throat. "I should kill him anyway for daring to touch you."

Kisah was torn between pleasure at his misguided protection and irritation that he seemed to believe he had the right to assume such a role. Gripping her skirts, she moved around the two men. "You presume too much. It is not your place to act as my protector. I could have summoned the guard if I had felt the need."

The thud of a body hitting the floor was the first indication Kisah had that Balian had abandoned Nkunda. Assuming he had returned to the festivities, she continued without a pause up the stairs. She was half way to the top when she was abruptly seized for the second time that night. Instead of being shoved into the stone wall, however, she was whirled and brought forcefully against a chest that felt nearly as unyielding. Off balance, she could do nothing but lean against him, gaping up at him in surprise. "You did not feel the need?" he asked through gritted teeth.

Kisah gulped. "What?" she asked stupidly.

"His attention was welcome?"

Her jaw dropped, but anger surfaced. "You have no right to ask that!"

His eyes narrowed. "Aye. I do. You are mine and I will allow no other to touch you."

His audacity knew no bounds. Before she could think of a suitable retort, he lowered his head and covered her mouth with his own. His kiss was hard, angry, possessive, his mouth hot with dark desire and forbidden pleasure. The taste of his tongue as it raked possessively along her own, the scent that was his alone, flooded her senses with the headiness of strong wine. Waves of heated pleasure surged through her veins.

He cupped her buttocks and pulled her flush against him, until sudden hardness nestled in the crux of her thighs. A groan rumbled in his chest and he thrust against her, hard, rough, pushing her back against the stone wall until he trapped her.

Kisah gasped into his mouth as he ground against her, his tongue thrusting in her mouth with near uncontrollable appetite. Wetness pooled between her thighs, blood rushing to pound like a frightened heartbeat in her clit.

The strangeness of some force beyond her ken swallowed her in its maw, depriving her of the will to resist. Magic, her mind warned her as she felt herself split into two, the one outraged by his boldness, the other curious, pleased at his mastery, encouraged by the pleasure his embrace promised her to yield completely.

Before she could gather her wits to protest his brazen assault, he released her as abruptly as he had seized her. He breathed heavily, watching her with a black gaze brimming with rough sensuality. His hands clenched into fists, and there was about him an air of barely checked passion that terrified her as much as intrigued. "Know this, Princess Kisah--you are mine."

He released her as abruptly as he'd grabbed her, leaving her feeling strangely weak.

Kisah was shaking when she reached her room--and thoroughly confused. It was madness to find pleasure in the man's arms, in his kisses, in his demands. Her destiny was in fate's hands. It was not her decision to make--and certainly not Balian's. The tournament would decide who was to be her mate.

It was disturbing to realize that the desire he had awakened within her gripped her still, disordered her thoughts, ached between her thighs. Of all the men who had come to vie for her hand, Balian was, perhaps, the most dangerous. It was foolhardy to consider even for a moment that she would have any control over such a man as he.

* * * *

Rest and composure had eluded her. Sleep had been slow to claim her and her night had been filled with dreams so real that she had awakened over and over, certain that she was not alone, that the lover who haunted her dreams with his tempting caresses lingered beside her still. A dull throbbing behind her eyes threatened to become a full blown headache by the time she had broke her fast and dressed to greet the day.

It took an effort to smile and pretend nothing had changed, in her, or in her world as she took her seat in the royal box. Fortunately, the excesses of the night before had not left anyone with keen senses.

The second day of the tournament was to be the turning point. The jousting the day before had eliminated more than half the lists and today only warriors of merit would do battle in single combat. The objective was not to deplete their warriors, and so the contest was not to the death. Rather, the men were to fight until they disarmed their opponent, or reached the point where a death blow could be dealt. The field had been divided into squares, a pair in each. Slowly, as the sun crawled toward its zenith, men fell one by one and were eliminated.

The men chosen to begin were given no respite, for the contest was to prove prowess, strength and stamina. Only those waiting on the sidelines for their chance in the competition arrived fresh.

Balian was among the first to be chosen to compete. Kisah did her best to ignore him, trying to concentrate on those contests nearest the box where she sat, but she found her gaze wandering to him over and over as the day progressed, found herself sitting stiffly erect, her fingers gripping the arms of her chair each time he stumbled or fell.

The servants brought refreshments, but Kisah found she

was in too much turmoil to eat more than a bite or two. Despite the decree that none were to me slain, a half dozen or more were mortally wounded, and none were unscathed. Even Balian, who seemed to wade tirelessly through one match after another, was smeared with blood from a dozen small wounds and she found herself, quite against her will, watching for any sign of weakness.

By mid-afternoon, the lists had been cut down, almost literally, to a dozen men. With relief, Kisah watched as her father rose and signaled an end to the day's competition. The crowd roared their approval as the twelve men stepped back and raised their swords above their heads in triumph. Kisah didn't know whether to be relieved or sorry that Balian was one of the twelve. Rising stiffly, she took her place beside her father and forced a smile of approval, waved, and then turned away with relief to make her way to her apartments to rest until the banquet.

To her surprise, she rested. She was so tense that she had expected to find herself as wakeful as she had been the night before, but once she had undressed and bathed, she lay down on her bed and was almost instantly asleep.

Conscious of her father's displeasure with her the night before, she made it a point to arrive on time. Smiling his approval, he waved her to her seat. She discovered herself surrounded by the warriors of the day. Balian, to her relief, and his obvious displeasure, had been seated far down the table from her on the opposite side, rather than beside her as he had been the night before.

He rarely took his gaze from her, even to eat, and she quickly discovered that she had been far more comfortable when he had sat beside her the night before, for his watchfulness was unsettling. She knew it was expected of her to behave graciously toward the warriors seated around her. Good manners compelled it, and yet she could not bring herself to flirt, as she had fully intended, to pit the men against each other, to draw them out to discover which among them seemed most promising as a future husband.

Nkunda, seated at her right, was at his most provoking, proving that he was even more stupid that she'd surmised, stroking her hand or touching her at every opportunity and then sending a triumphant smile in Balian's direction.

She should be glad. Of all those present, Nkunda had

seemed most likely to succeed--at least until Balian had arrived. Now, she wasn't nearly as certain. Of the two, however, she rather thought Nkunda most nearly matched the qualities she had been looking for. He was a fierce warrior, too dull-witted to be a ruler and fairly easily manipulated. If he won, he would be gone more than he was with her, for he was the perfect Wyvern warrior, far more interested in fighting than anything else and she would be free to rule when her time came to ascend her father's throne, unencumbered by his unwanted attentions except upon rare occasions.

Balian's assault upon him the night before had pricked his manhood. He had fought fiercely throughout the day, dispatching his competition quickly and viciously in each match, mortally wounding three men and killing two others outright.

He should have been disqualified on those grounds alone. Instead, her father had seemed pleased at his ferocity.

It seemed probable that the competition between Balian and Nkunda was destined to be a death match. It disturbed her to realize it, and disordered her mind that she should care one way or the other. The fact remained that she did, however, and, that being the case, she did not want to encourage the animosity already brewing between them by seeming to favor one above the other.

Nkunda was either immune to her attempts to discourage him, however, or more likely, completely oblivious to everything beyond taunting his rival.

Kisah found that she was looking forward to the final day of the tournament with far more dread than she had expected. On the morrow, her fate would be decided. On the morrow, one man would die.

Chapter Six

Her father seemed as bent upon provoking a deadly rivalry as Kisah was in preventing it. Once the food was cleared away, he summoned musicians and leaned close so that none would hear save Kisah. "It is time to remind your suitors that you are the greatest of the gifts that will be bestowed upon the winner. You must choose a dance partner."

Kisah glanced at her father, but kept her expression carefully neutral. It was an order, not a request, she knew. Nodding, she rose, taking care not to glance at either Nkunda or Balian, she smiled at the warrior seated directly across from her. "Sir, I find I have a wish to dance tonight."

The man, she could not seem to summon a name to place with his face, leapt to his feet immediately. "Princess! Would you do me the honor?"

She smiled a little more comfortably, feeling for the first time in a long while, more like her old self. "Thank you. I'd be delighted."

It took no more than a few moments once they'd reached the dance floor for her to realize the man was no courtier, for he could not carry on a conversation and mind his steps at the same time. Each time she distracted him by trying to draw him into conversation, he trod upon her foot or her gown. It was a relief when the dance ended.

She quickly found that her relief was premature, however. The dance had no more than ended when yet another of her suitors was bowing before her.

Balian, she discovered, merely watched as his rivals presented themselves one by one for their turn around the dance floor, and she began to feel a swell of resentment. He behaved, for all the world, as if she was indeed his already, so that she could not even relax sufficiently to flirt even a little, not that she was inclined to--but she knew very well that her father expected it of her, that he was not so interested in allowing her to get to know her suitors as he was in provoking a more fierce competition for the final test of the tournament.

It irritated her even more when she realized that she was becoming anxious as time progressed, anticipating the moment when Balian would approach her.

Nkunda, although he had seemed miffed for a time that she had chosen another to bestow her first dance upon, was not slow in approaching her. Before she had even finished her second dance, he was elbowing the others aside to reach the front of the line. For several moments, it looked as if a battle would break out among the men at the edge of the dance floor. Kisah glanced at her father, but he merely lifted his brows and looked away.

She had to rethink her previous assessment of Nkunda when he seized her without so much as asking and began to drag her about the dance floor. He was no less, nor any more, graceful than the others. Moreover, he was determined to hold her far too close for decorum, try though Kisah might to force some distance between them. The battle of wills distracted her, at last, from her preoccupation with Balian, but she found very shortly that that was not necessarily a good thing, for she was not prepared when Balian abruptly appeared beside them.

Nkunda stopped abruptly, glaring at him balefully. "My turn, dog! Take yourself off."

Balian's eyes narrowed. His expression, if possible, became more stony. "Not without my leave."

Nkunda gaped at him for a moment before his face darkened with rage. "Yours? That blow to the head today has rattled your brains. The princess is all but mine now."

Balian leaned forward until he was looking directly into Nkunda's eyes. "Go. Now. Or I will not wait till the morrow to rip your heart from your chest."

Nkunda blinked. Abruptly, a vacuous look descended over his features and he turned away. Moving unsteadily toward the table, he sat, lowered his head to his arms and began snoring.

Smiling, Balian bowed and offered his hand. In a daze of confusion, Kisah held her hand out. Slipping his arm about her waist, Balian whirled her about the dance floor as the musicians struck up once more, almost frantic now that it seemed the offer of violence in their midst had passed.

"You ensorcelled him," Kisah said accusingly.

Balian shrugged. "I did not think that you would care for a violent confrontation, and I did not wish to do anything that might result in injury to you."

Kisah gaped at him. "You don't deny it?"

"I do not admit it."

"It was you," Kisah gasped.

He looked at her questioningly.

"You stole into my room the other night. You placed some sort of spell upon me!"

Balian chuckled. "Have I?"

"What?"

"Placed a spell upon you, beloved?"

Kisah's eyes narrowed. "You will not distract me with sweet words! You did not answer my question."

"You asked a question?"

"You came into my room. You placed a spell upon me."

"I never like to argue with a lady, but that is not a question."

Kisah ground her teeth in annoyance. "Did you place a spell upon me? Is that why I feel so strangely? Is that why I have dreamed such ... unusual dreams?"

A slow smile curled his lips. A gleam entered his eyes that was part desire, part triumph. "Do you feel strangely, my love? Tell me, what have you dreamed."

Kisah found that she was blushing profusely. "You must know, for you put them there!" she said tightly.

"Alas, not by some magical spell, for I would have enjoyed them myself, I think."

She would certainly not tell him that he was the lover who haunted her dreams. "It is forbidden to use sorcery in the competition."

His brows rose. "I've no need of sorcery to best the bumbling morons that have pitted themselves against me. As you see, I am unscathed."

Briefly, surprise filled her and she spoke without consideration. "But ... you were wounded. I saw...."

A pleased smile dawned. "You watched me then? I confess, I had been positioned so far back upon the field that I had thought my efforts went unnoticed."

The blush that had barely died, washed into her cheeks once more. "I caught a glimpse, no more," she lied irritably.

He chuckled. "You need have no fear for me, love. I have promised that you will be mine."

* * * *

As if their conversation the night before had settled into her subconscious mind, Kisah dreamed of Balian when at last sleep claimed her that night. Unlike the dreams the night before, where she had only believed in her mind that the shadowy lover was Balian, she saw and felt and heard him as potently as if he lay with her, stroking her body and kissing her until her body was alive with sensations she had never felt before, never imagined, and she moved restlessly, begging him with sighs and moans of pleasure to cease tormenting her and give her surcease.

She was bare but could not remember disrobing. Her skin tingled as though stroked with lightning, prickling fine hairs along her body. Silken sheets slid over her skin like rose petals, as warm as soft lips. They caught on her breasts, pulled tight against the peaks, drawing over her. Hands joined them, their callused palms cupping the curves of her body, smoothing across her nipples until they hardened painfully, pleasurably.

Kisah arched her back, pushing toward him, wanting, needing to feel more, hovering on the edges of consciousness, in a drowsy state of arousal. She wanted to open her eyes, know if it was real or not, but a longing engulfed her, spread through her belly, making her fear to dispel it if it was indeed just a dream. Her cleft spasmed with achy need, growing wet with desire, until it dampened her thighs. She clutched at the bed sheets, needing something to hold on to, wanting to touch him, but afraid.

Palms skittered down the line of her belly, lower, on her hips. She gasped in surprise, jerking as his thumbs skimmed her bare cleft and moved to push her thighs gently apart.

Fingers nudged her nether lips apart, smoothing the cream of her arousal up around her clit. She moaned and jerked on the bed, tried to hold still.

Hair roughened thighs grazed her own, abrasive against the soft flesh of her inner thighs. She felt his heat, felt his fingers stroke her clit, rounding the nub with deliberate strokes. A foreign hardness suddenly pushed against the opening of her core, burning like fire, searing her nerves. Her eyes flew open on a strangled gasp.

She was alone.

Chapter Seven

The tension that had gripped Kisah from the moment she arose tightened as she reached the box and took her place beside her father. The last of six poles were being erected. Once it was secured, heavy chains were brought out and lain out at the foot of each. A peg, bent to form a horse shoe shape, was driven into the ground at the foot of each pole that grounded the chain while still allowing it to slide back and forth.

The objective was to reach the top of the pole and retrieve the pennant there. There was only one way to do so, however. The contestants must shift and fly to the top. The only way they would be able to reach the top, given the length of the chain and the peg, was to immobilize their opponent.

There had been a time, according to legend, when the Wyvern had been capable of shifting into great birds and they had become rulers of the skies, but that had been long ago and the ability had been lost. Now, although most were still capable of shifting wings, their ability to fly was extremely limited. The contest was designed to prove they had that trait to pass to their offspring.

Once the preparations were completed, the contestants began to file out onto the field, pairing off according to their positions attained during the contests on the preceding days of the tournament. As Balian walked onto the field, the people crowding the stands leapt to their feet and began to chant his name. Kisah's heart seemed to hammer in her chest in time to their praise. As he reached the pole that had been designated, he halted, holding up his arm to show that he wore her favor still.

The chant disintegrated into screaming, clapping, stamping feet and whistles of approval before it slowly began to peter out as the servants came forward and fastened the heavy manacles at each end of the chain to the two combatants facing off.

When all had been secured, the warriors turned to face the royal box, saluted with their swords and shifted.

Kisah's heart seemed to stop in her chest. She was scarcely aware of the collective gasp of shock that went through crowd, but her gaze was turned upon Balian just as all eyes had been.

He had shifted wings, but they were unlike anything anyone had ever seen. Instead of the beautifully feathered, elegant wings all were familiar with, Balian's were dark, leathery. Spines ran the length of the wings, sprouting sharp talons at the tips of each.

Kisah could only stare at him in dismay, a sense of foreboding slowly swelling inside of her. Finally, she turned to look at her father. His face was chalk white, his expression a mixture of terror and rage that she found incomprehensible. A deadly silence fell over the amphitheater. Almost in slow motion, he rose from his seat and moved to the front of the box. For long, agonizing moments, he simply stood there, staring down at Balian. Finally, to Kisah's relief, he gave the signal that the games were to begin.

Kisah gripped the arms of her chair in white knuckled fists as the heavy clang of metal against metal echoed through the unnatural silence of the theater. Balian seemed unperturbed by it, focusing his attention completely upon the battle at hand. Within moments, he had disarmed his opponent. For several moments, everyone watched the two men, waiting to see if Balian would strike the unarmed man. Abruptly, he launched himself into the air, ascended to the top of the pole and snatched the pendant from its perch. Everyone simply stared as he circled the pole, holding the pendant triumphantly, unable to take their eyes from the wings that spread and flapped above him. Belatedly, a half hearted cheer went up, swelling slowly through the crowd.

There was an air of slowly growing hysteria, however, that was nothing like the thrill of blood lust that had gripped everyone before. Sensing it, Kisah glanced around at the people, seeing the fear written on their faces despite their efforts to retain the gaiety of before.

The captain of the guard approached her father at a signal from him and bent low as her father spoke quietly to him. Nodding, he stood at attention, saluted her father and left the box.

A cold fear swept through Kisah. She felt as if a band were tightening around her chest, making it difficult to breathe, squeezing her heart so that it thudded painfully against her chest wall.

Returning her attention to the field, she saw that, one by one, the combatants had subdued their opponents and retrieved the pennant atop the poles, eliminating six of the remaining twelve.

A roar of half hearted approval went up from the crowd as the winners held up their swords for acknowledgment. Long moments passed, and everyone had begun to look at each other curiously, but finally the servants came forward and unlocked the manacles. Those defeated walked, or were carried from the field. The six remaining were pitted against each other, their manacles replaced. At her father's signal, the combatants clashed.

Kisah was scarcely aware of the battles being waged between the men, however. Movement at the edge of the field had caught her eye. As she watched, soldiers began to enter the field through the gates, lining up on either side of the field.

She glanced at her father, but his gaze was focused on the fighting men, his expression unreadable. The people crowding the stands began to fall silent as they, too, watched the soldiers line up in battle formation on either side of the field. Pages began running from the gates, each loaded down with shields. Kisah frowned, watching curiously as they scurried down the line of soldiers, handing out the shields they carried, but she was more puzzled, not less so. The shields looked nothing like those the soldiers usually carried. These were nearly as high as the men themselves, and as broad, covered by some strange material she was unfamiliar with.

Again, she glanced at her father, but she could tell nothing from his expression.

He stood abruptly. In the field below, the combatants, increasingly aware of the activity around them, had ceased to fight.

"Leave, daughter. It is not safe for you here."

Kisah leapt to her feet. "What is it? What's wrong?"

He turned to glare at her. "Do as you're told!"

Kisah gaped at him, stunned, but finally signaled for her women to move toward the exit at the back of the box. Shooing them ahead of her, she, too, moved toward the back, but she did not leave. Instead, as her father moved toward the front of the box, she slipped surreptitiously closer.

Lifting his hand, he pointed straight at Balian. "Seize him! He is a dragon!"

Kisah turned to look at Balian in horror as the soldiers, holding their shields before them, rushed upon him. He made no attempt to defend himself. He made no attempt to escape. He merely dropped his sword and waited, his gaze on her as he disappeared beneath the wall of soldiers.

Chapter Eight

Shock permeated every part of Kisah, cutting her off from emotion, corrupting her thoughts as she paced her room. Balian had been taken to the dungeon. Tomorrow, he was to be executed as an enemy of the people.

She shuddered at that thought, trying to shield herself from the horrible visions that swarmed through her mind. They would not give him a quick, clean death. His torture and execution would be a public display and they would draw his execution out as long as possible for the entertainment of the crowd---the same people who had showered him with honor with each battle he had fought and won would be there to enjoy his execution.

Revulsion filled her.

She hated them, all of them, she realized with a jolt of surprise. He was not Wyvern--he might well be dragon, as her father claimed, though she could scarcely believe it when she had been told her whole life that the race of dragons had been wiped from the face of their world. He had not come to them as an enemy, however. He had done nothing to deserve what her father had planned for him.

Why had he done nothing to defend himself? Why had he not tried to escape? The dragon of legend had possessed unimaginable magic. They had been a fierce, mighty beast people. The Wyvern had only triumphed over them through trickery, overcome their magic with the aid of the most powerful wizard of all time and slain them as they slept beneath the wizard's spell. Surely, if Balian was any of those things he could have saved himself?

Just as importantly, why would he have come at all to the land of his enemy ... alone?

Fear stabbed through her at that thought, but she

dismissed it. He must have come alone. If others had been with him, they surely would have revealed themselves when Balian was captured.

It was ludicrous, she finally decided. Despite the strange wings, no dragon had been sighted in her lifetime, nor for many lifetimes before her. Even if it were remotely possible that he was dragon, of what threat was he to the Wyvern? If there were enough of the dragon people left to be a threat, they would have known it long since.

Moving to the window, she stared out into the night. The sun had set long since. How long until he would die? She wondered. How many hours of peace would he be granted before they began to drain the life from him, bit by bit, stripping his flesh from his bones inch by inch?

She felt ill at the thought and it occurred to her that she simply could not stand by and do nothing. Indecision assailed her almost immediately. Her thoughts were treasonous. Princess or not, she would very likely take his place on the executioner's block if she helped him to escape.

She shook the thought off. If she was clever enough, no one would discover her treachery.

Turning away from the window, she began pacing once more, formulating and discarding plans. Her chatelaine would gain her access to the dungeon, but only the dungeon master held the keys to the cells, and Balian would almost certainly be locked in a cell as well as manacled considering their fear of him.

She would have to have some sort of distraction, she saw. She might also have to try to pick the locks she had no key for--unless she could get her hands on the dungeon master's keys.

She decided she could not count on getting the keys. She would have to take something she could use to pick the locks.... And what then? Assuming they had not beaten and tortured him already to the point where he could walk out--how?

She suspected he had some ability, but she was not certain. There was only one way in or out of the dungeon. If he could not use magic, he would have to fight his way past the guards. Once past them, she could lead him out through the servants' passages. As late as it was, they would almost certainly be deeply asleep.

She stopped in the middle of her room. If, if, if---he would die while she if'd. Moving to her dressing table, she found a long hair pin and tucked it into her bodice. She had no weapon to give him beyond her eating knife. She did not dare go to the armory for anything else.

Moving into the room beyond her bed chamber, she shook Edna awake, cautioned her to silence and led her back into her own room. Edna blinked at her owlishly, looked at the darkness beyond Kisah's window, and then around the room curiously.

"I have always felt you were most loyal to me of all my ladies?" Kisah said questioningly.

Edna's eyes widened, but she nodded. "Yes, my lady."

Kisah studied her a moment. "How loyal?"

Edna looked taken aback. Again, she looked around the room, as if she was searching for some clue of Kisah's meaning. "I would give my life for you, lady."

Kisah nodded, wondering if she dared trust her life to the maid, but she had no choice, really, except to abandon Balian to her father's mercy. "I find I must see Balian ... tonight. I must know if what my father says is true."

Edna's eyes widened. "But.... if it is true, it would be dangerous for you, mistress!"

Kisah began pacing again. "I do not believe he would harm me ... but I can not let him go to his death without knowing."

Edna looked at her doubtfully. "What would you have me do, mistress?"

"Go with me. I need you to serve as a distraction so that I can have a few moments alone with him.... To speak with him."

Edna thought it over for a moment, realizing that Kisah had undoubtedly noticed that the dungeon master, Kilan, was sweet on her. She found him revolting, but she did not like to think that she might bring about his death. Finally, she nodded.

They took the back way down, the stairs and hallways designed for the servant's use. With relief, but little surprise, they met no one, though, from the sounds filtering through to them, there were still a great number of castle folk lingering in the great hall, reveling ... and still Kisah's fingers shook when they reached the dungeon till she could scarcely fit the key into the lock.

A soldier came to attention the moment the door was opened. From the look of him, he had been sleeping. "Who goes there?"

Kisah flipped the hood of her cloak back and his eyes bulged. He bowed. "Princess!"

She nodded at him. "I have come to see this man my father says is dragon."

He paled. "I have orders to allow no one to go near him, lady! It is far too dangerous. He could shift, burn you to cinders! He might use magic against you."

Kisah summoned a depreciating smile. "That is absurd! If he had those abilities, wouldn't he have used them to prevent his capture?"

The young man frowned. "I had not thought of that ... but my orders...."

Another man, obviously awakened by their voices, staggered to the entrance of the tiny cell just off the main room. "What's this?"

Edna surged forward, smiling. "My lady wishes to see the prisoner, Balian."

Kilan's chest swelled with self importance. "Alas, this can not be. No one is to see him."

Edna's smile became coaxing. "But ... surely it can not hurt only to get a peek? He is to be executed in the morning. We will never get the chance to see another dragon!"

Kilan looked torn. Finally, he glanced sharply at the guard. "You were sleeping!"

The guard paled. "Nay!"

"Indeed you were, useless dog. Sleeping so deeply you did not see anyone pass this way."

The young man gulped. "I might have gone to relieve myself and missed them."

Kilan nodded. Reaching up, he took a ring of keys from the wall and nodded for the women to follow him. Kisah frowned. She had hoped to leave Kilan and Edna in the main room, but she saw no way to manage that. Feeling as if her plans were already crumbling, she trailed along behind Edna and Kilan, trying desperately to hatch a new plot while Edna chattered gaily to Kilan.

She had no time to formulate one, for they had not gone far when they reached the tiny cell where Balian was being held. Kilan removed a torch from a sconce nearby and held it so that it illuminated the cell and Kisah surged forward.

As she had thought, he was manacled to the Traitor's Cross, an x shaped configuration of beams used to secure the most dangerous captives and designed so that it could be positioned for optimal torture, either raised completely vertical, or horizontal or any point in between. The Traitor's Cross was fully vertical and Balian hung limply from it, held in place by the wrist and ankle manacles.

Her heart sank. He could not be merely sleeping, or he would have awakened at their approach.

"Oh!" Edna gasped. "But ... this can not be the dragon, surely? He does not look dangerous at all!"

Chapter Nine

"Indeed," Kilan said. "It is the one they call dragon. For myself, I can not see it. He has been like this for hours, and if he were dragon, he would have healed himself."

"You have tested him then?" Edna asked with pretended interest.

"Aye. I tested him myself."

Edna feigned disappointment. "Well, there is not much to be seen here. Have you no more interesting prisoners?"

Kilan thought it over and finally shrugged. "I am not sure you will find any of our 'visitors' interesting, but I would be most happy to show you around."

Edna slipped her arm through his. "Would you? I have never been down here. It gives me shivers."

Kilan chuckled and patted her hand. "You've no need to fear, my dear. I would allow no harm to come to you."

Edna turned to glance at Kisah as Kilan led her away.

Kisah nodded. As soon as they had turned upon another corridor, she fished the hair pin from her bodice and began working at the lock. Fortunately, it was a simple lock, since it was not necessary for any elaborate device to prevent escape. Most prisoners were manacled to the floor inside their cell and since the cells contained nothing more than straw and a bucket to relieve themselves, they would have no means of picking the lock themselves. Moreover, the only entrance to the dungeon was inside the main keep. Even if a prisoner could escape his cell, he would have little chance of escaping the castle itself.

Dismissing the thoughts, Kisah opened the door cautiously and moved quickly inside, but, even as she did so, she wondered what the point was. Balian was in no condition to escape even if she removed his manacles. She could not carry him out. She was no weakling, but the man was easily twice her size.

She moved toward him, feeling a mixture of pity for his state, and his situation, and frustration that she could do nothing to help him. Perhaps all that she could give him was the means to a quick death.

Moving closer, she touched his cheek. He did not so much as stir.

She glanced over her shoulder, listening. She could still hear Edna, but her voice was distant now. "Awake!" she whispered fiercely. "I can not carry you from here!"

Still he did not stir and she reached for his shoulder, shaking him slightly. A sigh of frustration escaped her when he did not react and she stood indecisively for several moments. Finally, she knelt and, using her hair pin, unlocked the manacles around his ankles. She looked up at him when she had released his ankles, wondering if a good dousing of cold water would bring him around. But, perhaps he was beyond even that.

Almost absently, she stroked the bruised skin where the manacles had bound him, realizing his state alone gave the lie to her father's accusation. Even with their own limited shifting abilities, they healed quickly. If Balian was dragon, as her father claimed, he would be capable of shifting fully--and he would heal far more quickly than the Wyvern.

Slowly, she rose, tracing a soothing finger along the welts and bruises that adorned his calves and thighs. He was completely naked save for the loin cloth he always wore. She hesitated, staring at it curiously, blushing at the impulse that assailed her.

Her maids had been giggling about his wondrous manhood. She could not help but be just a little curious ...

all right, more than a little.

It could not hurt just to take a peek, to assuage her curiosity, surely? Who would know?

She could just 'accidentally' flick it back, maybe brush it with her fingers.

She had already reached for the edge of his loin cloth when he spoke. "No peeking."

Kisah jerked her fingers back as if burned, nearly jumping out of her skin.

Balian was looking directly at her and there was no sign at all that he had been anything beyond completely alert. As it dawned on her that he had been neither unconscious nor sleeping, anger replaced her shock. "You were feigning!" she snapped accusingly.

A slow smile tipped the corner of his mouth up. "I was."

Kisah gaped at him. She'd expected him to deny it. "Why?"

He shrugged. "I was enjoying it."

Rage surged through her. For several moments, she could do nothing but stammer half sentences. "I risked my life to help you escape," she hissed at him, "and you waste time...."

He looked pensive. "I did not consider it a waste of time. Besides, you were curious. I did not want to discourage you."

Kisah was tempted to box his ears. "You are *insane*! They are bent on torturing you to death come sunrise! I've a good mind to simply leave you to their tender mercies!"

"I was never at their mercy.... Only yours."

Kisah gaped at him blankly, her anger deserting her. "What?"

"I've been waiting for you to come to me."

She stared at him in confusion. How could he have been waiting when she had spent hours pacing and wondering if she even dared attempt it? A suspicion arose. "Have you placed a spell on me?"

He frowned. "I would not, even if I could. You must accept me of your free will."

Kisah plunked her hands on her hips. "Accept? You presume far too much, barbarian! I came because ... because this is unjust, not for any other reason!"

He frowned, doubt flickering across his features. In a

moment, however, the doubt vanished and determination took its place. "It is enough ... for now, that my life has value to you."

He frowned, clenching his fists and his manacles popped open.

Kisah gaped at him as he stepped away from the Traitor's Cross, rubbing his wrists. She shook herself after a moment. There was no time to waste in further argument or speculation. She could allow it to tease her mind later--that he had pretended unconsciousness when he was not, that he had allowed himself to be captured, tortured, manacled when it was obvious he could have prevented it at any time he chose.

Pulling her dagger from her belt, she held it out to him. "This is not much, I know, but I could not get weapons for you without risking capture before I could even free you. Come. I will show you a back way out of the castle. We must move quickly if you are to win your freedom."

Balian's eyebrows rose nearly to his hairline as he stared in bemusement at the tiny dagger. His lips quirked, but he refrained from smiling. Instead, he took the dagger and slipped it into the band that secured his loincloth. He caught Kisah's arm as she turned to lead him from the cell, tugging her back so that she half fell against him. Capturing her face in his palms, he leaned down and kissed her lightly on the lips. Heat went through her at his touch and for a moment, Kisah clung to him.

With an effort, she opened her eyes to look up at him when he lifted his head.

"Sleep, my princess," he murmured softly.

Chapter Ten

Kisah felt a darkness descend over her, felt herself falling, as if she were drifting into sleep. Only half conscious, she felt him lift her into his arms. She wanted to protest, but found she could not give voice to the words clamoring to free themselves from her lips. She could not fight off the strange lethargy that had fallen over her.

Dimly, alarm surfaced when they reached the outer room of the dungeon and she heard the guard shout a command to stop.

Balian murmured something and the man dropped like a stone.

In a dream like state, she was aware of Balian climbing the stairs and moving toward the main hall. "No," she managed to murmur with a great effort. "Kill you!"

Either she did not manage to say the words aloud, or he ignored her, for the doors to the great hall burst inward with a resounding clatter that drew an instant, deadly silence over the room.

For several moments, Balian merely stood in the doorway, surveying the assemblage.

"To arms! Stop him!"

Abruptly, Kisah became aware of a tingling heat that seemed to vibrate around her. With an effort, she lifted her heavy lids to look around her. The chest she was cradled against was no longer that of a man, but instead the scale hide of a dragon. He had shifted, her mind screamed, but she could not force herself to feel alarm.

"Be still!" Balian roared, looking about the room. Around him, everyone froze, captured by his spell, alert, but unable to move so much as a hair's breadth. "If not for my love for my princess I would slay you all for what you have done to my people, but I will not hurt her by taking my revenge, nor will allow you to bring harm to her by attacking me.

"Be assured, however, that you will die if you think to take her from me."

He strode through the room then. The outer doors of the castle burst open as he approached them, and then darkness washed over them and the chill of night as Balian held Kisah tightly to him and launched himself into the dark sky.

Kisah shivered, cold, frightened by the nightmare that held her in its grip.

"You need not fear, my love. I will keep you safe."

The words were soothing, but they rumbled from the chest of a great beast that held her in a taloned grip. She struggled, trying to shake the nightmare from her mind, trying to awaken.

"Sleep deeply, love."

* * * *

Despite the nightmare that had gripped her the night before, Kisah found that she was reluctant to leave sleep behind and face the morning light that nipped at her eyelids.

Finally, unable to escape into sleep once more, she opened her eyes and looked around.

Her heart slammed into her chest when she realized nothing around her was familiar. The bed she lay upon was enormous, far larger than her own, and covered with creamy, silken sheets. Above her, she saw that the bed hangings were of a similar material. Slowly, she sat up, realizing only as the sheets fell away that she was bare to the skin.

It had not been a nightmare then. She had not dreamed that she had been captured by a dragon--she had been.

She must have been.

Almost reluctantly, she moved to the edge of the bed and drew the drapery back. To her relief, she saw that she was alone in the room. Sliding to the floor, she was instantly aware of the chill of the stones against her bare feet. Looking around, she saw her shoes had been discarded beside the bed and slipped her feet into them.

The gown she'd worn the night before when she had gone into the dungeon had been lain out carefully on the foot of the bed and she snatched it up and quickly dressed herself. Without a maid to assist her, she had some trouble securing the ties at her back, but finally managed it to her satisfaction.

Who, she wondered, had undressed her? And how, when she had no memory of it?

A fire roared in the hearth across the room and she moved toward it, warming herself as she looked around curiously. The room was stark. Beyond the bed, a single chair before a small dressing table which held a comb and brush, and the mirror above the table, it stood empty. Frowning, she moved at last to the single door in the wall opposite the bed and tested it. To her surprise, it opened readily. She peered outside. A wide corridor lined with burning sconces and bereft of anything else, greeted her vision. After a moment's indecision, she stepped outside and turned to her left, wandering along the corridor for some time. She came upon several doors, none of which were locked, but all were empty. The corridor ended at a wide, arched window, but it was covered with colored glass and she could not see outside.

After a few moments, she turned and retraced her steps. When she reached the room she had awakened in, she hesitated and then moved on, coming at last to a wide stone staircase that wound downward. Keeping close to the stone wall, she followed the stone stairs. When she reached the bottom, she found that the stairs ended at a wide, arched doorway. Beyond the stone arch lay a cavernous room. At the far end, two great windows had been set into the wall that looked like eyes--dragon eyes.

Below and between the windows sat a throne on a raised dais--a throne carved of stone and fashioned like a great, crouching dragon.

Balian sat upon the throne, staring into the fire in the brazier beside the dais. At her entrance, he lifted his head and looked at her.

Kisah's heart executed a little free fall, though she wasn't certain whether it was fear, or something else. After a moment, she moved toward him, coming to a halt as she reached the dais.

"You slept well?" he asked, his voice and expression neutral.

Kisah frowned. "Why have you brought me here?"

Balian looked away, staring at the leaping flames for so long that she wondered if he would speak at all. A shiver went through her. He seemed ... different, not like the suitor who had wooed her, or yet like the dangerous warrior who had so unnerved her when he had nearly choked the life from Nkunda for daring to touch her.

"Beyond concealing my identity," he said pensively, "I used no subterfuge in wooing you. I went to win a bride. I won."

Kisah blinked. She could hardly dispute his claim. Her father had offered her up as prize to the winner, and though he had been captured before he had fought his final battle, there could have been no contest, no doubt that he would have won, that he had every right to claim her. Nor did she see any point in arguing the matter. "Where is everyone?" she asked instead, curious and more than a little unnerved that she had seen no one at all since she'd woke.

"This is no one here save me ... and now you."

Not even servants? But then, if what she'd dreamed was true, then it could not have been a simple matter to acquire servants. "You are a dragon?"

"You are still in doubt? Or, perhaps, it's denial?" He did not look at her, but continued to stare musingly into the flames.

Kisah bit her lip. Maybe it had been denial, but she still found it difficult to accept. "It's just ... I don't understand. I had always heard there were no dragons left."

He turned to look at her then, studying her for several moments. Finally, a wry smile curled his lips. "Behold--the last."

Try though she might, she could not prevent the empathy that swelled inside her in a suffocating wave of pain. Finally, she understood the deep sadness she had sensed in him. She had not imagined it then--it must have been nearly unbearable. How long, she wondered, had he been alone in this vast, empty castle? It would have been a mercy to have slain him, as well.

Maybe that was why he had not struggled? Maybe that was why he had not tried to elude capture? Had he gone to the heart of his enemy to seek peace? Or for revenge?

"That does not explain why you have brought me here. It is revenge, is it not? For what my people did to yours?"

"My need for revenge died with my youth."

She stared at him, but she could see no reason for him to lie--and yet, nothing else made any sense. Why would he choose the daughter of his most hated enemy if not for revenge? Particularly since she was not even of his kind? "We are not the same."

His gaze wandered her length, lingeringly, and she was reminded of the fact that she had been naked when she woke. He had said there were no servants. "Curiously enough, the Wyvern were our brothers--the closest beings on this world in kinship. No. We are not the same, but we are ... compatible ... at least in the sense necessary to me."

Kisah flushed, but it was not altogether from insult. As denigrating as it was to be considered of no importance beyond breeding offspring, it was also inescapable when one was born female. Regardless of who had been chosen as her spouse, she would have been of no more importance. Surprisingly, however, the blatant sexuality of his inspection also sent a shaft of desire through her.

She ignored it. She must remember that he was her enemy. However much he might protest it, there was no doubt in her mind that revenge was his underlying motive for stealing her away. Fool that she was, weakened by sympathy for his plight, she had placed herself at his mercy.

Chapter Eleven

Balian's castle was enchanted. Kisah had been mystified that Balian could live in such a monstrous place with no servants whatsoever and maintain it, but when he had taken her arm through his and led her around to show her his domain, it became almost immediately apparent that he had no need of them. Magic permeated the very walls and all that needed to be done was done instantly, perfectly, without fuss.

It unnerved her. She had never seen more than silly tricks performed with magic. Mortiver, the legendary wizard who had once served her father, who had been so powerful that he had been able to overcome the magic of the dragon folk, had died long ago. Ironically, it was said that it was the destruction of the dragon folk that had brought about his own mortality, for the effort had drained his magic away and left him vulnerable to the aging of mortals.

It was almost as unnerving to hear nothing but the echo of their own footsteps through the halls, the rustle of their own clothing, their voices and no others. She, who had always been surrounded by people, had valued the few, precious moments of solitude she was only occasionally granted, but she had never, truly, been alone, for there was always someone within the call of her voice.

Perhaps his grief and solitude had made him mad?

If she had nursed any doubt at all that Balian was by far the most powerful being she had ever met, she could doubt it no longer. He was physically strong in his human form, and many times that when he shifted into his beast, and beyond that, he possessed inconceivable magic. Why bother with the charade of competing with beings so inferior in so many ways to himself? If he had merely gone to find a mate for himself, as he claimed, then why had he not simply taken her that night when he had come into her room?

The only answer that came to mind seemed ludicrous.

He had courted her. Could it possibly be that he had thought to win her heart? To win acceptance?

Was it conceit that made her think so?

She was uncomfortably conscious that that seemed likely, despite his protestations of love. She did not think it too farfetched that he had found her attractive. She was not beautiful, but neither was she plain---to a man who had lived alone for so long, it was hardly flattering, but very conceivable that he might consider himself smitten.

She could not escape the fact, however, that he had come to join the tournament, never having set eyes upon her before. It seemed far more likely that he had heard of her father's proclamation and considered competing for her hand a form of entertainment as well as revenge.

It should not bother her so. The others, she knew, had come for her riches. His motives had been no more pure, but no more insulting.

The question was, what, if anything, was she to do about it? What could she do?

She had no idea where she was. Balian had put some sort of spell upon her and she could only recall the events afterward hazily, as if she had dreamed it. Even supposing she could escape the enchanted castle, how would she find her way home?

And what dangers lay between here and her home?

She had never left her own land. Shadowmere was peopled with immortals of all sorts, and abilities--they were allies against mortals, but enemies still because of their varied natures. She could not travel alone in safety through the lands of other peoples. She could shift, but she could not fly for any appreciable distance and she felt certain that Balian had taken her far away from her own land.

It went against the grain to merely wait docilely and hope for rescue, but she was no fool. In truth, she had no option, at least not at the moment.

The day passed pleasantly enough. In truth, despite her best efforts, she found, once Balian had shaken his strange preoccupation, that he was an entertaining companion. As he escorted her around the castle, he told her the history of his people, but she could not help but notice that he spoke only in generalities, that he told her nothing of his own youth, or of his family. He became withdrawn and pensive once more as they shared the noon meal, but he shook off the mood afterwards as they left the castle and wandered the grounds.

Kisah's interest perked as they left the gloom of the castle and she looked around with keen attention, wondering if she might see an avenue of escape. To her disappointment, there was only one horse in his stables, a great, dangerous beast that eyed her with threat in his eyes and nuzzled upon Balian as if he were a kitten. She doubted very much that the stallion would allow her on his back, let alone carry her away.

"You can not leave this place," Balian said abruptly when they left the stable.

Kisah glanced at him sharply. "You brought me here against my will," she reminded him. She knew, even as she said it, that that was not entirely true. He had brought her without asking what she wanted, but she was not altogether sorry that she had been whisked away from the intolerable situation her father had placed her in. Particularly when she realized that, if he had not, she would have been forced to accept Nkunda. She had seen enough of his nature to know without doubt, that she had not wanted Nkunda for her husband.

"Was it? You came to me."

Kisah's lips tightened. Nothing was more annoying than having someone throw the truth in your face when it threatened your pride to admit it. "You have twisted my pity against me."

He caught her upper arms, hauling her against him, his face suddenly stony with barely leashed rage. "Pity?" he demanded through clenched teeth. "You feel nothing for me beyond pity?"

Frightened as she was by the abrupt, dangerous shift in his mood, Kisah felt her own anger surge forth. "Not even so much as that ... now!" she retorted bitingly.

For a moment, she thought she had gone too far, that she had goaded him past his rein on his temper. Then, before she could think to say anything else, he leaned down, capturing her mouth beneath his own. Forcing her lips to part, he thrust his tongue into her mouth, invading her--her body, her senses. His mouth was hot, moist, his taste and scent intoxicating, disorienting, so that she felt drained, weak. A bolt of pleasure shot through her at the first, possessive rake of his tongue along hers. Waves of heat and desire permeated her entire being as he explored the sensitive inner surfaces of her mouth thoroughly so that she felt more fully aware of every inch of her flesh than ever before, yearned for the caress of his hands like nothing else in the world.

Weak, needy, unable to think, incapable of anything but reveling in the sensations he had awoken, she clutched at his tunic as he carried her to the ground, rolling so that he was half atop her. She was barely aware of his knee forcing her thighs apart until she felt it pressed against her aching femininity. Pleasure, so sharp it made the muscles low in her belly clench, knifed through her as he nudged her there and she arched against him instinctively.

Releasing her mouth, he bit gently at the sensitive skin along her jaw, along her throat, moving downward until she felt the heat of his breath caressing the tops of her breasts. Her nipples tightened, stood erect, pushing against the fabric of her gown. She felt a tug, and then heard the rending of cloth and the coolness of air as he bared her breasts impatiently, but her protest became a moan of encouragement as his mouth covered one pouting peak. He nudged the sensitive tip with his tongue, cupped it around her nipple, suckled. She gasped as heat and moisture flooded her womb.

As abruptly as he'd begun, he pulled away, staring down at her, his breath harsh, labored, his face a mask of desire and hard won restraint. "I would rather have your hate," he snarled angrily.

Kisah blinked, still too wrapped up in the sensations he had created inside of her to react at first, but the disappointment that filled her brought with it a wave of outrage as she realized he had only aroused her desire to prove a point. "*That*, I give you freely!" she snapped.

She could have bitten her tongue the instant she gave voice to her childish petulance at having her treat so abruptly withdrawn, for the pain she saw in his eyes, however briefly it flickered there before he hid it, was not feigned.

As badly as she wanted to, she could not call it back and, in any case, she saw he would not listen. Thrusting himself away from her, he got to his feet and strode away.

Kisah sat up and watched him, so confused by the emotions roiling through her that she could not sort them. The remark had been stupid and thoughtless, however angry she had been at that moment. There was no use in lying to herself. She knew, in her heart, that he cared something for her. She had known it would hurt him, else there would have been no point in saying it.

She was still angry. He had made her feel things she had never imagined--things she had not wanted to feel--and then he had simply stopped, as if it had had no effect on him at all.

He had ripped her bodice! Never mind that she hadn't cared at the moment he had done so, that she would have torn it away herself only to feel his touch.

What was she to do now? She had nothing else to wear. He had stolen her away. He had not been thoughtful enough to pack her bags for her.

Pulling the tatters of her bodice together, she stalked into the castle, lifted her nose and stomped through the great hall and climbed the stairs.

She wasn't at all certain that he had returned to the great hall--she hadn't wanted to be caught looking for him--but if he was there she wanted him to know she was insulted and furious with him.

She was a princess. How dare he roll in the grass with her as if she were nothing but a kitchen maid!

She sulked until darkness fell and her stomach began to gnaw at her backbone. She was still angry enough to torture herself, however. The hunger would pass. She would stay in the room until she starved to death before she tucked her tail between her legs and went begging for food.

The uplifting sense of martyrdom had begun to wane, however, by the time the door crashed open, slamming against the wall. Kisah jumped reflexively and then turned to glare at the fire breathing dragon that stood upon the threshold.

Chapter Twelve

"We dine at dusk," Balian said coolly.

Seated before the dressing table, the brush still in her hand, Kisah didn't bother to turn, but her eyes narrowed upon his reflection. "I do not read minds," she retorted icily.

His anger vanished abruptly. For a moment, he looked sheepish. "Your dinner awaits, Princess."

She was slightly mollified, but not enough to allow him to get off so easily. "You have ruined my gown. I have nothing to wear."

He looked her over and the beginnings of a smile tilted the corners of his mouth. "Nothing would suit me."

Kisah turned to glare at him, but the effort was wasted, for he had turned upon his heel and strode away. Her eyes narrowed, she stared at his retreating back for several moments, unwilling to let go of her anger. "It would serve him right," she muttered, drumming her fingers on the dressing table.

A wicked thought entered her mind and she chuckled. The idea refused to be shaken, however, and the more she thought about it, the more it pleased her. After a moment, she stood up, loosened the tie at the back of her gown and pulled it off. The loin cloth she wore beneath it was little more than a scrap of cloth, tied at the waist with a thin length of leather. She studied herself in the mirror for several moments and finally pulled the pins from her hair. Unbound, her hair fell to her hips in deep, golden brown waves. Truthfully, considering the state of her bodice, she was nearly as well covered with her hair--maybe more so, but it would never have occurred to her before to do anything so brazen.

She was torn between delight at the prospect of shocking Balian, the pleasant notion of teasing him with what he'd so callously discarded earlier, and the unnerving thought that he might decide to finish what he'd started.

She almost lost her nerve then.

Sternly, she reminded herself that she was Princess Kisah. She might be his prisoner, but she would not allow herself to be treated as he had done earlier.

He was sorely in need of a lesson.

Lifting her chin, she strolled from the room, resolutely ignoring the chill in the air.

Balian's reaction was all she could have hoped for. He had been pacing back and forth before the brazier, so deep in thought that she was halfway across the room before he noticed her presence. He turned and froze.

A jolt went through him and his face sagged with shock.

Pretending an ease that she was far from feeling, Kisah approached the small table now set before the brazier and stood waiting for him to pull out her chair for her. Balian only gaped at her, obviously too dumbfounded to kick his brain into gear. Finally, a deep blush rose from his chest, climbed his throat and then his face, all the way to his hair line. He opened his mouth, closed it, cleared his throat and opened his mouth again.

Kisah smiled at him coolly, but she saw he would not take the hint and pull out her chair. She lifted a brow and glanced at the chair.

He looked at the chair. After a moment, he moved around the table and pulled the chair out for her. Kisah sat, trying to ignore the fact that he remained where he was, unmoving. Finally, she leaned forward and looked over the food. "Mmm. I'm starving. This looks good," she said casually.

Balian moved around the table and gripped the back of his chair. He did not pull it out, however. He merely gripped the wood in white knuckled fists for several moments, his eyes narrowing as anger warred with rising desire. "You will find, my love, that it is not at all wise to tempt a starving man," he growled. "You may discover that you are not at all happy with the results."

Kisah gave him a feline smile. "You will find, my beast, that a princess can not be treated in the manner of a low born trollop."

Growling, he pushed away from the table. As he stalked

toward the door, his dragon wings sprouted from his shoulder blades, unfurling, lengthening. He lifted his hands and the great main door burst open, slamming back against the wall resoundingly. Before she could do more than gasp in surprise, he launched himself into the air and, with a flurry of flapping wings, disappeared into the darkness beyond.

"He might at least have closed the door," Kisah said with a sniff.

At that, the door slammed shut.

A shiver went through Kisah. She found that both her appetite and her anger had vanished, leaving a strange hollowness in its place. She ate anyway, though it tasted like ashes, wondering why it was that she felt so absolutely dreadful. She was a captive. She was well within her rights to torment her enemy.

She supposed, after a while, that she felt horrible because she did not feel like Balian was her enemy. She felt badly because everything she had done, and everything she had said, was a lie. She had not come naked to his table to taunt Balian. She had hoped to tempt him beyond reason. Instead, she had only driven him away.

His self-restraint in the face of her lack of it had challenged her to push him beyond it, but she had not intended to retaliate in kind, as he must have thought. She would have yielded to him gladly, wholeheartedly. She might have many doubts, but that was not one of them. She wanted him. It might be no more than pure animal attraction, but that alone was as potent and impossible to ignore as the strongest magic.

He had earned the right to claim her. She was willing to accept it. Why did he hold himself back?

Because she had wounded his pride to save her own?

In truth, she had not meant it the way it must have sounded to him. She supposed, though, that she could not have chosen a poorer choice of words. He was a proud man. He had every right to be, for he was exceptional in every way. How could she have guessed that one word would prick him so deeply? He had seemed so self-assured, so thick skinned, that it had not occurred to her that she *could* wound him.

After a while, when she saw that he would not return, she

left the table and climbed the stairs once more. She sat at the window of her room for a while, uncaring that Balian might think she was watching for him--which she was--but finally, dejected, she climbed into the bed and slept.

She woke the following morning determined to find a way to make amends. Balian, she discovered, was not to be found, however, and she spent most of the day wandering the castle in search of some task to occupy her mind. To her dismay, she discovered there was nothing that needed attention. Thwarted of honest occupation, she began exploring exhaustively. By the time she fell into bed that night she had arrived at only one certain conclusion--it was nothing short of amazing that Balian had lived so many years alone in this great heap of stones without going mad.

He returned the following day, but he remained coolly distant and Kisah could not bring herself to bend her pride enough to approach him more than once. When her one attempt to draw him into conversation failed, she withdrew into her own cold silence and her remorse degenerated into anger once more.

Almost a week had passed when she awoke one morning to discover that everything had changed. Her first thought was that she had dreamed everything that she had thought had happened since that fateful night that she had decided to free Balian--or that Balian had rethought her desirability and returned her. Surrounding the bed in which she lay was every stick of furniture, every cushion, wall hanging, even down to the smallest, most insignificant object that her room had contained--and all arranged exactly as it had been in her own room.

The exception was Edna, who had never slept on a pallet in her room, but who lay curled in a tight little ball in one corner, shaking as if she were freezing to death. Kisah's heart leapt joyfully at the sight of her maid. "Edna?"

Edna's head jerked upwards. She stared at Kisah for several uncomprehending moments and finally leapt to her feet and rushed across the room. "Princess Kisah! Oh, my lady! I am so happy to see you!" she said, laughing and crying at once as she fell to her knees beside the bed.

"How...." Kisah stopped. She knew how. She just wasn't certain why.

Sliding to the edge of the bed, she patted Edna's shaking

shoulder consolingly. "Were you very frightened?"

"I thought I would *die* of fright, mistress! His *is* a dragon! Oh mistress! Will he eat us?"

Kisah gave her a look. "Don't be absurd! He will not harm you."

"But--"

"Hush! I will not hear you speak ill of him!" Kisah said sharply. "He is my lord."

Edna's jaw dropped. "But ... he stole you away."

Kisah slid off the bed, knelt beside her trunk and pulled out a robe, then drew it around her and moved to the dressing table. "By my father's decree, I am his," she said sharply.

"You will wed that...." Encountering Kisah's narrow eyed glare, she stopped mid-sentence. "Man?" she finished weakly.

Kisah frowned. In truth, Balian had said nothing of wedding her. Perhaps it was not a custom the dragon folk practiced? When she glanced up, she caught a glimpse of Balian's reflection in the mirror and her heart fluttered uncomfortably in her breast. He was standing in the doorway, studying her, his face expressionless. She had not heard his entrance, had not heard the door open nor his tread. How long, she wondered, had he been standing there? "I will honor my father's word ... even if he did not."

Was it her imagination, or did some of the tension ease from his stance?

"You are pleased?"

Edna shrieked when Balian spoke, scurrying into a corner. Distracted, both Kisah and Balian turned to look at her, Kisah with irritation, Balian with a good deal of surprise.

Frowning a warning at the maid, she turned to Balian. "I am ... most grateful for your thoughtfulness."

He nodded. "Will you break your fast with me?"

Kisah smiled wryly. "If I can coax my silly maid from the corner to help me dress."

Balian glanced toward Edna once more, nodded, and departed, closing the door behind him. When he had gone, Edna darted from the corner and rushed to Kisah's chest, nervously jerking first one gown and then another from it. "I will wear the blue, Edna," Kisah said coolly, wondering if it would be more comfortable if Balian simply returned the poor thing. As thoughtful as it had been for Balian to bring the girl, Kisah was not certain she really wanted Edna around if she was going to quake like a mouse and squeak every time she saw Balian.

Glancing nervously toward the door, Edna carefully laid the dress that Kisah had chosen out on the bed and smoothed it, then rushed across the room and took the brush from Kisah's hand and began brushing her hair. Trying to contain her impatience, Kisah bore with her, though the girl created almost as many tangles as she removed--some forcefully--from Kisah's scalp.

"Peace, Edna! Or you will have me bald."

Glancing toward the door once more, Edna leaned close. "They are coming for you, Lady," she whispered.

Chapter Thirteen

Dread was not something Kisah would have guessed that she would feel to learn that her father intended to rescue her, but it swept through her in a cold tide. A dozen questions collided in her mind making it difficult to decide which to ask first. "Who? How? How do you know?" She didn't bother to ask why. Her father would have had Balian slain rather than to allow his enemy to take his daughter.

"I overheard your father speak of it to Nkunda--for you must know that it was he who triumphed at the tournament."

Kisah felt a sick feeling in the pit of her stomach. "They went on with the tournament after I had been ... after I left?" she demanded, outraged.

Edna gaped at her. "The dragon was disqualified. A winner had to be chosen," she said reasonably.

Kisah's eyes narrowed. There was nothing reasonable about it to her way of thinking. Obviously, her father had been devastated by her loss, she thought sarcastically. "So ... my father plots with Nkunda to ... rescue me?"

Edna nodded eagerly.

"Nkunda is no match for Balian."

Edna cast another look toward the door. "Nay, not as he is, but the king knows of a way wherein Nkunda can use the powers of Mortiver to overcome the dragon."

Kisah gaped at her. "And he dead and buried nigh three centuries ago? What do they expect to do, resurrect him?"

"T'was a secret your father kept close to his heart these many years, should the need arise for the powers once more. For it may only be used once, and briefly at that. The essence of Mortiver's powers remain. Once consumed, they will give his power to whomever does so. And though it would only be for a day and a night, Nkunda would need no more than that, surely, to defeat such a one as Balian?"

Kisah got up, pacing, but she knew there was no point in railing against her father. He would not listen to any plea she might think to make even if she had been able to speak to him directly. It was worse than useless to consider sending a message to him, even if she had the means to do so.

"Even if what you say is true," Kisah muttered, more to herself than to the maid, "they can not know if it will even work. Mortiver, from what I have heard, was boastful. It may be nothing more than a story put about to ensure his immortality in the memory of the people. And Mortiver had been so weakened by the spells he cast upon the dragon folk that it led to his death. What might he pass along beyond the little he had left to him? Which was not even enough to preserve his own life."

Edna shrugged. "Your father the king did say that Mortiver had not exhausted his powers, he had merely weakened his physical self ."

Kisah wasn't certain whether she did not believe it, or if she was afraid to believe it. For, if it was true, then Balian would die.

She did not think that she could bear that, but was it within her power to do something about it? Finally, she decided that she must try to reason with Balian, warn him at the very least, if he would not listen.

Dressing quickly, she made her way downstairs. He was standing before one of the windows staring down at the sea beyond when she crossed the great hall. At the sound of her tread, however, he turned to look at her. Fleetingly, a look of pleasure crossed his features, but then he seemed to recall the discord between them and the pleasure faded, replaced by a look of polite coolness.

Kisah bit her lip. He had not forgiven her, she thought, but as he came forward to help her with her chair she realized that she was wrong. It was not so much that he had not forgiven her as it was that he had erected a barrier and withdrawn behind it. She had not realized until his withdrawal that he had never shown her anything other than openness and honesty.

She had lost--no, thrown away, something of great value, she realized with a sinking heart.

The food, as usual, was delicious, but it might as well have been mud. She saw now that his peace offering had not been an attempt to thaw her heart, but merely a courtesy to her comfort. He must think her heart wrought of ice and impervious to warmth.

They had finished their meal before it occurred to her that she had come down with the intention of warning him of her father's plot. Somehow, she could not bring herself to simply blurt it out. Now, they had a truce of sorts. If she told him, would he not interpret it as doubt of his ability to protect himself? Might he consider it a threat, instead of a warning?

She had not thought to ask Edna when they planned to come for her. Perhaps the maid knew, perhaps not. In any case, she had no notion of whether or not she had time to consider how she might break the news.

If she said nothing, and Nkunda attacked, catching him off guard....

She stood up indecisively. "Will you walk with me in the garden?" she finally asked.

Something flickered in his eyes that she could not read, but he nodded and offered his arm. She took it, but her mind was so filled with how she might broach the subject of her father that she could think of no polite chitchat to offer and an uncomfortable silence settled over them as they left the castle to walk in the garden.

When they had taken several turns around the garden, Balian led her to a garden bench and urged her to sit. Only a little beyond the bench, a low wall edged the cliff edge that fell sharply into the sea. Kisah looked down at the crashing waves below for several moments and finally sat.

"You are very quiet," he said, breaking the strained silence at last.

Kisah glanced up at him and decided to simply take the plunge and hope for the best. "My maid brought news of home."

Balian frowned and looked away. "This is your home."

"I meant...."

"I know what you meant." His lips twisted. "I had thought that I had learned patience, but perhaps I have been alone too long."

Kisah reached for his hand when he started to rise. He looked at her in surprise, aborted the movement and lifted her hand to his lips. Brushing his lips along her knuckles, he lowered her hand to her lap and released it, then stood abruptly and moved to stand looking down at the sea.

Frustrated, Kisah turned to study his back, clasping her hand where it still tingled from his touch.

"I had so little time, you see."

Kisah felt a stab of anxiety at his words, though she had no idea of what he spoke. She was on the point of prompting him to continue when he spoke again.

"In but a few days the time will be upon me when I might breed offspring. Another century will pass before my time comes again and.... I feel a desperation to know that I will not die, knowing that my kind has passed from this world forever."

The urge to weep for his pain was nearly overwhelming. She supposed she could not truly understand or feel what he felt, for she had not endured the life that he had, but she had been in the dragon's lair fully long enough to have a taste of what that loneliness must have been like.

Rising, she moved to stand beside him. "I will honor my father's decree. I will bear your children gladly, but...."

He looked down at her, smiling faintly, but there was great sadness in his eyes. "You are Wyvern. We are not the same."

If he had slapped her, she could not have felt more rejected. "It did not seem to matter to you before," she said stiffly, and turning, began to walk quickly back to the castle.

He caught her before she reached the garden gate, forcing her to turn and face him. "You do not understand."

"No," she said tightly. "I do not!" She tried to tug her hand free, but he would not allow it.

"We mate for life ... and only when love is mutual. It can NOT be otherwise, else I would happily accept what you offer."

Kisah discovered that there were tears streaming down her cheeks. She dashed them away angrily. "I do not understand!"

"And I can not make you understand, any more than I can make you love me!" he said harshly. "It happens ... or it does not."

He released her then, so abruptly that she staggered back a step before she caught her balance. "Then take me home!" she cried in frustration, in too much turmoil to make any sense of his words, unable to think at all beyond the blow to her pride. It was unthinkable that she, Princess Kisah, had offered to bear his child and been flatly rejected, only because she was no starry-eyed child who imagined respect, admiration and lust equated to some higher emotion.

"No."

"Why?"

"Because I am a selfish monster," he snarled. "Because I want you and I will not allow another to have you."

Chapter Fourteen

Rage was welcome, for it forced out all other confusing emotions. "They will come for me!" she said.

A stillness settled over Balian. "Who?"

"Nkunda!" Kisah snapped, flinging the name in his face like a challenge.

"The one whom you favored?" he asked, his eyes narrowed, filled now with an anger that seemed to surpass her own.

It was, perhaps, the last thing that she had expected him to say and it sent a jolt of surprise through her. Quite suddenly, however, she recalled that she had done just that, though it had not been her intention to favor Nkunda so much as it was her determination to show Balian that she would not simply drop into his hands like a ripe plum because he demanded it.

It was unfortunate that she had not been born with the gift of foresight. She had not expected when she had done it that it would come back to haunt her. Faced with the prospect of angering him even more, however, she could not bring herself to answer.

Apparently, he took her silence as an affirmative, for he leaned close. "I will take pleasure in killing him."

Kisah paled, realizing abruptly that she had, once more, completely bungled everything. Instead of warning him as she had intended, she had thrown it out as a challenge in her anger. "I do not care," she said a little weakly.

"You lie," he said through gritted teeth.

Kisah gaped at him. Reaching out as he turned away, she grasped his tunic. "Nay! It is not a lie. I only meant to warn you."

He pulled her hands free and thrust her away from him. "You beg for his life."

"I swear to you on my mother's soul! He means nothing to me! Balian! Do not be careless because I have made you angry! They have found a way to endow him with the powers of Mortiver!

"Take me home, please! I can not bear the thought of having your blood on my hands."

He studied her a long moment. "I could almost believe that you think that would be an end to it."

Kisah stared at him in dismay, but she knew he was right. It would change nothing. Her father's hatred of the dragon folk was absolute. He would not rest knowing that even one had escaped. "It would be," she said, almost to herself, trying to convince herself that, if she only had the chance to speak with her father, she could end the blood letting.

He shook his head. "You truly do not know, do you?"

"What?"

"We were allies once ... brothers. It was my kind that taught yours how to shift into their human form, for the Wyvern did not know this power. For centuries we lived side by side, in harmony ... until the king of the Wyvern fell in love with a dragon princess. But she had already given her heart to another--the dragon king.

"Enraged, he slew her mate, thinking, perhaps, that he could win her heart if only he could be rid of the one she truly loved. Instead, he found that he had slain her, as well, for dragons mate for life and when she had lost her mate, she lost her will to live.

"When she died, he turned his rage upon my people, and slew them one by one until he believed he had slain them all."

Kisah was shaking her head. "This is not true! It can not be true! It was my father who....."

"It *is* true. I know because it was my mother he coveted, my father whom he slew."

"But ... you could not have been more than an infant! How could you know this? How could you have survived?"

He shook his head. "I was a boy. I remember it all quite well. I survived because my mother hid me, placed a spell upon me that kept even Mortiver from finding me. Centuries passed, the world changed and I with it. My mother was wise to bind me so long, else I would have sought out your people and destroyed them as they had destroyed mine ... or died in the trying. By the time that I was released, my need for revenge had burned itself away and acceptance for what I could not change had taken its place."

Kisah found that, as badly as she wanted to deny all that he'd said, she could not doubt him. Another thought occurred to her, however, and she found she needed to know the truth of it. "Had it?"

His brows rose questioningly.

"This need for revenge? Did you not seek me out to have your revenge upon my father?"

To her surprise, a faint smile curled his lips. "I sought you out because the seer, Syrian, told me you were my destiny. I knew when I first beheld you that he was right. There could be no other for me. Alas, it seems the rest of his prophecy was true, as well."

"What did he say?" Kisah asked fearfully.

"That you would bring me great joy--or sorrow. That, in loving you, I would give my life into your hands."

Kisah stared at him for several moments, feeling desperately unhappy that she had made such a mess of everything. It gave her no solace that she had never intentionally caused him pain, that she was not directly responsible for much of it, for she had spoken thoughtlessly, said things she could not call back. How, she wondered, could she convince him that she cared nothing for Nkunda? No matter what she said now, her actions before gave the lie to it.

Perhaps actions, not words, were what she needed now?

The thought had no more than crossed her mind when she moved toward him. Stopping only when she was standing toe to toe with him, she placed her palms against his chest and slid them upwards, rising up on her tiptoes and lifting her head so that she could brush her lips against his. He caught her waist in his hands. For a moment, she thought that he would push her away. She slipped her arms around his neck, tightening them, pressing more fully against him.

In the next moment, his arms closed tightly around her, his mouth opening over hers hungrily. A thrill of triumph went through her even as a heady rush of desire flooded her. She kissed him back with equal fervor, entwined her tongue with his when he thrust it into her mouth.

Abruptly, he pulled away. Before she could protest, he scooped her into his arms, bent his knees and launched them both into the air with the flurry of flapping wings. Landing upon the balcony that overlooked the sea, he thrust the doors open with his mind and strode inside, down the corridor and into her room.

Edna shrieked when the doors flew open.

"Out!" Balian commanded and she ran from the room.

Kisah tilted her head up, gazing into Balian's eyes as he strode into the room and laid her upon the bed. His eyes blazed with need, his muscles bunched with restrained power. He wouldn't release her, couldn't cease touching her, just as she could not cease touching him.

She feared if she let go, the spell would be broken, that he would somehow leave her in anger.

Balian sank with her onto the bed, his arms propped on either side of her, crushing his body against hers, down into the mattress. She was surrounded by him, by his scent, his skin, the warmth of his flesh. One hair roughened thigh fell across hers, trapping her to the heat of his groin pressed into her hip. She felt melded to his body, the hard planes of his chest, the rippled muscles of his stomach. She ran her hands up his back, marveling at the musculature, the silken strength, craving to touch him everywhere, to feel him everywhere.

Her gown was little barrier to the heat and strength of his body, but suddenly it was too much, too much covering her. As if reading her mind, he lifted and tore the gown away as his mouth came down on hers.

Kisah gasped in surprise, allowing him entrance. He thrust his tongue into her mouth, possessive, sweeping aside her small protest. Kisah whimpered into his mouth as he ravished her tongue and cupped a breast, pinching her nipple as his tongue tangled with her own.

Kisah felt dizzy, assaulted from all angles by swift, searing desire. He tasted sweet and wild, dangerous, intoxicatingly exciting. When he groaned into her mouth, she consumed his breath, his life force. Her senses heightened, raging out of control. Her blood sizzled as though on fire, burning down to her core. What had begun so simply was escalating farther and faster than she ever dreamed possible.

She couldn't think straight, knew only that she needed him inside her, plumbing that empty space that begged for satiation. Liquid heat trickled in her sex, soaking her, dampening her thighs, molten moisture that increased the burning of her loins instead of quenching the fire. He broke suddenly from her mouth, and she groaned at the loss of wet heat, moaning as he blazed a trail of kisses along her jaw to her ear. He nipped the sensitive lobe, swathing her with his tongue, breathing hotly into her ear. Goosebumps chased across her flesh, making her shudder beneath him.

Her thighs parted of their own accord, instinctively allowing him nearer, nudging him closer as he moved between her splayed thighs. She squirmed, unable to lie still another moment, needing something … something she couldn't name.

He suckled her neck, hard, kneeling between her legs, moving forward until the foreign length of his cock nudged her bare cleft, parting her swollen folds. Kisah stiffened at the hot, hard invasion, wondering when he'd lost his loincloth, wondering how she could be so crazed as not to notice they were both naked.

He sensed the change in her, and he went rigid, ceasing the caress of his hands at her breasts, his mouth at her throat. A shudder went through him, called forth from his bones and very soul. His voice guttural, pained, he asked against her ear, "Do you want this to stop?"

"No, please don't," she whispered, cupping his neck, urging him for another kiss. He lifted his head, gazing into her eyes, unreadable save for the dark flash of passion and pain. Would this be their only chance? How much time had she wasted acting like a child? She could not go back now-- there was no going back.

He bent and kissed her lightly, nipping her lips in a teasing nibble that stoked the flames of need high in her belly. Her sex felt drenched with it, and she couldn't imagine waiting any longer. She clutched his shoulders, eager for him to proceed, but he pulled back, moving down her body, denying her.

He slid his tongue down her throat, down the valley of her breasts, nipping her breasts with lips and teeth. She reached for him to beg him to stop, to not torture her, but he grasped her wrists and pinned them to her sides as he closed his mouth around one taut peak.

Wet heat latched onto her nipple, sucking hard, burning and aching and bliss in one potent combination. It lanced through her breast, deep in her belly, pulsing between her legs. Ecstasy nudged her, teasing the edges of her mind. Kisah gasped as pure pleasure arced through her body. Her insides coiled around it, begging for surcease.

He raked his teeth over her distended flesh, freeing one wrist as he thrust one hand down to cup her sex roughly, plunging into her cleft to find that swollen, achy bud. She groaned as he stroked her, suckled her. Her nails dug into the mattress trying to hold on as lightning jumped through her veins and scorched the shroud of sanity.

"Please … no more … I cannot take it," she gasped, writhing beneath him, desperate for completion.

He tore his mouth from her breast, freeing her other wrist to cup her buttocks, raising her hips from the mattress. "As my lady commands it," he murmured huskily.

Kisah wrapped her legs around his hips, jerking toward him as he propped on his arms, looking down at her with smoky, passion filled eyes. His cockhead nudged the opening of her womanhood, stretching the edges. He closed his eyes, his brow furrowed with pain, damp with perspiration. He pushed forward and the dull ache became pain, burning, damning pain.

He was huge, too large to fit. Kisah panted with exertion, trying to hold back her gasp of agony, trying to hold on to consciousness.

He whispered strange words that tickled her mind, twisted in her ears like cobwebs. Words of magic….

The pain eased, became no more. Only pleasure hovered now … and the vast emptiness of her soul. The slickness of her cleft eased his passage, and he edged inside her, moving infinitesimally.

His arms shook as he stood above her, sliding inside her, so slowly she thought she would die before he was fully inside.

"Balian … hold not back. Give yourself to me," she breathed, smoothing her palms up his taut arms and the tense line of his shoulders.

Her words broke him. A strangled groan tore from his throat as he plunged deep inside her. Kisah arched her back, screaming with the ecstasy, the stretching fullness.

He breathed brokenly above her, holding still, his breath so ragged, her heart ceased to beat. He lifted his head, staring into her eyes. She shuddered at the sadness there, the longing.

She felt wetness on her face, her own tears.

She cupped the back of his neck and pulled him down for a kiss, moving her lips tenderly across his.

He nibbled her hungrily, rotating his hips. She whimpered, her muscles spasming, clenching his cock. He withdrew, sliding out and then in with long, torturous strokes, grinding his pubic bone against her swollen clit, making her jerk with the sensation.

"I will never let you go," he breathed against her lips, watching her with eyes aglow with passion, plunging into her.

He set a tempo, short and fast, potent. Each stroke had her arching, quivering with sensation. Her muscles twitched as he withdrew, gushed with wet arousal, and welcomed him inside her core with pulling, sucking muscles that clenched hard around his engorged cock. She could feel every rippled vein, the taut muscles of his thighs and hips, the hardness of his buttocks against her crossed calves.

He moved faster and faster, never taking his eyes from her, until she felt he captured her soul with but his eyes. Kisah couldn't look away, watched him as tremors climbed inside her with each pounding second.

A stillness engulfed her, blocking out sound, obscuring her vision save for the glow of his eyes, dulling touch save for the ecstasy pounding deep inside her. Her heart galloped, her lungs froze. Sudden, soul shattering bliss stole through her like a lightning strike. It echoed inside him, she could see it on his lips as he threw back his head. His skin glowed golden, blinding her with light. Light all around, everywhere. It came from him, her own skin, surrounding them as the waves of orgasm crashed and engulfed them in searing, painful pleasure.

Kisah tried to scream but she'd lost her voice, lost everything but Balian. He anchored her to the world. She wrapped her arms around him, holding him tight as he plunged into her and spewed his hot seed deep in her belly.

Kisah found her breath, breathed weakly against his temple, dropping her arms from his body as she collapsed feebly against the mattress.

The tears renewed themselves in her eyes, streaking her face. Balian lifted his head, his expression unfathomable.

He raised a hand, stroked his thumb across her bottom lip, calming the rage of emotion in her soul. She didn't know what to say, didn't know what to feel anymore. Her heart tripped over itself, her breath caught in her throat.

His eyes grew dark, shadowed by pain. "I will never let you go," he whispered.

Chapter Fifteen

Kisah was not so naïve` as to believe that their coupling, however wonderful, had erased past mistakes, or would ensure harmonious future between them, but she was deeply reluctant to allow the world to intrude so quickly upon the heels of such a wondrous experience. As important as she knew it was to decide what was to be done about the trouble brewing upon the horizon therefore, she set it aside for a later time.

"You shift with such ease I find that I am impressed. I can barely shift at all."

Balian rolled onto his side and propped his head upon his hand, studying her. "This is something my parents taught me when I was very small. Your people have forgotten what they were taught and can not teach it to their young. Or, perhaps, they did not feel that they wanted, or needed, the gift.

"There are strengths, and weaknesses, to both forms, the human and the beast. You have it still, but you make little use of it. It is the gift of shifting that allows you to heal yourself, and slow aging--else you would live no longer than any mortal man."

Kisah rolled over so that she was facing him. "That much, I know."

Rolling from the bed, Balian held out his hand to her. After a moment, Kisah slipped to the edge of the bed and placed her hand in his. He led her from the room and to the balcony they had entered by, then faced her once more.

"You will find your beast inside of you if you but look for it. Close your eyes, seek it."

Obediently, Kisah closed her eyes, but she was not certain of what she was seeking. Finally, she opened her eyes again and shook her head. "Perhaps I was born without my beast?"

Balian shook his head. Lifting his hand, he brushed it lightly over her eyes, leaned close and whispered in her ear. "Close your eyes to the world and open your inner eye. Allow your mind to seek what lays dormant, waiting to be awakened. It is that part of you that yearns for freedom, that feels a fierce need to soar through the skies in search of prey."

Something stirred inside of her, an excitement not unlike the thrill of pleasure that washed through her when she and Balian coupled, but there was a wildness to it that went beyond. Her heart thundered in her chest as she felt it growing, consuming her. Frightened by the strange sensations, she jumped back, blinking at Balian in surprise. "You placed a spell upon me."

He shook his head. "Nay. I did not. I merely showed you your beast."

"I am not certain I want to yield to it," Kisah said shakily.

"You must free it from restraint before you can learn to control it."

Turning away, Balian climbed atop the balcony rail. Before Kisah even knew what he was about, he leapt into space. Shifting even as he plummeted toward the ground below, he swooped away, caught a current of air and soared upward.

Kisah's heart thundered in her chest as she watched him, but it was not all fear. Partly it was admiration, for he was a noble creature--and partly it was a yearning to soar as he soared, to feel air beneath her wings. With an effort, she climbed upon the balcony as he had. Balancing precariously, she closed her eyes once more, seeking that part of herself that Balian had shown her. Slowly, it built inside her once more, filling her with a fierce excitement. Heat rushed over her. Her skin prickled almost painfully, fire shot through the muscles of her body, so intense it almost seemed that she was melting. She shied away from it, closing her mind to the pain.

At once, she felt it receding, felt fear fill her mind in the place of the fierce excitement she had felt before. She wobbled on her perch, knew the moment that she lost her balance and screamed as she felt herself falling.

Balian caught her. In the blink of an eye, the talons that had gripped her became human arms, the plated dragon's chest was transformed into the smooth flesh of the man. Gently, he set her on the balcony once more. "My baby bird has not learned to fly from her nest," he said teasingly.

Amusement lit his eyes when she looked up at him, but she saw something beyond that--love. Why had she not realized it before? Why had she not believed his words of love?

Because, she realized, she had not felt it herself and had not recognized it for what it was. When, she wondered, had her feelings for him changed? She could recall no moment in time when she had felt something that should have told her that she loved him, but she realized that she should have known it when she realized that she could not bear it if her father executed him. Instead, she had dismissed it as nothing more than sympathy. She had convinced herself that it was merely the injustice of the situation that had driven her to commit treason and plot to free him instead of accepting that he had stolen his way into her heart.

Balian frowned. "What is it, love? I did not mean to frighten you. I would never allow harm to come to you."

Kisah smiled with an effort. "I know you would not."

He caressed her cheek. "What then?"

"I am afraid."

Wrapping arms around her, he held her tightly a moment. "You said you trusted me."

Kisah shook her head, gripping his arms tightly. "Fool! I am not worried for myself."

Balian pulled away, looking at her in surprise.

"If you were not blind, you would have seen what I took such great care to hide even from myself. I love *you*, Balian. I am afraid for you."

His lips tightened. Releasing her, he stepped away. "You say this to protect Nkunda."

Kisah stamped her foot. "That is not true! Do you think I went to free you from my father's dungeon because of my concern for him?"

"Did you?"

Kisah gaped at him. "How could you even think that?"

He frowned. "I could not meet him in the final match when I was seized and imprisoned."

"Exactly! And if my concern had been for him, then I need not have concerned myself further. If I did not love you, I would not have warned you of my father's plot."

"You said that it was pity for my plight that drove you."

"I *lied*!" Kisah snapped angrily.

His lips twitched, but he shook his head. "I could not tell. How am I to know you are sincere now?"

Kisah gasped in outrage. "You want me to *prove* it!" she demanded.

"I would like that, yes."

She didn't know whether to laugh or hit him, but, despite his banter, she saw that he still doubted that he could trust her. She stepped closer to him, slipping her arms around his waist. "How am I to do that?" she asked, laying her cheek against his chest, listening to the comforting beat of his heart.

"Wed me ... in the ceremony of my people."

She pulled away to look up at him, smiling. "Yes."

To her surprise, instead of looking relieved, he frowned, looking away from her. "No. I should not have suggested it," he said, pulling away from her and pacing the length of the balcony.

She stared at his back, rigid now with tension as he stared at the sea. "Why?"

"Because, if you lie ... you will die."

Chapter Sixteen

Kisah's heart seemed to stand still in her chest. "What are you talking about?"

"Only two, pure of heart because of their love for one another, can stand upon the joining stone and exchange their vows. They must become as one, and that can not be when their hearts are divided."

Dismayed, Kisah could only stare at him blankly for several moments, but she no longer had any doubts. Perhaps it was he who doubted?

"I am willing."

He shook his head. "I can not chance it. You are too dear to me."

"You can not deny me this!" Kisah said angrily. "You doubt me, and yet you will not even give me the chance to prove that you are wrong?"

He turned upon her angrily. "If I am wrong, you will die!"

"That is my choice!"

"It is *my* life! I would rather live with doubts than lose you forever."

Kisah studied him for several moments. "You will lose me forever if you do not. I will not suffer your doubts. I will not stay with you."

"You can not leave!" he roared angrily.

"I can and I will!" she shouted back at him.

Surprised at her vehemence, he was silent for several moments. "Then we will go together tonight ... and we will leave together as one ... or remain together in death as we could not in life, for I am weary past bearing of existing alone."

* * * *

The full moons had risen high in the sky when Kisah met Balian in the great hall. She was nervous, but she was excited, as well. Tonight she would wed Balian before his gods. Somehow, she would convince her father to accept her choice of husband.

Taking her hand when she reached him, Balian pulled her to him and simply held her for several moments. Finally, he pulled away and turned to the throne. It quivered as he stared at it and began to move backwards, revealing a stairwell that wound down into darkness. The absolute blackness of the pit unnerved her, but in a moment, light flickered, almost seeming to beckon to them.

Balian led her to the stairs and they began to descend, on and on it seemed until at last, when it seemed they must have gone down into the very bowels of the world, they at last reached the bottom. A single, arched doorway led out from the stairwell. Beyond it was the same utter darkness that had greeted them when the stairs were first revealed. As before, however, torches sprang to life, illuminating the cavern beyond ... for it was a cavern, rough hewn, lined with stalactites and stalagmites that jutted from the floor and ceiling like great, sharp teeth.

Kisah shivered slightly as Balian led her through the cavern, and then through a tunnel and into yet another, smaller cavern. Beyond that, lay yet another cavern, this one far larger than the first. A river of molten fire flowed through the heart of the cavern, forming a pool at one end. Beyond the pool, the wall of the cavern had been carved into the shape of a crouching dragon. A rough hewn altar stood within its gaping jaws.

Balian led her to stand upon the altar. Facing her, he grasped both of her hands. His face was ashen, his hands as cold as her own. "I invoke thee, Hermantee, goddess of the dragon folk. Look down upon us and give us your blessing to unite."

Kisah's heart skittered painfully, fearfully, at his words, but that was as nothing when she saw what rose from the pool beside the altar, for it was a creature of fire, as beautiful as it was deadly.

Balian closed his eyes. "Hermantee, I love this woman with all of my heart, with all that I am. I give to myself to her, without reservation, beseeching you to make us as one."

Kisah swallowed with some difficulty when he opened his eyes once more and looked at her, waiting. "Hermantee," she said in a quaking voice, "I love this man with all of my heart, with all that I am. I give myself to him, without reservation, beseeching you to make us as one."

Silence fell. Kisah had begun to wonder what would happen next when the creature spread its arms, reaching out to them. Balian gripped her hands tightly as Hermantee's arms closed around them. Expecting to burst into flame the moment it touched them, Kisah was surprised to find instead that peace and joy filled her, and beyond that, something far more extraordinary. Her beast rose within her, without her summoning. The pain she'd felt before as her body contorted, rose, but she closed her mind to it, allowing it to engulf her.

You are no maid, said a chiding voice.

Kisah looked around before she realized that the voice was inside her head. *Nay,* she replied in kind, *for I gave myself to the man I love.*

Balian.

Aye.

I sense doubt.

I am afraid for him. I fear my father will have him slain, as he slew Balian's father.

Your love for Balian will overcome that and bring peace between your two peoples.

Hope surged through her. *How? Please ... tell me what I must do!*

When the time comes, your heart will tell you.

Frustration surged through her. She needed wise counsel.

Amusement flooded through her, as if she could feel the laughter of the god Hermantee. *You will give birth to a new race, Kisah. You must be strong. Use the gift you were born with and all will be well.*

What gift? Wait! Tell me! But she sensed the goddess had withdrawn. To her surprise, when she looked down at herself, she saw that she was human once more. Or, perhaps, she had not shifted at all?

Balian, she saw, had dropped to his knees. He looked up at her for a moment and then pulled her to him, holding her tightly. "I thought she would take you from me," he said hoarsely.

"You should not have doubted me," Kisah told him, but it warmed her that he had been so fearful for her safety.

He chuckled. "I should not have." Releasing her at last, he rose and pulled her to her feet. "We have faced death together. Now we must face life."

Kisah smiled at him, but her heart clutched painfully in her chest at his words. He seemed to have no reservations that he could face the powers of Mortiver and triumph, but she had plenty enough for the two them.

He led her back the way they had come, up into the castle and her room.

He faced her toward the mirror, sliding the sleeves of her gown down her shoulders, following the path of the fabric with his mouth.

"You are beautiful, wife. I want you to see yourself as I see you when we make love."

Kisah shivered, watching as he drew the gown down and let it drop to her feet. His lips trailed warm, moist kisses down her back, along the curve of her buttocks, his hands following around her belly, moving low on her hips.

He touched the top of her slit, nuzzling the bottom cleft of her buttocks as he dipped a finger inside her cleft to touch her clit.

Kisah bit her lip to halt the moan from escaping, breathing sharply through her nose as he nudged her legs wider with his face and fingers. His tongue snaked out, shockingly hot and wet against her folds, spurring a gush of liquid arousal to dampen her sex.

She gasped as he found her core and plunged his tongue deep inside her, flicking his fingers across her nub as he lapped the edges of her womanhood. Kisah jerked back against his mouth, arching her head back, clenching her hands into fists.

Pleasure climbed in her body, threatening to buckle her knees as again and again, he plumbed her core. He released her suddenly, rising on his feet, whirling her around. He bent and kissed her, and she could taste herself on his lips, smell her sweet arousal and his own heated response. He cupped her buttocks and lifted her, spreading her legs and guiding his cock to her opening.

He hovered a moment, building the anticipation, making her insides squirm with expectation, until she was desperate to feel him.

He plunged deep inside her with one stroke, and she cried out, tears blinding her as her muscles were stretched to the very brink of acceptance. She arched her head back as he blazed a molten trail down her throat, lifting her up and down on his cock, grinding against her in short strokes that had her orgasm racing toward her femininity. She caught it, spiraling out of control as the exquisite nirvana wrapped her in its arms, shimmering through her veins with blinding intensity. He came inside her at the same instant, his body in tune with hers, his cock pulsing and jerking deep in her core.

He held her there, against him, protective, loving. The high of pleasure receded, warming her muscles with residual heat.

Kisah trembled, kissing him, touching his face, loving the feel of him still inside her. She couldn't get enough of him. She felt starved, thirsty … for him and only him.

He carried her to the bed, easing them down, massaging her cheeks as he laid them down on their sides.

"I hungry for you, Kisah. My soul was empty until I found you," he murmured huskily.

"As was mine, my love," she whispered.

He made love to her again that night, and every time she awakened. She felt no weakness from his loving, only exhilaration, and on the third night, she felt the quickening that told her Balian's child had found a home in her womb.

Chapter Sixteen

The chill that brushed Kisah's skin woke her and she sat up groggily, looking around. Balian, she saw, was standing before the window, staring out into the night. "What is it?" she asked fearfully, dreading his answer.

He turned to look at her. "They have come."

He strode toward her when she would have leapt from the bed, pulling her into his arms. "Nay. You can not see. They are beyond the boundaries yet, but I sense the barrier weakening."

"Let me go. I can speak to my father, make him see reason."

"You can not! He is more like to slay you for what he sees as your treachery than to listen to anything you have to say."

She would have argued with him if she had not feared as much herself. "You must at least let me try. He is not an evil man ... and I do not want harm to come to him anymore than I would have him harm you."

"I know this. I promise that I will do all that I can to make peace ... or if that can not be had, I will try to do him no lasting harm."

Kisah clutched at him. "Nay! Don't promise me that! Promise me that you will do what you must to protect yourself."

He caressed her cheek. "I will promise ... if you will make a promise to me."

"Anything!"

"Then promise me you will guard the life of our child. No matter what happens, promise that you will do all that you can to see him into this world and into manhood.

"Anything but that!" Kisah gasped, horrified. "You would not ask me that if you planned to keep your own promise!"

He smiled faintly. "I will not yield my life willingly. I've a mind to give my son siblings to grow up with."

Kisah relaxed fractionally, leaning against him. "Take me with you. At least, if I am there, there is a chance that we can make peace without bloodshed."

Balian stroked her hair. "Sleep, my princess. All will be well."

The moment he murmured the words over her, Kisah felt her consciousness slipping away, felt as if she were falling through a dark tunnel. Distress filled her, for she knew that he had placed a sleeping spell upon her. She struggled against it, but it seemed the harder she struggled, the deeper she fell.

She drifted for a time, aware that Balian had left her side. Faintly, a voice seemed to whisper to her. *Use the gift you were born with and all will be well.*

The gift? What gift? She wondered, trying to jog her sluggish mind to solve the puzzle.

Her beast! She knew suddenly that that was the answer, but she had never summoned her beast. She wasn't certain that she could. She could not see how it would help her even if she managed to do so.

She could not awaken from the spell Balian had cast upon her, however, and it occurred to her finally that she had never been more distant to her human consciousness than she was now. Searching, she found her beast, rousing it, summoning it to take her. Dimly at first, and then more strongly, she felt her flesh prickle, felt the burn in her muscles as they changed shape and as the pain built, so did her consciousness, the lethargy lifted as energy surged through her.

She woke abruptly, as if from a nightmare.

Looking down at herself, she saw her arms were now tipped with three talons instead of five fingers and covered with feathers that gleamed palely in the dim room. Rising from the bed, she strode quickly across the room, freezing as she caught her reflection in the mirror on the wall. Her figure was much the same, but covered with feathers. Great wings had sprouted from her shoulder blades. Her head was not hers at all, but the head of a bird of prey, her eyes now golden, fierce.

Turning away, she ran from the room to the balcony at the end of the corridor, leaping from it without thought and flapping her wings. The wind raced past her as she gained speed and altitude.

In the distance, much further than her human eyes would have seen, she saw a great dragon locked in battle with two beings much like herself. On the ground below them lay dozens more and the ground was red with blood.

Her father had brought his army.

Uttering a cry of rage, Kisah flapped her wings, searching for and finding air currents to help speed her along, but she saw Balian fall even before she came close enough to realize her brethren had not shifted as she had. Instead, they were merely winged men, armed with swords.

Contempt filled her. The blood lust of her beast consumed her as she burst into their midst with a flurry of wings, ripping at them with her talons, diving at them and rending their flesh with her hooked beak.

They cried out, turning upon her, but she was fully shifted, far faster, and far more deadly. Within moments she had sent three plummeting toward the ground. As she looked around for more prey, however, she saw Balian and her father below her. As she watched, horrified, the great dragon's knees buckled and he fell to the ground, shifting, becoming a man once more.

The ragged remains of her father's army surged forward, swords drawn and as they did so, Kisah dove for them, crying out her rage and agony, for she knew then that Edna had not lied about that much at least, her father had somehow summoned Mortiver's sleeping spell to drain Balian's strength.

The soldiers ducked and ran as she swooped down upon them over and over, tearing at them with her talons and beak, but she knew in her heart that there were far too many for her to overcome them all. Finally, having chased them to a safer distance, she landed by Balian's side. Already he was cut and bleeding, unable to heal himself because he was unable to shift.

Kneeling, she lifted him into her arms, hoping that she might carry him away, but he was far too heavy for her to lift. Wrapping her arms around him she held him to her, rocking him, weeping as she felt the life blood seeping from him. She didn't even notice when she shifted, becoming human once more.

"Daughter?"

She lifted her head at the sound of her father's voice, looking up at him with hate in her eyes.

"We came to rescue you!" he cried out in anguish at the look on her face.

"You did not! You came to slay my husband! And you have done it! He grows cold. I feel his life flowing through my fingers and I can not stop it!"

"You have wed him?"

"I carry his child! Slay me, as well, father, for you can not slay the last dragon without putting your sword through my heart."

Her father dropped his sword arm to his side and fell to his knees. "Daughter, I would sooner fall upon my own sword than hurt you."

Kisah shook her head. "Can you not see that you have hurt me past bearing? I love him!" Turning away from him, she tilted her face to the sky. *Hermantee, help me!*

Tell me what I must do! You said that I would know!

You do know, Kisah. Look into your heart and you will find him there.

Kisah's heart skipped a beat. Balian had told her that they would become as one once joined. Was that it? Could she help him to find his beast and break the spell as she had broken the spell he had placed upon her?

Clutching him more tightly to her, she turned her mind inward, seeking her beast, summoning it, calling to his. She felt her beast awaken, straining to break free of her human form. Slowly, almost distantly, she heard her mate's call as his beast stirred.

Come with me, my dragon! Awaken! Come to me!

She felt it more strongly then. Even as her own body shifted, she felt the coolness receding in his human body, replaced with a growing warmth. He stirred against her and she lifted her head to look down at him, watching with growing hope as his muscles rippled, elongated, changed structure, watching scales appear where only human skin had been before. The bleeding slowed, ceased. The gaping wounds began to close, the flesh to seal itself and then become whole, as though it had never been pierced.

He groaned, opened his eyes at last and looked at her uncomprehendingly for several moments. "My love?"

A gurgle of relieved laughter fought its way up her throat. "Yes, husband?"

He frowned, slowly pushing himself up, looking around at the soldiers who moved back nervously, at the king, who eyed him distrustfully. "You broke the sleeping spell?"

Kisah gave him a look. "Aye, love, I did. But I will slay you myself if you ever try that on me again! For I was almost too late to save you!"

He grinned a toothy dragon's grin, his eyes narrowing. "Nay, love. Next time I'll pull the covers over my head and send you in my stead!"

Kisah laughed, throwing her arms around his neck. "I love you, Balian! Take me home!"

Epilogue

Balian paced the floor like a caged beast. In all his life, he couldn't recall a single time when he'd been as frightened as he was now.

Kisah had been holed up in her room with her maid for most of the day. The maid had been in and out a dozen times or more, but she was always in a hurry and would only tell him that everything was going as expected.

That left a lot of room for his imagination to torment him. Although, he supposed her comments were supposed to reassure him. He hadn't been allowed in the room with Kisah. The one time he'd tried to stick his head in to have a look at her, Edna had slammed the door in his face and nearly took his nose off.

He was certain he couldn't take much more of this, but he also knew if he left, Kisah was almost certain to call for him, and there would be hell to pay.

Faintly, a strange noise filtered through the door.

He stopped in his tracks, listening intently. It came again, more pronounced now. He moved to the door, reaching for the handle, wondering if he dared open it.

The door was snatched open before he could turn the knob. Edna stood, beaming in the doorway. "You've a fine son, my lord."

Balian felt a knee weakening relief. "Kisah?" he asked.

"She's fine too. You can come in now."

Now that he'd been invited, he wasn't absolutely certain that he wanted to go in. He moved into the doorway and peered around the edge of the door. Kisah was sitting propped up in bed. She looked exhausted but happy as she studied the bundle in her arms. As if she sensed his presence, she looked up and smiled at him.

Relief flooded him. He strode across the room and knelt beside the bed, taking her hand. "All is well?" he asked.

Kisah chuckled. "Now it is. Would you like to see your son?"

Balian nodded. She held the bundle out to him, urging him to take it.

A cold sweat broke out on his brow. He smiled at her a little sickly. "He's beautiful," he said, refusing to take the tiny bundle.

Kisah gave him a look. "You can't even see him."

Thus urged, he reached to twitch the bundling back. A red-faced urchin met his gaze. Sprouting from his forehead was one thin lock of hair that curled over his brow.

Balian tried, really hard, to think of something positive to say. "He's got good lungs."

"He's beautiful," Kisah said challengingly.

Balian forced a smile. "Uh huh."

"He looks just like his daddy."

"Uh … what? Think so?" He peered at the squalling, red-faced thing more closely. In truth, it resembled nothing so much as an over-ripe tomato. Beyond the gaping, squalling mouth, he could see nothing but a tiny button for a nose and wrinkles for where the eyes would be if they'd been open. He knew Kisah was waiting, however. And she would expect her effort to be appreciated, regardless of the outcome.

"Thank you, love," he said.

The End

Printed in the United States
31587LVS00007B/12